OBELISTS
FLY HIGH

DOVER MYSTERY CLASSICS

OBELISTS FLY HIGH

C. Daly King

DOVER PUBLICATIONS, INC.
Mineola, New York

Bibliographical Note

This Dover edition, first published in 1986 and reissued in 2015, is an unabridged, unaltered republication of the work originally published by William Collins Sons & Co. Ltd., London, 1935.

Library of Congress Cataloging-in-Publication Data

King, C. Daly, 1895–1963.
    Obelists fly high / C. Daly King.
        p. cm.
    Summary: In a mystery that ranks with the best of Ellery Queen and Agatha Christie, shots are fired at a policeman aboard an aircraft on which a murder has already occurred. Will the officer survive, and will anyone emerge from the now-plummeting plane? With its intricate plot and "locked room" scenario, this masterpiece of detective fiction was hailed by The New York Times as "a very thrilling story."—Provided by publisher.
    ISBN-13: 978-0-486-25036-6
    ISBN-10: 0-486-25036-9 (pbk.)
        I. Title.

PS3521.I51402 2015
813'.52—dc23

2014034666

Manufactured in the United States by Courier Corporation
25036902   2015
www.doverpublications.com

For Muriel and Fred–whose previous cries of anguish have purchased this easy one.

CONTENTS

List of Characters
importantly involved

AMOS CUTTER, M.D.	*A famous surgeon.*
FONDA MANN	*One of his nieces.*
ISA MANN	*Another.*
HOOD TINKHAM	*His assistant.*
DR GESELL	*At the College of Physicians and Surgeons.*
HUGH L. CRAVEN	*A literary man.*
PROF. ISADOR DIDENOT	*A professional philosopher.*
THE REVEREND MANLY BELLOWES	*A successful clergyman.*
DR L. REES PONS	*An integrative psychologist.*
MICHAEL LORD	*Captain, New York Police Department.*
MARJORIE GAVIN	*Stewardess.*
'HAPPY' LANNINGS	*Senior pilot.*
HAROLD E. LOVETT	*Junior pilot.*

Diagrams

OBELISTS
FLY HIGH

Epilogue

Pong! Pong! The two shots came in quick succession; they sounded hollowly in the metal cabin forming the central section of the 'plane's fuselage. Captain Lord spun a quarter-turn around in the narrow aisle, grasped at the back of the seat beside him. Irrelevantly he was wondering which of the shots had hit him, the first or the second.

It seemed a long time before he heard the clatter of his own automatic as it fell uselessly to the flooring. Bungled, the whole case irretrievably bungled! His right shoulder was curiously numb, the entire arm and hand without sensation. No pain; must have been hit through the shoulder, though.

He was swaying – or else the 'plane was swaying. No control over his knees . . . So he had found the criminal – his solution was right. Pretty late in the day for the right solution, with the criminal firing up the cabin from the aft partition, shielded by the pretty, little plump stewardess. Her body, grasped fiercely around the waist and held where it would receive any answering bullets, was large enough to cover every vulnerable spot except the right side of the head. She was kicking, fighting vainly against muscles stronger than her own. The neat whipcord of her uniform was crushed in folds between her body and the encircling arm, and her short skirt, dragged upward on one side by the struggle, revealed a brief but shapely leg, the gartered top of sheer hose and a line of rumpled lingerie above an inch of white skin.

Right hand out of it, gun on floor, no knee control – part of Lord's mind was busy working out that problem. He must get the gun in his left hand, and he couldn't bend over to find it because of those unmanageable knees.

Pong! What was that for? No one in the cabin was armed except the detective and his weapon had fallen. Why fire again? Was the criminal out to do more damage? The tinkle of glass in the cockpit door answered the question. Pong! Pong! Two more shots into the cockpit. Of course! The pilots were armed, and the criminal knew it. This would keep them in the cockpit and bring the 'plane down, perhaps out of control. A forced landing would provide a chance of escape; a disastrous one would kill them all, along with the felon.

Right hand out of it, gun on floor, no knee control – he must fall to the floor where he could reach the gun with his left hand. But things were happening so slowly, like a slow-motion moving picture. He swayed backward, then bent at the waist; gradually the chair-tops rose above him. He was managing to fall backward, then.

He was sitting on the floor and that hardness in the small of his back was one of the eight-inch-high lateral braces across the aisle. His left hand was groping for the automatic. A chair-leg. No, that's not it. Two men, he saw, were on their feet. No use; no good trying to rush the criminal. The rear of the confined cabin was accessible by three routes only – over the tops of the two rows of seats down its sides (but they were occupied) and along the aisle, but little more than eighteen inches wide and impeded by cross-braces every three or four feet of its length. It couldn't be done. Lord was dizzy and his senses were blurring with the effort of keeping his left hand searching along the floor.

Then his senses cleared momentarily as the rear end of the cabin tilted and rose high above him. There seemed a sudden and devastating silence as the motors were cut. Pong! That sway was not in him; it *was* the 'plane that was swaying now. In a great arc the after-end of the

cabin moved leftward and up, as Lord felt the gathering
acceleration of the whole 'plane downward . . .

7100 FEET

The senior pilot was speaking with San Francisco . . .
'Dew-point six, one; probable hail squalls south-east
Reno . . . ' The ear-phones were clamped on his head
and he held the microphone close to his lips.

'Altitude seven, six hundred, field – '

A tinkle of glass behind him interrupted his report,
and he glanced sharply around. For a moment he stared
uncomprehendingly at the broken window, then at the
splintered edge of the instrument panel in front of him.
In the seat at his right side the junior pilot seemed suddenly to be manipulating the controls in a peculiar
fashion.

The senior snatched off his ear-phones and half rose in
his seat; he sank back as first one, then two more holes
appeared in the flooring between the dual 'Dep' controls.
'Pong . . . ! Pong! Pong!' came faintly to his ears. With
one hand he drew his safety belt across his seat and
reached for his own 'Dep.' The cockpit lurched forward
and down to the left while he spoke rapidly into the
microphone in his other hand. 'Firing in cabin. Taking
over ship. Controls may be hit . . . Port aileron controls
gone. Ship falling – going into spin . . . ' He dropped the
microphone and both hands became busy with his controls, while his lean, competent face gradually whitened.

The junior pilot was out of his seat, clutching its back
with one hand as the cockpit swung leftward in ever-
decreasing circles and the nose of the ship edged over
and down. His right hand pulled his revolver from its
holster and his right foot sought and found the instrument panel behind and now below him. In the whirling

cockpit he braced himself for a leap toward the door to the cabin.

5400 FEET

From the floor of the cabin, close to the cockpit doorway, Michael Lord regarded his own feet above him up the aisle. If only everything didn't go so slowly! A portfolio, tilted out of a rack overhead, was falling (it seemed to drift) on to the girl beside him, who had turned in her seat and was clinging to the back of it, looking up the aisle.

Suddenly his hand found the automatic, wedged against the lateral brace at his back. But could he use it? He was a poor shot with his left hand, and he was dizzy; he knew he was dizzy. He couldn't take the chance of hitting the little stewardess. She had struggled free now, but she was holding to the last chair in the cabin, and the criminal's body was still more than half covered by hers, although the criminal, too, was striving to keep upright by grasping the same seat with both hands.

No, he couldn't do it. What a mess, what a damned mess! He had bungled everything – the whole case from beginning to end. And now at the end he had passed the game over into the felon's own hands. And the felon, more alert than himself, had seized the offered instant, had shot him and wrecked the 'plane. For there was no mistaking the ship's movement; through the deceptive slowness of his own sensations, Lord realised that the angle of the cabin, the circling of its after-end and the sighing rush of wind he heard almost unconsciously, meant just one thing – a spin.

So this was the finish. They would all die, he reflected bitterly – all of them. He hoped there would be a crushing impact, and oblivion. No fire; dear God, no fire!

A galling rage swept through his veins, and with gritting teeth he managed to raise himself partly on one side. Even if they did die, he would kill that – With a thundering roar both motors cut in and the cabin was jerked forward and down from under him. His head swung forward, then back, and above his face a tongue of flame leapt out with a terrific c-rash!

He was losing consciousness; mustn't do that. Dizzy, it was blurred. Was his head rising? Blurred. Finish; he had bungled it; this was the finish. As if he were following a book that is written or hearing a story that is told, he saw the whole case successively spread out before him, saw its incidents re-enacted, heard its characters speak, including that character which he recognised impersonnally as Captain Michael Lord, Special Officer attached to the staff of the Commissioner of Police of the City of New York . . .

Part I – Preparation

It began in the office of the Commissioner of Police.

The dingy April morning accented the Victorian drabness of the high-ceilinged room on the third floor of the old building on Center Street. The room was spotlessly clean; its drabness was that of a period of little physical grace and even less graceful architecture. On the large desk in the centre of the apartment a single daisy in a high-stemmed holder made the only spot of colour in the furnishings.

An identical daisy in the lapel of the Commissioner responded to the first one. Oliver Darrow, the current incumbent of the office, always wore a fresh daisy on his nine a.m. appearance. According to instructions its counterpart greeted him from the desk on his arrival, to be placed in turn in his buttonhole about noon. In a city as dirty as New York it was necessary.

The Commissioner has just come in and his secretary had, likewise, just placed before him the tentative schedule of his day. Tentative, because the breaking of any serious crime in the large community for whose safety he was responsible, would interrupt it, might even sweep it entirely off the desk and into the waste basket. Few of his schedules ever did see complete fulfilment, as a matter of fact. Still, they made a background, if only for the unexpected; they were invariably prepared.

Commissioner Darrow bent over the present one. 9.45: the line-up; the Marchiotti gang and 'Spud' Nicholas (he wanted to hear them both questioned by the detectives, and they would not appear until that time). 10.30: Conference with His Honour at City Hall (arrangements for the reception and protection of a foreign Royalty and for his safe, and relieving, dispatch to Washington). 1 p.m.: Advertising Club luncheon at the Waldorf (address by the Commissioner). 2.30: Three churchwomen on a matter of vice conditions on West Forty-Seventh Street. ('My God,' groaned the Commissioner.) 3 p.m.: Conference with Captain Burrow of the Homicide Squad on the progress in the Mandable investiga –

'What is it, Felix?' Darrow raised his head and looked over at his secretary, to whom a police captain had entered and stood talking at the small desk across the room. Both men approached. The officer saluted smartly (Darrow's war record had made him a strict disciplinarian) and the secretary laid a small card before the Commissioner. 'Amos Cutter,' announced the card; and, as an afterthought, '878 Park Avenue.'

'Cutter?' asked the Commissioner, after a brief glance. 'Not the Secretary of – '

'No sir. Not the Secretary; his brother, I believe. The surgeon. Very well known; you'll remember he's the man who operated on the President last year.'

'Of course, yes.' Darrow spoke almost absently. 'Did you tell him, Captain Dennis, that I see visitors only by appointment?'

The usually good-natured officer drew himself up and stared straight ahead, stonily. 'I told him, sor. He insisted. He nearly pushed past me. He'll be outside now, though.' A small degree of satisfaction crept into his voice. Then he added, coldly, 'Said his time was important, but he'd have to wait.'

Darrow drummed on his desk with the fingers of one hand, thinking of the reports he wished to clear from it before 9.40. Finally, 'H'm . . . Well . . . No use having a fuss with Washington . . . Show him in, then, Captain.'

Disgruntled, Captain Dennis saluted and walked away stiffly, while the Commissioner's secretary turned on the visitor's light overhead, an ordinary-appearing ceiling fixture, but arranged in such a way that the figure in the comfortable chair opposite the Commissioner's desk was clearly illuminated at the scarcely noticeable expense of the other parts of the room.

Darrow rose as his caller entered, but found it unnecessary to offer his hand. 'How do you do, Dr Cutter? Will you take this seat?' He placed himself again behind his own desk, courteous but restrained. The dignity of the Police Department was at least equal to that of a Cabinet Officer's brother.

The visitor, as he sat down, was seen to be a tall man, as tall as the Commissioner, but somewhat heavier. His hair and his short beard were grizzled, he was probably between fifty and sixty, and the large, strong lines of his face stood out in bold relief. In comparison with his involuntary host his clothing was untidy, slightly wrinkled and already ashed with cigar droppings. Unexpectedly (for the Commissioner's visitors seldom did this) he came brusquely to the point.

On the edge of his chair Dr Cutter leaned farther forward and, without preamble, his harsh voice cut short Oliver Darrow's uncommenced inquiry. 'You are a busy man, Mr Commissioner, and so am I. I have received what the tabloids call a death-threat. I have to come to place it in your hands.'

Darrow, taken a little aback by this succinct statement of his caller's business, said, 'Yes, Dr Cutter,' almost perfunctorily. Then, with more interest, 'I am glad you have come to us at once. If more people would do that . . . In what form was this threat made to you?'

The surgeon produced his wallet and took from it a large envelope. From this he carefully withdrew a smaller envelope, which he passed over to the Commissioner. 'Came in the late post last night,' he stated briefly. 'Mailed at Grand Central some time before four o'clock, as you see.'

The Commissioner of Police accepted the envelope

and scrutinised it in silence. The postmark bore out Cutter's information; for the rest it was merely a cheap envelope with the address printed in capital letters and bearing no other marks whatsoever. With a pair of pincers from his desk drawer Darrow drew out the enclosure and spread its single fold. On cheap, ruled paper, such as is found in thousands of pads, there was printed, also in capital letters, the following sentence:

YOU WILL DIE APRIL THIRTEENTH AT NOON EXACTLY CENTRAL TIME.

A precise announcement. Nothing superfluous except, perhaps, the one word, 'exactly.'

'A hoax?'

The surgeon's grating tone interrupted Darrow's examination and he looked up. 'I take it you think not,' he countered, 'or you would not have brought it here so promptly. Have you some suspicion as to the source of this note?'

'None at all. I take it seriously for an entirely different reason. My abilities are unusual,' Cutter stated without the slightest self-consciousness. 'They are about to be employed in a most important matter.'

Darrow said, 'Of course I can guarantee you complete protection at noon on the thirteenth, if you will place yourself in my hands. A cordon around your house and two of my men inside – '

'Will not be of the least use.' From the same wallet the surgeon extracted another paper and handed it across. This time it was a telegraph blank:

Amos Cutter   Reno, Nov. 11-4-34. 12.11 p.
878 Park Avenue
New York City

PATIENTS CONDITION ALARMING OPER-

ATION IMPERATIVE WITHIN ONE HUNDRED
HOURS.

MacKenzie.

To Darrow's inquiring glance Cutter grated,
'Patient's my brother. The operation is a serious one;
there's only one other man in this country who could
make it without pretty certain failure, and he's in
Europe. In the present juncture of affairs my brother's
life is of some moment.'

'I am aware that your brother is Secretary of State, Dr
Cutter. And I am certain that, aside from personal
consideration, his life is extraordinarily valuable, especially just now. But is it not unusual that you intend to
operate upon him yourself? I had always thought a
physician outside the family – ?'

'Can't help it. I'd have had Schall, if he'd been here.
As it is, I'm the only one who can do it without taking
chances.'

'Do you really mean, doctor, that there are only two
men in the country competent to perform this operation?'

'I really mean it,' Cutter replied, and Darrow's ear,
attuned to the nuances of his callers' utterances, detected
plain impatience. 'This is a – well, no use bothering you
with Latin names. I have great surgical ability; not
particularly proud of it, but there it is. If Schall and I
were both in Europe, I'd advise MacKenzie, the man
who is with him, but I tell you frankly it would be taking
chances. So out I go.'

'And you're leaving at once?'

'Can't leave till to-morrow; I've an operation this
afternoon. I'm going from here to the Amalgamated Air
Transport and get my accommodations; going out by
'plane. That will get me there in time . . . If Dr Mac-
Kenzie says a hundred hours from yesterday noon, that's
right.'

Darrow leaned back, elbows on the arms of his chair and his fingers came slowly together in front of his body. 'And to-morrow is the thirteenth. You'll be en route, out of my jurisdiction. Why, you'll be in the air, if you're flying out – in no one's jurisdiction at all, for practical purposes.'

'Up to you,' rasped Cutter. 'I've come to you for protection. I don't know the details of this sort of thing.'

'I don't mind telling you,' the Commissioner smiled, 'that I don't know much about sky protection myself. However,' he added seriously, 'I can do this: I'll send one of our best men out with you, and there are other measures I can take, also. The less details you know, the better, perhaps.' He motioned to his secretary. 'Felix, have Captain Lord step in, please. Tell them not to hold the line-up for me; we'll be busy here for some time longer . . . And put this through the works.'

With great care the Commissioner's secretary placed the death-note and its envelope in a prepared box which he took from a small stack near his desk, and went out. The door closed quietly behind him.

Michael Lord was tall, dark-haired, twenty-eight years old, and several not unsophisticated young ladies had already found him much to their several tastes. In a less blasé age he would undoubtedly have been the answer to the maiden's prayer. He was wealthy, he was a fine shot and a first-rate boxer. His father, who had died some years previously, had been Oliver Darrow's closest friend, and the latter, when appointed Commissioner, had put Lord on his personal staff, on trial.

Lord's first rank, of Lieutenant, had been merely complimentary. Now his rank was Captain and no longer a courtesy one; he had caught a notorious malefactor on the *Meganaut,* and he had solved the crimes on the Transcontinental Limited, single-handed and far from the aids and benefits enjoyed by the lowest precinct detective. He was already the Department's crack man for foreign service (meaning by foreign service anything outside the territorial limits of the City of New York).

Now he sat in the chair that he had pulled up beside the Commissioner's desk, having met the man he was detailed to guard, and having just read over Darrow's copy of the threatening note.

The Commissioner leaned forward, his arms now resting on the surface in front of him. 'Let's get down to business, Dr Cutter. Will you please tell us anything which you can think of that may have any bearing at all on the present situation? Are you going out to Reno alone? What will be your rôle when you get there? Doctor and patient, simply?'

'*If* I get there.'

'*When* you get there, doctor. We shall get you there; I promise you that, with one very important proviso: I shall expect you to follow explicitly any directions or instructions that Captain Lord has occasion to give you during the trip.'

'I'm not a child, Mr Commissioner. I can take care of myself under ordinary circumstances.'

'These are not ordinary circumstances.' Darrow paused and added with all the impressiveness he could muster, 'Dr Cutter, I must insist that you place yourself unreservedly in our hands and follow without hesitation anything we direct.'

The surgeon's face was disquietingly non-committal. His answer was a grunt.

'Now, as to the situation.'

There was a sound like an old-fashioned automobile going into second gear as Cutter cleared his throat. 'The general situation probably has nothing to do with our business, but I shall give you some idea of it. There is more in Reno than just my brother, although I should not be going out except for him. My brother and I are bachelors, but we have a sister who married a scoundrel, and after putting up with him like a fool for more years than I care to think of, we have finally persuaded her to get her divorce. She is getting it in Reno now.

'That is one reason why James was there when he became ill. Congress, of course, is not in session, and my brother took the opportunity to visit the western states, especially California, where they are more excited about Oriental affairs than elsewhere. On his way back he stopped off at Reno for a few days to visit our sister. Then, we're a Reno family, too, you know. Born there, brought up and died there, most of us. So he has plenty of friends in Reno; the mayor's an old crony of Jim's, and he would probably have stopped to see him, if for nothing else.

'Anyhow, he stopped, and came down so suddenly that there's nothing for it now but the knife. Luckily MacKenzie was in Denver and went right up to him. I can pull him through, but he's a sick man to-day – so sick that I'm taking Fonda and Isa out with me, although we didn't want them in Reno just now.'

Darrow interrupted. 'Who are Fonda and Isa?'

'My nieces. Sister's daughters; they live just around the corner from me, over on Fifth Avenue. Anne – that's my sister – lives with them, of course, when she's here, which isn't often. Fonda and Isa Mann. Too bad they have to bear that rascal's name. Maybe we can change that now, though . . . I can't see how this bears on it . . . '

The surgeon's voice ceased and, though they waited some moments, he seemed in need of further prompting. Lord spoke. 'And your own establishment, doctor? Can you give us some idea of that? Whom you live with – servants, and so on?'

'Bachelor apartment; a few rooms, an office and a small laboratory. I live alone. That is, I have a man; he gets my meals when I want 'em, and does for me gener-

ally . . . I have few friends here, no intimates. I'm a busy
man, as I told you. I specialise in difficult operations
and, aside from that, spend all my time in research,
mostly at the College of Physicians and Surgeons. Been
studying *encephalitis lethargicus* for years.'

'So, outside your sister's family and your servants, no
one comes into your own home, or is familiar with your
plans?'

'My assistant, of course, drops in all the time.'

'Name?'

'How's that?'

'What is your assistant's name, doctor? I take it you
know him well; *he* must be more or less of an intimate, at
any rate.'

'He is,' Cutter acknowledged. 'His name is Tinkham.
Young fellow, about thirty, I'd say, though I've never
asked him. Been with me for the last five years. I found
him doing post-graduate research at P & S, and his work
was so good that I asked him to help me. Since then he
has become so proficient that I never do a really serious
operation without him. Taking him with me this time,
naturally.'

'H'm . . . Let's get this straight. You received your
telegram about one o'clock yesterday ("Quarter past,"
Cutter interjected) and there are only four people who
would be in a position to know anything about it from
this end. They are your nieces, Fonda and Isa Mann,
your servant and your assistant, Tinkham. Now, which
of these people *did* know about it?'

Cutter considered for some time, but when he answered, it was apparent that he had not been concerned
solely with the Commissioner's question. 'What has that
got to do with it?'

'It's perfectly plain, doctor,' explained Lord, 'that
whoever sent you that threat knew all about the telegram, and even knew when you intended to leave New
York. "Noon, Central Time." That means, of course,

that it was known you would be in the Central Time area
to-morrow.'

'Or,' Darrow contributed, 'that it was intended to
keep you out of it . . . We'll come back to that. The first
question is, who knew of your plans?'

'They all knew of the telegram. Tinkham and I were
eating, Sven was serving us, and Fonda and Isa came in
with the telegraph boy. I told them what we'd do,
immediately. But it's ridiculous,' Cutter expostulated,
'to connect them with this note. Sven has been with me
twenty-five years or more, Tinkham's wrapped up in our
work, hasn't thought of anything but surgery and
neurology for I don't know how long) and, as for my
nieces, we don't see eye to eye in everything, but a death-
threat – No, it's absurd,' Cutter grunted in disgust.

'Has it occurred to you, doctor, that this threat might
be directed against your brother, rather than against
you?' It was Lord who made the suggestion.

'Eh?'

Darrow half-smiled his appreciation of the point.

'Yes, Dr Cutter,' he said, 'it's certainly possible. We
must accept that your brother's life rests largely upon
your prompt arrival. Therefore, if by threats you can be
prevented from undertaking this journey to-morrow – '

'Hell and damnation! I'm not a schoolboy, Mr
Darrow. Why, of all the damned impudence I've ever
heard of! No one who knew me would have tried that
trick.'

'Nevertheless, I'm afraid we must consider the possibility.' The Commissioner once more leaned back in his
chair and placed his fingers together in a characteristic
gesture. 'Supposing, now, that the threat is directed
primarily against your brother. Has he any personal
enemy who really desires his death?'

Cutter was emphatic. 'None at all, I'd swear. Jim's a
friendly fellow, much more so than I am. Hundreds of
friends, and not an enemy that I know of; politicians

have to be hand-shakers, anyhow . . . Unless you'd call
that Mann skunk we're getting rid of an enemy.'

'Well, what about him?'

'Oh, he probably hates our guts. We've had it in for
him for a long time. But the last I heard of him, he was off
to Africa with one of his women. He certainly didn't mail
that note to me yesterday afternoon.'

'So . . . That leaves us just the foreign angle, then,
doesn't it? We're not on the inside of the Administration's policies here, naturally, but it's fairly common
knowledge that, quite apart from Asia, there is at least
one Power in Europe which would be delighted with
your brother's – shall we say retirement?'

'Hrgh!' Cutter's voice grated with surprise, and it was
evident that this aspect of the matter had not occurred to
him. 'Never thought of that,' he admitted. 'Frogs, eh? I
never did like 'em, with their weasel manners and
appeals to the world. It's no secret that Jim's the back-
bone of the anti-French policy. Still,' he paused and
considered briefly, 'that's a bit fantastic, isn't it? I can't
quite see them sending me a note to keep me from going
out for this operation. International intrigue stuff – bah!'

'Perhaps it's fantastic, perhaps it isn't. We'll look into
it, anyhow, in the time we have left. And now, doctor, we
will let you go along for the present; we shall have a good
deal to do before to-morrow. We can reach you at your
apartment, I presume – ?'

The surgeon got up and held out his hand, hesitantly.
To tell the truth, he was feeling more than a little foolish,
for the first time in many years. 'I – No doubt there's
nothing in all this. Mountain out of a molehill. I
wouldn't have bothered you, except for the importance
of this operation . . . I'll be getting along to the Amalgamated for the tickets . . . '

'No, Dr Cutter,' Darrow's voice was suavity itself as
he extended his hand. 'You will go from here directly to
the Grand Central and procure accommodations for

your party on the Transcontinental Limited, leaving to-morrow night. Not to-night – *to-morrow* night.'

Cutter's mouth almost dropped open. 'But – but – that's impossible – I – there isn't time – I shall certainly not have my plans interfered with by this note-writing nincompoop!'

'Captain Lord will get your real reservations on the 'plane,' said Darrow calmly.

'But – why, this is absurd. I'm not a child. I'll get my own tickets.'

'Please, Dr Cutter.' The Commissioner raised his right hand slightly and his voice was incisive. 'We are taking this matter seriously. It is *necessary* that you follow our instructions. If not for your own sake, then for that of your brother. I want you not only to take your passage on the Transcontinental, but to procure the actual tickets, and I want you to be sure they are seen when you get home. Your nieces and your assistant are to be told of this apparent change of plan as soon as possible. You will please not fail us.'

The surgeon still looked somewhat dazed, but after a moment, grunted his acquiescence. 'All right. It's your job. Always make my own patients do what I tell 'em. I'll get them.'

'Thanks.' The Commissioner bowed slightly as his visitor moved toward the door. 'Captain Lord will call for you and your party in the morning to take you to the air field. We'll let you know the time. Kindly be sure that all of them expect to leave on the Transcontinental to-morrow night . . . We'll see you through.'

As the door closed, Darrow was pressing three buttons in succession, among the row of buttons at the side of his desk. Far down the gloomy hallway outside, an annun-ciator board glowed briefly: 'T-blank-p-blank-blank-3 (Tail-protection-three).' Around the corner of the hallway came a nondescript-looking man, chewing a large black cigar; he ambled into the elevator just behind

Dr Cutter's bulky proportions. On the street below, a well-dressed gentleman got into a taxi and drove off just ahead of the surgeon's cab; the nondescript man, after lingering momentarily at the curb and thus overhearing the words, 'Grand Central,' turned and made off rapidly toward the Grand Street subway entrance. Behind Cutter's taxi a mechanic on a motor-cycle chugged carelessly through the traffic, sometimes half a block in the rear, at other times drawing up nearly level . . . The procession disappeared up Lafayette Street, heading north . . . .

In the Commissioner's office, Darrow was just taking up his gloves and stick. 'Of course, Lord, this may be a hoax. It *may* be. But that was a fairly businesslike note, to my mind. Our doctor's an important man; we can't afford to take chances with this. There's a lot to do and you'll have to step. Get busy.'

G-2

His first step, Lord decided, could be taken right where he was. 'Get me G-2 on private, will you, Felix?' It was a private police line, leading from the Commissioner's office to the Customs House, but whether it led then to some obscure office within the customs building, used by the Federal Secret Service as its New York headquarters, or to some other part of the city, not even the Commissioner himself knew. Beyond its entrance into the Customs House, it was maintained by others; even to that point it was entirely unconnected with the commercial telephone system and was considered non-tappable.

Lord, the receiver to his head, heard a click, and a quiet voice said, 'G-2, two twenty-four.'

'Captain Lord, police. Seventeen hundred and seventy-six, less seven.'

'Check. Information or assistance?'

'Information.'

'Go ahead.'

'Are any foreign governments interested in the health of James Cutter, Secretary of State?'

'All of them.'

'Any dangerously interested?'

'Nothing special on him now, so far as I know, if that's what you mean. What's it about?'

'James Cutter is seriously ill in Reno – '

'Check.'

'His brother, Amos, is leaving to-morrow by 'plane to operate on him. Amos has received a note threatening him with death, which may be an attempt to prevent his departure. Our information is that the operation is so delicate as to be probably fatal, unless this one man performs it.'

'Interesting. How soon do you want anything we can get?'

'The sooner the better. Before to-night, if possible.'

'O.K. You will be met, southern end of the Mall in the Park, six thirty-five this afternoon. Our man will use four matches to light his cigarette.'

'Thanks.'

'Check.'

Click.

AIR FIELD

The card that Lord sent in to the President of Amalgamated Air Transport bore simply the notation 'Jonathan Jones. Representing Cunard Steamship Company.' It didn't work. It did, however, secure enough interest to produce the president's personal secretary. Lord found himself admiring the Personnel Department of Amalgamated. He then displayed a small golden badge in the palm of his right hand. The young lady disappeared, only to return almost immediately. He was ushered in.

In his sumptuous office, behind his enormous desk, the president's tiny figure was almost lost. An old-young man, smooth-shaven. 'I suppose your call is important, Mr – er – '

'Captain Lord.'

'Yes, yes, to be sure. Captain Lord. I was about to drive out to the field.'

'You are going alone, sir?'

'Yes. Well, no. My secretary is coming. I inspect at odd times.'

'I see. If I might drive out with you, we could save time.'

'Excellent, excellent. If the matter is confidential Miss Spedie can sit with the chauffeur. Yes, that will do very well, very well.'

On that drive, through the Holland Tunnel and out over the Elevated Highway across the Jersey meadows, in the back of the president's limousine, with the forward partition raised, Lord spoke frankly, but not too frankly.

'We are interested, Mr Marley, in four passengers who will fly with your company to Reno to-morrow.'

'A gang of crooks?' The president fingered his chin nervously. 'Gamblers?'

Lord smiled. 'Not exactly. No, I wouldn't call them a gang of crooks. Dr Amos Cutter, his two nieces and his assistant. Dr Cutter is flying out unexpectedly to perform a delicate operation on his brother, the Secretary of State, who is seriously ill in Reno.'

'Ah!'

'As you will appreciate, the trip is most important. I intend to accompany the party on your 'plane.'

'Dear me, is there any danger?' asked the president doubtfully. 'Perhaps it would be better if he went by train.'

Lord realised that, gently as he was leading up to the subject, a change of approach was necessary. Mr

Marley, it was evident, possessed a certain timidity of outlook. Indeed, he was continuing, 'We should not care to have any unpleasantness on one of our 'planes. We have not lost a passenger in over ten years. Our business is ordinary, prosaic transportation, as safe as any other kind. But we still have to be very careful, very careful. If there is any danger – '

'Well,' said the detective, 'is there any? Of course, if you consider the trip too hazardous, we shall have to consider that aspect fully.'

His companion exploded protestingly, and Lord silently congratulated himself. 'No hazard at all, none at all. We haven't lost a passenger in ten years. A lighted boulevard from coast to coast, from coast to coast. Seventeen airports, seventy-nine intermediate fields, over a hundred lighted emergency fields, over five hundred beacons, two-way radio, weather reports every – '

'Just as I thought,' said Lord. 'An ordinary, every-day matter, flying now.'

'Sixty million miles' experience in handling passenger traffic,' said the president.

'Of course, I'm going simply as a precautionary measure. In a case so important as this one . . . Under the circumstances . . . '

'Yes, yes,' said the president of Amalgamated, who knew nothing whatever about the circumstances, but who had achieved his present office largely by appearing wise under all conditions. 'To be sure, yes . . . What 'plane are you taking, Captain Lord?'

'That I don't know yet. The earliest to-morrow, and the fastest. Speed is essential. I must attend to that for the whole party as soon as we reach the field.'

'Bless my soul, we're nearly there now.' The big limousine slid down an incline from the elevated structure to a broad arterial highway which continued across the Jersey fields, flashed past a large arrowed sign – 'Newark Airport' – and turned left around a traffic circle.

'Our early 'plane leaves at nine o'clock, gets you into
Reno before two that night. San Francisco, four a.m. . . . .
So we can reach Los Angeles before seven. Competi-
tion . . . Well, well, here we are.'

Mr Wiley, the manager of Amalgamated's eastern terminus, had a small office to himself just beyond the
broad waiting-room and ticket counter. 'Every
consideration, Mr Wiley,' said the president, 'every
consideration. Anything he wants.' The president
smiled a thin smile and bustled off for his inspection;
Miss Spedie undulated behind him, a closed but ready
note-book in her manicured hand.

The detective made known to Mr Wiley his desires as
to reservations. Mr Wiley pressed a button. The reservation card of to-morrow's nine a.m. cross-continent 'plane
appeared upon Mr Wiley's desk.

'You're in luck,' he said. 'Not always easy to
accommodate five people on that 'plane as late as this.
Only four booked so far, though. I'll have our offices
notified that five more places are taken . . . Five, you
said?'

'Said five. Amos Cutter, Fonda Mann, Isa Mann,
Tinkham (don't know his first name) and myself,
Michael Lord.'

'Oh, going yourself?'

'Yes. By the way, who are the four passengers who are
booked already?'

'H'm. That's an unusual question. Still, you're the
police.' Mr Wiley drew the reservation card slowly
toward him.

Lord had been appraising the manager closely, and
now concluded that he was a different type than the
president. 'I am going to confide in you,' he decided.
'This is confidential – I mean it. For no one else, either in
your company or out of it . . . We have information that
an attempt may be made to injure Dr Amos Cutter
during his proposed trip. I am going along to protect

him, if necessary. You will see that every precaution must be taken. That is why I asked you what I did, and why I shall have several other things to ask you.'

The manager hesitated. Then, 'Will the 'plane be in any danger, Captain Lord? I must insist that you be perfectly frank with me about that.'

'No. We have no reason to suppose that there will be any danger whatsoever to your 'plane. The threat, such as it is, is directed entirely against Dr Cutter. Just the same, I will speak about the 'plane in a minute. But first, about the other passengers?'

Mr Wiley now appeared thoroughly interested; as the president had inferred, his was a prosaic life. He hitched his chair over and placed the reservation card between himself and the detective. 'There they are,' he pointed out. 'Isador Didenot, Hugh L. Craven, L. R. Pons, Rev. Manly Bellowes. Just names; that's all I know about them.'

'Well, of all – ' Lord was staring at the form in front of him with every appearance of astonishment. After a moment's silence he asked, 'You say you know nothing but their names? You don't know whether this L. R. Pons is Dr L. Rees Pons, for example?'

Wiley grinned ruefully. 'Guess I spoke out of turn,' he admitted. 'I don't know whether his name is L. Rees Pons or not, but I have seen him. He's the only one I have, though. He made his own reservation at the field here, yesterday, I think, and I showed him over the place. A large man, two hundred and eighty pounds, I'd say; affable, moon-faced. Do you know him, Captain?'

'I should say I did. Just by chance he was with me on my two most successful cases. This looks like a good omen . . . Well, well, Dr Pons, journeying again . . . Did he have grey hair, by the way?'

'Yes, this man had grey hair. I noticed it especially because he seemed too young for grey hair.'

'That's the man, all right. And you're correct; he is

only about forty. Now these others. Let's see, Manly Bellowes – there can't very well be more than one of those.
He must be the fellow with the church on Fifth Avenue –
or is it Park Avenue? I've never heard him myself, I'm
not much of a church goer, but I believe he's something
of a sensationalist – got a big following for a minister
these days.'

The manager did not commit himself; doubtless he,
too, held no records for attendance at public worship.

'And Hugh L. Craven,' Lord continued, 'will turn out
to be the English novelist, unless I'm much mistaken. So
there would seem to be three of your passengers out of
the running for any criminal honours right off the bat.
The Didenot man I've never heard of, however . . . Just
as a matter of routine, can you let me know when and
where each of them made his reservation?'

'Sure I can get that for you. When do you want to
know?'

'Oh, any time this afternoon. If you wouldn't mind
telephoning it over to Headquarters for me. And now, I
wonder if I can look at the 'plane we shall be taking, or at
one like it. Just to familiarise myself with the arrangements. What are they, tri-motors?'

'No.' The manager's voice deepened with unexpected
pride, as he prepared to lead his visitor forth from the
office. 'We fly nothing but twin-motored Boeings on the
cross-continent route now. They're the fastest transport
'planes in the world – two Wasp motors rated at 550
horsepower each, seventy-four-foot wing-spread, with a
cruising speed of 170 miles an hour. You'll see, they're
the sweetest ships yet.'

The immense hangar, into which they emerged
directly from the passage behind Wiley's office, arched
high above them, its cantilevered roof, mostly transparent, letting great shafts of sunlight through to splash
the wide floor area with brightness. The day had cleared
now and was warmer, and both ends of the hangar, made

up entirely of folding doors, had been thrown open. Except for an aviation show he had once attended, Lord had never seen so many 'planes under one roof. Single-seated open mail 'planes, two-seaters, cabin 'planes, and no less than four of the big transports seemed to his surprised eyes to be almost stacked on various parts of the floor. On several of them mechanics were working with the aid of spotlights dangling from the roof, despite the general sunlight.

Across an open space the manager led the way to one of the transports; with its silvered wings spread widely and gracefully from beneath its streamlined, torpedo fuselage it seemed, even under the hangar roof, as if poised for flight. The detective felt something of Wiley's enthusiasm for this beautiful machine. Stepping in front of it, he noticed the long tapered snout with a hinged door at its forward end, probably for mail, and the two big rotary motors protruding one from each wing, a short distance on either side of the fuselage. 'Landing lights,' said the manager, as Lord stopped to look at the transparent sections on the leading edges of the wings. 'The navigation lights are here,' pointing to the red and green glass sections, also inset in the wing surfaces at their tips.

The pilots' covered cockpit was just visible above and at the rear end of the snout, with an unobstructed view in four directions, forward, to starboard, to port and upward. Behind, and slightly below it, the windows of the cabin stretched along the side of the fuselage to the single door on the starboard side, half-way down the 'plane's body. To this door they walked and, Wiley having unlocked it, pulled themselves into the interior.

Now the cabin itself lay before them; it was longer than Lord had supposed, and narrower. Along each side was a line of seats, five in each line, a window beside every seat. The seats, he found, were adjustable to any inclination, even the almost horizontal; in the wall beside them were individual reading lights, individual ventilators (for the windows could not be opened), and a combination cigarette lighter and ashtray. Also safety belts. Lord looked up from his inspection of a cigarette lighter.

'Oh, yes, you can smoke. Except for the carpet and some wood and felt sound-insulation behind the walls, these are all-metal 'planes.' Wiley showed him the system of general, as contrasted with individual, ventilation, and how it warmed the 'plane in winter and cooled it in summer. 'The dome lights are out late at night, of course, but you can still read with your own light, if you want to.'

Lord pointed to a round, stiff paper carton in a holder beside each seat. Wiley grinned. He said, 'If you get sick. We have other measures, too.' He produced a shallow box of small glass bulbs, rather like small electric light bulbs. 'You break one of these in a handkerchief and inhale. It's a gas of some kind; harmless, but does the trick for most people.'

'Is that so? That's ingenious. Never heard of it. Can I try one?'

'Sure thing. Here.'

Lord took the tiny object, dropped it into his handkerchief. As he hesitated, the manager extended thumb and forefinger. 'This way.' Lord crushed the nut-like hardness and bent his head quickly, breathed in. He was surprised at the absence of any distinctive odour, but a wave of cool clarity swept through his nostrils and throat. Or he thought it did.

Up the aisle, past the six lateral braces across it, over which they stepped awkwardly, they came to the cabin's forward partition. A narrow door here, with a glass window; on one side a large clock, on the other an altimeter. Wiley held the door open, and the detective looked in. The pilots' cockpit. To right and left he saw intricately adjustable chairs, with the inevitable safety belt, and tilted forward in front of them, the dual control shafts sticking up from the flooring, surmounted by what looked like half an automobile steering wheel; half a circumference, its open ends joined by a diameter. Buttons on the shafts. Between the control sticks a box-like contrivance from which short levers protruded, and directly ahead the instrument panel, crowded with dials, pointers, gauges. He motioned toward an unusual one at the top, a large dial bearing a shaded cross-bar, over which hovered a miniature 'plane behind the glass.

'The Sperry Artificial Horizon. All these 'planes are completely equipped for blind flying.'

Metal struts across the glassed sides and over the glass roof. Lord found himself gaping without comprehension. 'Thanks. Let's go back.'

They came again to the back of the cabin, with its three doors; the one by which they had entered, and in the rear partition one on the left (shelves, Thermos flasks, sandwich trays, coffee cups, blankets), and one on the right to a tiny wash-room and toilet. 'There's nothing beyond this but the baggage compartment and, behind that, the control wires through the tail. The baggage compartment does not connect with the rest of the 'plane; has its own door on the other side of the fuselage.'

They came back, the manager carefully closing the doors behind them. They jumped from the cabin door to the concrete of the hangar. Just opposite them the president stood pointing with a small stick at a replica of the 'plane they were quitting; he was dictating fussily to his graceful secretary.

Lord grinned.

COLLEGE

He rode back to the city, alone, in the biggest limousine he had ever seen. 'Amalgamated Air Transport,' it announced to all it passed. 'Amalgamated.' 'Amalgamated Air Transport.'

It was just as they were leaving the Holland Tunnel that he experienced a sudden idea. He thought it over; and the more he thought, the better he liked it. At Thirteenth Street and Seventh Avenue he knocked on the back of the chauffeur's partition and had himself put down. As the man drove on, Lord was disappearing into a subway entrance – 'Uptown.'

At the college of Physicians and Surgeons his card – his own this time – secured immediate attention at the office. Not so immediate was the appearance of the man to whom he was eventually directed. Dr Gesell, finally located at the end of a gloomy corridor, regarded the detective with watery eyes peering through thick-lensed spectacles.

'*Er ist ein braver Mann,*' said Dr Gesell. '*Sehr* skilful, a gr'at surgeon. Who would wish to hurt him I do nodt know. Sometimes,' said Dr Gesell, 'life, I think, it a bad dream iss.'

They talked.

Half an hour later they were standing on the steps of the old building, already partly deserted for the new quarters of the College at the Medical Centre still farther uptown. Dr Gesell's old-fashioned frock coat flapped slightly in the breeze, and his bald head was now covered by a grim bowler. 'It iss the time; it is nodt the rest,' he murmured. 'I vill see.'

'*Gut* morning, sir.' Dr Gesell began a progress, ungainly but somehow dignified, along the sunlit street.

ARMY BUILDING

Downtown again, where the shade of deep chasms still held chillness and the wind blew briskly between skyscrapers. The mouth of Wall Street, sucking in and gushing forth pedestrians simultaneously between its brand new lips, two great despite-the-depression towers that flank its entrance. The end of Broadway, with its open plaza and little park, a reminder of the old days when Broadway was broad. Past the north end of the Customs House and down a slight decline toward water.

Whitehall Street.

Colonel Swickerly was the best dressed army officer of Lord's experience. No less than four rows of ribbons decorated his breast, just above the embroidered wings. His boots, incredibly polished, like mirrors at an amusement resort, reflected everything in the room distortedly.

'You're not giving us much time.' The colonel's small, pointed moustache twitched with his smile. 'We can do it, of course, but must have that request in writing from the Commissioner . . . Meantime, I'll get on to Washington for final authority.'

Lord got up. 'Thank you, Colonel.'

'Good hunting, Captain Lord.'

AND HEADQUARTERS

The only times when Police Headquarters show no lights are those rare occasions when the main fuses in the cellar are blown, but not always are there lights in the Commissioner's office. To-night, however, there was a subdued glow from his windows high above the street. The glow was reflected from the yellow flood that, spreading downward from its two green-shaded points of origin, made the Commissioner's desk a pool of brightness in the large dim room.

Darrow, in informal evening dress, leaned back in his chair, his white shirt-front gleaming in the full rays of the desk lights. Lord still wore his mufti of the morning; in

fact, since his rendezvous in Central Park late that afternoon he had had no more than time to snatch a hasty
dinner and return to Center Street. The daisy in the
Commissioner's lapel, he noted absently, seemed as
fresh as its early morning counterpart. Number three
daisy, no doubt.

Darrow said, 'It's nearly nine o'clock. Let's see where
we stand. Now here are these reports.' He shuffled
through the pile of papers stacked neatly beside him.

'In the first place the threatening note is a blank.
There are no prints on it. The paper cannot be identified;
the three big pad companies all make that grade, and
probably a dozen or so smaller companies put it out, too.
Same for the envelope. Waterman's Fountain Pen Ink
was used, probably with a #2 Spencerian nib. A good
many people have ink and pens of that description; as a
matter of fact, a number of hotels, and not only the large
ones, supply their public writing desks with Waterman's
Ink. Printed capitals, of course, effectively disguise the
handwriting; they're even less characteristic than a
typewriter, nothing there.

'So there's not much meat in the note. The only
conclusion I can see is that the person who wrote it is not
an ignorant tramp or anyone of such a category, but then
there is no attempt to make us think so. The cheap paper
is plainly a device to avoid tracing, that's all. Either the
combination of means employed in preparing the note
was exceedingly lucky, or else, which seems more likely
all around, the writer is quite clever enough to write
untraceably.'

Darrow laid aside the laboratory report and spread
before him several other papers – the reports of his three
operatives, together with a combined résumé. 'Cutter,'
he continued, 'went directly from here to the Grand
Central, bought his tickets and then went home. His
assistant arrived at his apartment about noon and they
came out together at two-thirty, took a cab to the Med-

ical Centre. He performed his operation, a long one; he left, again by cab, at 3.48. He then went to the College of Physicians and Surgeons, downtown, remaining until 6.30, when he left, stopped in at the University Club for a few minutes and proceeded to a restaurant in the East Fifties, where he had dinner. A report has just been telephoned in that he has now returned to his apartment, apparently for the night. Two other plain-clothes men are taking over now, to see that nothing happens to him.'

'Hasn't seen the rest of his party, then?'

'No, he hasn't seen his nieces. But he made a 'phone call about 12.30, which was traced to their apartment; undoubtedly he told them then about the new reservations on the Transcontinental . . . So there's a harmless day. He was approached by no one in the least suspicious, there were no mysterious messages or other communications detected.'

'What about the rest of these people?' Lord asked. 'I turned that over to Captain Dennis before I left this morning.'

'Nothing much,' the Commissioner sighed, reaching for yet other papers. 'Hood Tinkham,' he read off. 'Born in Columbus, Ohio, 1902. Parents both dead. He came to New York in 1920, worked his way through Columbia, then through medical school, and has a medical degree. Cutter took him up in 1928, as he told us; uses him as a research assistant and also in his operations. Tinkham has no money of his own, but Cutter pays him well, practically supports him. The opinion is that he gets his money's worth, however, and is enthusiastic about Tinkham's ability. That's all. Tinkham lives quietly at a hotel on the west side, has no habits, bad or otherwise, spends all his time in research.'

Darrow paused, took up another sheet. 'Anne Cutter, the sister. A famous beauty about the turn of the century. Her first husband died in 1904, and she married Wotan Mann – there's a name for you – in 1909. He is of

German extraction, seems to have independent means and one big hobby: he hunts – large tough animals and small, frail ladies. About half and half; sometimes he combines the two as at present. He left for Africa a month ago with a little show-girl named Mitzi. There is no doubt about the grounds for divorce.

'Fonda and Isa Mann, just what you'd expect. Carefully brought up, finishing school and so on. Fonda is twenty-four and Isa twenty-two. Modern and independent, live in their mother's apartment, which is practically their own, for she has spent most of her time travelling or visiting in Reno since her estrangement from her second husband, their father . . . Sven Dahlgren,' Darrow grunted in exasperation, 'just nothing. Goes to the movies. Naturalised years ago. Been with Cutter since 1908.' He spread his hands. 'So there you are.'

'Well, it isn't much,' Lord acquiesced, 'is it?'

'No. It's a curious thing how little these routine reports tell you about anyone except a professional crook. Nothing at all about amateurs. It might be any of them.'

'Or none of them. There certainly isn't anything there to indicate our note-writing friend.' Lord stopped and lit a cigarette, this conference was informal. 'Well, I've had a busy day.'

Darrow smiled. 'I don't doubt it. Let's hear about it.'

'In the first place, which was the last on my programme, the Secret Service reports that there is no activity directed towards Cutter's brother, the Secretary of State, so far as they know. They assure me that they very probably do know, and that, in any event, such activity on the part of any foreign government in times of peace would be most extraordinary. On the other hand, they tell me that so indirect a menace as this threat against his brother, who is to perform a serious operation on him, would be not entirely unbelievable on the part of at least two Powers under present conditions. They promise to continue working on the idea until they get the "All clear" from us. There they leave it and, as they know nothing definite, I suppose that's all they can do.

'In order to guard against this foreign angle I have taken two precautions. First, I went to the Army Air Service, as you know – '

'As I don't know,' interrupted the Commissioner. 'I've given them some kind of a written request that they wanted, but I don't know what it's all about.'

'Perhaps I'm putting on extra steam there,' Lord admitted, with a grin. 'But it struck me, when I was looking over the route we would fly, out at the airport this morning, that there were plenty of places on it where a strange 'plane could find us and take a crack at us. Bring us down; maybe burn us up.'

Darrow said mildly, 'Isn't that just a trifle far-fetched, Michael?'

The other shrugged. 'Maybe it is. Yes, to tell you the truth, I do think it is. Just the same, why leave it open? . . . Anyhow, I went to the Air Service and told 'em we wanted the route patrolled, and why we wanted it patrolled. Result, they'll patrol it. There will be an army combat 'plane, sometimes two of them, in sight of us the whole way out, with orders to warn off any inquisitive neighbours and, if necessary, to fire on them and put them out of business. For this purpose they have arranged that our 'plane will carry the army insignia on top of both wings and will display what I gather is an unheard-of yellow light on the roof of the cabin at night.'

'But how can they tell your 'plane from one of their own, if you carry their insignia?'

'Because there aren't any Boeing transports in the Air Service now. Of course, all these transports are convertible into army bombers, in case of war, but they're not converted yet. The army pilots know all types of army 'planes, and most of the others; when they see ours, they'll know what it is . . . The orders won't go out to the army fields until first thing in the morning, so there will be no chance of a leak and a phoney 'plane with our markings. Incidentally, they seemed delighted with the opportunity of doing something besides taking joy rides, for a change.

'Well, that's the first thing I did. The second has to do with any possible tampering with the 'plane itself, and I ought to tell you what the ordinary precautions are as to that. An hour before any Amalgamated transport 'plane goes up, it is completely gone over by their regular mechanics, and then it is warmed up and tested under the direct supervision of the chief mechanic of the air field in question. A half-hour before it leaves, it is gone over again by the pilots who are to take it up – there are two of them, senior and junior – and it is warmed up and tested again. Fifteen minutes before departure, the pilots taxi it out to the starting point and continue testing until the 'plane actually leaves. That seems pretty thorough, but it wasn't enough for me. After all, I don't know the chief mechanic; he may be all for Amalgamated, but bribable as regards Cutter.

'So all this routine will be gone through with the regular 'plane which would naturally go out to-morrow morning, but that one won't be the one that goes. Our 'plane, extra thoroughly inspected and tested beforehand, will come over to Newark from Hadley Field at New Brunswick just fifteen minutes before we leave. There is a 'plane due from the west at 8.30, and ours will come in with three or four dummy passengers in it, so it will look to anyone interested like a section of the trip from the west. But it won't be; it will be the one we are really going out in.'

'This seems,' Darrow hazarded, 'very elaborate.'

Lord stated, 'It's as elaborate as I could make it. I couldn't think of anything else to add. I admit I don't know much about foreign spies, but I think I'll give them a run for their money if they are really involved. And it won't be ostentatious – that's certain. I doubt if the other passengers have a hint of any of it.'

'Ah, the other passengers.'

'Yes, there is the matter of the other passengers. But there we are playing in a little real luck. There are only four of them; with our party that makes nine for the 'plane, which carries no more than ten passengers, anyhow. The Amalgamated people have consented not to sell the other seat for this particular trip, and so the four already booked are all we shall have to think about. Of these four, one is Dr Pons, the man I told about who was on the Transcontinental when Sabot Hodges was killed; and he was on the *Meganaut*, too.' Lord smiled reminiscently. 'He's a psychologist, the fellow who wished the "intrextroversion" method on me. There is certainly no possibility of his setting out to put a hole through Cutter.

'Another one is Manly Bellowes, from the church uptown, and still another is Hugh L. Craven, the English novelist and dramatist. So, unless we are going to look for hobgoblins in our overcoat pockets, they're out, too. I just can't see either of them as our criminal, even though amateur.'

The Commissioner's, 'Well-l,' was long-drawn. 'That *is* a bit of luck. Look out for your Bellowes man, though. I heard him a year or so ago; he's a holy terror.'

'Hot stuff, eh? I only know he has one of the largest congregations in town.'

'He gets them by scaring them,' Darrow averred. 'His line is hell and damnation, brimstone and fire. If his pulpit manner is any criterion, his name is belligerency. He's far from a typical minister; there aren't many like him left nowadays. As for me, I prefer the clergy somewhat more dignified, as most of them are, of course . . . In any event, I'm sure you can count out both Bellowes and Craven. But what about your fourth passenger?'

'His name is Isador Didenot, and that's all I know about him – yet. But there ought to be a report here for me from the field; that may tell us something.'

Together they bent over the Commissioner's stack of papers, and almost immediately turned up a sheet in his secretary's handwriting, headed: 'Information for Captain Lord, from Amalgamated Air Transport.' It was the telephone message from Wiley concerning the reservations. From this it appeared that Pons had made his reservation the day before, as Lord knew already, and that Bellowes had done the same, but in New York. The Englishman's reservation had been made for him by a lecture bureau some two weeks previously; and a place had been held for Didenot by the American Philosophical Society no less than three months before. Recourse to a reference book showed Isador Didenot to be listed as a member of that organisation, and a 'phone call to one of the newspapers disclosed that the society was about to hold a convention in San Francisco. 'So there's his explanation,' Darrow commented, 'and he is almost certainly as harmless as the rest. In any event, he planned to take this 'plane three months ago, and that is long before James Cutter was taken sick or had even gone to the west. Also, it's even longer before Amos Cutter had any idea of going. Yes, your Didenot man is out, too. It strikes me forcibly,' he continued, 'that of all the people on the 'plane, Cutter himself is the one who is likely to give you the most trouble.' He paused, as if struck by a sudden thought. 'He can't possibly be up to any hanky-panky himself, can he?'

Lord considered the suggestion for several minutes in silence. Then he said slowly. 'No, I can't really believe that possible. Whatever you can say about him, he surely is not an unbalanced neurotic. He would never plan to do himself an injury and then tell the police about it in advance.'

'Of course not,' agreed Darrow. 'It was a silly idea.

What I started to say was that he is an obstinate old codger; all his remarks about his "not being a child," and so on. You'll probably have a fine time making him follow orders.'

'You're right on that. I had a chance to stop at Physicians and Surgeons this afternoon for a few words with some of his colleagues. He's crabby and obstinate, without a doubt. Gesell, the man I spent most time with, seemed definitely hostile to him at first; but then, when I told him what the purpose of my inquiry was, he changed completely. He said there was no question but that Dr Cutter was a man of the highest attainments professionally, and couldn't imagine that anyone would try to injure him seriously. I couldn't help noticing that he went further that way than he had the other; I can easily believe that Cutter is hard to get on with, though, and, of course, Gesell didn't know that there was anything dangerously wrong, to begin with.

'As a matter of fact, this man Gesell helped me work out an idea I had for Cutter's own protection, but one that I'm not going to tell Cutter about, I assure you. I think he needs to be protected from himself, and here's what I propose to do . . . '

Darrow, a moment later, had opened his eyes widely. Then he chuckled. Then he congratulated Michael Lord. 'Of course,' the latter added, 'the idea primarily is to balk whoever may be trying to injure him.'

'Well, let's see what else.' Darrow drew out a small page of notes and regarded it for some moments. 'We've been over the passengers and we've been over the members of Cutter's own party. I've a note regarding them. You remember, when we suggested to Cutter that someone might be trying to injure his brother by keeping him – Amos – away by threats, that he said, "Nobody who knows me would have tried that trick." Aside from the fact that we haven't been able to turn up anything to implicate his nieces or his assistant, it seems to me that his remark was pretty nearly correct, and that they all know him fairly well. For what it's worth, it's in their favour, don't you agree?'

'Yes, if the threat is really against his brother, or if it is against both of them. If it's only against Amos Cutter, of course, the point doesn't mean so much.'

'H'm. Yes, that's so. And yet this certainly seems an innocent party all around, if ever there was one. We haven't left anyone out of – '

'But we have,' Lord interrupted gently. 'The crew of the 'plane.'

Darrow grunted with chagrin. 'My word! That's right. Naturally.'

'However, they are as innocent-looking as all the rest. Even more so. We change ships at Chicago and at Cheyenne; they used to change pilots oftener than that, but with these new and faster ships the pilots are only changed when the ships are changed. There are always two pilots, so that's six on the way out. Most of the senior pilots employed by the Amalgamated were army flyers in the war, then air mail flyers; nearly all of them have around 10,000 hours of transport flying to their credit, and even the junior pilots hold the highest-class Department of Commerce Transport Licences. Of course, they all have to have Federal Licences as radio operators.

'That's as to their regular abilities. To-morrow we start out with the veteran senior pilot, as would have happened in the ordinary course of events, anyhow. The ones we pick up later have been specially transferred to this trip out of turn, and I am assured they have the highest rating the company can give. As to the stewardess we have from Cheyenne to Reno, I can't get up much alarm about her. Among other things, she is a graduate nurse, as all their stewardesses are.'

Darrow said, 'A match, Michael?' and offered him a cigarette lighter. 'These aeroplane companies do it up brown, don't they? But won't this ship-changing thing interfere with your plans? I should think it might.'

'No,' the smoker smiled, 'that's arranged, too. By the way, did you know the amount of authority these senior pilots have? While they're in the air, they are just like ship captains on the high seas; whatever they say goes, including landing or not landing, regular stops or irregular, make 'em or skip 'em, or do anything else they judge best. They have more authority than ship captains, really, for there isn't even a traditional code about anything as yet, except, of course, the safety of the 'plane and its passengers. But they're fully authorised to sacrifice one, or some, for the rest, in a hypothetical case. Pretty absolute.'

'H'm. Might effect you, mightn't it, if your criminal should manage to persuade one of them to land somewhere or do something else?'

'They are to be instructed to accede to no requests or demands from any passenger unless I have passed on it first, this time. For the rest, their authority is higher than mine while we're in the air, but my opinion is that their judgement is likely to be pretty trustworthy. They are armed, of course, because these 'planes carry United States mail. In a pinch I can't think of any class of man I'd much rather have with me.'

There was silence for some minutes. Both were thinking, trying to seek out some point that might have been overlooked; and neither could do so. Darrow stirred, finally.

'I can't think of another thing,' he confessed. 'Your own party, the passengers, the crew. If there *is* a potential criminal among any of them, it must be in Cutter's party.' A frown appeared on his forehead. 'And I still think there may be; there probably is. *I don't believe that note was a hoax.* God knows we've seen enough of them here to be able to judge, and I believe that that one was no fake . . . Well, you've got two jobs. The first, naturally, is to protect Cutter. And the second is to bring in the person who threatened him. But Cutter first, of course.

'Now, here's what has been done. On the foreign theory, which does appear a little far-fetched to me – but I'm no stranger to the unlikely – your route will be patrolled and your 'plane guarded from outside all the time; you've arranged for an extra careful inspection of the 'planes themselves and, when you start, it will be in a 'plane that has been substituted for the one that would go out in the ordinary course of events.'

'The relay 'planes will be substituted ones, also,' Lord cut in.

'Good again. Furthermore, the Secret Service will continue to work on this theory and take any measures that may suggest themselves. Certainly that angle is covered. As to what we can call the domestic theory, your fellow passengers could scarcely be less dangerous for a trip like yours. We have done our best with the note Cutter got, but that's blank. We have turned up what we could on his own group of people, in the time available; it isn't much and there, if anywhere, lies the risk. But they expect to go out by train now and, if any plans have been made, they have to be changed hurriedly at the last minute, which will hardly be an advantage to the planner. We shall send you anything more we can get, but in any event you will be in the 'plane yourself, watching them. In a small cabin, where everyone has to sit almost all the time in two lines of five chairs each, I don't see how much opportunity for a crime can arise, if you're on your toes. And I happen to know that you will be.'

Across the flood-lighted desk Darrow and Michael Lord looked at each other steadily.

'Never have I known a man better safeguarded than this one,' said the Commissioner. 'He *can't* be reached.'

Part II – Operation

The morning of 13th April was bright, cool and breezy. From the end of the Elevated Highway, just before it declined to the ground, the flat fields of Newark Air Port stretched away southward, while the Highway turned in a great loop to the west, meandering off into Jersey distances. To the left, beyond the series of enclosed parking spaces that bordered the main approach, squatted the row of broad hangars, one behind the other, each with its western side merging into a low administration building of offices, ticket booths, passengers' lounges, pilots' billets, recreation rooms. Some were brick, some stucco, one was modernistic concrete, but all possessed their porches or esplanades from which footways ran, past trim hedges, to the flagged areas in front, the embarkation points of the 'planes. In the early sunlight the names, painted large above the hangar doors, stood out clearly – Colonial Airways, United Air Lines, Amalgamated Air Transport . . .

In the north-west corner of the field stood the buildings of an air school, two repair hangars, and a high control tower, like a lighthouse with its four glass walls. Between this cluster and the transport buildings opposite lay the brown expanse of the field itself, patched with the green of spring grass.

Lord's car, a hired limousine bearing non-official New York plates, rolled past the public parking spaces, turned right, sped on behind the first few hangars, turned right again and, picking its way between a big transport and two cabin 'planes already in front of the hangar doors, stopped beside the automobile entrance of the Amalgamated offices. Lord stepped down and held open the door for the rest of the party. Out they came,

Fonda and Isa Mann first, then Tinkham, Cutter last of all. They stood for a moment in a small knot, while Lord paid off the chauffeur and then turned back to them; no other cars were near, no sightseers stood about, there was, in fact, no one else at all outside the Amalgamated building. It was just eight-thirty.

'We might as well,' said Lord, 'go in.'

They were already mounting the two low steps to the entrance when Fonda interrupted. 'I'm going to take a look around,' she announced in her clear, velvet voice. 'Come on, Isa.'

Isa's voice was husky, without strain. She said, 'O.K.'

The three men made their way inside, to find a broad, empty lounge. Large wicker chairs on a parquet floor, several settees, three palms in tubs and cretonne hangings along the tall windows made a foreground for the long counter behind which a single clerk in uniform smiled cheerfully. Tinkham wandered to the counter where stacks of coloured folders drew his attention, while Lord and Cutter sought chairs. The surgeon lit a cigar.

Now that they were out of sight, Lord found himself wondering about the two girls. Fonda was beautiful; she had a full figure and dark-yellow hair that glinted brightly when touched by light. But she was definitely not the small, pretty, blonde type; for one thing, she was too tall for that – a good five feet six, Lord conjectured – and, for another, her features were too regular for prettiness; despite this regularity, however, her face was animated, her blue eyes vivacious. She wore a smartly-tailored suit; about her neck a bright scarf relieved the sombre colour of her suit and was fastened in front by a large, spade-shaped clip in which a sapphire gleamed, matching her eyes. On her small hat another ornament responded to the clip. No, he decided, she was not pretty – she was beautiful.

She had been petulant when she met them at the

canopy of her imposing Fifth Avenue apartment house. The, for her, hurried change of departure, of course. Very petulant indeed, until Lord followed her uncle out of the car and was presented. She had given him a quick, attentive look, and the pouting frown had been instantly replaced by a wavering change, then a bright smile. 'I'm *glad* we are going by 'plane,' had said Fonda.

Lord grinned with the wisdom of his twenty-eight years, and sought an adjective for her behaviour. He selected captivating. 'I'll lay my hat,' he wagered, 'that Pons labels her captivating before we're up half an hour.'

Isa was a contrast. She was as tall as her sister, maybe a little taller; she was slender, with an impression of hard muscles beneath her clothes. Not pretty, certainly not beautiful, just as certainly not homely. Lord fumbled about with his vocabulary. She was handsome, he decided finally, but not quite old enough to be handsome yet; about to be handsome, that was it. At that, she *looked* older than Fonda. And her attitude had made it clear that she was, if anything, bored – bored with the trip and not interested at all in young men, good-looking or otherwise. Assuredly not in Lord. Pons' presumptive description could be left to Pons.

With a start Lord wondered how long he had been thinking about those girls. It was his job to get acquainted with this party as soon as possible, and he had better make use of opportunities that were present rather than absent. Tinkham was present, and Tinkham even now was wandering away from the counter across the room. Lord got up and joined him where he had halted before one of the windows that looked across the flying field.

'We've good weather for our start, at any rate,' the detective opened.

Dr Cutter's assistant glanced briefly around, then looked back through the window. 'Good, bright day. Excellent light for dissections.'

'Dissections?' Lord was puzzled. 'Did you say dissections?'

Tinkham did not smile; his voice, though he recog-
nized the other's bewilderment immediately, was
entirely solemn. 'I was thinking of the past few days. We
have had to use artificial lighting for our dissections,' he
explained. 'Sunlight is always better for microscopic
work. To-day would have been excellent.'

'Ah, I see.' With an effort Lord brought his attention
from flying to surgery. 'I suppose you do a good deal of
experimental work. I've often wondered what you use for
the kind of research you and Dr Cutter do. The dead
bodies of animals, or – er – real bodies?'

'I suppose by "real" bodies you mean human bodies.
We don't use cadavers at all; we dissect living animals –
rats, guinea pigs, sometimes cats or monkeys. We have
two monkeys at P & S now with well-developed malign
encephalitis. Except for this trip we would have been at
them to-day.'

'I see you believe in vivisection.'

Tinkham shot the detective a glance as cold and
impersonally appraising as if the latter had been himself
under one of the assistant's microscopes. 'Naturally. It's
the greatest tool experimental surgery has ever been
offered. Vivisection has solved many major problems
already; its competent use will give us solutions to a great
many more. Why, if we could trepan those monkeys to-
day, by to-night we might be ready to confirm a major
clue to the nature of *lethargicus*!'

'I've no doubt it *has* value,' Lord admitted doubtfully.
'I've never like the idea of it myself.'

'I fail to see what liking has to do with it. It is a technique for the acquirement of knowledge, without relation to emotional fancies. Knowledge is important, but
all sorts of fools are emotional . . . I am entirely in favour
of extending the technique to human beings.'

Lord speculated momentarily on the possibility that

his leg was being pulled, although Tinkham's tone, while emphatic, continued sober. He would explore further, he decided. 'What do you mean by that last remark, about human beings?'

'Why, just what I say!' Behind their glasses, Tinkham's eyes widened with frank, or assumed surprise. 'I am in favour of extending vivisection to human subjects. Because of the silly prejudices of a lot of half-wits, we should have to begin with condemned criminals. We could put them under an anaesthetic, perform the indicated vivisections and then administer a lethal dose, that's all. It is not important to me one way or the other, but for the sloppy humanitarians it would certainly be better than burning out their brain cells with electricity. And it would be of the utmost benefit to science. In addition to the condemned criminals, I can think of a good many other subjects whose only usefulness can be achieved in the same way: idiots, incurables . . . That would have to come later, when public ignorance has become accustomed to a rational procedure.'

There could no longer be any doubt that Tinkham was in earnest. The subject was evidently of special significance to him, for his voice had become slightly strained in speaking, and the detective, still somewhat surprised, asked if the view just expressed were his private one, or if it were generally held among his fellow-workers.

Tinkham started to answer, then considered, as one who wishes to give exact weight to the strength of the opposition, for his own rather than his hearer's benefit. 'We are not so many as yet, but we are united and we are determined. The medical profession is full of old fogeys and some of them have great influence because of past reputations. Naturally our first struggle is on the floor of the national medical convention. The annual convention comes next month, and we must win there before going to the public. But not even all the old men are against us; Gesell at P & S is one of our strongest leaders, and plans to make an address for us.'

Lord's notice was caught by the familiar name. So that mild old gentleman who had helped him yesterday, he remarked with a slight feeling of wonder, was engaged in this crusade for the right to dissect living human bodies. From his experience with psychological cliques (or 'schools,' as they liked to call themselves) he knew to what lengths some of these scientific controversies could go; this one, perhaps, was more than usually bitter, inasmuch as it was not mere theory that was in question, but a definite course of action. He found it difficult to visualise the rôle of a man like Gesell . . . But Cutter, he considered suddenly, what a fighter he would be, on one side or the other, with his aggressive disposition and his great surgical reputation. He found himself momentarily curious as to Cutter's allegiance, and made a mental note to inquire. Without much question, though, Cutter must have aligned himself with the vivisectionists. Lord caught the end of the assistant's continuing words.

' . . . We can and must prevail,' he was concluding. 'Nothing can be allowed to stand in our way. The history of science is the overwhelming of just these sentimental prejudices. From Galileo on we have fought and we are still fighting. Nothing can prevent for long the free search for knowledge.'

At some loss as to a fitting response to these assertions Lord was beginning, 'And what position does Dr – ?' when a subdued roar drew their attention through the window beside them. One of the big Boeing transports was taxi-ing up to the flagging in front of the building with intermittent spurts of explosions from its twin motors. Porters appeared beside the runway as if by magic, and a small mail truck whirled around the corner. The cabin door was opened, and down the accommodation steps now before it climbed half a dozen sleepy-looking travellers. Behind them appeared a stewardess, wideawake and neat, carrying three Thermos flasks in her arms.

Lord, scanning the expanse of the field, saw another big 'plane circling for a landing half a mile away across the level earth.

Fonda pointed a slim finger at the spark plug that a grease-covered mechanic had just withdrawn from one of the nine cylinders of the motor he was working on. 'Does it explode?' asked Fonda.

The man turned, hesitated, suddenly realised he had been addressed.

'Huh?'

'Does that little thing explode?'

The mechanic gaped. 'No, lady, it don't.' Fonda was no more bewildered by this small part of the motor than was he by the abrupt sight of the two girls before him. His whole expression indicated clearly that he would have liked to stay and hear some more; but habit prevailed, and he walked away toward a repair bench across the hangar. From there he continued to look over his shoulder as long as they remained on the floor.

The girls also walked on, although not until Fonda had tried several times in vain to open the locked cabin door of the transport whose spark plug had been found wanting. They were examining a small cabin 'plane, almost a sport model, at the other end of the hangar when they became aware of the approach of another man, this time in a well-cut business suit. 'Are you young ladies interested in anything particular?' Mr Wiley inquired pleasantly. 'I am the manager; if there is anything I can do?'

They both looked up, and Isa said, 'No, my sister always likes to poke around. Our name is Mann. We are going out on one of your 'planes in a few minutes.'

'Oh, yes. I remember your – '

Fonda favoured him with a deep blue stare. 'We are going out because my uncle is very ill. But Uncle Amos will fix him up all right.'

'Of course Amos will fix him up.' Isa's matter-of-fact words were plainly addressed to her sister. 'And while we're out there we'll see that Anne goes straight through with her divorce.'

Fonda chose this moment to decide on one of the lightning-changes she found so effective; from the naïve ingénue she became in the twinkling of an eye the woman-of-the-world. So tiny a tinge of hauteur might have been in her tone that one could never be really sure, as she said, 'You know perfectly well, Isa, that I do not consider the fault entirely on one side regarding the divorce. And I am sure that this gentleman can scarcely be interested in mother's plans.' She smiled at Mr Wiley as one sophisticate to another.

The manager was, in fact, not interested in the divorce of whose incidence he had just been apprised; he was a happily, if a bit prosaically, married man, but at the moment, it must be confessed, he was thinking neither of his wife nor of Mrs Mann. He was thinking, as most men in his position did think, of Fonda. In addition, he was astonished and rather embarrassed.

To relieve the latter emotion he pulled out his watch and, without considering the consequences fully, proposed, 'Your 'plane is leaving in about ten minutes. I must get up to the control room. Would you care to come with me?'

'Oh, yes!' cried Fonda brightly, before Isa could object. The ingénue had returned; she did not spring into the air, or even move at all, but the impression was of a very lovely little girl jumping up and down with glee. 'Can we, really?'

A rather strangled noise came from Isa's throat, an inhibited snort at these tactics of Fonda's which always affected her unhappily, no matter how often she witnessed them; but the manager, as he led the way toward a side door with a smiling, 'Come along, then,' felt unquestionably relieved; his masculine egotism was suddenly bolstered by the display of childishness, which was Fonda's intended result, along with getting into the control room.

At the end of their climb into the cupola atop the administration building they found a relatively small room, almost entirely large windows. There were several desks, on two of which Teletype machines were clicking busily, reporting 'plane positions and miscellaneous data. The Amalgamated 'plane dispatcher sat at one of the other desks and two men in pilots' uniforms stood looking at the six a.m. weather bureau synoptic map spread across one section of the sharply sloping ceiling; on the section next it were a series of eight smaller maps, the winds aloft charts of the weather bureau, showing by numbered arrows the direction and velocity of the wind from sea level to 13,000 feet, over the whole United States.

'But you don't go up that high, do you?' asked Fonda, who was looking at the numerals on the last of the charts.

The manager indulged a superior smile. 'Our transports have a ceiling of 20,500, Miss Mann, and an ordinary service ceiling of 18,400. Of course, flying west we ride much lower because, as you will notice, the prevailing winds at high altitudes are west winds. They always are.'

He glanced at the large chronometer in the panel between two of the windows, and abruptly called, 'Time!' The two pilots left the weather map and walked across to join him at one of the Teletype desks. 'The hourly weather report comes in at 8.50,' he explained in an aside to the girls.

Suddenly the Teletype ceased chattering. For thirty seconds it was silent; and then the reports started coming in. In turn the fourteen stations between Newark and Cleveland reported the conditions as observed within the last five minutes – Whitehouse, N.J., Northampton,

Pa., Numidia, Sunbury, Hartleton, Woodward Pass, Bellefonte, Kylertown, Greenwood Club, Brookville, Lamartine, Mercer, Bristolville, O., Cleveland. They reported, thought Isa, as she watched the Teletype figures transferred to the clearance sheet, plenty: general condition, ceiling, ground visibility, wind direction and velocity, temperature, barometric pressure and miscellaneous, including sometimes the dew point. It came over the Teletype in symbols and she couldn't understand most of it, but she did make out that the weather was clear except at Cleveland (where it was overcast but clearing), the barometer ranging around 30.1 and the ceilings almost all 'unlimited.'

The pilots' expression made it plain that they considered the reports propitious. 'Duck soup,' murmured the younger. The manager bent over a typewritten form which read, 'I, Frank Wiley, consider conditions suitable for the scheduled flight. Signed —, Manager,' and signed it. The senior pilot, an older man with a tanned, wind-bitten face, affixed his name to a similar slip.

'All right,' said Wiley, 'let's get below. Five minutes to departure.'

In the passengers' lounge bustle had replaced calm. Not only had several of the incoming passengers lingered at the counter on various errands, but one of the enormous Amalgamated limousines had stopped at the entrance simultaneously with the arrival of the 'plane from the west and discharged the outgoing passengers who were to leave with Lord's party.

With the entrance of the first newcomer the detective had hurried back to Cutter's side; in the midst of company he considered his position to be beside the man he was guarding. The note, of course, had specified 'noon, Central Time,' but that was no excuse to take chances regarding a possible anticipation. Closely but covertly he scrutinised all who came into the room, and his right hand had dropped carelessly into the side pocket of his coat. Captain Lord was on duty and, from now on, it was up to him.

The occupants of the room, however, evinced nothing but the most innocent intentions. All but one of the arrivals seemed plainly sleepy, and the exception was a young man carrying a portfolio who walked briskly through the lounge and closed the opposite door smartly behind him. With some curiosity Lord saw the door open again and three of the passengers from New York file in. Pons was not with them, but through one of the side windows he saw his friend waiting behind the limousine, from whose capacious rear trunk the hand baggage was being lifted. There was no mistaking the large form and grey hair of Dr Pons, who already was mopping his face with an outsize handkerchief.

Lord's first impression of the three who were coming in was simply that they were all tall men, and in the next moment he saw that two of them were slender, almost thin, while the other was well filled out, though by no means stout. At this earliest glance, across the airport lounge, he strove to place them, to decide which was which. One of the lanky men with the tweed suit and the brown, grained shoes, must be Craven the novelist, and the other thin one must be the philosopher; he wore a black artist's tie, a sack coat with trousers that did not match, and his face, along with his figure, was thin and ascetic. That left the well-built man for the rôle of the Rev. Dr Bellowes. Well, there was nothing against it; he had on a conservative suit of dark material, across which ran a heavy gold watch-chain and around his neck hung a broad black ribbon that disappeared into an upper vest pocket and doubtless ended in a pair of glasses.

Interrupting further observation, Mr Wiley appeared at the other end of the room, accompanied by the two girls. He looked about, then spying Cutter and the detective, raised an arm and beckoned them toward the exit to the field. Lord turned to his companion. 'I guess it's time we were on our way; the manager seems to want us. Oh, Tinkham, we're going out to the field.' He hoped Wiley had seen to it that there would be no last-minute hitch in the arranged programme.

But as they followed Fonda and Isa out the door and looked down the footway to the embarkation point, he saw that he need not have worried. The genuine arriving 'plane had been taxied away; a twin transport stood just behind the big Boeing now at the end of the path, and several men were engaged in transferring mail sacks and hand baggage from the 'plane at the end of the footway to the one behind it. Lord found time to admire Mr Wiley's efficiency; even the mail had been loaded into the decoy departing 'plane. There were only these few minutes in which anyone who might have planned harm to the ship could realise what ship would really be used; and these few minutes would avail such an evildoer little, with the manager of the Amalgamated terminus standing watchfully in front of the second transport.

As they stood waiting while the deceptive 'plane was taxied back to the hangar by a surprised mechanic, Lord remembered the question he had noted for the surgeon. He turned to the man beside him and said, 'By the way, Dr Cutter, I was discussing vivisection with Tinkham just now, and I gathered that there is a considerable controversy on the matter, especially as concerns the possible use of human subjects. I wondered how you stood on the point, but I suppose you support your assistant's party.'

Cutter, who had been watching the manoeuvring of the second 'plane, which had now drawn up opposite them, said, 'What . . . ? Oh, vivisection. Yes, Captain, I have done a great deal of vivisection in my time and been a hearty believer in it; Tinkham has probably gotten a lot of his enthusiasm from me. I used to think it our most promising technique, but – '

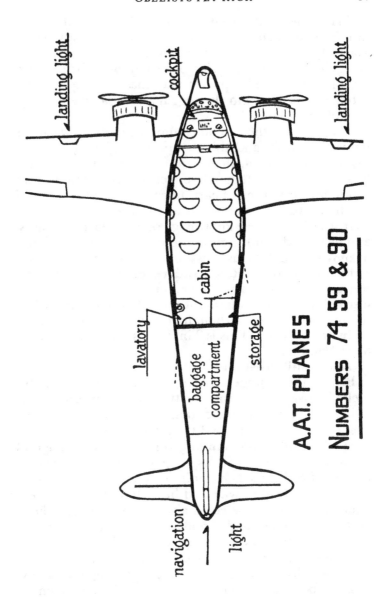

landing light

landing light

cockpit

cabin

lavatory

storage

baggage compartment

navigation

light

A.A.T. PLANES
NUMBERS 74 59 & 90

'What the devil are you trying to do?' cried the assistant from just behind them. Lord and Cutter both turned abruptly, to see Tinkham and an attendant apparently struggling for the possession of a small black bag carried by the former. The porter was maintaining that all satchels must go into the luggage compartment in the rear of the 'plane.

'But you say there is no communication between the passenger cabin and this compartment,' Cutter's aide expostulated. 'Well, then, you can't have it, and that's final. This bag contains a hypodermic and a new glonoin solute for Dr Cutter's heart, in case it becomes affected by the altitude. It goes with me, in the cabin.'

It was Lord's first knowledge of any heart weakness, and he looked inquiringly at the surgeon. 'Yes,' the latter acknowledged, 'it's just possible that I might experience a slight heart attack if we go high enough. Most unlikely, but as a precaution we have agreed to take out some nitro-glycerine as a stimulant. I was bothered once when mountain climbing, although that was certainly brought on by the exertion. This is Tinkham's suggestion, really; he insisted on it.'

'And I still insist on it.'

Before the younger man's emphasis the attendant melted away, and the party proceeded down the pathway to the accommodation ladder before the 'plane. Just inside the cabin stood the junior pilot; he was grinning cheerfully and handing out a small package of chewing gum and an air log map to each passenger who entered. Lord placed Cutter in the rear seat just forward of the entrance doorway and himself took the rear seat opposite. Tinkham selected a seat several places ahead of the detective, and Fonda and Isa took the two foremost seats in the cabin on opposite sides of the aisle. In a moment the other four passengers came stumbling in awkwardly, making a difficult progress up the narrow passage between the chairs. Dr Pons, the last to enter, did not recognise Lord in the dimmer light of the cabin, and the detective thought this moment of departure not the one in which to greet him. Of the ten in the cabin, it was the chair in front of Lord that remained vacant. The junior pilot had gone forward to the cockpit and, passing up the two steps from the cabin, had left open the small connecting door. A porter had removed the accommodation ladder and just outside the entrance stood Wiley, watch in hand. 'Time!' called the manager, then glanced within, hand on the door. He smiled across at Lord. 'Good luck,' he said in a low voice.

The door slammed.

The motors roared; the tail of the 'plane slewed around and it began taxi-ing slowly away from the buildings. Around the cockpit partition appeared the head of the junior pilot. 'Please adjust your safety belts everyone, for the take-off; you can release them when we are in the air.'

It seemed a long time bumping across the field to the opposite side, but finally the 'plane swept around once more, facing nearly in the direction from which it had come, and stopped. With the landing-gear brakes clamped tightly the motors were opened to full throttle, the r.p.m.'s, oil and fuel pressures and temperatures tested and the radio and other instruments checked. All this took scarcely a minute.

The final tests had been made, the brakes released. The roar of the motors diminished, then rose again as the 'plane moved off in response to the 'All Clear' signal from across the field. Gradually it gathered momentum, and the bumps became harder. The field, Lord noticed, was not as smooth as it looked. Outside, the ground was speeding past, and suddenly, although there seemed no difference through the windows, he realised that the bumps had stopped. They had taken off.

Then the nose of the 'plane lifted perceptibly; they began to climb and the ground fell away rapidly. Lord looked at the altimeter on the cockpit partition and saw that the pointer was moving. He was just in time, in glancing back through the window, to see the hangar roofs sweep away beneath them, to see the lines of parked automobiles already tiny below and a stretch of the Elevated Highway he had travelled this morning, as the 'plane tilted slightly in a bank and the horizon lifted above the top of his window.

'PX,' chattered the Teletype in the Amalgamated control tower, '74 LEWIS CV D9.03 NK.'

(Position report. Airplane No. 74. Senior Pilot Lewis. Destination Cleveland. Departed 9.03 a.m. Signed: Newark.)

'PX 74 LEWIS CV D9.03 NK.'

3750 FEET

The junior pilot stepped down into the cabin from the cockpit. He came the length of the cabin and opened the locker door on the starboard side; when he returned he carried a shallow cardboard box. After an hour's flight the noise of the motors had already become accustomed, and everyone heard his raised voice without difficulty.

'We are in the cross-currents over the Allegheny Mountains. It will be a little rough for half an hour or less. By that time we shall have come into smooth air again, but in the meantime I will pass these aromatic buds around for any of you who may feel uncomfortable.'

He came slowly down the aisle, pausing to instruct the partakers in the use of the little bulbs whose acquaintance Lord had made the previous morning. Most of the passengers partook, for the peculiar motion that a 'plane gains when flying through disturbed air was becoming noticeable.

The well-built man in the dark suit, who had been the

first to re-fasten his safety belt when the motion had
begun, reached out his hand as the pilot approached.
'Thank you,' he said. 'I know how to use 'em. A bit
bumpy about here, what? Air pockets.'

The pilot, radiating cheerful unconcern, recognised
an experienced air traveller. 'We used to call them pockets, sir. Of course they're not pockets, really – just billows in the air, pretty much like billows in water. We ride
up and down on them.'

'Quite.' The passenger was brushing the tiny frag-
ments of glass into the ashtray beside him. 'I didn't know
that. Interesting. Thanks.'

Dr Pons needed instruction, and welcomed it. He sat
now in the vacant seat in front of the detective and,
because he had screwed himself around in it to look
backwards toward Lord, with whom he was talking, had
not fastened his belt. His face, as he held to the back of
the seat, was pasty, but after he had been shown how to
inhale the contents of the offered bulb, and had relieved
himself of a tremendous sneeze immediately afterward,
his appearance showed marked improvement. The pilot
adjusted the belt loosely around his liberal waist and
departed forward. At the head of the cabin he entrusted
his box of restoratives to Fonda, in case they should be
wanted during his absence in the cockpit, and only
remembered, after he had taken his own seat again, that
he had originally meant to leave it with the more
competent-looking Isa across the aisle. Somehow, in
coming up the cabin, he had not noticed anyone but
Fonda.

'Yes,' said Pons, 'I'm going out to Hollywood. They
pay good money for technical advice. Of course, it's a
racket, but I know the ropes now; I've been there before.'

'Why fly, though? I don't believe you really enjoy
flying. Do you?'

'Oh, I don't mind it. I had to this time, anyhow;
they're making a picture about two girls in love with

each other, and they have got into a jam and need to be helped out. They're in a hurry, spending thousands of dollars a day to keep everyone on location, until I get there . . . Besides,' Pons added with a return of his customarily broad, good-natured grin, 'if I had known about this, I wouldn't have missed out on it for anything. I suppose we can expect the shooting to start any minute now, old man.'

Lord permitted a slow smile to crease the corners of his lips. 'Just because you saw some shooting on the *Meganaut* you don't need to expect gunfire to follow me around like a pet dog, doctor.' He added more seriously, 'As a matter of fact, this excursion isn't exactly in the nature of a joke.'

'No? I suppose not. What *is* it about, anyhow? Can you tell me?'

The detective had found that while it was possible to be heard the full length of the cabin, and that without shouting, it was also possible by employing a correct modulation of the voice, to make one's words audible for a distance of no more than two or three feet. Employing this tone, he said, 'I know you can be trusted to keep quiet, doctor. Confidentially, I am guarding Dr Cutter, just across the aisle here, on this trip. He has received a death threat. Now, you know as much as I do.'

Dr Pons pursed his lips for a soundless whistle. 'You don't say so?' He lowered his voice and turned to eye the man in the seat opposite. He saw little more than a large shoulder, a grizzled cheek and the end of a beard touched with grey; Dr Cutter was sitting quietly looking out the window beside him.

After a pause Pons turned back again to the detective. 'You're just guarding him on the trip?' he asked, his voice still subdued. 'Yes? Well, it doesn't look so difficult; I don't see how anyone could very well get at him where he is, and I suppose it will be like this all the way out. If you keep watching these people as you are now' (for Lord, even while talking to his companion, had been letting his eyes rove continually along the two lines of seats ahead), 'I don't see how anyone can turn around or get out his chair to start something, without giving you plenty of warning . . . Have you any idea whom to look out for? It's someone with us, I suppose?'

'I don't know who it is, or whether he or it is even with us. I'm just beginning to get acquainted with Cutter's own party, and I haven't even spoken to the rest of these people; don't know much about them . . . By the way, who is the man just ahead of Cutter, in the tweed suit?'

'I can tell you that; I rode out with them from New York. The man in the tweed suit is some sort of philosopher, I understand. The fellow farther up, with the funny black tie, is a minister – Blows, Belows, something like that; and the dark suit ahead of you is an Englishman called Craven. None of them seemed desperate characters when I was talking to them.'

Pons paused and Lord smiled, then explained that he had guessed them all wrong when he had first seen them entering the airport lounge at Newark. 'Let's get them right now,' he added. 'The lanky tweed is Isador Didenot, philosopher; the long thin one with the tie and the coat and trousers that don't match is Manly Bellowes, and the big man of the gold watch-chain is Hugh L. Craven, English novelist.' He murmured the names over again, while he inspected as much as he could see of the three passengers.

'Ugh!' cried Pons, shaking in his seat. 'Gosh, what a jolt! How much longer do you think this will keep up?'

'Don't know. But there,' his friend pointed through the window, 'that ought to be Bellefonte, according to the log; we're half-way through the mountains, at any rate.'

Dr Pons craned his neck around and, peering through the glass, saw a valley in the Allegheny hills opening out beneath them. As he watched, it spread out right and left, and the 'plane swam steadily across it; almost directly below, as the cabin tilted momentarily, appeared a marked-out field, a tower, a radio mast, a large yellow number painted on a black background – 52 B.

'That's Bellefonte, all right,' Lord confirmed, consulting his air log. 'The field is 745 feet by this map, but there's still some higher ground beyond before we ease off for Cleveland.' While he spoke the motors took on a slightly deeper note, and the nose of the transport lifted gently as it climbed to surmount the greater altitudes around Clearfield thirty miles ahead.

'Those three men,' he continued, 'have you come to any psychological conclusions about them, doctor?'

The psychologist, glad to have his attention withdrawn from the motion, said, 'Not very many. From what I know of the minister, I'd say he was out for personal publicity. I don't know anything about Didenot, except that he's a philosopher, and a philosopher – Well, I used to be interested in philosophy as an undergraduate, but I gave it up and, really, I just can't think in those terms any more – don't know what they're talking about. My own approach is entirely different . . . The Englishman is typical. Silly aloofness; gives me a pain . . . That's not much, I guess, but I didn't know about their possible importance when I was riding out with them. From what I've seen, I wouldn't pick any of them as your assailant, but then, of course, I haven't seen enough of them yet.'

'I don't consider them very seriously myself, except that, so far, it may be anyone. I think the threat meant business, and I can't afford to play favourites at this point; it would be too costly to be wrong.'

'What about your own party?'

'Cutter's assistant and his two nieces. Innocent enough looking, too.'

'H'm. Well, maybe.' The psychologist considered,

and Lord knew what was coming. 'Two girls and a young man. Any love affair there? Jealousy? Avuncular objection to a suitor?'

'Not that I know of. But we'll discuss it later.' Dr Cutter, Lord noticed, had become restless and was casting inquiring glances in his direction. He loosened his belt and prepared to get up.

'Just as you say.' Dr Pons was unabashed as he began screwing himself around forward in his own seat. 'One of them might be upsetting. That girl up in front, in this line of seats, I'd say, is a real captivatress.'

Lord grinned broadly, but to himself; he had been right in one guess, at all events.

2800 FEET

Cleveland lay behind them. They had spent only a few minutes there, while the 'plane was refuelled and the pilots had visited the administration building. It had been almost exactly eleven o'clock, Central Time, when they had sped across the field and taken the air again for the hop to Chicago. Sixty minutes to zero hour, Lord had thought, mentally turning back the hands of the cabin clock which had then still registered Eastern Time.

They had flown to the south of Toledo without pausing, while the air field Teletype reported their passage. Now they were flying over western Ohio, approaching the Indiana line, clear enough on the map, but unlikely to be identified below. To the south appeared a little cluster of buildings – Archbold, said the log map – while out the starboard windows the outlines of Intermediate Field No. 18 could just be glimpsed to the north.

Lord sat in his seat as alertly as ever. His preparations had been made, every preparation he could think of, and the time of their testing was drawing near. Across the aisle Dr Cutter rode, chin in hand. He pressed his lips together, stretching them tightly across his teeth; it made of his mouth a clear-cut scar above the beard, like those which his deft surgeon's fingers so skilfully made in the tegument of human bodies. His face, lean and square, beneath whose surface the muscles formed the hard, harsh angles of modernistic sculpture, was turned forward along the parallel rows of seats coming down the cabin from the rear wall of the pilots' cockpit.

Up the cabin he saw, without noticing, the backs of his nieces' heads beyond those of the other passengers. Fonda's hair, a bright, marcelled profusion escaping from underneath the right side of her pert little hat; Isa's hair, close-cut beneath the brim of a masculine felt. Both girls were dressed in travelling suits, tailored; Fonda, of course, would discard hers for something far more alluring at the earliest opportunity, but Isa would keep hers on. All her clothes were equally severe, as close an approximation of male attire as the most high-priced and faddish couturier would permit.

Out the window beside the surgeon the sky was bright and, far below, lay the map-like expanse of fields, roads and towns, moving past with deceptive slowness. There were dark clouds away to the north, but it seemed certain that the 'plane would skirt to the south of them and skim contemptuously beyond their menace. That scene, too, he saw without being aware of it.

His thoughts were altogether concerned with the mission toward which he was winging at so high a speed. Well, he could do it, if that detective fellow – what was his name, now, Lord? – got him there all right. Very dangerous and very delicate, that operation; almost certain to fail if conducted by an ordinary surgeon. But he could do it. He had done it before, he could do it again; he had, and always had had, plenty of confidence. He could pull the man through, brother or not, if he reached him in time, and if he got there alive.

He had never felt fear in his life, so he thought, and he did not feel it now. But he couldn't deal with assassination. The threat of it merely angered him, and anger he knew to be an inefficient, blundering emotion. His mind was tempered to deal with clear, hard facts; before threats, however definite, from the nebulous unknown he was helpless. He was a realist, and so he had taken his warning seriously; but there he halted. As an expert, he had put his problem into the hands of other experts. It was up to Captain Lord to see that he reached the man he would save, in a fit condition to save him.

An air bump changed the direction of his thoughts. Lucky he had brought his assistant, young Tinkham. A brilliant young man, the best assistant he had ever had, although foolishly apprehensive about that heart attack business. Already Tinkham had pestered him twice, despite the low altitudes at which they were flying, and the third time, no doubt, he would have to take an injection, just to keep the man quiet. There he was, up ahead, just visible from Cutter's own seat, the last in the cabin and almost against the wall of the small compartment behind, which was occupied only by inanimate supplies. Tinkham ahead and Captain Lord in the chair directly across the narrow aisle.

It had been rough for the last hour, ever since leaving Cleveland, uncomfortably rough. If it kept on much longer he would have to fasten his safety belt again. Unexpectedly the stations had commenced reporting unsettled weather from all directions. Spring vagaries, local storms; those clouds out the window were one of them. Already on this hop the passengers had passed back the box containing the little glass bulbs that did so much to overcome air nausea. He glanced at the clock in the cabin's forward wall and was surprised to see that it now showed a few minutes before noon; he remembered its having been retarded an hour from Eastern Time just

as they were passing over the southern outskirts of
Toledo. But that was the time; twelve noon, Central
Time, was the threatened hour of his death!

A succession of sharp bumps and a giddy little slip
caused general discomfort along the cabin. He was
beginning to feel a trifle sick again, himself. Opposite
him the detective – Lord – was leaning forward and passing up the word for another trip of the box of tiny bulbs.
It was somewhat slow in coming back; three of the
passengers, he did not notice whom, availed themselves
of its assistance before handing it along.

Now Lord had it. He took out one of the bulbs, broke
it, inhaled, then leaned over and offered one to Cutter.

He didn't need it. He shook his head; but the detective, with a significant glance toward the clock, pressed it
on him. 'Better take one now, while I have them here.
The effect will last for some time.'

Well, perhaps he had better. Nearly twelve o'clock.
He felt but very slightly upset, but it would be better to
feel perfectly fit if anything *did* happen at noon. He saw
Tinkham rising from a chair ahead; coming back, probably, to be on hand beside his seat when the hands of the
clock coincided at twelve. He nodded and said, 'Might as
well.' He took the bulb.

At the first long inhalation he stiffened sharply. There
was a momentary burning sensation from his lungs; then
blankly, like the dropping of a colourless curtain –
nothing. He slumped forward, swaying in his chair. His
body fell into the aisle, where it lay curiously huddled at
the detective's feet . . .

On the forward wall of the cabin the hands of the clock
were vertical.

Part III – Titillation

In the face of emergency Captain Lord acted quickly and
calmly. Standing directly above the body in the aisle, he
quickly adjusted the surgeon's seat to its recumbent
position, and with Tinkham's assistance lifted Cutter
and placed him upon it.

Tinkham, his fingers on the surgeon's wrist, said, 'No
pulse. Severe heart attack,' and started to open the small
bag he had brought with him when approaching Cutter's chair. He had already extracted a hypodermic
needle and was in the act of rolling back his patron's
sleeve when the detective interrupted him curtly.

'No injection,' said Lord sharply.

Tinkham paused, stared. 'What?'

'Dr Cutter is not to be tampered with in any way.'

'What do you mean, tampered with?' The assistant's
face was pale with anger and his voice had taken on the
same strained timbre Lord had remarked when he spoke
of vivisection. 'This man is seriously ill. Have you forgotten that I am a doctor? I shall examine him and treat
him at once.'

'You will neither examine him nor will you treat him,'
Lord answered with complete certainty. 'Possibly you
have forgotten that my authority is final in this matter.
Possibly also you are unaware that, with very few exceptions, everyone in this 'plane is suspect of having done Dr
Cutter the violence he has already suffered.' The detective raised his voice. 'Dr Pons! Will you come back here,
please?'

Dr Pons rose with alacrity and it was apparent that
Lord's voice need not have been raised to summon him.
The attention of all the passengers was focused upon the
group at the rear of the cabin, and a protest was, in fact,

already rising from the direction of the Rev. Manly Bellowes at Lord's interference with Tinkham. Pons, on his
way down the aisle, took occasion to silence it by
announcing, 'This man is a detective of the New York
Force. I have known him for years, and you may take it
he knows what he is doing.'

As the psychologist approached, Lord cut short the
assistant's angry remonstrances and turned to the man
in the seat directly ahead of Cutter's. He pointed to the
surgeon's handkerchief lying in the aisle where it had
fallen. 'Professor Didenot,' he requested, 'will you kindly
take that handkerchief and sniff it. Be careful, don't get
your nose too close to it. Just a sniff.'

Didenot, surprised at being addressed by name,
leaned over and retrieved the handkerchief. Undoubtedly he brought it too close to his nostrils when he
raised it, for he swayed and grasped at the back of his
chair, then commenced to cough and retch violently.

Lord nodded. 'I thought so. Cutter had no heart
attack at this altitude. He was poisoned by the bulb he
inhaled . . . Put your face to the ventilator, Didenot, and
don't do any more sniffing.' The advice was
unnecessary; the philosopher was already leaning
against the side of the fuselage, with his nose to the
ventilator, continuing to cough – but gradually recov-
ering. Lord took the handkerchief from his limp fingers,
folded it carefully and put it in his wallet.

'I insist,' began Tinkham, 'on examining – '

'Just a minute. Pons, take a look at Dr Cutter, will you,
and see what you make of his condition.'

Pons stepped forward, his weight easily pushing the
smaller assistant out of his path. He bent forward and
scrutinised the prone form of the surgeon closely,
searched for a pulse, felt of his skin and finally turned
back one of the closed eyelids.

'I'm not a physician, as you know, Lord,' he said,
straightening up, 'but I think there is no doubt at all that

this man is dead. I can assure you of my own knowledge, also, that he did not die of a heart attack, for I happen to be familiar with the symptoms of that. That's about as far as I can go for you, I'm afraid.'

'You see,' Tinkham's voice cut in with angry emphasis, 'this man is not a doctor. I insist upon examining Dr Cutter at once and rendering whatever assistance may be possible.'

Michael Lord turned and eyed the young man coldly.

'We may as well have a showdown right now.' he said incisively; then, raising his voice, 'Gentlemen, I want no one to be in any doubt as to the situation which has arisen. First of all, I am Captain Lord of the New York Police Department; I intend to have my badge passed around the cabin, so that no one shall have any excuse for doubting my credentials.' He drew a small gold badge from his pocket and handed it to Didenot who, after a brief observation, silently passed it on to the man ahead, as the detective added, 'The pilots are already aware of my identity, as is Dr Pons, and that constitutes more corroboration than is necessary for anyone.'

He continued, 'Dr Cutter has received a threat of death and I have been accompanying him in order to protect him. It is apparent that I have failed, but I assure you that I shall discover and arrest his assailant before this trip is over. When we reach Chicago no one is to leave this cabin until I give my permission; and if the culprit is not then found, the passengers will transfer directly to our next 'plane under guard.

'There is no question but that Dr Cutter met his death through the agency of the small bulb which he broke in his handkerchief and inhaled. That was the means used by the criminal to attack him. The first thing is to discover the origin of that box of bulbs. Will someone see if the junior pilot can step back here for a few moments?'

Isa Mann, with a set face but dry-eyed, got up from her seat and opened the door to the pilots' compartment.

Across the aisle from her Fonda sat in shocked immo-
bility, her hands twisting in her lap, but without any
other apparent sign of emotion. As Isa's head disappeared around the narrow doorway, the detective added,
'I have full authority to handle this situation as I think
best. I am armed, and you may count upon it that the
pilots, who are also armed, will back me up in any decision I may make. For the time being you will all please
consider yourselves under my orders. There is a murderer in this small company, and it will alleviate a very
bad situation if my instructions are obeyed promptly
until this criminal has been discovered.'

Lord's voice ceased, and the passengers, who had
watched and listened silently, were unquestionably
impressed. Their varying expressions indicated everything from comprehension to fear, and, as his concluding
words were heard, more than one involuntary glance of
suspicion was cast among the fellow-travellers. The
junior pilot, his youthful face stern, came down the aisle
just as Professor Didenot handed back the badge, which
had now made a full circuit of the cabin.

'Is everybody satisfied as to our present status?' Lord
demanded.

There was no dissenting reply; there were, in fact, no
replies at all and, taking the silence for acquiescence, he
addressed the pilot. 'Can you tell us anything about the
box of aromatic buds we have been using in this 'plane?'

The pilot was plainly surprised. 'What about them?'
he asked.

'Mainly, where did they come from? Who put them on
the 'plane? Who has had a chance to tamper with them
since they were put on and before we commenced to use
them?'

'Oh, why, I put them on board myself. I drew that box
from the Commissary myself just before we left Newark
and locked it in the supply cabinet before anyone else
had gotten aboard. When I brought it out, just before we

passed Bellefonte, the box was still sealed, so no one could have been fooling with it up to then. But why? What about them?'

'One of them contained poison gas of some kind. Dr Cutter, who inhaled it, has died from its effects.'

The pilot stiffened as if suddenly stung. 'What! Is this passenger dead? I thought he was just sick.' The young man's hand went unconsciously to the holster at his side. 'Who did it?'

'That is what we are trying to find out. First, we must eliminate any chance that this poison bulb was brought into the 'plane in the box with the rest of the bulbs. Fortunately you can tell us where the original box came from. Was it an ordinary issue, just as usual, or was there anything out of the ordinary about the box when you got it?'

'Nothing at all out of the ordinary about it, sir. It came off the top of the stack that's always in the Commissary. The clerk just turned around, took the top one and handed it to me. I put it under my arm and brought it aboard. It looked just like every other one to me.'

'I see. That means that the poison bulb was substituted, then, by one of the passengers some time after you first opened the box and passed it around near Bellefonte. By the way, here is the box. I want you to lock it up and when we reach Chicago, the remaining bulbs will be turned over to the police department for examination.'

The pilot, having fulfilled this instruction and returned the keys of the locker to his pocket, asked, 'What do you want done, Captain Lord? We have orders to follow your requests so far as possible. Do you want to land, or shall we go on to Chicago? We're less than an hour from there now.'

'We shall go right through to Chicago – and beyond.' Lord paused and considered. 'I want to get the history of that box as clearly as possible. With whom did you leave it after you first passed it around? It was only passed around once by you, wasn't it?'

'Yes, I only passed it the first time, when I told the passengers how to use the bulbs. I don't know how many more times it was used, of course. When I had finished I went up the aisle and left it – ' Suddenly the young man's face flushed and he caught his breath perceptibly. It was quite evident that he had abruptly recognised the bearing of the question. He stammered, 'I don't know – I've forgotten who I left it with.'

'You left it with me,' said Fonda Mann in a choking voice, but with a look at the pilot that plainly said, 'Thank you just the same.' The young man's face became redder than ever.

Isa's voice, without any emotion at all, asserted, 'And I had it part of the time. Twice after it had gone around, anyhow.'

Lord repressed a smile at the expense of the discomfited pilot. Never had he seen a clearer instance of beauty interfering with the pursuit of an investigation. 'That's what I thought,' he said. 'Miss Fonda Mann had it after its first trip around, and after that Miss Isa had it until it came back for the last time. Well, it's hardly conclusive of anything; everyone in the cabin has had the box at one time or another with sufficient opportunity for substitution.'

He turned once more to the pilot. 'Can you send a message for me?'

'Yeah. I mean, sure. I mean, of course, sir.'

'To whom will it go?'

'It will go to the Chicago field. We wouldn't be calling them for another fifteen minutes or so, but I can get them any time.'

The detective scribbled rapidly on a page from his small note-book . . . 'Stretcher to meet us on field. Also detail of eight police to form cordon around 'plane and escort passengers to departing ship . . . ' He handed the sheet of paper to the pilot.

The latter took it, read. 'You want these messages sent right away?'

'Please. Send them to the manager of your field and sign them with my name: Lord, Captain, New York Police Department. Be sure they are understood. If there is any doubt, let me know.'

As the pilot made his way forward, Cutter's assistant got up from the seat across the aisle into which he had subsided when pushed aside by Pons. 'Now, this non-sense – ' he began.

Lord turned to him in some exasperation. 'Tinkham,' he said, 'I've had enough of it. There is nothing stupid about you; you understand clearly my position and my authority. If you continue your interference, I tell you plainly I'll handcuff you, and you can ride that way to Chicago, where I shall place you under formal arrest.'

The eyes of the two men met and held, Tinkham's obviously hostile, the detective's appraising. Lord continued, 'I have made no charge against you, and I am not prepared to do so – now. Nevertheless, you are one of several suspected people, and you will certainly have no special privileges and no opportunity to meddle with Dr Cutter's body. Someone gave Dr Cutter a poisoned bulb, and until that person is found, you, like everyone else in this 'plane, will obey my orders. I assure you I mean every word of it.'

Tinkham's voice, icicled, said, 'You are the man who handed him that bulb. I saw you.' He turned on his heel and walked back to his chair up the cabin. He sat down, placed his bag across his knees; his posture assumed the rigid, immobile lines of repressed animosity.

3000 FEET

Lord returned to his own seat and Dr Pons, who had stood aside to the rear during the preceding exchange, sank into the vacant chair just forward of the detective's. There was a pause: the passengers sat silently for the moment, digesting the significance of the drama in which they so suddenly found themselves involved. Then gradually conversation sprang up, first in one place, then in another. The Rev. Bellowes, whose chair was directly behind Isa's, leaned forward and tapped her on the shoulder.

Professor Didenot arose and was standing beside Lord's chair, somewhat timidly. He looked pale and his breathing, either from embarrassment or from the remaining effects of his sniff at Cutter's handkerchief, was slightly irregular.

As the detective looked up, he spoke in a low tone. 'I – I should like a few words with you. I think – I – to tell you the truth, I think the man you were just talking to is the one you want.'

Pons glanced around. Then, realising to whom the professor was alluding, 'Oh, you mean the young doctor?'

'What makes you think that, Professor Didenot?' asked Lord. 'Here, wait a minute.' He reached behind his chair and brought forward a small, collapsible stool which was provided for the comfort of a stewardess in the tiny open space at the rear of the cabin. Since no stewardess travelled with them on the daytime flight to Chicago, it had been leaning against the metal wall behind the last seat. The philosopher accepted it and, placing it at the end of the narrow aisle, leaned forward confidentially.

Lord's tone was casual, almost careless. 'What reason

have you to accuse him, Didenot?'

'I would scarcely – scarcely accuse him. But it seems to me he is the only one aboard who might rationally be suspected. It is plain to reason from the nature of the action that he is the only one who could have performed it.'

'How so?'

'That – is surely obvious.'

'Not to me,' Lord admitted. 'No, I'm afraid it's not at all obvious. But I have no objection to listening. Go ahead and tell me just what is in your mind.'

'Well,' began Didenot, 'so far as I am concerned, I have never seen – seen the victim of this attack before. It is pure chance that we are on the same 'plane at the same time. That can be established. I am sure that it is also true of the other passengers, who, I have gathered, are a minister, a writer and this gentleman here,' indicating Pons, 'whose profession I do not know, but who, I believe, is a scientist of some kind. Until this morning we had never seen each other, and I am confident none of us is even acquainted with the murdered man.'

'Well?'

'But the only other people are two young ladies and yourself. It is fantastic to suspect you, in view of – your identity; and it is almost as fantastic to suspect either of the young women.'

'Why do you say that?' Pons interrupted. 'I am a psychologist, and I assure you there is nothing fantastic about the idea that women are capable of crime.'

'But – but not this kind of crime. Oh, I know poison is supposed to be a weapon congenial to women, and if it had been arsenic or some simple drug the case would not be so clear. But a poison gas! Where could they get it? How could it be introduced by a woman in such a fashion?'

'You are a philosopher, I believe, professor?' It was Lord who put the question.

'Yes,' agreed Didenot, 'I am a professional philosopher. And as such I am acquainted with the techniques of modern science in a general way. Science has greatly changed our view of reality in recent times, and I am a realist who accepts the findings of exact science for the larger purposes of philosophy. I am afraid,' he added parenthetically, with a glance toward Pons, 'that I cannot accept the findings of psychology so readily. They are too – random. The first task of any scientific inquiry is selection; the answers found depend greatly on the questions asked. It is not by asking random questions of nature that we can expect essential knowledge.'

'Quite right,' Pons grunted. 'I agree with you.'

'To get back to the present case,' suggested Lord.

Didenot said, 'Yes. I have been using the process of elimination, a proper method of logical deduction. From the time of Sherlock Holmes, I believe it has been a method widely used in your profession – Captain? Eliminate the impossible, and what is left is the answer sought. An inductive process will lead – to the same conclusion. We have the use of an unusual poison, in a gaseous state difficult to obtain. Moreoever, this gas is enclosed in a small glass bulb which itself is a counterfeit of similar harmless bulbs in commercial use. Then either the poison bulb must have been specially made or an ordinary bulb obtained, from which the harmless gas was exhausted and into which the poison gas was introduced. Last of all we have a doctor, a research man, I understand, to whom the facilities for such work are at hand in a laboratory. Professionally, also, he has access to a wide range of poisonous materials. I – I can only repeat that to suspect a young woman of this achievement, when all the inductive particulars point to a research man who is also present, is fantastic. Deduction and induction both point to the same man, and the probability of error in such a case is logically negligible.'

'That's impressive so far as it goes,' Lord admitted. 'But have you any more concrete evidences for your suspicions?'

'When logic gives us as clear a reply as at present, it is supererogatory to ask for further evidence.'

The detective shook his head. 'I'm afraid not. Supererogation of the kind you mention is precisely a passion with most trial judges.'

Didenot paused, and it was evident that he sought to bring his thoughts down from the abstract to more primitive considerations. Just as Pons was about to break the short silence he said, 'Yes, there are corroboratory facts. This man used the box of bulbs as it was being passed back, for I saw him do so. He could have put in his poison bulb then. And his extraordinary persistence in attempting to "examine" the body may well have been intended to give him an opportunity to do away with the evidence of the poison, so that he could insist upon simple heart failure as the cause of death. He certainly tried hard enough to do that.'

'By the way,' Lord spoke with increased interest, 'did you happen to notice anyone else who made use of those bulbs the last time they were handed back, just before Cutter took his?'

'Yes. The very good-looking young lady up front took one first. Then this gentleman took one, and, last of all, the man Tinkham. Of course,' Didenot considered, looking at Dr Pons with speculation in his eye, 'this gentleman is a scientist, also. Do you do research, sir?' he asked suddenly.

'Ah – ugh,' said Pons in a startled fashion. 'Yes, I do research. So what?'

Lord grinned involuntarily. 'You may dismiss your fears, professor,' he told his informant. 'I can vouch for Dr Pons personally. It would be impossible to convince me, much less a jury, that he is involved in this matter, except as a possible witness.'

'Ah! It was only a sudden idea. I apologise, doctor. After all, logic points inexorably to the other man.'

Lord's attitude was not at all that of one convinced, but rather that of one interested in another's attempt to solve a puzzle. He said quietly, 'However inexorable your logic may be, Didenot, you have failed so far to explain a very vital point. How did Tinkham, if it was Tinkham, manage to get his poison bulb into Cutter's handkerchief?'

'He was the last to use the box before it was passed back. Of course. All he had to do was to put the poison bulb on the end of the row, and it would be the next one taken out.'

'That doesn't follow; but, granting it, how could he know that Cutter would be the next one to use a bulb? Why not you, for instance? He certainly couldn't tell that. As a matter of fact, I not only picked out a bulb and gave it to Dr Cutter, but I myself used one after Tinkham did and before Cutter did. And also, as a matter of fact, I didn't take the bulb on the end of the row in either case.'

'Well . . . I have not considered that aspect. Maybe he just took a chance.'

'Oh, come,' Pons contributed. 'Took a chance? You can't possibly mean that. Think of your own theory of probabilities. If Tinkham put a single poison bulb into the box, intended for Cutter, and it was in fact the one to reach Cutter under the circumstances that existed – No. Why, the chances would be millions against one!'

The philosopher acknowledged the point with a slight motion of his hand. 'You are right about that. I do not profess to explain the actual method by which he got the proper bulb to his victim . . . But perhaps he put in several of the poison kind. Or maybe he changed them all; there were only a few left in the box as I remember it. Yes, that would bring the probability to unity, or certainty.'

'No, he couldn't have changed them all,' Lord pointed

out. 'I took one after he had had the box, and it was genuine.'

'Several, then.'

'It still leaves the probabilities against you – especially as he could not possibly know who would take the next bulb. And if anyone but Cutter had taken the poison, there would go his last chance of getting the man he wanted to get. I'll wager no one takes another of those bulbs this trip, out of that box or any other we may get at Chicago.'

'When logical considerations point so – '

'Excuse me,' Lord interrupted abruptly. He half rose from his seat and across the still body stretched on the opposite chair looked through the starboard window beyond it. Below them lay a flat expanse with clusters of buildings dotted upon it haphazardly; a network of converging railways traced their spidery lines across it, and far away to the north he thought he could catch a glimpse of silvery brightness where the sun shone on water.

'Have you got your air log, Pons? Where are we?'

The psychologist fumbled among the batch of envelopes and papers stuffed in the inside pocket of his coat. 'Only a minute ago,' he offered, 'I saw a big "3" on the roof of a building out this window. I suppose that's one of the intermediate fields . . . Yes, here you are.'

Lord, the log in his hand, ran a finger down the printed notations beside the map. ' "3." Yes, there it is, just south of McCool.' Again he peered through the glass, inset in the metal wall. He had never flown to Chicago before, but several times he had crossed the plain beneath on one of those thin, tiny lines that were railroad tracks. Even from this unaccustomed angle he recognised the drab, cheerless, industrial approach to Chicago. The water to the north was much plainer now, and against it the towering stacks of great steel mills made a small, jagged comb. Gary. He glanced at the clock on the forward wall of the cabin; three minutes past one o'clock.

'We're getting in. I shall have to step ahead and speak to the pilots for a moment. Pons, will you stay here until I come back, and see that no one touches Dr Cutter? In any way at all. If anyone tries to, yell for me.'

He turned to Didenot. 'I'm obliged for your ideas, professor, and I will grant you that they are perfectly logical. At the same time, I cannot agree with you that they are sufficient even for an arrest. Whoever succeeded in getting that bulb to Cutter will have to be shown to have used a means that had practically no chance of allowing the poison to go astray. Somehow he must have insured that Cutter, and only Cutter, would get that one poisoned bulb, and only that one bulb. For I shall be very much surprised if any of the others are found to be altered . . . Murderers don't plan a crime, warn their victim, and then just trust to chance that, out of nine people, they will be lucky enough to reach their individual victim, by putting one black marble indiscriminately into a bag of white ones . . . The method will have to be clearly shown. If such a means occurs to you, I should be very glad to hear of it.'

With a nod, that somehow managed to combine brevity and courtesy, the detective made his way quickly up the still unsteady aisle. As he opened the cockpit door, the geometrical designs of city streets were beginning to slide beneath the 'plane.

600 FEET

The big Boeing circled the Municipal Air Port twice, while the pilots observed the cone on the Control Tower, veering sharply in the blustery winds, then turned their attention to the mechanically operated 'Tee' on the ground which served as an auxiliary indicator of landing direction under just such conditions as the present.

Far below them the airport siren shrieked and howled; and from the headphones on the senior pilot's ears the voice of the field manager spoke: 'Lewis in 74. Lewis in 74. Land with the "Tee." Land with the "Tee." All clear. Go ahead, Lewis.'

The junior pilot's head appeared in the cockpit doorway. 'Everyone adjust safety belts for the landing, please. Everyone.'

The 'plane banked, receded from the airport, banked again and slanted down toward the field in a long glide. The altimeter arm began moving steadily; 2800 . . . 2500 . . . 1800 . . .

At 1500 feet there was a whirring sound that rose rapidly to an angry buzz, then as rapidly faded out; a small, single-seated combat 'plane, bearing the army insignia, flashed past them, dived again, finally straightened out and touched the field at between ninety and a hundred miles an hour. The dust thrown away from its three bounces made little spurts against the earth.

A minute later the transport settled down gently at less than sixty miles. It, too, made one slight, long bounce, and, with intermittent bursts of its big motors, taxied across the wide expanse toward the Amalgamated buildings.

Some little distance away from them it stopped, the pilots having brought it directly behind an identical transport, then letting the motors go dead. Close to the 'plane ahead, its propellers already turning slowly and evenly, a considerable gathering stood about. There was a squad of police headed by a lieutenant, whose gold embroidered bar glinted brightly in the sunlight; and there were several porters, one of whom supported a collapsible stretcher, as well as two mechanics, a pair of post office men with dangling automatics to transfer the western mail, or deliver that for Chicago to their main office. Their small truck stood near the nose of the forward transport.

The Amalgamated manager disengaged himself from the group and walked across to the arriving 'plane. An accommodation ladder was placed next the fuselage, and he produced a key and unlocked the cabin door. Lord stepped down.

They shook hands, and Lord said, 'First of all, before anything else is done, I want Dr Cutter transferred to the new 'plane. Can he be put in the rear baggage compartment?'

'Yes, but – '

'He will be safer there than in the cabin.'

'But you know,' the manager protested, 'once you are in flight you can't possibly reach him. There is no communication between the cabin and the rear baggage compartment.'

'How long is our next hop?'

'To Omaha. About three hours. Then Cheyenne; that's about three and a half. You get another 'plane at Cheyenne, a little after seven, Mountain Time.'

Lord considered. 'That's all right – to Cheyenne, anyhow. In an emergency the pilots will land at my request, won't they?'

'They have been told to follow any request you may make, provided it does not endanger the ship. They understand that you are in command of the cabin.'

The police lieutenant was now approaching; the detective, being in mufti, stepped forward and shook hands with him, rather than exchanging salutes. 'Swain,' said the lieutenant. 'This is a hot one, Captain – new to me. The Commissioner says we will waive jurisdiction as a matter of courtesy to your Department. I don't believe he's too sure he has any jurisdiction to waive, at that. I have a squad with me – at your orders until you leave.'

'Thanks, Lieutenant. The first thing is to get Dr Cutter transferred.'

The task proved far from easy. Two of the porters, their expressions plainly evidencing their distaste for the assignment, finally managed to place the surgeon's body on the stretcher and to lower it through the narrow doorway. After much panting and tugging it was accomplished without mishap, and the stretcher borne away toward the 'plane ahead, in company of the police, who regarded both porters with evident suspicion.

'Please close the cabin door again,' Lord requested. 'No one can get out with that door closed, I believe?'

'Not a chance,' grinned the manager, slamming it shut. 'It has an automatic lock. The senior pilot has a key, and I have one here. No one else can get through it either way once it's shut.'

'By the way, I'll want keys for the cabin door, and also the baggage compartment of the new 'plane. Can I have them?'

The manager assented cheerfully and immediately. 'Sure thing. I don't know how you did it, but I'm told to let you have anything you want . . . Here, Ainsworth,' beckoning to one of the mechanics, 'duplicate keys for 59.'

'Now, Lieutenant, I wish you would have your men form two lines at intervals, making a lane between the cabin doors of these two 'planes. The passengers are to pass directly from this to the other. I'm afraid,' turning to the manager, 'that it will be impossible to permit them to go into the buildings, even for a quick lunch.'

'Yes,' the latter returned, 'I got that from your message. We have put a stewardess aboard 59, so she will serve lunch to all of you as soon as you go up. She will go right through with you now, on special service.'

'Thanks very much; that's considerate . . . Lieutenant, will you take charge of transferring the passengers?'

As Lord and the manager walked off toward the transport ahead, Lieutenant Swain, having formed his men as

requested, was bawling through the again opened cabin
door, 'Come out, you. Come on! Step on it,' in a tone
quite other than he had employed up to the present.

At the baggage compartment entrance the two
policemen were relieved to note Lord's approach; they
had very little idea as to what it was all about. Lord
peered in. The compartment was quite large enough to
hold the stretcher and leave a considerable space over; it
had been securely lashed to the starboard wall and to
two rings in the fuselage flooring. Dr Cutter's body in
turn, had been strapped to the stretcher. The detective
climbed into the narrow space and tried all the fasten-
ings. They were firm, and he turned his attention to the
baggage. Only the personal effects of the travellers had
been transferred. These were not many; they were lashed
together and tightly secured at the rear of the compartment by strong bonds. Satisfied, he climbed out again.

'Here are your keys,' the manager told him as he
dropped to the ground. 'This one is for this door, and the
other for the cabin door.'

Lord thanked him and closed the doorway he had just
quitted. Immediately he tried the key he had just been
given. It fitted; the door opened easily.

The lieutenant appeared around the tail of the 'plane.
'Everybody in,' he announced in a satisfied tone. 'Pilots
and stewardess, too. There was a minister of some kind
in the gang who made a fuss. Thinks he's a tough baby.
He ain't.'

'Well, I guess we're ready to go, so far as I am concerned.'

'Oh, a couple of messages for you, Captain.' Swain
reached into the recesses of his uniform. 'Hell, I nearly
forgot them, what with that minister and all.'

Lord took the messages. The first was from Darrow,
and had already been decoded for him by Chicago. It
contained nothing of immediate importance: the Secret
Service had turned up no new lead. Fonda Mann was

reputed in her own set to have had a continuous series of love affairs, commencing when she was yet at finishing school – 'probably harmless episodes,' Darrow believed. Anne Cutter had been engaged to Dr Gesell long ago, before she had married even for the first time; Gesell had been an intimate of the Cutter family then, but after the engagement was broken the friendship had waned, although there was still an apparently friendly acquaintanceship. 'Good luck,' the message concluded.

He opened the next one, an ordinary telegraph form, and regarded it with some surprise. 'Does all go well?' it asked. 'Wire Physicians and Surgeons. Gesell.' He read it again; somehow it was the last thing he would have expected to get. His impression of the elderly German had not indicatedso much solicitude. Yet the occurrence must have been an unusual one for him; and of course if he had once been a close friend –

At Lord's side appeared a leather-coated aviator, as suddenly as if he had sprung from the ground. 'Is this Captain Lord? I'm Captain Thrumm of the Air Service; going to take you as far as Des Moines. If you'll let me know when you're going up, I'd like to take off a bit ahead.'

'All set now, I guess.' Lord looked inquiringly at the manager.

'All clear, I believe. You can be up in a few minutes.'

The aviator smiled, waved a hand, strode off rapidly toward a hangar at the far end of the field where his tiny 'plane had been refuelled. Two minutes later he was taxi-ing rapidly across the field; he whirled his 'plane round in a sudden turn, was off ahead of the dust-cloud from his own propeller, zoomed sharply, flattened a little, zoomed again, was high above the airport.

The transport followed him, rising far more slowly, sweeping thunderously over the Control Tower with the roar from its powerful motors, banking toward the west.

'PX 59 STRUTHER OM D1 : 36 CH'

3400 FEET

The passengers sat at luncheon. Tomato juice cocktail, hot broth, club sandwiches, coffee, fruit and biscuits, more coffee. Not a bad luncheon at all, in a sky flecked with fleecy clouds, blustery but not uncomfortably rough. The stewardess moved deftly up and down the aisle, replenishing plates or bearing a steaming Thermos jug.

Captain Lord and Dr Pons now occupied the two rear seats, but it was the one in front of Pons that was vacant this time. They were both making an excellent meal; Pons, indeed, might be said to have been making a super-excellent one.

'We seem fated to eat together on these trips, Lord,' suggested the psychologist, thinking of another meal they had had at ground level not far from their present location. 'Or was that west of Omaha? . . . You missed a grand row when you got out at Chicago and left us all cooped up in here.'

'Ugh,' grunted Lord between mouthfuls of club sandwich. 'I suppose you mean the minister?'

Pons looked his astonishment. 'How did you know that?'

'Swain. The police lieutenant . . . Told me.'

'Oh, I didn't mean that rumpus.' Pons' eyes twinkled with amusement. 'The Reverend Whatsisname has been taking it rather neatly on the chin – not that I object. He's a pompous fool, trying to buck a tough Chicago cop. But that was only an aftermath. He got his dominance all worked up taking on young Isa before we were herded out of the cabin. An appetitive type, on the make, just as I guessed.'

Lord, commencing his second sandwich, raised

interrogative eyebrows.

On his side Pons took an enormous bite, swallowed and went on: 'I don't know how it started. I rather gathered when I went back to my seat – I was just opposite him, you know – that he had already made some advance to the girl and had been rebuffed. He was just trying again when I sat down.'

'Don't tell me he is taken with Isa Mann's charms?' Lord regarded his companion quizzically, for he had been unable to discern these attractions himself.

'Eh? Oh, hardly. She's almost masculine, and he is a typical appetitive male. No, quite different motivation, I'd say. They're a prominent family, and he thought he saw a chance to worm himself in with one of them. That's what I mean; that type are continually on the make, never let an opportunity slip . . . What is the fellow's name, anyhow?'

'Bellowes,' said Lord. 'Manly Bellowes.'

'Hah . . . Well, he was trying to give her some nonsense about condolences. "My dear young lahdy," ' Pons strove in vain to attain unctuousness, and merely succeeded in achieving an unpleasantly querulous tone, ' "in this time of sorrow," and so on. The Mann girl said she thought she had told him once to pipe down, and what business was it of his. What damned business, I think she said. He now-now-ed her a bit, and then she turned around in her chair and let him have it. Told him just what she thought of ministers in general, and of him as a particular example. Called him a voodoo doctor, without even the excuse of believing in his own voodoo. V.D., she said he ought to be, not D.D. Playing off a cheap superstition against what he could cadge from his wealthy parishioners. Corrupt politicians, she trusted, would find themselves at a rather higher level in hell than he would. And more to the same effect. Hot stuff. Couldn't have done better myself, although perhaps I should have been a bit more technical.'

Pons paused and Lord inquired, 'How long did this go on?'

'She ran out of breath just before we were let out. Bellowes was beginning the counter-rebuttal when your cop started yelling at us. That's what started the fuss between those two. I imagine Bellowes had some retort up his sleeve that he believed would restore his dignity and put the girl to shame; and the policeman wouldn't give him time to pull it off. Isa just walked away from him, and you can see she is now as far away as she can get.' This was apparent. The Rev. Bellowes now occupied the seat Fonda had had to Chicago, while the latter sat in Isa's former chair at the head of the starboard line. Isa, however, had moved to the rear, choosing the seat just ahead of the vacant one beyond Pons.

Lord noticed her changed position for the first time. 'My word, Pons,' he admonished, 'I'll wager she's heard everything you've been saying.'

'Not that I care,' the psychologist returned. 'And I don't believe she does, either.'

They sat in silence for some minutes, finishing their luncheons. The stewardess brought them fresh plates and fruit. She was small, blonde, plump and pretty in her freshly-pressed, short-skirted uniform. 'What is your name, if you don't mind?' asked Pons, regarding her appreciatively.

Her blue eyes scrutinised the big scientist carefully, observing his pleasant face and genial appearance with increasing favour. 'Miss Gavin,' she remarked coolly after a short moment. 'Marjorie Gavin to you, sir.'

'Hah!' Pons seemed the slightest bit flustered at this frank reply. He thought of a pun, started it, abandoned it abruptly. 'I am Dr Pons,' he told her, 'and this is my friend, Michael Lord, the boy detective. A master mind,' he finished, and thought it pretty laboured himself.

Lord smiled. 'Let me know if he annoys you,' he requested. 'Big but harmless.'

OBELISTS FLY HIGH 101

'Most of them are,' the girl assured him, departing forward. On her way she almost collided with the junior pilot, who was coming aft with a piece of paper in his hand.

The pilot came directly up to Lord and said, 'A telegram has just been relayed from the Chicago field, sir. It is addressed to Dr Amos Cutter, and we thought it had better be given to you.'

'Quite right,' answered the detective. 'May I see it?' He held out his hand.

The paper changed possession. Lord spread it out on his knee. It was a sheet from the pilots' notation pad, and the writing was in pencil: 'Dr Amos Cutter, care Amalgamated Air Transport, Chicago. Patient sinking rapidly Stop My opinion operation necessary immediately Stop Communicate. (Signed) MacKenzie.'

'H'm.' Lord leaned back, and his gaze wandered toward the ceiling. 'This tells us something.'

Pons had been looking over his shoulder at the message and added, 'I should say it does. It tells us there is probably going to be a vacancy in the President's Cabinet before the sun goes down.'

Lord's glance came back, to settle almost idly on the doctor's expression. 'No . . . I didn't mean that . . . However people in New York may have been misled by our preparations, it is plain that Reno has always known Dr Cutter would be coming out by 'plane. They even knew approximately what 'plane, for this telegram was addressed to Chicago just about when we were actually there.'

Dr Pons said nothing; he was unacquainted with the New York ruse concerning Cutter's departure. His friend thought in silence for a few moments, and presently took out a fountain pen. Unscrewing the cap and turning the paper over on his knee, he wrote: 'Dr Mackenzie, Reno Hospital, Reno. Operate only if absolutely necessary. Advise delay if possible. Your opinion to govern. – Cutter.'

The pilot, when he had read, looked at Lord doubt-fully. 'You're sure this is all right, sir? You have signed a dead man's name to it.' He glanced perplexedly from the paper to the detective.

'It is perfectly all right, pilot. You don't know all the circumstances of this case. Please get that off just as fast as you can.'

The young man, reassured by the authority in Lord's voice, hesitated no longer. 'Very well, sir. I don't want to be mixed up in it. I'll send her off this minute.' He passed up the aisle toward the cockpit.

Dr Pons broke the silence with a low whistle. 'You don't care whose life you take a chance with, do you, Lord?' He surveyed the detective's calm face with a very speculative eye. Lord returned his gaze without any change of expression.

4700 FEET

Omaha had been passed, and they were mounting above the rising ground ahead. The farms were fewer below them now, for they had passed from the Middle West into the real West.

Lord had spent the hour and a half before their last stop, sitting silently, with an occasional glance out the window at his side, thinking. Pons, meantime, had made tentative advances to Isa Mann, moving for this purpose into the vacant seat behind her. Surprisingly, he found himself welcomed, not very heartily, it must be admitted – but, still, welcomed. Isa wanted to talk, apparently, and the psychologist's friendly but common-sense approach succeeded where Bellowes' more wily technique had failed. They had talked steadily for more than an hour.

At Omaha Lord and the pilots had left the 'plane. Pons, begging at the last moment to be allowed to stretch his legs, had been permitted to do so, for the detective was not the man to fear making an exception he knew to be justified, and Dr Pons was the only passenger on the 'plane of whom he was absolutely sure. They had descended together behind the two aviators, and Lord had made certain that the door was closed and locked behind them.

His first concern had been the baggage compartment. He made his way there immediately and, producing his key, opened the entrance. Climbing in, he had knelt in the low compartment and bent over Dr Cutter. The surgeon's face was bloodless as he lay still and rigid on the stretcher; grey lips, blue-grey eyelids, ashen cheeks. Lord examined the straps fastening him and the lashings by which the stretcher was made fast. He found them all as firm as when they had left Chicago. There was nothing more he could do, and he backed slowly out of the compartment.

On the ground, as he closed the door and tested its security, he found Pons awaiting him. The psychologist, somewhat near-sighted, had been peering through the opening, endeavouring to make what he could of his friend's activities. In this he had succeeded.

'All fast?' asked Pons, when they stood together beside the 'plane.

'All fast. We stay here until the ship is ready to leave.'

'What for? I don't get this, Lord. What can happen to Cutter now? A dead man is in a fairly conclusive condition, after all.'

'Who knows what can happen to him?' the detective replied affably. 'There is such a thing as an autopsy, you know; and I'm not at all sure that one attempt has not already been made to alter the effects of whatever he took in that bulb.'

'Yes, and that's another thing I don't get. Why didn't

you have him taken off the 'plane at Chicago? That was
the place for the autopsy. The longer you wait, the
harder you make it for your own surgeon. I'm surprised
the Chicago people let you go on.'

'A special courtesy from them to us with love and
kisses. As a matter of fact, it's a question where the
jurisdiction lies in a case like this. Ohio might even claim
it, but we're handling the case from New York, and I
don't think there will be any interference until an arrest
is made, anyhow. As to taking Cutter's body along, it
will have to be brought to Reno in any event, for that is
where their family burial ground is, and you haven't forgotten that there is a criminal in that cabin still to be
caught. I couldn't very well hold everybody indefinitely
in Chicago. With Cutter out of it, I still have the job of
arresting his enemy; and I don't know yet who his enemy
is. It might be any one of them. This is the easiest way to
keep them together until I'm sure . . . So there you are,
doctor.'

'Hmph,' commented Pons noncommittally. He began
a short promenade up and down between the wing and
the port elevator on the ship's tail, while Lord leaned
negligently against the baggage door and lit a cigarette.

Presently he paused in his pacing in front of the detective and remarked, 'It's surprising how fast these things
travel. Remember the last time we were in Omaha, on
the Transcontinental? Took us two full days from New
York, and a few hours over; and what a storm when we
pulled out of her in the middle of the night. I'm glad we
haven't got it now . . . Well, we left Newark at nine this
morning, and so far, as I make it, that's just about seven
and a half hours.'

Lord nodded. 'They travel fast, no doubt about
that . . . Ah, there's the pilot. Cabin door hasn't been
opened, has it?'

The flyer strolled up, ground out his last cigarette for
the next three and a half hours. 'It's closed up tight,' he

assured Lord. 'All clear to start; we're a minute and a half late, as a matter of fact. It's raining at Lincoln, ceiling 3000. Clear beyond, but squally at Cheyenne.'

The other glanced behind him doubtfully. 'Think he'll be all right in there? The lashings are fast enough now.'

'Oh sure. It won't be very rough, at the worst. Probably calm, anyhow, by the time we get to Cheyenne. I wouldn't have told you if there had been anything to worry about.'

They made their way around to the other side of the 'plane. Another little mail truck was just backing away from the ship's protruding snout as they passed; it slipped into first, skidded into a turn and dashed away. They entered the cabin.

Lord sat now in his accustomed place, as Bellowes advanced ponderously down the aisle. He watched the approaching clergyman with prophecy in his heart. Nor was he mistaken, for Manly Bellowes stopped at Pons' chair opposite and asked in the resonant voice that had thrilled four hundred worshippers simultaneously, 'Would you object, sir, to exchanging seats with me for half an hour? I believe it my duty to communicate certain facts to the authorities.'

Dr Pons glanced up in a manner which he made no attempt to pretend was friendly. 'I'm not so – ' In looking up, his eyes had fallen across the clergyman's chair, the most forward one in Lord's row; just opposite sat Fonda Mann, her shoulders drooping disconsolately, gazing out the window. 'Very well,' said Pons, 'I'll try it. I may want my own seat again before the next half-hour, however.' He walked off without further remark.

The Rev. Bellowes observed him with surprise, gave a dignified shrug and sat down. When he spoke, his voice was unctuous, causing Lord for the first time to realise what the psychologist had previously been trying to imitate. 'I am a man of God. You sir, I presume, are a

God-fearing man.'

'Is that the information you desire to give me? I am an officer of the New York Police Department, and at present engaged, as you know very well, upon the solution of a crime.'

'A mortal sin has been committed on board this 'plane,' Bellowes announced sternly.

'All right, you can call it a sin, if you want to; I call it a crime. The point is, what do you know about it?'

'There is a woman on board this 'plane who is an infidel and an atheist. She espouses feminism, that modern disease which would even go so far as to place women in God's pulpit, thus sinning against the Holy Ghost. She has aspersed the revealed Word of God, and she has raised her piping voice against His minister, she is a sinner and capable of deadly sin.'

Lord's first surprise, having given way to a slight amusement, was now giving way to something else. It was difficult to be amused with the cold, light eyes of Manly Bellowes boring into him and the righteous indignation of the clergyman's voice hammering at his ears. He said evenly, 'Dr Bellowes, it is neither my duty nor my interest to take any part in your controversy with Miss Isa Mann. Most assuredly I am not inclined to take any steps against her in order to convert her to what, I may tell you frankly, I consider your private prejudices.'

The minister looked with quick suspicion at the detective. His voice was no longer unctuous, as he demanded, 'Are you a God-fearing man? Do you believe in the revealed Word of God?'

'I am not a Christian, if that is what you mean.'

'You are an infidel, sir; a blasphemer!'

'Have it your own way, and good-day. There are more important matters to claim my attention just now.'

'You refuse to hear my information?'

'If you have any information bearing upon the crime which has been done, I shall be glad to hear it. However, you shall have to confine yourself specifically to that. Do I make myself entirely clear?'

'Your soul is lost,' declared Bellowes grimly. 'I doubt if God, who is a jealous God, will forgive your grievous blasphemy . . . Nevertheless, it is my bounden duty to tell you of the transgressor whose iniquities have now had a fatal result . . . That person is the Mann woman.'

'Indeed?' Lord regarded the man opposite him coldly. 'Is this a formal accusation? I presume you are acquainted with the law of libel?'

'I am well acquainted with it. There can be no libel in laying a charge against a confessed criminal.'

'Are you telling me that Isa Mann has confessed to this crime? I don't believe it.'

'She has confessed inadvertently. Her sins have betrayed her. That is the information I have to lay before you.'

'Very well; but let me tell you first what you will have to show. You will have to show that Isa Mann, in substituting the poison bulb, adopted some means whereby just that single bulb would eventually reach her uncle, alone of all the passengers in this 'plane. Do not forget that I myself was the one actually to select the bulb for Dr Cutter, and that the box had passed from her hands through several others, some of whom took bulbs themselves.'

'That is not the issue at all. That was simply a matter of chance.'

'I have some knowledge of murderers, Dr Bellowes. They do not operate by chance.'

'She did not intend to kill her uncle. You do not understand the situation at all, sir. It was the Almighty who made her his executioner against a trespassing sinner. Her own intended sin, however, was as heavy.'

Lord was frankly puzzled. He said, 'I'm sorry, but I don't know what you are talking about. Do I understand you to assert now that she didn't care who was killed?

That some supernatural force decided that of those in the
cabin, it was Dr Cutter who should take the fatal bulb?'

'I am not unaware of the activities of Dr Cutter.' The
minister dropped his voice to an austere murmur. 'He
was an infidel who gave his life to seeking the Spirit in the
coarse texture of men's bodies. Almighty God would not
permit so wicked a life to go unpunished.' His voice rose
again resonantly. ' "Vengeance is mine," saith the
Lord.'

Michael Lord said, 'Now, see here, I am not going to
be drawn into a fruitless discussion. Your suggestion is
monstrous; it is more blasphemous than anything your
opponents have ever said of you . . . If you have definite
information regarding a confession of Miss Mann's,
inadvertent or not, kindly give it to me at once.'

'She has confessed. Her sin has betrayed her.'

'So you said. In exactly what words,' demanded Lord
with exaggerated patience, 'has she confessed to the purpose of murdering anyone on this 'plane?'

'She told me,' Bellowes answered sternly, 'that she
would rather die than live longer in a Christian community.'

'But what in – '

The minister hurried on over Lord's interruption. Dr
Pons, returning, had just sat down in the vacant seat
ahead and was giving his undisguised attention to the
recital. Across the aisle, the novelist who sat in front of
the detective had obviously been listening for some time,
while Isa also had turned in her chair, the better to hear
what was said.

Bellowes' words came faster now, but his tone was
solemn, thoroughly in earnest. 'As she has to live in a
Christian community, she plainly intended suicide. It
was the judgement of God upon her sinfulness. For a
long time I had noticed her with the box of bulbs open in
her lap, fingering them, examining them. There is no
doubt that she had placed a poisoned one among them

with which she intended to take her life. But time and again her courage failed her; she has no recourse, no help in time of trouble, and, suddenly, while she was still hesitating, the box was called for and she passed it back automatically. Only then did she realise that the fatal bulb was still among them, but she dared not make an outcry and give herself away. Possibly she trusted chance would bring her back the box with her bulb unused; but the Almighty interfered and another transgressor perished in his wickedness.' Bellowes' voice, raised as he had made his points, ceased, and the drone of the motors became audible in the silence.

For some moments the detective sat with his mouth partly open, too surprised to speak. 'I did no such thing!' Isa cried out suddenly. 'That is as cheap a lie as even he has gotten rid of in a good long time.'

Dr Pons turned forward and patted her arm. 'Don't take him so seriously, my dear.' He turned back to Lord. 'Michael,' he said slowly, 'you know of my work, and I believe you even have a certain admiration for it. I am not infallible, as you also know, but I will stake my professional reputation on the fact that this young woman is as far from a suicidal type as can well be found . . . As to the man you are talking to, he is so definitely abnormal that he ought to be shut up for the benefit of society.' Pons glared at the minister next to him with every evidence of active hostility.

'Have you given me all the evidence you possess for your remarkable accusation?' Lord demanded of Bellowes.

The latter had risen, and towered in the aisle above the others. 'The Lord has made me the discoverer of the sins against His name. I have given you the truth, as was my duty. Do you or do you not intend to act upon it?'

The detective looked up at the man beside him. 'Certainly not,' he replied shortly. 'It's ridiculous.'

'Then I wash my hands of the whole matter,' Bellowes' stern accents returned, as with a dramatic gesture he suited the action to the word. 'You are no more than a pack of infidels, pitting your puny strength against God. "Those that live by the sword, shall perish by the sword." '

With this cryptic sentence he stalked stiffly forward, as Lord remarked pleasantly, 'I remind you once again, Bellowes, about that law of libel.'

Hugh L. Craven, novelist and playwright, swung one long leg over the other. He was observing the scene with interested amusement.

5900 FEET

6.55 Central Time, 5.55 Mountain Time. In the Control Room at Cheyenne the dispatcher sat with his eyes on the airway clock, a large affair with letters and numerals scattered along its outer edge. The hand ticked to the minute; opposite the minute stood the letters, 'W.B.,' westbound 'plane. It was time for one of the three-times-an-hour routine reports. He pressed the transmitter button.

'Cheyenne Amalgamated calling Struther in 59. Go ahead, Frank!'

There was a moment's silence, then the pilot's voice crackled into the headpieces and the loud speaker. The dispatcher repeated the message in a habitized monotone. 'All right, Frank. You are approaching Ogallala at 5900 weather clearing ceiling unlimited rain over North Platte, okay, Frank. I am calling you again at fifteen past at fifteen past okay.'

He cut off the transmitter and sat with the headpieces still clamped over his ears. There was no minute in the hour, no hour in the day or night when the Control Room could not be called by any 'plane in its division.

In the cockpit of 59 the senior pilot dropped the micro-phone into his pocket and leaned forward to switch on the instrument lights. The sun had fallen behind the rearing mountains to the west, leaving a short twilight, orange and violet bands across the westward clouds. Below them the earth was merging into a uniform dark-ness, with here and there the twinkle of a tiny light. To the south a succession of twin tin-points where automobiles followed the invisible Lincoln Highway. Still farther south a series of minute, red spark-showers as a big freight locomotive strained at the head of its unseen cars.

Except for the glow of the shaded lights behind the instruments the cockpit was dark, the door to the cabin closed, its window covered by a snap-down shade . . . suddenly, directly ahead and underneath, a brilliant, white beam, the light beacon at Ogallala, followed by a red dot-dash signal giving its number. Beyond and slightly southward another white beam flashed, and beyond that another; the Big Springs and Chappell beacons were sparkling along the airway, and in the far distance away to the west came the intermittent reflec-tion of the Sidney flash. On both sides of the cockpit, where the motors jutted out from the wings, the flick-ering of the exhaust flames showed up weirdly.

In the cabin the stewardess had turned on the lights, and despite the falling temperature outside, it was bright and warm within. Lord closed the ventilator at his side and looked at the clock on the forward wall. An hour and a half, more or less, before they would reach Cheyenne. He leaned forward, tapped Craven's shoulder just ahead.

'Have you any ideas about what has happened?' asked Lord conversationally. 'Have you seen or heard any-thing that might be of use to me?'

The Englishman turned sideways in his chair, stretching his long legs into the aisle, his back against the fuselage wall. 'Scarcely my affair, is it, old chap?'

'Oh, I don't know,' the detective answered easily. 'It's more or less the affair of all of us, I'd say. It might turn out that I'd have to hold everybody as material witnesses when we get to Reno,' he added pleasantly.

'That *would* be embarrassin'.' Craven smiled, seemingly not greatly disturbed.

'Cutter had an enemy on this 'plane,' Lord went on. 'That enemy is still here with us, and I can't let this little company disperse until I find out who that person is.'

'Quite.'

'Well, do you know anything at all about the situation?'

'Of course,' Craven considered, 'I could hardly help knowing something. After all, I've been here all the time, and I couldn't help overhearing one or two conversations . . . Damned interestin', as a matter of fact; right along my line, a situation like this . . . Still, I'd rather thought it wasn't up to me to push in.'

'Forget that,' Lord advised him, 'and let me hear what you think about the whole thing. How did you like the last theory we heard, about someone slipping up on a proposed suicide?'

'My word, I don't put anything on it! The girl never did anything of the kind. You don't think so yourself. Fella's a fanatic, that's all. Wouldn't give it another thought, if I were you.'

'Well, I don't know.' The detective brought out cigarettes, offered one to Craven, who declined, lit one for himself. 'Oh, you're right about Bellowes, of course; he's a belligerent wind-bag making his last stand with a system that's done for. But the theory – consider that; never mind for the moment to whom we apply it. There is a suicide on the 'plane; the man's upset, nervous, going over his reasons and arguments again and again in his mind. Naturally he's not normal; might do anything in a state like that. Finally, while he still hesitates *his* bulb gets mixed up with the others and comes to Cutter merely by chance. You know, that's the one hypothesis so far that accounts for the fact that I, who was guarding him, actually gave him the fatal bulb.'

Craven, busy with a pipe, did not answer for so long a time that Lord turned to Dr Pons across the aisle. 'What do you think of the suicide notion, doctor?'

Pons stretched and yawned prodigiously. Finally he said, 'Oh yes, you're entirely correct. That is the only theory – so far – that explains how the bulb reached Cutter.'

Lord remarked, 'You don't sound very convinced. Have you an alternative hypothesis, by any chance?'

'Afraid not, Michael,' was the response. 'No, I haven't any hypothesis for this case. No suggestions at all. Sorry.'

6000 FEET

In the cockpit Struther had taken over the 'plane, while his co-pilot, with ear-phones adjusted, was checking the beacons, watching the instruments, observing the night sky for the lights of other 'planes. Cheyenne was reporting freshening winds from the north, clouds banking up in that quarter also.

Abruptly another voice rasped into the junior pilot's ears, arresting his attention. 'Amalgamated 59. Amalgamated 59. Where is your yellow light? Show your light, 59. Lieutenant Philips, Army Air Service, speaking.'

The pilot reached for his microphone with one hand while closing the unaccustomed little switch clipped to the lower edge of the instrument panel with the other. He pressed the microphone button.

'Lieutenant Philips, Air Service. This is Lee in 59, Lee in 59. Sorry about the light; we forgot it. Is it okay now?'

After a moment the 'phones crackled again. 'Okay, 59. Light shows up well. I am escorting you at 7500. There is a 'plane dead ahead proceeding northward. Are you landing at Cheyenne, 59?'

'59 is landing at Cheyenne, landing at Cheyenne.'

'Okay, 59.'

'Okay, Lieutenant.'

Silence once more in the cockpit. Droning motors. Lee dropped the microphone back into his pocket, shifted slightly so that his automatic dangled down over the edge of his chair. Through the semicircle of glass the 'plane seemed to be suspended motionlessly in a dark void. The scattered lights below approached so slowly that their movement was scarcely perceptible; as they quietly vanished under the wings, others rising from the distant horizon took their places. The beacons flashed, beckoning the 'plane across the night. Steadily the big transport throbbed onward . . .

6100 FEET

In the bright cabin behind the cockpit the novelist had got his pipe going at last. Ramming down the burning tobacco, he took a long draw and raised his eyes to Lord's.

'That suicide theory is' – puff – 'foolish,' he drawled. 'I'd count it out.'

'And just why would you do that?' the detective wanted to know.

'Because it's too far-fetched, under the circumstances. You would have to stretch a super-imagination to credit it . . . You told us all that this man Cutter had received a warning or a threat of some sort. Somebody was after him, and after him hard enough for you to take a two-thousand mile journey purposely to guard him. Then, when he's killed, it is suggested that quite another person, some entirely unsuspeced suicide, made a mistake, and that Cutter only died by chance. I can't see that.'

'Too much of a coincidence, you think?'

'Rather!'

'Well, there is something in your idea, certainly.'

'By the way,' Craven continued, 'how specific was this threat? Was any time mentioned, for example, in regard to the attempt to do away with the man?'

'Yes, there was,' Lord had to acknowledge. 'Twelve o'clock, Central Time.'

'And when did he take that bulb, as a matter of fact?'

'Twelve o'clock, Central Time. Or so close to it as to make no difference.'

'Well, you see.' The novelist shrugged expressively. 'What's the use? It's much too pat. Simply impossible that his death should have been accidental in view of all this.'

Lord admitted the point smilingly. 'But just consider,' he suggested, 'where that leaves us.'

'It leaves you,' Craven declared, 'just where you were. Somewhere there is a criminal, right enough; but I don't think you are going to find him, no matter if you keep us all together for a fortnight. Incidentally, there is a British Consul at Reno, and I don't believe that I shall be delaying there very long after I get in touch with him.'

The novelist's tone had been a pleasant one, but Lord realised that in all probability the prophecy was far from idle. He remarked casually, 'Of course, this criminal might conceivably be none other than yourself, Craven.'

'Oh rather.' Craven's tone was now emphatically disinterested.

'No, I'm serious,' the detective pursued. 'How do I know that you are not in the employ of some foreign government? Cutter's brother, you know, is our Secretary of State. He is desperately ill, and the surgeon is one of the few men who can save his life.'

For the first time the Englishman looked surprised and genuinely interested. His voice was no longer so slow a drawl. 'So that's it, eh?' he surmised. 'I wondered why we have been under escort of a combat 'plane all the way out . . . But that's as far-fetched as the other theory. You're not serious, really?'

'Why not?'

'Well, really, y'know. Foreign spies are all right in magazines. I have a colleague who writes about little else, but in actual life, I imagine, they are fairly small fry; certainly in peace times. We read about "spy rings" being discovered in Paris or Warsaw, but I'll lay a wager the whole show is mostly Latin imagination. What could these music teachers or what-not find out that cannot much more readily be turned up in the standard reference books? I have never heard much about "spy rings" at home, or over here, either, for the matter of that. Pshaw, we're not on the films, old boy!'

Lord leaned back in his chair, comfortably relaxed, as he observed the other with an attentiveness which he succeeded well in concealing. For some time the cabin had been tilted slightly upward; now its forward end rose even more noticeably as they climbed into higher altitudes. The pointer of the altimeter showed 8900 and was still moving.

'It is true, of course,' Lord remarked, 'that, spy or not, the *modus operandi* of getting that bulb into Cutter's handkerchief remains the crux of the problem.'

'Oh, that. No, that's simple enough, if you would only stop being far-fetched and use common sense.'

'You don't say so?' It was now the detective's turn to show interest, and he sat up straighter in his chair. 'I should be very glad to hear you explain how you believe that was done.'

'No,' said Craven slowly. 'I don't think I shall tell you.'

'Ah! You know but you won't tell me. May I ask why not?'

'I know, certainly. There is only one possibility in the present case. As to why I won't tell you, that is merely because you would not believe me if I did. You are hypnotised, Captain, just as almost everyone else is; you cannot and will not admit to yourself facts which stare you in the face and which, except for this hypnotism, would be as plainly perceived as they are plainly evidenced . . . But you can't see them, so why enter into a bootless argument?'

Michael Lord sat up straighter yet. 'You interest me, Craven,' he acknowledged sincerely. 'I should like to have you go on very much indeed, and don't be too sure about my being hypnotised. I don't claim to be a genius in any sense, but it happens that in a couple of my cases I have been thrown into several fields of theory, psychology and economics, for instance. In addition, I chance to have a fairly broad, general acquaintance with modern science.'

'Yes, that's what I meant. I have no doubt you would believe anything a "scientist" told you.' The novelist pondered briefly, then shrugged. 'Well, you will see. You really are hypnotised, you know; but it will pass the time . . . However, if I'm to tell you what I think about your case, you will have to let me go what may seem a little far afield, to begin with. I shall have to acquaint you with an aspect of the situation that I don't think you know.'

'Glad to hear of it.' Lord nodded, and the other drew several times on his pipe before continuing.

'Wotan Mann,' he said then. 'I am entirely unknown to the Cutters, to all of them, but I have met Mann. Met him on a hunting trip once. You probably know that he is separated from his wife, who is the sister of the man who has been killed, and I suppose, though I am not sure, the mother of the two young ladies who are with us. Now,

Wotan Mann is not as bad as he has been painted, by a long throw. He likes women, yes; but then they like him, too. And he has a terrific temper. Any woman who married him with the idea that she'd have a domesticated husband around the premises must be quite stupid enough to deserve a rude awakening. Not that I'm saying Anne Cutter expected to find him tame; his quarrel, as I made it out, was with her brothers rather than with her.

'We made a longish trek together, and he told me a good part of the story, for there's nothing like a camp fire late at night to bring out confidences. To make it brief, his side of it was that his brothers-in-law were a pair of moralistic prudes – although he had a stronger name for them – who interfered between him and his wife. According to him she was quite content with his wanderings, both geographical and erotic, because he always came back from them sooner or later; but she was a somewhat weak personality, and the brothers, forever at her, began by causing quarrels, and finally succeeded in bringing about a definite estrangement. He resented this the more, inasmuch as he confessed to an unusually strong attachment to his eldest daughter, and if that is she up forward, I can well understand it. He was also, I believe, sincerely fond of his wife, and had no desire whatever to abandon her, except temporarily.

'As I said, Wotan Mann has a dangerous and uncontrollable temper; when he goes into a rage he is a killer. I have seen him in a rage and I have seen him kill. I have also seen him sit and brood for an hour or longer when something angered him; then, like a flash, he jumps up and fights. When that man hates, he hates so violently that one can feel a definite physical emotion from his presence.

'I may add that he resented very strongly what he called the meddling of the Cutter brothers in his life. His bitterness against them was extreme, and I am certain that the full force of his hatred was turned in their – '

Craven broke off as the cockpit door opened and the junior pilot stood in the entrance. 'Ladies and gentlemen,' he called; and all conversations ceased abruptly as the passengers looked toward him, startled.

The pilot smiled. He said, 'I didn't mean to frighten you. Nothing is wrong. We are about to land at Cheyenne. It is the highest airport on the North American Continent, over 6000 feet in altitude. We must therefore land at a much higher speed than usual, since at this altitude the air is less dense and has less ability to support the 'plane. I want to make sure that everyone's safety belt is properly adjusted for the landing. It is also necessary that the cabin lights be extinguished while we land; it will only be for a few minutes . . . Will you kindly adjust your belts? The stewardess will inspect them and report to me.'

The pilot's head withdrew and he closed the door.

6058 FEET

In the brilliant glare of the airport Captain Lord ushered the passengers carefully from their second 'plane to the third. He counted them out and counted them in, permitting no more than the short walk to where the new ship waited, a glistening silver bird under the bright lights, in all respects like the one they had just quitted; and then Lord locked the cabin door.

The Cheyenne airport was enormous; lines operated from it to north, south, east, west, south-west, north-west, north-east. 'Planes arrived and departed continuously. It was also the main operating base of the Amalgamated system, with the result that it was the assistant manager of the line who presently made his appearance.

'Is everything all right?' he asked cheerfully when he

had found the detective. He motioned to the 'plane that would carry them farther. 'We have just substituted 90 for 77, the ship that would have gone out ordinarily. 90 is a new ship; it has been thoroughly tested, of course, and we have been tuning it up all day. You'll find it in perfect shape, I think.'

When they came to transfer the surgeon's body, the manager's jaw dropped. 'My God!' he ejaculated. 'Have you had violence on the 'plane? Is the man dead?'

Lord indicated the ashen features under the heavy blankets on the stretcher. 'He looks it, doesn't he?' he asked grimly. As the lashings were made fast, inspected, tightened again here and there, he added, 'The next stop is Salt Lake City, I understand. How long will it take us to reach there?'

'Three hours, almost exactly.'

'Well, that's all right. He'll be safe in there, will he?'

'We'll make sure he is.' The manager climbed into the new baggage compartment and checked all the lashings himself. As he dropped to the ground again, he swung his arms briskly in the cold air and rubbed his hands together. 'You may find it a little rough over the Rockies to-night. There are some storms around, too, farther on, although you ought to miss them, but you needn't worry about the stretcher; I'll guarantee it won't budge an inch, or the man on it, either. We have to fasten things down tight in this service, and we know how to do it . . . I gave you the duplicate keys to the doors, didn't I, and took the keys to 59?'

As they rounded the tail of the 'plane (where a mechanic stood on guard, as did another at the nose) they saw a telegraph boy at the cabin door. Lord walked up quickly.

'Telegram for Dr Amos Cutter.'

'Yes, Dr Cutter is on this 'plane. I'll take it.'

He tore open the yellow envelope. 'Operation success-

ful,' he read. 'Patient's condition critical, but every hope
for recovery. MacKenzie.'

Stuffing the form into his pocket, he looked up to find
that the managers had been joined by the two new pilots.
Introductions were effected. 'Lannings . . . Lovett . . .
Captain Lord of the New York Police . . . Of course,
they've nicknamed Lannings "Happy." '

Lord found himself looking into two tanned faces.
Piercing blue eyes above a long nose and lean jaw; that
was Lannings, the senior pilot. Lovett's eyes were brown
and his face chubbier, but both men were tall.

Lannings drew the manager slightly aside. 'The storm
at Rock Springs is clearing,' he said in a low voice, 'but
there is light snow at Parco and cloudy at Medicine Bow.
Ceiling's only 2000 there now. We had better get started.
I think we can pass Parco before it gets bad, if we leave
right away.'

The little stewardess was coming across the field from
the Administration Building, her arms loaded with fresh
Thermos flasks and boxes. Behind her a porter bore a
heaping pile of blankets.

'Hello, Hal,' she greeted the junior pilot. He grinned
happily. ' 'Lo, Margy. I'm glad it's you. Lucky transfer,
this trip.' The girl smiled back at him.

Lord was glad to open the door and enter the warm
cabin. Despite his overcoat the cold winds blowing
across the open spaces of the airport had chilled him
uncomfortably. The belts were adjusted and the
stewardess was just about to turn off the lights when the
noise of the motors, rising to taxi the 'plane out on the
field, fell abruptly, as the big propellers idled. In the
comparative quiet there was knocking on the cabin door.

Lord opened it, at a word from the stewardess, to find
another telegraph boy outside. This time the envelope
was blue and the telegram addressed to the detective.
'Did you receive previous wire. Is all well. Please answer
216 West Ninety-Seventh Street. Gesell.'

Another telegram from the little German. Lord remembered, with a start of compunction, that he had not answered the first one. 'Have you a blank?' he asked the boy.

The boy hadn't; he had left his blanks behind when running out to catch the 'plane. 'I'll get one in a minute, sir.'

The junior pilot had come back through the cabin. 'Sorry,' he advised the detective, 'but we shall have to leave now. Can't wait for him. We've got to beat some weather.'

'That's all right. Never mind, boy.' Lord closed the door. 'It's not important. I can send it later.'

Now the lights were out, the ship bumping across the ground. Then came the deep-throated roar as Lannings gave both motors the gun. Smoothness replaced the bumps; the 'plane began a long climb upward. As it swung above the first of the mountain ranges, it picked up the Laramie beacon, north-west.

9200 FEET

Supper was finished high above jagged peaks. It was not a lengthy affair, rather resembling the luncheon in its courses; moreover, a tumultuous wind was sweeping across the Rockies, and the transport, big as it looked on the ground, was none too steady in the vast spaces it now traversed. No one ate very much.

Some of the seats had been changed again. Dr Pons now sat beside Fonda Mann at the forward end of the cabin and Tinkham, who had gotten in last, had taken the chair opposite Lord at the rear. He sat in a stony silence, his face set in cold lines. Since his earlier clash with the detective he had addressed no word to him, and apparently had no intention of doing so. As before,

Craven occupied the chair directly ahead of Lord.

The latter turned to the novelist. 'We were inter-rupted,' he pointed out, 'by landing at Cheyenne. You were telling me your view of this case, and, I believe you said, were about to show that I was hypnotised.'

'You put it a bit bluntly,' Craven smiled. 'But – well, I think I had rather finished telling you about Wotan Mann.'

'You said you understood the means by which the poison bulb singled out Dr Cutter, I think?' Lord sug-gested.

'Oh, yes.'

'Perhaps you will tell me now. Who gave Dr Cutter the bulb?'

'Why, you did, old boy. I thought you admitted that yourself.'

Across the aisle Hood Tinkham, for all his assumed withdrawal, might have bent slightly toward the conversationalists. He continued to stare straight ahead, but Lord, who was still observing everyone he could, sus-pected, perhaps unjustly, that his ears were alert to catch the words opposite.

'You believe that I poisoned Cutter?' Lord continued to Craven.

'No, no, of course not. Why all these fantastic supposi-tions?'

'But you say I gave him the poisoned bulb.'

'I said you gave him the bulb. Unless I am mistaken, that is the plain fact. I did not say you gave him poison.'

Opposite them Tinkham unfastened his safety belt, got up, and without a glance in Lord's direction made his way unsteadily into the little lavatory behind. The detec-tive watched him go, watched the tiny door close after him. In a flash he was on his feet and, leaning across the aisle, had snapped open the assistant's small bag, reposing on the chair opposite. He looked quickly within, withdrew his hand. In a moment he was back in his own seat and going on with Craven as if nothing had happened.

'But Dr Cutter inhaled that bulb and was poisoned.'

'Well, well,' Craven responded, 'where is your common sense, man? You gave him the bulb. The bulb was not poisoned because you were the last person in the world to attack the man you were specifically guarding, but when he inhaled it he inhaled poison; therefore, the gas in the bulb was poisoned *after you gave it to him but before he inhaled it.*'

Michael Lord said slowly, 'I gave him the bulb. He put it into his handkerchief and broke it immediately. There was no time for anyone to monkey with it – not even Cutter himself.'

'How long a time do you think, Captain, is required for the completion of a chemical reaction?'

'That depends upon the reaction in question. Some, of course, take place in a few instants, once the critical point is reached.'

'So then there was plenty of time for the gas in the bulb to undergo a reaction. It probably did not react until it was actually in his nostrils.'

Lord was completely puzzled. He played for a moment with the notion of a gas so prepared that it would remain innocuous until in contact with human nostrils, but that, again, would involve a specially prepared bulb. Or – '

'Then why did not this gas react in a similar fashion in the nostrils of the rest of us?'

'Because there was no force present to bring about the reaction.'

'And such a force was present in Cutter's case? What was this force? Where did it come from?'

'It was,' the novelist told him soberly, 'the very violent, the very malignant hatred of Wotan Mann.'

'Ah! Ah, yes, I see.' Lord leaned back in his seat. 'Are

you a Christian Scientist, Craven?'

The other burst into a frank laugh. 'Good heavens, no, Captain. I am merely a man whose common sense, by some fortunate chance, has not been hypnotised by the current scientific superstitions.'

'It is evident, at any rate, that you believe thought can influence matter.'

'Now there is just what I should call a gross instance of superstition, Captain, if I may say so. I don't know what thought is, and I haven't the foggiest notion as to what you may mean by matter. I am also sure that you don't know, yourself. If you will dip into a few books by modern physicists, you will find that they possess no remotely intelligible description of "matter." You said you were acquainted with modern psychology, I think? Then you must know that psychological discussions of thought do not even make verbal sense . . . The fact is, y'know, that we exist in a unitary world where everything bears some relation, however remote, to everything else. There are no such opposites as the material and the immaterial; there is the more or less homogeneous realm of the material-immaterial, or of the immaterial-material, if you prefer it that way. In other words, there is no thought and there is no matter; what exists is thought-matter or matter-thought. Ours is a hyphen existence.'

'What you describe is a somewhat complex view,' Lord observed, reaching out a hand to steady himself as the 'plane took a sudden drop and bumped. 'Professor Didenot, our philosopher, ought to be interested.'

'Philosophers,' chuckled Craven. 'No, thank you. They're the most superstitious of the lot. They have a fashion now of "accepting the findings of modern science." That means that they accept a smattering of pseudo-science and build an airy structure of speculation on that doubtful foundation. Result, there isn't any philosophy nowadays at all; there is only a little bad science embellished with primitive, traditional beliefs . . . Y'know, Captain, we're havin' a bit of weather now.' He nodded toward the windows across the narrow cabin.

Lord glanced at his own window, then pressed his face against it, cupping his hands around his eyes. In the light streaming out from behind him he saw snowflakes streaking past; tiny flakes in their thousands and thousands, with occasionally a little hailstone pinging against the 'plane. The flakes that struck the glass wetted it, started to freeze and melted, the drops running across the window almost horizontally in the wind tearing past the 'plane.

10,800 FEET

In the dark cockpit Lannings' face wore a serious expression as he turned the ship over to Lovett, drew on his earphones, plucked the microphone from his pocket.

He pressed the transmitter button. 'Amalgamated 90 calling Lieutenant Philips in escort 'plane. Amalgamated 90 calling Lieutenant Philips, calling Lieutenant Philips.'

At the second call the answer crackled in Lannings' ears. 'All right, 90, this is Philips. What will you have?'

'Can you see us, Philips?'

'Lost you about a minute ago, 90. Hope to pick you up again between flurries. I am flying at 11,300 north-west by west. Almost no visibility now.'

'Are you equipped for blind flying?'

'Hell, no. I can just get the directional beacon, though. I'll pick you up again, 90.'

'We will keep in touch with you every few minutes. Visibility fading out here. You had better go to 15,000, Philips; we are going up to 12,500. Our air speed now approximately 150 m.p.h., course north-west by west, 10,800, and going up. This is Lannings in 90, Lannings in 90.'

'Okay, 90. Afraid of ice higher, but I'll try it. Keep in touch. This is Philips, this is Philips.'

'Okay, Philips.' Lannings released the button, but kept the transmitter in his hand. He stared ahead into blankness, the little hailstones whispering over the glass above his head.

11,900 FEET

'Nothing much we can do about it,' Lord observed, inspecting the buckle of his safety belt. 'Can't say I'm fond of these bumps we're getting, but I might as well hear the rest of your story. I take it you believe that Mann's hatred of Cutter was so violent that it actually affected the gas Cutter was inhaling. It's hardly a case I could take into court, but it's highly original – I'll say that for it.'

The novelist encircled the back of his chair with a long arm and braced a foot against the floor. 'Oh, no, you can't take it into court.' He grinned. 'If you could have done, I should not have told you, for my sympathies happen to be with Mann in the matter . . . But you compliment me too highly with originality. Have you never heard of Charles Fort, Captain? His was one of the very few free minds in the world to-day. I happen to be a Fortean.'

'You have me there, I'm afraid,' Lord had to admit. 'Who was Charles Fort, and what did he do?'

'He collected evidences – and drew the obvious conclusions. Obvious, that is, to any unhypnotised person. Of course, the vast majority are always hypnotised by some system of primitive beliefs. For a thousand years the Church did it, with a gentilised Hebrew religion out of Genesis; we were just treated to the arguments of one of the last survivors. That's on the way out now, but the scientific superstition is on the way in. Unless the whole western show goes to pot, we shall have some hundreds of years of as dark taboos and as rigid orthodoxy as priests ever fostered. Priests and scientists are blood brothers underneath, really.

'Charles Fort collected evidences. He put a lot of them together in the *Book of the Damned* a number of years ago. The "Damned," of course, are all those phenomena, fully reported and amply witnessed, which are deliberately deleted by the orthodox. I have heard it said that science is selective, but that is only true in a passive sense. Actively, science doesn't select, it damns and disregards; it deletes from the evidence everything that won't fit its childish little theories, and what is left is therefore "selected." You will find some hundreds of the deleted items in the *Book of the Damned*. I'll give you one.

'Einsteinism is a current fad in the general superstition called science. Prof. Freundlicher reported to the Physics Association at Berlin in 1931 that the displacement of the stars during the 1929 eclipse was quite other than would accord with the Einstein equations. Deleted. There is, of course, much more actual evidence, mathematical, physical, astronomical, against Einsteinism than for it. Deleted. Authorities find it very easy to be believed. I'll wager you believe them yourself, Lord – take them on superstitious faith.

'Another of Fort's books is *Lo;* but that wouldn't interest you particularly. In that one he mines the astronomers and touches off the mine. But *Wild Talents* is right to the point; it reports scores of authenticated instances of what we had on the 'plane this morning. Abilities, mostly unsuspected, held by particular persons, with definite results. The man they couldn't hang, the dog they couldn't stop howling, the inventor whose machine would only function in his own presence. Transmediumisation; a Fortean term meaning the passage of phenomena from one medium of existence to another. For example, from mind-matter to matter-mind, the essence of the situation being not a passage at all, but merely a change of emphasis, since all phenomena are hyphenised anyhow.'

'Go ahead,' said Lord as the novelist paused to adjust his grip more firmly on his chair. 'I don't believe you, but I think I shall obtain one of those books.'

'Of course you don't believe me,' Craven agreed good-naturedly. 'Hypnotised. I recommend *Wild Talents* to you. I would especially direct attention to the many cases of objectified hatreds recorded there. People burned to death while fully clothed and their clothes not singed. Bodies burned in beds, and the bedclothes not even discoloured by the smoke. Murder at a distance. Visualisations that worked. Most of these abilities to project visualisations objectively are probably unconscious, but I doubt that all of them are. They are not much mentioned, however. Science is as ardent in hunting out and persecuting "witch-craft" to-day as ever religion was three hundred years ago.

'Well, there's my case, Captain. Consciously or unconsciously Wotan Mann has been projecting strangulation, suffocation, some violent form of asphyxiation upon Cutter. I would say consciously, in view of the correspondence in time between threat and execution; and, by the way, I should look upon the other brother's illness with some suspicion, too. Wotan Mann's energy is tremendous, but in our case here it was not quite sufficient to produce real-unreal effects under usual circumstances, that is, when Cutter was breathing ordinarily; but the sudden change in Cutter's nostrils from ordinary air to whatever is in these bulbs was the catalyst that precipitated the phenomenon Mann was visualising. Or maybe not. Maybe the bulb part really was coincidence, coming just at the threatened time . . . Cutter died, but you will never solve this murder, Captain, and if you did, you could never bring Mann into any court for prosecution, unless you wanted to lose your job. Imagine bringing this kind of murderer before a judge who is paid every month to uphold the final absurdities of orthodoxy and to denounce the deleted with as much noise as he can muster.'

Craven chuckled. Then, 'Y'know, old chap, I shall have to turn around and strap myself in here . . . This isn't funny any longer . . . There's my solution. Don't forget those books.'

'I won't,' Lord assured him. He looked up the cabin, to see almost everyone holding to their seats with various grasps, despite the safety belts. The operation of the 'plane was becoming definitely erratic. It plunged and swayed, steadied for a few moments, bumped, rose, dropped. Tinkham, emerging from the lavatory, just managed to get into his chair and fasten the belt. The passengers were shaken out of any further possibility of conversation. Marjorie Gavin, the stewardess, sat strapped in one of the vacant seats, a smile that was too obviously a set one stamped across her pretty face.

6058 FEET

The Amalgamated dispatcher in the Control Room at Cheyenne sat at his desk, with intermittent glances at the airway clock and the Teletype tape. Out of the black night voices came to him from North Platte, Ogallala, Bushnell, from Laramie and Parco and Rock Springs. Along the tape ran word from all these places, and from others.

Suddenly the dispatcher bent forward over his desk,

and strain crept into his features. He beckoned to the assistant manager, who crossed the room with quick, light strides. '90 is in trouble south-west of Medicine Bow.'

The manager sucked his breath in a swift intake. 'How bad?'

'Don't know. This is the first I've heard.' The dispatcher held up a silencing hand ... 'Okay, 90. Cheyenne Amalgamated standing by. You are calling Medicine Bow, calling Medicine Bow. Go ahead, "Happy." '

The dispatcher lowered the transmitter from his mouth, turned to the manager. 'They are in a snow storm. Lannings reports line squalls and estimates their position about over McFadden. Medicine Bow has just reported snow over the tape, and Parco reports heavy snow, with a gale. No visibility at Parco, and ceiling 1500 at Medicine Bow. No visibility from 90; they have lost sight of their escort 'plane, which is not equipped for blind flying. Lannings is keeping in touch with escort 'plane by radio, but the snow is freezing on his wings and interfering with radio transmission. He is losing altitude at about 100 feet per minute.'

'What's their altitude?'

'10,600.'

'My God, and the worst place on the whole route, just this side of the Continental Divide. Elk Mountain just ahead of them, over 11,000; the Laramie Mountains on the other side. Christ!' he cried bitterly. 'When will we ever learn anything about weather? I could have sworn it was nothing but a few snow flurries, and here's a nasty storm. Too damn nasty.'

The dispatcher's hand went up again ... his voice was harsh even before it reached the microphone. 'Cheyenne Amalgamated calling Lannings in 90, calling Lannings in 90, calling Lannings in 90. Could not get message, "Happy," could not get message. Repeat message, 90, repeat message. This is Cheyenne Amalga-mated.'

'What the hell?' The manager's voice tensed abruptly.

'Something about Medicine Bow. Faded. Couldn't get it.'

The manager snapped, 'Clear the air . . . ! Clear the tape!'

'Cheyenne Amalgamated calling all ships. Cheyenne Amalgamated calling all ships, calling all ships. Amalgamated 90 in trouble south-east Medicine Bow. Clear the air for ten minutes, clear the air for ten minutes; for ten minutes! This is Cheyenne Amalga-mated, Cheyenne Amalgamated.'

With his right hand the dispatcher reached toward the Teletype machine and tapped out on it the repeated symbol for 'Clear.' For thirty seconds the incoming machine chattered on. There was a final click; silence.

For thirty seconds more the Control Room was dead quiet, as the dispatcher pressed the earphones against his head. The third occupant of the room, a pilot who had just come in from Colorado Springs, walked softly across to stand beside the manager, questions in his eyes.

Then, 'Okay, 90. This is Cheyenne Amalgamated. You cannot get Medicine Bow. We are telling them to floodlight on the tape, to floodlight on the tape. We are telling Medicine Bow to floodlight on the tape. Go ahead, 90.' His hand tapped rapidly against the Teletype keys.

Out of the side of his mouth the dispatcher spoke to the men beside him. '90 is stil losing altitude. Now 10,200. Can't get any answer from Medicine Bow, and want the field floodlighted. Have to land; no out now. Position undetermined, due to line squalls for last half-hour. The air is cleared, but that last call was so faint I hardly got it.'

Silence once more closed over the Control Room. To north and south and west other pilots, themselves careening through the black void, were listening tensely. The knuckles of the manager's hands gleamed whitely under the lights.

10,100 FEET

'What do you say, Lovett? Shall we take a chance? We only have four of them.'

There was no hesitation in the junior pilot's voice. 'Sure, take it. The poor bastard's escorting us, isn't he?'

Lannings pressed the button. '90 calling Philips, calling Philips. We are releasing parachute flare, releasing parachute flare. Watch out, Philips. This is Lannings in 90.'

He pulled one of the little levers between the sticks and, a few seconds later, a brilliant glare burst brightly several hundred feet below the transport. Hotly it burned in the midst of swirling snowflakes, spreading its light in all directions, yellow to white to grey to dark grey, merging finally with the darkness. A globe of brilliance in the stormy skies.

' . . . Okay, Philips, you think you saw us. We are proceeding direct north-west from here, direct north-west from here. Landing at Medicine Bow if we can find it, landing at Medicine Bow if we can find it. You will follow direct north-west. Okay, Philips.'

Danger was in the cockpit, danger surrounded the 'plane; but the pilots' expressions, while serious, showed no touch of panic. Lannings muttered, 'Hell, we're below Elk Mountain, falling below Laramie Peak. This damned ice . . . Cheyenne estimates the wind at fifty to sixty, west . . . Can you get the directional beacon, Hal?'

'Nope.'

Lannings listened intently. The directional signal

came only intermittently, fading out almost as he caught it. 'D-a-s-h . . . dot . . . d-a-s-h . . . dot . . . d-a – '

'Port rudder, Hal,' murmured Lannings, and listened.

Nothing. Then, 'D–a–s–h, d–a–s–h,' fading almost at once into, 'Dot . . . d-a-s-h . . . dot . . . d-a-s-h . . . dot . . . d-a-s-h.'

'Starboard rudder. Oh, hell, never mind; we're away off the course, anyhow, nine chances out of ten. The beacon may take us smack into Elk Mountain . . . We ought to be in the valley. If we're not . . . Give her the works, Hal, north-west, and watch for the field. They're floodlighting it over the tape.'

9000 FEET

Not all the swaying in the cabin was due to the elements. Every now and then the junior pilot banked the 'plane to port or starboard to get a better view below. Blackness everywhere. Lannings reached behind him, opened the door to the cabin. 'Lights out,' he said calmly. 'All belts. We will be landing soon.' He closed the door. 'I hope,' he said to himself.

And blackness everywhere. 'I'm taking over the ship,' said Lannings quietly. 'Turn off the instrument lights, will you, Hal?'

'The instrument lights? You mean that?'

'Yep. Can't bother about anything now except landing. We've got to find that field.' He took a last look at the compass and the altimeter. They vanished. Blackness . . . The motors droned steadily and powerfully, drawing the 'plane across the wind, cutting a way through air that tore at the ship, tossing it to starboard, pushing it down, boosting it in senseless zooms . . . To the straining eyes in the cockpit came blackness . . . Nothing else . . .

Both of them saw it at once. 'Is that – ?' 'Try it, it looks – '

The faintest suggestion of a tiny glimmer, almost beneath. Then the wind threw the port wing up and forward, and the ship dived; he pushed it to the left, extending his right foot against the rudder with all his force. The 'plane responded, circled downward.

Yes, it was somthing. It was different from the universal blackness. 'It's light!' Lovett cried, excitement in his voice for the first time. Suddenly came a flash; they were lower now, they could almost glimpse a suggestion of red, following the flash. 'That's the field!'

Lannings said, 'Give him another. We'll go up some, if we can.'

Lovett said, 'Sure,' and brought the transmitter to his lips. '90 calling Philips, calling Philips. The field is below us. Wait a minute, Philips.' He switched the instrument lights on and off. 'This is 90, 90. Medicine Bow Field below, our altitude, 9000. We will climb if we can and give you another flare, another flare. Say when ready, we will give you another flare . . . Okay, Philips, here she goes.' He pulled the lever.

Nothing on the earphones. The flare burst out below them, was carried rapidly to the east, dwindled into darkness. The seconds passed . . .

'Hell, we can't leave him,' ground out Lovett. 'This is 90 calling, Philips. Did you get it, Philips? . . . Okay, Philips, you didn't get it. Try flying west for a minute and a half, then circle. We will release another flare in two minutes, in two minutes. Our altitude now 9100. This is 90 calling, 90 calling. Okay, Philips.'

It was a long two minutes. Lannings murmured, 'Hell, I've lost it . . . Ah, got her again. We can't go any higher, even if we wanted to . . . ' Lovett pulled the lever.

They waited, bearing westward, thrown east as they circled. A little too far before they turned and the oblong

glow below faded into nothing almost instantaneously . . . 'Okay Philips, you got it. This is 90, our
altitude now 8900. Field just west the flare. We will go a
little west and drop another – our last flare, our last flare.
You must land with this, Philips. Hurry up, Philips,
hurry up. This is 90.'

The transport tossed ahead until the light beneath had
almost vanished. Lovett pulled the lever for the fourth
time. They banked and scudded back. They watched.

Suddenly between the two glows, the one from the
ground and the one slipping rapidly eastward, a small
shadow flitted. As the junior strained his vision through
the hail-marked glass, it dived, straightened, zoomed
abruptly into an Immelmann. It crossed between the
transport and the falling flare. It banked and dived once
more, its little wings outlined for an instant as it passed
into the parachute light . . . Five seconds . . . A tiny
shadow crossing into the glow from the ground . . . Not
reappearing.

'He's down.'

The transport flew eastward with motors partially cut.
Then they roared, opened full, as it banked and headed
west again, diving for the light . . . Now they were
nearer; the glow loomed brightly through snow-filled air.
Suddenly Lovett closed the landing-lights switch, and
brilliant twin swathes, joining beyond the snout, cut
through the whiteness ahead. A gust pushed them to
starboard and Lannings gave her port rudder. There,
there were the green border lights, faintly at the edges of
the field, the big floodlight streaming brightness almost
directly ahead. He pushed the stick forward . . . Bump!
The wheels hit hard; the transport recoiled into the air,
and bumped again. They were racing across the field,
diagonally. The border lights approached, braking
wouldn't stop the 'plane in time. Port rudder, starboard
ailerons, depressed elevators. It slewed to port, starboard wing up, port wing-tip scraping the ground; the

tail swept round in a great skid. Headed east once more, with brakes clamped tightly, the transport shuddered to a shaking stop.

Over the Teletype into the Cheyenne Control Room came a 'PX.' 'Amalgamated 90 landed apparently without damage, 8.28. Escort 'plane landed first. (Signed) Medicine Bow.' The assistant manager wiped the perspiration, hitherto unnoticed, from his forehead. He groped behind him for a chair and sat down limply.

6200 FEET

For some minutes the passengers remained quiet in the darkness of the cabin. They were jarred and shaken; they had also had a first-class scare. The lights of the field played strangely through the windows, showing drawn faces, peculiar shadows in the closed fuselage. In the cockpit the pilots were looking over the instruments while the motors idled, deciding not to take the 'plane up the field.

Marjorie Gavin was the first to recover in the cabin. As the propellers went dead, she undid her belt, got up and turned on the cabin lights from the rear partition. She rubbed her left arm where it had been bruised when she had turned them off.

Michael Lord was next. He opened the cabin door, to find the army flyer already outside. Lieutenant Philips looked green with cold, but Lord had no time to stop for that.

'Hello, Lieutenant. See that no one leaves the 'plane except the pilots and the stewardess, will you, please? I mean that; no one else, and, yes, here's a message for a man in New York. Would you see that one of the pilots gets it when he comes out – to be sent off right away? The name is Gesell; I think the rest of it legible.' He hurried off into the scurrying flakes.

Around the nose of the 'plane. Under the port wing, into the shadow it threw along the side of the fuselage. Lord fumbled with his keys; the lock of the baggage compartment door was small, and at first he couldn't fit the key into it. Then the cold struck his fingers. It was numbing cold; he must get the key fitted before his fingers became useless.

He pressed the point of the key over the lock's surface with his left hand, exerting slight pressure along the key's shank with his right thumb and forefinger. At last the door was open. He prepared to climb into the compartment.

Behind him a figure hurried, noiseless in the snow, around the tail of the transport. An upraised hand and arm. A blow. Lord sank silently beside the 'plane.

The figure pushed the prone body before it, slightly out of the way under the fuselage; but not before it reached into the detective's pocket and procured his flashlight. Then it climbed into the baggage compartment, leaned over Cutter's body strapped to the stretcher. The compartment was pitch black. The movements were hurried but careful. Again a raised arm, a jabbingly lowered hand, this time.

Not until then was the light, so hazardously obtained, used. Dim behind it, the figure played the flash over the surgeon's body, giving it a close inspection. And straightened with an abrupt exclamation . . .

Part IV – Cerebration

The junior pilot came down the cabin. He was grinning. The stewardess still stood in the little space behind the chairs. 'Good girl, Margy,' the pilot said. 'You sure brought us luck that time, kid.'

She was white and she was trembling a little, now that the landing had been made. She said, 'I – I didn't think you were going to make it, Hal. I guess – '

He shot a warning glance toward the passengers, now stirring in their seats, getting out of the safety belts. He leaned down, bringing his lips close to her ear as he squeezed a cold little hand. 'Didn't myself for a bit, kid.' Then he kissed the ear.

Marjorie Gavin blushed violently and jumped to one side, but did not forget to squeeze back with her hand. 'Go along, boloney. You just did it to scare me. I know.' However, her appearance was completely transformed. She smiled a real smile and pushed the pilot toward the door.

He looked out, preparing to jump down. 'What the hell's this?'

Beside the entrance the figure of Lieutenant Philips lay on its back in the snow. Lovett sprang out, lifted the flyer's head with an arm around his shoulder, just as Lannings' face appeared in the doorway above. 'Hey, "Happy," he's fainted. Exposure, I guess; he's practically green. What did he come out here for, anyhow?'

Between them the pilots lifted the fallen man and began carrying him slowly across the frozen ground toward the little house of the keeper at the edge of the field. Not until they had laid him on a sofa in the small front room did they notice the paper still clutched in his hand. Lannings loosened it and read the dampened message.

'H'm. He's got a message from Captain Lord here; must have seen him. Where the dickens is Lord, anyhow? Lord!' There was no answer to his shout, and the pilot regarded the message doubtfully. 'He must have given it to Philips to have it sent. I think this ought to go out.'

Lannings stepped into the tiny office and put the wire on the Teletype while Lovett chafed the lieutenant's wrists, administered brandy and made him as comfortable as possible by loosening his clothing. The passengers from the 'plane commenced straggling in.

Lannings came back into the stuffy little room. 'Well, folks,' he announced, 'we may be going up again presently, unless the snow is too deep on the field. This is the funniest storm I've ever seen. Looked like a blizzard half an hour ago, and now Parco reports on the tape that it is clearing rapidly there.' He peered through a window. 'Not coming down as heavily here now, either, I'd say.'

They stood about, most of the passengers huddling around the stove in the corner, although the room was warm, even hot. On the sofa Lieutenant Philips had regained consciousness and was struggling up on one elbow. 'Take it easy for a few minutes, Philips,' Lovett adjured him.

Lannings looked around the room; everybody was present except Lord. 'Where the dickens is Captain Lord?' he demanded again.

No one answered. Then Philips said, massaging his stinging hands, 'I saw him. He was the first out of the 'plane. He gave me a message to – '

'Yes, that's all right. I sent it while you were still out. But where did he go then, after he gave it to you?'

'I haven't a notion. I think he went up toward the nose of the 'plane, but I didn't watch him particularly. He seemed to be in a hurry. I must have fainted almost as soon as he left me . . . My God!' cried the flyer suddenly. 'What are all these people doing here? Captain Lord told me especially not to allow anyone off the 'plane except the pilots and the stewardess. He was emphatic about that.'

'I don't get it.' Lannings shook his head in puzzlement. 'You say he went toward the nose of the 'plane. But what for? And where could he have gone, then? There is nothing around this field but wilderness. There is nothing he could have gone for.'

Dr Pons spoke up. 'Maybe he went to look after Dr Cutter's body. In the baggage compartment.'

'But it can't have taken him all this time to look in there. Where the dickens could he have gone, then?'

'I think,' said Pons, 'we had better go take a look for him. Come on, let's go.'

At the doorway, just as the pilot and Pons were stepping out, Michael Lord came staggering up through the now thinly drifting flakes. 'We were just going out to look for you . . . Man, what's the matter with you?'

The detective made a negative motion with one hand; he wanted to save his breath. He came into the room and leaned heavily against the wall beside the doorway. 'Who's not here?' he snarled.

Lord's appearance contrasted entirely with the calm he had exhibited during the previous journey. He had no hat, his clothes were wet with the snow he had lain in. On the side of his head there was an ugly bruise, from which a small trickle of red disappeared underneath his crushed collar. His eyes held pain, and his expression was angry and menacing.

Someone said, 'Everybody is here.'

'Who came in last?'

Apparently no one knew. Pons asked, 'What is it all about, Michael? You look as if someone had hit you.'

'You're damn right someone hit me,' grated the detective. 'Someone knocked me out at the door to the baggage compartment, and then someone went in and murdered Dr Cutter.'

Everyone in the room appeared thoroughly astonished. 'But – but he was killed this morning,' Fonda gasped.

'Hell, no. He wasn't killed then. That was a specially prepared bulb I gave him, all right, but it didn't kill him; it just put him in a trance.'

A chorus of bewilderment greeted the terse statement. 'In a – ' 'What do you mean?' 'But – I'm going out – ' Alone of those present, Dr Pons seemed not entirely amazed. 'I thought there was something phoney about this set-up all along,' he murmured to himself. He nodded his head sagely.

Isa Mann repeated, 'I'm going out to him. Are you sure he is dead? How was he killed?'

'Stabbed,' Lord answered bluntly. 'You're going nowhere, and neither is anyone else. The lot of you are staying right here.' He turned to the army man abruptly and snapped: 'And what the hell happened to you, Philips? I told you to let nobody off the 'plane. If you had tended to business this wouldn't have happened.'

The lieutenant said in a low voice, 'I'm sorry. I fainted.'

'Is that so? Isn't that queer?' Into the detective's jumbled thoughts swam notions of foreign spies in the American Army. 'Sure you didn't follow me around the 'plane, pull the job and then come back and fall in the snow?'

'That's not fair, Lord,' Lovett protested. 'He came out there when he was just about all in, to thank us for getting him down to the field. I saw you go out the cabin door as I was coming down the aisle. It was less than a minute when I got out myself and found him unconscious beside the 'plane. He was out all right; it took us over five minutes to bring him around after we had gotten him to this house. He couldn't have done anything.'

Lord looked at the two flyers with eyes that were clearing. 'Give me some brandy,' he demanded. He gulped the drink, shuddered involuntarily as the hot liquid went down his throat, pulling himself together. When he spoke again his voice had returned to its normal tone. He addressed the two flyers on the sofa. 'I see. That let's him out, all right. Rather a wild idea of mine, I guess. Sorry, Philips, old man; it's pretty plain you couldn't help it.' He paused a few moments, then looked appraisingly around the small room, confirming for himself that everyone who had been in the 'plane was present. 'All right, ladies and gentlemen,' he continued grimly. 'I've been bluffing so far on this trip, but I'm not bluffing now. If I have appeared to consider matters lightly, it was because nothing outside my own pre-arranged plan had happened. What about my telegram to New York?' he asked suddenly. 'I wrote out a message that everything was O.K., but probably that hasn't been sent if Lieutenant Philips fainted.'

Lannings spoke up from the window through which he was watching the storm. 'It's gone, Captain. As I recall it, it said, "Everything O.K. according to plan." I found it in Philips' hand when we brought him in here. I put it on the Teletype for you . . . Looks as if it was out of date already. If you want to send another, it can go back to Cheyenne on the Teletype any time you say.'

'No, I guess not. Not right now, anyhow; there will be plenty of time for that later. Now,' Lord went on, 'up to the time we landed here no crime had been committed. A crime has been committed now, and the crime is murder. Let me make it perfectly plain to all of you that from this point on I'm not fooling . . . We'll be here for the night, I suppose, Lannings?'

The senior pilot shook his head doubtfully. 'I don't know. It's certainly letting up some now; and farther

west they report it practically clear. If the snow stops
presently, and if we can clear a track across the field, we
may be able to go on again in a few hours.'

'H'mm . . . Well, the first thing is obvious anyhow. I
intend to interview everybody separately, and find out
where they have been and when. Is there a room in this
house I can use for the purpose?'

It appeared that the little house boasted three rooms:
the one where the passengers were now gathered, and
from which the entrance door gave access to the field,
and, opening off this to the left and rear respectively, the
tiny office with its Teletype machine and weather instruments, and a fair-sized bedroom. Lord chose the bedroom for his investigations.

'I'll take the pilots first,' he announced from the
doorway in the rear wall. 'So they can be free to make
any arrangements they want about our going on.'

Neither Lovett nor Lannings, however, who went in
after him, could supply any information of value. They
had been the first out of the 'plane after the detective;
they had found Philips in the snow and carried him to the
house, where Lannings had sent off Lord's telegram. By
the time this had been done, and Philips had shown signs
of returning to life, a number of the passengers had
already arrived, but neither of the pilots had noticed
exactly who was present and who absent. 'I don't think
either of the girls were here then,' Lovett contributed;
and Lannings added, 'Nor the big man with the grey
hair. I'm not really sure, though.' The one point on
which they were certain was that no one had left the
cabin of the 'plane before they did.

'All right,' Lord acknowledged, making a few entries
in his open note-book. 'If that's all you can tell me, then
that's all. Too bad,' he murmured, 'because you two and
Pons are the only ones I can completely trust. And the
stewardess, of course. By the way, do either of you
happen to have known Miss Gavin for any time? I *can*

trust her, I suppose?'

The senior pilot said nothing, but Lovett was emphatic. 'You bet you can, Captain. Margy's a swell kid, and bright as they come. Anything she says goes.' The flyer's face took on a slight flush, and Lord noted in his book, 'Lovett – Gavin (?)'

'O.K. Thanks. That's all just now, then. Send in Philips, will you please?'

The army man limped in and sat down on the bed, but his testimony was even more meagre than that of his fellow pilots. Apparently he had fainted at almost the very moment when Lord had left him beside the 'plane. He could only say that when he had come to on the sofa in the front room there were a good number of people already there from the 'plane, but he was not acquainted with the passengers or their appearance, and was unable to make any conjecture as to the individuals who may not have been in the room.

'Who is that man in the corduroy trousers and the mackinaw?' the detective asked.

'That's the field keeper, I guess.'

'I see. Ask him to step in here for a few minutes, will you?'

Lord looked up as the keeper shuffled into the room. He was an awkward, ungainly man of middle age and plainly upset by the unexpected invasion of his accustomed solitude. He advanced from the doorway, halted, stood first on one foot, then on the other, obviously ill at ease.

'Come in,' the detective invited with a friendly smile. He pointed to the recently vacated bed. 'Have a seat. It's your mattress, after all. Will you let me know your name?'

'Ginty.' The man sat down gingerly on the very edge of the bed.

'All right. My name is Lord. What can you tell me about this situation, Ginty?'

'I dunno. Reckon I can't tell you much, mister. What you want to know?'

'Well, first, let's see where you were. Did you come out to the 'plane when we landed?'

'Naw.'

'I see. Have a cigarette, Ginty?' Lord extended his pack, and the keeper took one. He snapped a match alight with his thumbnail and took a long draw on the detective's Piedmont. The diversion appeared to put him somewhat more at ease. 'Where were you when we landed, then?'

'I was standing in the door to the house. Didn't want to go out on the field and get hit when you come down.'

'And you stayed here all the time?'

'I'll tell you, mister. It's thisaway: At eight-twelve I got a message on the tape to floodlight the field, that 90 wanted to land. The snow has bolluxed up the radio somehow. So I lit up and went to the door to watch for you. I seen your flare. Then first the little 'plane come down; and then you come down after it. So I went in and sent a "PX" off on the tape sayin' you'd landed. When I got back, and started across the field toward you, I seen the pilots comin' across carryin' someone, so I jest helped them bring him in and put him on the sofa.' Ginty drew a deep breath and expelled it in a loud sigh after his lengthy speech.

'I suppose you know the exact time when we landed? You put the time on the teletype, don't you?'

'It was eight-twenty-eight, mister.'

'And then what did you do?'

'Then I hung around. The senior pilot come into the office to send off a message on the tape, and I come in with him. I was lookin' out of the window while he was sending it, but I couldn't see the 'plane across the field for the snow. It's way down the other end, far away as it can get. Then I come back in the front room with him, and I been there ever since.'

'Now tell me this, Ginty: When you came back into the front room from your office, was anyone else there besides the three pilots? Had anyone else come in yet from the 'plane?'

'No, but a couple of gents come in just after we went back to the front room. And then pretty soon the rest of them come in.'

'You wouldn't know who the first two were, would you?'

'Naw.' The keeper shook his head, then his eye brightened. 'But the first one had a funny tie, like a black muffler, and his pants and coat was different.'

'Bellowes,' said Lord. He thought a moment. 'Do you remember what time it was when Lannings sent off that message for me from your office?'

'Sure, I know that. I know them tape times by habit. It was eight-thirty-six.'

Lord wrote in his note-book: 'Bellowes arrives house 8.37 (keeper). Some other man behind him.' He looked up again. 'And that is the only one you noticed, the man with the black tie?'

Ginty scratched his head. 'Yes, I think so.' He seemed to be struggling with some further memory. 'Oh, yeah; I seen a woman comin' along through the snow when I was lookin' out the office window.'

'You're sure of that?'

'Yep, I seen her all right coming across the field . . . But that's all, I guess.'

Into the note-book went: 'Woman approaching house, 8.36 (keeper).' But that *was* all, for the keeper had now been induced to part with all the information he possessed.

Isa came in stiffly and sat down stiffly at the foot of Ginty's bed. She spoke before Lord could say anything. 'I want to go out and see my uncle. It is possible that if he has been stabbed there may still be something that can be done for him.' Her lips were set in a straight line, and to the detective it appeared that she was labouring under a considerable stress.

Lord answered her quietly. 'I am sorry, Miss Mann, but that is quite out of the question. I don't want to upset you further with an account of the details, but, if it will relieve you at all, I can assure you from the nature of his wounds that Dr Cutter is beyond any help whatsoever.'

Isa said in a dead voice, 'It's terrible. I thought he had been killed this morning; but to find out that he was really all right, and then to have this other – ' She stopped abruptly.

'You were closely attached to your uncle, Miss Mann?'

'No . . . No, I am not "closely attached" to anyone; but I admired him; and it is imperative that he should get to Reno. For the divorce. Anne will never go through with it unless she is pushed. You don't know my mother.'

Lord admitted his lack of acquaintance with Cutter's sister by a nod. He said, 'Naturally, I am in the dark about that, but I take it you are anxious, at any rate, to assist me in finding out who stabbed him. Will you please tell me exactly what you did from the time the 'plane landed until you reached this house? You realise that, by checking everyone up, I may be able to make some progress toward the criminal.'

'I suppose so,' the girl replied abstractedly. 'Although I don't see how you can find out much. It was confused after the way we came down. I wasn't paying a great deal of attention to the others.'

'Let's just check up on what you did. You can tell me that.'

'Yes, I unfastened my belt and went out the door. It was open. I started across the field, not quite in the right direction. Then I saw the house, and came over to it. That's all.'

'You got right up as soon as the 'plane landed? Right after I did?'

'I think so. I didn't notice you, I'm afraid.'

'Well, let's see.' The detective bent over his book. 'The 'plane landed at 8.28. You left your seat immediately, we'll say 8.29; 8.30, out the door. It takes two or three minutes to reach the house from the 'plane; I've timed it. So you would have been on the field from 8.31 to 8.34, when you probably reached the house here. You walked directly across?'

'Yes, except that I started in the wrong direction, as I said.'

'In that case it may have taken you another minute or so. It might have been 8.36 when you were at the door of the front room?'

'I imagine so. I don't know.'

Lord consulted his note-book: 'Woman approaching house, 8.36 (keeper).' He said, 'Yes, I think we can say you reached the house at 8.36. That would give you a long time on the field, though – six minutes. You must have gone quite out of your way.'

'I don't know, really. I was thinking about the divorce and what I could do about it. I thought Uncle Amos was dead then, you know.'

'And when you reached the house, who was ahead of you? I mean, who was already here when you arrived?'

'I'm afraid I can't tell you that, either. Oh, some people were in the room when I came in. The pilots, I guess. I think some others, too; but I'm not sure. I tell you I was thinking all the time about affairs in Reno.'

Lord considered. Finally, 'If you can't remember, you can't. It's better than guessing and leading me astray by making me take your guesses seriously. Very well, Miss Mann, I should like to see that man Tinkham next, if you please.'

Isa got to her feet, said, 'I'll send him in,' and closed the door behind her. The detective turned a fresh page in his note-book and made parallel columns for each passenger, ruling off a space for every minute beginning with 8.28, when the 'plane had landed. He proceeded to fill in the columns so far as he could with the information he had now obtained. Presently he glanced around, to see Tinkham seated in turn on the bed opposite. The latter had come in so quietly that Lord had been unaware of his entrance. He observed the surgeon's assistant speculatively, wondering how far he could trust the other's hostile attitude.

Tinkham's bearing, however, had undergone a considerable change. To Lord's surprise, the assistant when he saw that he had the detective's attention smiled and began, 'We may as well forget our quarrel, in view of what has occurred. I see why you objected to my examining Dr Cutter this morning. As I understand it now, you had administered some drug to him which rendered him unconscious, in order to put off any possibility of his being attacked by the person who sent him that threatening letter.'

'You are perfectly correct,' Lord admitted.

'Under the circumstances, I realise why you could not afford to have an examination made. You must see, though, why I insisted, knowing nothing of the real situation. Probably you do not appreciate how much I admired Dr Cutter, or how concerned I was about his condition.'

'Ah, I see. Well, we can forget the incident, so far as I am concerned.'

'I owe Dr Cutter a very great deal,' Tinkham continued earnestly. 'My whole professional career up to now, practically speaking. That means something, Captain Lord. And, aside from these personal considerations, he was a man whom experimental surgery can ill afford to lose. My admiration for him was as great as my gratitude.' The man's voice held the sound of sincerity, and the detective could not but admit to himself the common sense of his statements.

'Very well. Let's forget it. I understand that you are

prepared to help me now in any way you can.'

'I certainly am.'

'You can help me by giving me your movements after the 'plane landed and by telling me what you can of anyone else's movements, but first your own.'

Tinkham leaned forward, regarding the floor between his feet. 'Let me try to be as accurate as possible.' He reflected for some moments, then said slowly, 'I sat still for a minute or so after we landed. Then I unfastened my belt and went out on the field, intending to find the house that I heard was somewhere about. When I reached the ground I saw some tracks leading off in the snow, and I followed them. I had gone some distance, when I suddenly realised that I had come away without my bag. So I turned around and came back to the 'plane again. The bag was on my seat where I had left it; I suppose I had been somewhat shaken by the kind of landing we made. As soon as I had gotten the bag, I came across to the house. I think when I finally got here that everyone except yourself had already arrived – almost everyone, anyhow.'

Under the column headed, 'Tinkham,' Lord had been making entries as the other talked. '8.28, seat 8.31, getting up. 8.32 out door. 8.33, field.'

'How long would you say you were on the field before you turned back to get your bag?' he asked. 'It takes about three minutes to go from the 'plane to this house.'

'I don't believe I can say with any accuracy; but I must have been nearly over here when I discovered that I had come away without it.'

'Suppose we say you turned back at 8.36, and reached the cabin again at 8.39? Do you think that likely?'

'It's possible.'

'How long did it take you to find the bag?'

'No time at all. It was right on my seat.'

'Then you were on the field again at 8.40, if you left at once. That would bring you to the house at 8.43.'

Tinkham said, 'No. It probably took me a little longer than the average time. I forgot to tell you, but as you are calculating this in minutes I must say that I dropped the bag in the snow on the way over. The catch must have been unfastened. The bag came open and, as I was grabbing it, it fell out of my hand. It wouldn't make much difference, of course, but picking it up and seeing that nothing had fallen out might have brought me here a minute later.'

'Scientific detail,' Lord smiled. 'All right, we can put it down at 8.44, then. Now, whom did you notice as you were going back and forth on the field? There must have been plenty of the others out there with you during that time.'

'There were,' the assistant admitted. 'But no one passed me close enough for me to recognise him or for him to recognize me, for that matter. It was snowing very hard, you will recall, when we got out of the 'plane – thick. I did see some figures through the snow both coming and going, but I couldn't say for certain who they were.'

'You are sure of that? Sure you didn't recognise someone's figure or gait? Can't you recall anyone at all?'

'No,' Tinkham said after a pause. 'There is no use my just guessing. Everyone on the 'plane is tall, even the girls. So height is no criterion, and I didn't notice any peculiarities; they were just vague figures through the snow. I don't believe I saw more than two, or three at the most. I simply couldn't identify them to you. It wouldn't be fair, and I really don't know.' He finished with a shrug.

'That is all you can tell me?'

'I'm sorry. That is every bit. I wasn't concerned with watching anyone, you know. I had no idea that anything serious was happening at such a time. To tell you the truth, I found myself a little let down after the tension of whirling around in the air before the pilots managed to bring us in. I imagine everyone must have been more or less self-centred just then . . . Except the person who attacked you and Dr Cutter, of course.'

'Can you recall definitely who was here when you finally got to the house? You said everyone, I think. Are you positive about your being the last to arrive?'

'Well – '

'Well, what? You must understand that these questions may be vitally important.'

Tinkham hesitated and when he spoke it was with obvious reluctance. 'No, I was not literally the last to come in. Miss Fonda Mann got here several minutes after I did. She was the last; but you would not have any idea of suspecting her, I'm sure.'

'Why not?' asked Lord. 'Why should I exempt anyone from possible suspicion? Don't you consider her strong enough to have attacked me? I was hit from behind, you know; there was no struggle at all.'

'What were you hit with? Do you know?' The assistant's voice was curious.

'Yes, I do know. It was one of the blocks for the wheels. There are four spares carried under the fuselage. One of them was in the snow beside me. I see no reason why a healthy young woman could not have swung it at my head.'

'Of course she is strong enough,' Tinkham said slowly. 'She plays a good game of tennis, plays a great deal; a hard game develops powerful arm muscles and fine co-ordination, but, seriously, you can't really suspect her; it's out of reason that a girl like that should murder her uncle in cold blood. Why, I wouldn't credit it for an instant!'

'Well, she is only one out of six. We needn't get excited about it yet. All I mean is that everyone is a suspect until I can prove him innocent. As far as I have gone, though, no one seems to have much of an alibi.'

'Alibis will be scarce, I think,' Tinkham hazarded. 'As

it seemed to me, we all scattered and came over more or less separately. I don't remember seeing anything but isolated figures myself.'

The detective said, 'Yes, it's unfortunate. I'll see what Pons has to contribute next. It can't be possible that everyone lost sight of all the others. Something may turn up yet.'

He watched Tinkham rise and make his exit. At the door the latter paused and turned. 'If I can help you in any way, you will call on me?' He was gone, carrying his bag, which he had brought with him, in his left hand. Lord's pencil made a further note about the bag.

Some minutes passed before Dr Pons' large figure appeared in the entrance. The psychologist came in with a sandwich in one hand, from which a bite had already been taken. As he crossed the room he swallowed, then asked, 'How are you, Michael? That looks like a nasty crack you got.'

'I have one hell of a headache,' the detective admitted, 'but it seems to be getting a little better. It's nothing serious. Where did you get that sandwich?'

'The stewardess – Majorie – brought over some eats from the 'plane. She is serving everyone out there. Shall I have her bring something in to you?'

'Not just yet. I'll get some later. I want to finish up these interviews first. I'm relying on you, doctor, for a little real information. I haven't gotten much as yet.'

Pons disposed of his sandwich with a final gulp. He said, 'What happened, anyhow? Haven't you any idea who hit you? Where was it?'

'You tell me your story first,' the detective invited. 'I don't want to put any suggestions into your head. What happened to you between the time the 'plane came down and the time you got to the room out there?'

'All right,' Pons acquiesced. 'We'll do it that way . . . Let's see, now. First of all I can tell you I sat a good long

time right in my seat after we finally got down. My good-
ness,' the doctor ejaculated, 'that was a regular whirlwind we got into in these mountains. I didn't think we
would get down safely at all; I don't see yet why the
'plane wasn't torn apart. I was dizzy; I was very nearly
sick. If I hadn't thought we were all going to be killed I
think I would have been sick. I was so glad to be on the
ground again that I just sat still and recovered myself.'

Lord asked, 'How long do you think this recuperation
lasted?'

'A good long time. Five or ten minutes.'

'Really? As long as that?'

'I know it's a long time,' Pons agreed. 'But I'm
familiar with time intervals from experimental work. I
am certain I sat there between five and ten minutes. I
can't get it closer than that, because I wasn't paying
special attention to the time.'

'Well, nearer to which? Nearer five, would you say, or
nearer ten?'

'It was well over five, I'm sure. And I'm quite sure it
wasn't as much as ten. If I were doing it, I'd split the
difference – say seven. That's the highest probability.'

Lord returned to his note-book, under 'Pons.' '8.28,
seat. 8.35, getting up.'

'So you got out of your seat at 8.35, we'll say? Then
what?'

'When I got up I walked directly to the back of the
cabin and came across the field to the house. I was the
last person to leave the cabin, if that is of any use to you.
Everyone else had gone – except the stewardess, that is.
She was still there, fiddling around with the storage
compartment by the door.'

'Yes. 8.36, out the door; 8.37 on the field. Did you walk
over rapidly or slowly?'

'Neither. Just an ordinary walk.'

'Say eight-forty for your arrival here, then. Now, can
you remember whether the tracks in the snow that the

others had made were all together, or was there no beaten track?'

The psychologist answered without reflection, 'Yes, I can tell you that, because I couldn't see the house, and I looked for a trail to it, but there wasn't any. There were footprints leading off in different directions, but most of them pointed in a general way toward here. They went out rather like a fan, and I took a course midway between the outside tracks. That was just about right; I came almost directly toward the house.'

'Did you notice anyone coming back to the 'plane as you were leaving? Tinkham says he returned to it later to get his bag. Or perhaps he came back before you had left?'

'No, he didn't do that; nor did I see him when I left, but I believe his bag *was* on a seat. I think I recall seeing it when I came down the cabin.'

'Anything else before you got to the house?'

'Yes. I met the Englishman just as I came to the door here. He came up from the right. I don't know where he had been; the 'plane was not in that direction at all. We went in together . . . And someone else came in right after us. Raven, or whatever his name is, closed the door and I heard it open again a second later, but I don't know who it was. I didn't look around; I was cold after coming across and I went right over next to the stove. When I did look around the room everyone was there except the two good-looking girls.'

'Who are the two good-looking girls, doctor?'

'The captivatress, of course, and Marjorie.'

'Fonda Mann and the stewardess, you mean?'

'Uh-huh. They came in quite a few minutes later.'

Pons waited until his friend had brought the note-book entries up to date; then he said, 'You probably know, Michael, that I've had an idea something was going on behind the scenes. I'll have to confess, though, that I hadn't guessed just what you were up to.'

'Yes,' Lord remarked, 'I am aware you smelled a rat. That was fairly plain when you refused to concoct any theory about the "poisoned" bulb. I did get some quite interesting theories from the others, though. I'd be glad to know just what put you on your guard, because the criminal evidently saw through the scheme, too. I must have made a bad mistake somewhere.'

'I'm not so sure I can help you there. I got it because you must remember that I've seen you at work before. Your attitude this time was entirely different than it was on the "Transcontinental," for instance. You didn't seem to me to be in earnest in the same way. There could be only two reasons for that: either you knew who the criminal was and were only waiting to grab him, or else there wasn't any criminal and thus there wasn't any crime. I couldn't see any reason for not making the arrest at Chicago if the first alternative were true; but you didn't, and so I plumped for the second, even though I didn't entirely understand it. The way you received the other theories confirmed it, too. I have heard you listen to some pretty wild ideas on other occasions, but you have given them far more serious consideration than you did to the ones you invited this time. It seemed to me you were only half listening sometimes; it was more like passing an hour or so than like seeking a necessary solution . . . Just the same, I can't believe that the real murderer could have gotten on to you as I did, unless he knows you well. Certainly the people who offered you solutions for something that didn't need one were all taken in, and, if they were, I don't quite see how the criminal found you out.'

'I must have made a stupid slip somewhere,' Lord repeated. 'If I can put my finger on it, it may point to the person who took advantage of it.'

'It's time you told me what happened after we landed,' the psychologist suggested.

'There isn't much to tell. Naturally I was worried

about Cutter after all those whirligigs we had done. I got out as soon as we stopped. Found Philips at the door and told him to let no one out of the cabin. So I thought everything was fixed and paid no attention to anything except getting to Cutter. I had a little trouble with the door of the baggage compartment, and I had just gotten it open when I was hit. When I came to, it was some time later. As soon as I could I crawled into the compartment – the door was still open – and found that my man had been stabbed in the throat. There wasn't much blood; in fact there was almost none, but his neck had been slashed deeply with some sort of sharp instrument. The wounds are curious. I could swear that no ordinary knife had been used; the slashes weren't clean enough for that. It was something sharp, but not as sharp as a knife; the flesh was torn in places as well as cut. Of course I searched for the weapon carefully, but I couldn't find a sign of it. I'm certain it was taken away by the murderer. After that I locked up the compartment again and came over here. The only thing I know about the criminal is that he – or she – came around the tail of the 'plane from the cabin door. I came around the nose, and there was a track in the snow leading around the other end of the 'plane, but the prints, of course, were too vague to imply anything.'

Dr Pons lit a cigarette. 'He, you said, or she?'

'Certainly. It may have been one of the girls, for all I know. Tinkham tells me Fonda plays a lot of tennis and has a strong tennis arm, and Isa looks as if she had good muscles with that wiry build of hers. I haven't anything against them, but I haven't anything for them, either. I can't seem to get alibis for anybody, and so everyone is still an equally possible suspect.'

'Hah,' said Pons. 'This will take some thinking. I have talked to both of them, and I find there is a first-rate mix-up and controversy in the Cutter family. You know about it, perhaps?'

'This business about the sister's divorce, you mean? I know only the general outlines of the affair.'

'It is not a mild disagreement by any manner of means. It's seriously important to several of them – probably to all of them. It will bear thinking about. It involves some very strong emotions and some fundamental ones.'

Lord inquired, 'You haven't formed a theory about it already, have you?'

'No, not yet. What I'd like to do is sit down by myself and go over what I know about it. Motivation is an excellent place to start from, and I have quite a bit of data on possible motives here. I'm not ready with it yet, though.'

'That sounds reasonable enough,' Lord admitted. 'Well, doctor, go ahead and work out your motives. You were pretty close to the correct solution on the *Meganaut,* I remember. I'll be glad to hear any ideas you may hit upon. We shall have to work fairly fast now, if Lannings is right about going up again.'

'He's right about that, I guess,' said Pons. 'The snow has stopped, and they are out there clearing off the field now, I believe.'

'All right, you work on motive for a bit and I'll concentrate on the other angles. The weapon and my own slip that must have told the murderer the truth about Cutter. Meantime I'll get on with these interviews and finish them up before there is any question of leaving here and going up again.'

'Right you are,' the psychologist assented cheerfully. 'I can use another of those sandwiches about now, then I'll sit down and see just what we have to go on . . . Whom will you have next, Michael?'

Lord consulted his chart. 'Didenot, I guess, and then Bellowes. Yes, I'll take them that way.'

'Hah! Bellowes won't do your headache any good, I'm afraid. Shan't I have Marjorie bring you a couple of aspirin tablets?'

'Not yet, no. I'm in a hurry to get through with this. I'll get some from her when I talk with her.'

When the philosopher had replaced Dr Pons, Lord got the first definite advantage of his questionings. Didenot could give Bellowes an alibi. As they worked out the times, he had gotten up from his chair at 8.33, been in the rear of the cabin at 8.34, descended from the 'plane at 8.35, started crossing the field at 8.36, and reached the house at 8.39. The significant part of his testimony, however, was that Bellowes had preceded him out of the 'plane and across the landing field. Didenot had seen the latter leave just before him and, since he had followed him toward the house, had not lost sight of him until he had entered the doorway. Bellowes had walked somewhat faster than the philosopher, however, and thus might possibly have arrived a minute or more earlier. Lord checked the information against Ginty's evidence of Bellowes' arrival at 8.37 and found an agreeable matching of the time. Didenot also confirmed that when he had entered the front room only the pilots, the keeper and Bellowes were already there.

With Bellowes, although the clergyman treated him with the greatest reserve and had to be cross-examined at some length before he disclosed his information, Lord managed to establish another alibi. He had noticed Didenot getting out of his seat as he passed down the aisle; he had also glanced back at least twice toward the 'plane after leaving it, and was sure that the other had followed him across the field. Moreover, he confirmed that Didenot had entered the house shortly after he himself had arrived, being the next passenger to come in. Although he could not be made to commit himself to any particular times, the detective calculated that Bellowes had risen from his chair at 8.32, started for the house at 8.35, and reached it – since he agreed that he had walked rapidly – at 8.37. It all checked nicely.

The minister left with his lips still set in a thin, straight line. He had washed his hands once of the whole sordid affair. He had no desire to consort further with the derelict sinners among whom he found himself for the duration of his journey.

Hugh L. Craven entered Lord's sanctum with his pipe drawing well and a sportsman's smile lighting up his face. 'Pullin' my leg a bit about that bulb, weren't you?' he remarked as he reclined in a relaxed posture on the bed at Lord's gesture. 'Just the same, I shouldn't be too sure if I were you, Captain; maybe you're pulling your own leg now instead of mine.'

'How is that?' asked Lord, leaning back more comfortably in his wooden chair and lighting a cigarette.

'Why, just that it may still have happened as I suggested. You admit now that you gave the man the bulb on purpose. It wasn't an injurious one, but that's all right; I assumed that it was harmless myself. It doesn't alter the fact that the fatal effect may have been projected just as I told you, and Cutter have been dead since this morning. This stabbing affair may have been quite superfluous. By the way, have you got the knife he was stabbed with?'

'No,' said Lord. 'The murderer still has that. Unless he has thrown it away in a snowdrift off the field somewhere.'

'Quite. On the other hand, how are you so certain that there is a knife? I take it there is a wound now; but how do you know that that isn't a projected wound also? You haven't the instrument you suppose caused it. What if there wasn't any instrument in the ordinary sense?'

The detective took his turn at grinning. 'What if it's all black magic, eh?'

Craven shrugged good-naturedly. 'Black magic is simply a silly label for what you don't understand. There have certainly been instances of secondary projection. Do you recall the circumstances of the death of J. Temple Thurstone, for example? His body was found burned to death, dressed in clothes that were not even scorched. No other signs of fire on the premises, but hours later further inexplicable fires broke out in the vicinity in such a fashion that no "ordinary" explanation sufficed. Then there was Lavina Farrar, also. She died of a stab wound to the heart; but her clothes were unpunctured. Some distance away was found a knife and a little blood; but there was no blood on her garments. Fully reported by competent witnesses. There are other cases.'

'From which you conclude, Mr Craven?'

'Both are instances of projected death. But more than that: they are also instances of *afterthoughts*. The original visualisations had been merely of the fatal attacks upon these persons, and the attacks had been inexplicably localised because that was all that had been imagined and projected. Then a realisation that inexplicable circumstances might lead to searching investigations. So in one case further fire projections (but likewise "unnatural") and in the other a knife and blood, but again in such a fashion that the knife could not have been withdrawn from the wound or the blood have issued from it . . . So here perhaps you have the original successful attack followed later by a further projection attempting to make the murder more plausible to contemporary superstitions.'

'Very clever,' said Lord, 'a most ingenious theory. However,' he leaned forward again and continued more briskly, 'in view of the actual wounds, which are far from imaginary, and also of the footprints of the criminal as he approached and left the scene, as well as a large bump on my head that I am quite sure was not "projected," I shall stick to a more usual hypothesis. Let us get down to what really happened following our landing.'

'Of course,' Craven waved his pipe in graceful retirement, 'I was certain, to begin with, that hypnosis is proof against proof.'

'I should like to have a summary of your movements. I

am collecting all of them, you understand, in order to establish alibis. Have you an alibi, by any chance? I hope so. It will reduce my work.'

'I'm afraid not, old chap. I walked over to look at the combat 'plane at the other end of the field, and I fear I neglected to take anyone with me. There was no one there, and I only met Dr Pons when I had left the army 'plane and was at the doorstep of the house.'

'And how did you happen to go over to the army 'plane, in the first place?'

Craven shrugged. 'Again no special reason, I'm afraid. I fly a great deal. I'm interested in 'planes, that's all.'

'I see. Well, let us try to get your movements down to definite times. Did you leave our 'plane soon after it landed, or did you wait at all in the cabin?'

'I can tell you that. I got down just after the pilots. I believe I was the first to follow them out; in fact I am sure of it. They were carrying the other flyer away to the house just as I reached the field.'

'8.31, then,' said Lord, 'for your descent to the field. How long did it take you to reach the other 'plane, would you say?'

'No idea, really. I had to find it first, and it was some distance from this house. Nearly as far as our own 'plane, I would say, although in quite another direction.'

'If you came in with Pons, you reached here at 8.40. Suppose we say four to five minutes to find the army 'plane. That would bring you to it at 8.36. Did you stay there long?'

'Only a minute or so. It was colder than I had thought. I merely glanced into the cockpit and looked at the instrument panel.'

'All right. About two minutes, probably. Then you would have left it about 8.38 and reached the house at 8.40. That would seem about right, would it?'

'Really, I can't say. In general I should think you were

about correct. I didn't notice the time when I arrived
here; but, by Jove, I did see the clock on the instrument
panel of the combat 'plane. Let me think; I believe it was
between 8.35 and 8.40 somewhere. I can't do better than
that for you.'

'That would check.'

'Probably it would. Just the same, I think you're
barkin' up the wrong tree. I don't know who has alibis
and who hasn't, but I don't believe any of these people
did a murder at that time. I've had a bit of experience
flying, as I said; and after a landing such as we had, no
one is likely to be prepared for quick action and meeting
unexpected emergencies as this theoretical murderer
must have done. I don't know whether you realise it, but
we were in a tight place for a bit up above.'

'Oh, I know that well enough. Nevertheless,' Lord
added grimly, 'someone did do it, so your objections, no
matter how good, are overcome.'

The novelist rose from his lounging position and
stretched. 'I can see,' he agreed, 'that you will have it
your way. I wish I had an alibi for you, but I haven't. I
should gladly tell you anything I could, but I can't even
give anyone else an alibi. In fact, I've said all I know, and
I can see it's not of much account; but it's the best I can
do.'

'O.K. Then send in Miss Fonda Mann, if you don't
mind.'

Fonda came in and flashed a brilliant smile at Michael
Lord. She brought a perceptible effect of brightness into
the dark little room with its one electric bulb above the
shabby bedstead.

'Won't you sit down, Miss Mann?'

Fonda sat down, straightening her tailored skirt over
her crossed knees. 'Must it be "Miss Mann"?' she
inquired in her low, rich voice. 'We seem to have become
rather closely' – she smiled again – 'involved together in
a very short time.'

Lord, surprised, adjusted himself quickly to her attitude; he had usually found it advantageous to meet witnesses on their own ground.

'May I have a light – Michael?'

'You may have a light, Fonda.' He crossed to her side, held a match to the tip of her cigarette, could not avoid noting the darkened lashes fringing her raised blue glance. 'Thank you, Michael.'

In his own chair again, with the girl leaning back gracefully on one arm while the smoke drifted out between her red lips, he said, 'Of course you surprise me. You do not appear as concerned over what has happened as I should have supposed. Would you object to telling me frankly your view of Dr Cutter, Miss Mann?'

'Fonda, please,' said Fonda.

'Fonda.'

The girl drew her features into a frown, rather an attractive one. 'I didn't like him at all,' she answered. 'He was a hard man, unreasonable and prejudiced. Half the reason he came out here at all was to force my mother into a divorce against her real wishes. Dr Mac could have done the operation just as well, no matter what he said . . . As to his death, I *was* shocked at first, but I have gotten over most of that. I have thought all along, you know, that he was killed this morning.'

'And how do you feel about your other uncle? I gather that he, too, is in favour of your mother's divorce. You understand that these personal questions are necessary under the circumstances.'

'It is perfectly all right; I don't mind at all . . . Uncle Jim is much nicer. He's not so – inhuman. Amos has always been breaking up mother's relations with the men she liked; I think he was just plain jealous of them. Uncle Jim doesn't really care; he lets people live as they want to. He was just talked over by Amos. I haven't seen him for some time, or I could have changed his position myself, easily. He won't do anything much by himself, you wait and see.'

'But you couldn't do anything with Amos, eh? He was hard-boiled.'

'He was a perfectly horrid man, Michael. Nasty, he was.'

'Just the same, he has been murdered. I don't suppose your animosity goes so far as to approve of that?'

'No–o.' She flicked an ash on the floor without taking her deep-blue gaze from Lord's face. He could not escape the realisation that she was one of the most beautiful girls he had ever seen.

He gave himself an inward shake, half angrily. She knew that, of course, and she was managing to put him in a position where it would be extremely difficult for him to take advantage of this intimate conversation to incriminate her, if she had had anything to do with Cutter's death. She was evidently a shrewd judge of character in addition to her other attributes.

'Now look here, Fonda Mann,' he said more sharply, 'a murder has been done – and murder is a dirty, cowardly, degenerate crime. I am going to find out who did it, and I am going to send that person to the chair. I may as well tell you that you are still a possible suspect along with the rest.'

'That's all right with me.' Fonda seemed in no way perturbed by the ominous information.

'Michael?'

'What?'

'Can I have another light, please?'

This time he tossed the matches across to her. She caught them deftly in her left hand. He waited until she had selected and lighted another cigarette.

'Now,' he said, 'I'm going to ask you some important questions, and I don't want frivolous answers.'

'You're so serious, Michael.'

'I am entirely serious,' he agreed.

'I like you serious. You look – oh, handsomely intense

that way, you know.'

'Quit it. I want these questions answered.'

'Yes?'

'Did you send your uncle the threatening note he received in New York?'

'Good heavens, no.' Fonda almost choked with surprise as she inhaled the cigarette. 'I never even thought of it, and, if I had, I wouldn't have sent it. It couldn't possibly do any good.'

'What do you mean?'

'I mean it wouldn't have kept him away from Reno. Probably have taken him out sooner. He was terribly obstinate, like most disagreeable men.'

'I see . . . ' Lord spoke abruptly. 'Did you kill him? Was he disagreeable enough for that?'

'Of course I didn't kill him. What an idea, Michael! You don't think female murderers are attractive, do you? I don't.'

'I have known them to be beautiful, however, and very calm and calculating.'

'Am I beautiful, Michael?'

'Indeed yes, Fonda. You are certainly beautiful. I should not rely upon that circumstance too far, though, if I were you,' Lord finished unpleasantly.

'Now you're angry.' The girl's bearing changed instantaneously. 'I'm sorry. I am, really. I shouldn't have been flip when you are trying so hard; and your head – Oh,' she cried suddenly, 'that's an awful bump you have on it! It's as big as an egg, and I'll bet it hurts like anything.' She opened her handbag and reached inside. 'Here, take these aspirins. Please.' She held out two white tablets in a slim, manicured hand.

'One way to get rid of the detective?' Lord suggested.

'I – Michael!' Fonda's voice rose, then dropped reproachfully. 'That's perfectly horrid of you.'

He looked into wide open, reproachful eyes that looked steadily into his. He felt automatically ashamed of himself; he simply couldn't help it. 'All right,' he said ungraciously. He accepted the tablets and swallowed them both.

Fonda smiled happily, and became serious. 'Now I'll answer your questions decently. Really, I will.'

Still somewhat distrustfully, Lord said, 'Tell me just what you did after the 'plane landed.'

'I sat still for a few minutes. Then I got up and asked that nice little stewardess where the pilots had gone. I saw them get out of the 'plane. She said to the keeper's house. So I jumped out and went after them. When I was almost there – '

'Wait a minute. How long before you left your seat? Three or four minutes?'

'I don't know exactly. About that maybe. It was a few minutes before I was ready to get up. I was frightened up in that storm, Michael.'

'We landed at 8.28. About 8.32 you got up?'

'I guess so. I don't really know.'

'Then you would have been on the field at 8.34, if you stopped to speak with the stewardess, and you reached here at 8.37?'

'But I didn't reach here.'

'Oh. Where did you go?'

'I came up to the house, but I didn't come in. When I was nearly here, my scarf blew off, and I saw that I had lost the clip for it. I looked around in the snow for it, and then I went back to the 'plane to look for it.'

'Why all the rush? I should have thought you would have been pretty cold after walking across the field. You could have come back later, after you had warmed up a bit.'

'I was cold, but I wanted to find the clip. It is rather valuable.' She pointed to the ornament, now holding the gay scarf securely below her throat. 'It has two real sapphires in it, you see.'

'So you turned around and went back again. Wait

now, you must have been near this house at 8.36 or 8.37, if you started at 8.34. Did you see anyone coming in here when your scarf blew away?'

'Yes. Someone opened the door and went in as I approached the house. The pilots, I suppose.'

'You're sure it wasn't anyone else? You must have been close enough to see.'

'I don't know. I was close enough, of course, but I had my head down against the snow that was blowing in my face. I don't know who went in. I only know that I was aware of the door being opened and then closed just as the scarf blew away.'

'So you came back. If you looked in the snow first, I should give you, say, four minutes for that. That would bring you to the 'plane again at 8.40. You found your clip in the cabin?'

Fonda nodded. 'Yes, I did. I had to search for it a little. Then I found it under the seat behind mine. It must have dropped off during the storm.'

'Are you sure of that – that you had it up to the time we ran into the snow over the mountains?'

'Why, no, I'm not sure at all. I was only guessing. I suppose it might have fallen off any time after we got into this 'plane at Cheyenne. Even when I was getting in, so far as that goes. I didn't notice it at all until my scarf blew away . . . Well, and then I came back here again with the stewardess. I helped her carry some of the Thermos bottles she brought over with her.'

'8.43, on the field again, and 8.46, at the house? Well, never mind; I don't suppose you noticed that, either. I can check it with the stewardess. Can you help me with anyone else's statements? Did you pass anyone on the field close enough to identify them?'

'No, I passed some people, I think, but everyone seemed to be going a different way than I did, and I had my head bent down. I can't say who they were.'

'And what else?'

'Nothing else, I think. That is what I did, and the only person I really met was the stewardess. Oh, but there's this. She and I were the last to come in here except you . . . I know, because I looked for you when we got here.' For the first time Fonda dropped her eyes. The lashes, Lord noticed, could be seen curving outward from the curve of her cheek. Why the dickens, he wondered, did he persist in noticing these things?

'That's all,' he said abruptly, and actually *felt* her blue eyes on him again as she looked up.

'I have to go now?'

'That's right. You have to go now.'

She said 'All right' submissively. 'I suppose you want to see someone else?'

'I want to see the stewardess.'

'Oh.'

Fonda slid to her feet in a single, graceful movement and stood looking down at him. 'I think she's very pretty, don't you?'

'No doubt,' Lord answered shortly.

'I'll get her for you.'

When she was almost at the door he stopped her. 'By the way, do you play tennis?'

'I do,' the low voice assured him. 'I play quite decently. Will you play tennis with me, Michael?'

'I should be delighted to play with you, Fonda. Let's hope nothing will prevent it.'

'Nothing will prevent it, Michael,' she said softly. She smiled invitation to him across the room. She opened the door. Fonda was gone, and the single light shone bleakly above the rumpled bed. Lord shook himself and muttered, 'What a damned fool *I* am . . . and maybe I'm not, at that.'

When the stewardess appeared, he said, 'Have you had anything to eat, Miss Gavin? No? Well, I'd like a little something, if you can scare it up, and if you haven't had anything yourself, why not bring in enough for both of us? I want to ask you a few questions, and we might as well have a bite together while I'm doing it.'

In spite of her blonde hair and her blue eyes, in spite of her prettiness, she seemed a complete contrast to the girl who had just left. She stood thinking a moment. 'Thank you,' she said. 'I'll do that, if you don't mind.' She had meant to eat with Hal Lovett after the detective had finished with her; but he was getting pretty fresh. She would give him his sandwiches and have her own in here. Of course, it might make the junior pilot even fresher the next time they were alone. Well, that was O.K., too. She disappeared through the doorway.

In a few minutes she was back again. They sat at opposite ends of the keeper's bed, a plate of sandwiches between them and a smoking Thermos flask of coffee on the floor at their feet. The detective, after his first bite, found that he was hungrier than he had thought. He finished off two large sandwiches before asking any questions at all. With the third, however, he put his chart on the cover beside him and looked over at his companion.

'From what I've been told, it appears that you stayed in the 'plane for some time after we came down – until after everyone had left, in fact. Is that correct?'

Marjorie said, 'Yes, that's right.' She had finished eating, and was sipping hot coffee from a paper cup. Her voice was cool and efficient. 'Two of them came back later.'

'Before we get to that, can you tell me anything about the order in which the passengers left the cabin originally? I'm trying to check up on the stories they have told me.'

'Yes; but I'm not sure I can remember just how everybody left. You went first and then the pilots went; they found the lieutenant lying in the snow outside and carried him off to the house. The man who speaks with an accent came next; I should think he was English.' The stewardess paused and was evidently searching her memory. 'After that I'm not entirely sure. The two girls came to the back of the cabin, and the one with the blonde hair asked me where the house was, I think. One of them left right away and one stopped for some minutes near the door before getting out, I think, but I wasn't noticing especially; I was busy straightening up the cabin and seeing what I had for a supper. While I was doing that the other men left, too, but I can't say in what order. The psychologist with the grey hair was the last; he stayed for some time after everyone else had gone. I don't think he was feeling very well at first, but he was all right when he finally got up.'

Lord was writing in his note-book, comparing the statement with his chart. 'That's pretty good,' he remarked. 'Better than I expected . . . And now what about the ones who returned? Especially the times when they came back, if you recall.'

'The first one to come back was the short man. He came in just a moment after the grey-haired man left.'

'Just a moment afterward, you say?' Lord asked. 'That's funny. Pons – your grey-haired man – said he didn't see anything of Tinkham as he was leaving.'

'That's queer.' The stewardess thought a moment. 'I'm positive there couldn't have been a minute between them, hardly half a minute. I was back in the rear of the cabin then, by the door. I don't see how they could possibly have missed each other.'

'There it is just the same. They did. I've known Dr Pons a long time, and his evidence is perfectly trustworthy. Well, we'll let it pass now. What did Tinkham do when he came in?'

'I don't know that, I'm afraid. I didn't watch him. I was counting sandwiches. But he was only there a minute or less. He got a bag he had left behind and went right out again. It was several minutes after he had gone when the blonde girl came in. She said she had lost a scarf clip and wanted to look for it. I helped her search, but I hadn't noticed it when I had gone through the cabin after we landed, and I didn't think it was there. I looked around the rear end and in the lavatory, but she found it up forward under one of the seats. Then we talked a little and she took some of the Thermos flasks and we left. I locked the cabin door after we had gotten out.'

'I don't suppose you noticed the time at any of these points?'

'Only when I finally left the cabin. I looked at the clock then. It was 8.42 exactly.'

Lord checked the time with his data, and found that he appeared to have calculated Fonda's movements remarkably accurately. After a pause he continued, 'You said that there were several minutes between the time Tinkham left and the time Miss Mann returned. I should say she must have come back at about 8.40 if you left at 8.42. Two minutes is quite a long time, even for a reasonable search; but if that is so, it would put Tinkham in the 'plane about 8.37. He himself put it later than that. Can you be sure about the interval between the two returns?'

'Well, I'm pretty sure about it. Of course, I can't be positive, but I should say there was a longer time between when he left and she came in than it took to find the clip. Yes, I'm fairly sure of that, as I remember it now.'

In the stewardess's column of his chart Lord put down 'Tinkham (?)' at 8.37. He asked a few more questions while drinking a second cup of coffee, but it was plain that he had now found out all she had to tell. She confirmed Fonda's statement that they had been the last except the detective to reach the house by saying that no one except him had come in later. As everyone had been present in the front room when he arrived, it amounted to the same thing. She began gathering up the papers in which the sandwiches had been wrapped and screwing the cover on the Thermos flask.

Lord said, 'Thank you, Marjorie, for the food and the information, both. I understand we may be going up again soon. Is that right?'

'I think so,' the girl answered. 'They have been clearing a track across the field and refuelling the 'planes. If that is all you want of me, I had better give the pilots something to eat before we start.' He nodded, and she walked quickly across the room to the door. A competent young woman, Lord thought as he brought his chart back to the chair. Pretty and attractive, too, but certainly matter-of-fact.

He sat down and looked the chart over attentively. It was filled now; everyone had been accounted for as far as was possible. Unfortunately there were fewer alibis than he had hoped; still there were some. He put down his own movements as he recalled them – 8.28, seat; 8.29, getting up; 8.30, out door; 8.31, nose of the 'plane; 8.32, baggage compartment door; 8.34, struck down in the snow; and from then on to the end of the chart, still in the snow. He knew he had not come to until 8.50, because he had looked at his watch at once on regaining consciousness. The chart, however, ended at 8.46 with the arrival of Fonda and Marjorie at the house.

He sat regarding his handiwork for some minutes. Then an idea occurred to him, and he ruled off with heavy lines the 'Crucial Period,' 8.33 to 8.37 inclusive. During this time the murderer must have been engaged in reaching the baggage compartment, knocking him out, attacking the helplessly unconscious Cutter and leaving the scene. He surveyed the spaces between the heavy lines. Fonda, Isa, Tinkham, Craven, they were all unaccounted for except on their own stories during this period. No corroboration. So that was that. Only Bellowes and Didenot had really been exonerated, and he had never thought seriously of them, anyhow. Too bad, but that was all his interviews had accomplished.

He sighed and set about marking with symbols such

REPORTED MOVEMENTS.

TELETYPE	TIME	LORD	FONDA	ISA	TINK-HAM	GAVIN	PILOTS	PONS	CRAVEN	BELL-OWES	DIDE-NOT	KEEPER
"PΛ" 90	8.28	seat	seat	seat	seat	seat	seats	seat	seat	seat	seat	house
	8.29	getting up	→	getting up	→	lights	→	→	getting up	→	→	field
	8.30	out door	→	out door	→	rear	Lovett in aisle	→	→	→	→	→
	8.31	nose	→	field	getting up	→	out door	→	out door	getting up	→	house
	8.32	baggage door	getting up	→	out door	→	carrying Philps	→	field	getting up	→	→
(Crucial period)	8.33	→	out door	→	field	→	→	→	→	rear	getting up	→
	8.34	snow	field	→	→	→	→	→	→	out door	rear	→
	8.35	→	→	→	→	→	→	getting up	→	field *	out door *	→
	8.36	→	approach house	□ house	turn back	→	house	out door	army plane	→	field	□ window
Lord's Message	8.37	→	return	→	(?) Tinkham	→	→	field	→	house	→	house
	8.38	→	→	→	→	→	→	→	field	→	→	→
	8.39	→	→	→	→	→	→	→	→	→	house	→
	8.40	→	cabin	→	field	Fonda	→	+ house	+ house	→	→	→
	8.41	→	search	→	→	→	→	→	→	→	→	→
	8.42	→	find and leave	→	drop bag	out door	→	→	→	→	→	→
	8.43	→	field	→	→	field	→	→	→	→	→	→
	8.44	→	→	→	house	→	→	→	→	→	→	→
	8.45	→	→	→	→	→	→	→	→	→	→	→
	8.46	→	house	→	→	house	→	→	→	→	→	house

times as his note-book told him could be checked by at least two witnesses. For Bellowes and Didenot he assigned a star – *; for the keeper who had seen Isa through the window at 8.36 a square – □; for Pons and Craven at 8.40 a cross – +; and for Fonda and the stewardess, when Fonda had returned to the 'plane, a circle – °.

Now it was completed, entirely completed. He gazed at it in the poor light as if the paper itself could perhaps tell him the answer. His head was aching and he was forced to admit that nothing very satisfactory had been accomplished. Fonda, Isa, Tinkham, Craven. One of them – one of them must by all reason be the criminal it was his task to convict – but which one? Irrationally and quite against his will he hoped it wasn't Fonda.

8900 FEET

They all trooped out on the field, following the pilots down the cleared runway to the transport at the eastward end of the snow-covered expanse. The ship had been swung around again, with its nose into the wind, and the cabin lights gleamed through the windows against the background of dark forest beyond the borders of the field. Next to the transport the little combat 'plane had been taxied and now stood waiting for its companion to take off first. Fed, warmed and entirely revived, Lieutenant Philips already sat at his controls, his motor idling slowly in the brisk wind.

Lord, walking behind the others, brought up the rear of the procession with Dr Pons. The psychologist was saying something about motives, saying it with emphasis, almost with enthusiasm. Lord's attention to his friend's remarks, it must be confessed, was not very close; he was trying to think if he had done everything that ought to have been done, back there at the house. The message to Headquarters in New York had been sent off under his own supervision, a long message, not only reporting the situation but requesting immediate information that would not be easy to obtain in the middle of the night; for a brief moment he wondered to whom that message would come, who would be on duty now to receive and deal with it. Someone with initiative, he hoped, for he needed the answer to his inquiry, and needed it soon. And his other message to Salt Lake City, that had gone off, too, clicking away over the wires of the Teletype system.

Ahead of them the others trudged dejectedly over the ground. They looked weary, some of them looked quite worn out. No conversation enlivened the passage. They came to the 'plane, and the pilots opened the cabin door and got in first. The rest stood clustered around the entrance as one of their number and then another clambered up over the high sill. He stepped forward and helped Fonda into the cabin with a strong lift. 'Oh, Michael – ' she smothered a yawn behind a slim, gloved hand – 'I'm so tired. I want to go to sleep.' Lord glanced at his watch and saw that it was five minutes past one.

Once in the cabin, no time was lost. The stewardess closed the door, walked up and down the aisle observing safety belts, and turned out the cabin lights. The motors roared, the transport shook itself into motion. Faster, bumping across the uneven field. Snow swirled past the windows, the motion smoothed itself out, they climbed into the air. Behind them the combat 'plane buzzed in their wake. It zoomed sharply, climbing faster than they, and passed them at 7500. It circled twice as the transport circled, then streaked out after them into the west. Clouds still were prevalent and the wind whistled fiercely through the pass between the mountains, but here and there a star peeped out of the night ahead.

In the cabin the lights came on again, and Marjorie

Gavin passed up the aisle with blankets. She assisted in lowering the seats to the reclining position, she adjusted safety belts once more as the passengers lay back, she tucked the blankets around their prone forms. When she returned and switched off the lights once more, leaving only the dim night-light above the lavatory door, the cabin was quiet, several of the passengers already asleep. The drone of the motors made a low undertone to the occasional movement of the ship, which for the most part seemed as if suspended without motion in black vacuum. The flicker of the exhausts outside played with eerie dimness through the windows over the two lines of stretched-out figures.

The detective, who needed rest more than any of the others, had no time for rest. Two and a half hours to Salt Lake City, and Reno only three hours beyond that. He had no solution of the crime that so unexpectedly had upset his careful plans; he had not even the beginning of a trail to the criminal. The weapon, he considered, nine chances out of ten, was still in the murderer's possession. By the same token, it was doubtless right here somewhere in this small cabin. Later, when sleep had claimed the others fully, he might make a quiet search along the seats.

He considered also the error by which he must have disclosed to some alert brain his ruse concerning the man now slain. He racked his wits, but for the life of him could not recall any obvious slip. Since noon he had steadily maintained to everyone that Cutter was dead, murdered. He had listened to no less than three theories regarding the method of the 'crime' and the identity of the hypothetical criminal, and apparently the three theorists had harboured no suspicions about the good faith of the event. Then why should anyone else not only have suspected, but have become convinced? Except possibly Craven. That Englishman, he thought, is a pretty slick piece of works with his transmediumisations and projections. The fellow seemed sincere enough, however, seemed really to believe in these strange Fortean notions. It was difficult to say, just the same. It was distinctly possible that he had been amusing himself – rather a macabre type of humour – at Lord's expense and that of a man supposedly dead. To go further, it was within the range of possibility that Craven's intentions had been somewhat more sinister than amusement.

Just now it was difficult, however, to follow the train of reasoning beyond that point. For one thing, it was no more than an unbased conjecture. For another, Dr Pons, who sat beside him, very plainly desired to discuss the matter of motives. They sat side by side on camp stools against the cabin's rear wall beneath the single light that still burned. They had persuaded the stewardess to lie down in one of the rear chairs they had vacated, by a promise to call her immediately if anyone stirred. Then they had withdrawn to their present position, from which the low tones of their voices were surely inaudible to even the nearest reclining passenger.

'Go ahead, doctor,' Lord murmured. 'I'm afraid I didn't hear much of what you said coming across the field. I was thinking about the messages I had sent off, wondering if I had left anything out of them.'

'Is that so? You didn't hear what I said about the sister?'

'I really didn't,' the detective admitted. 'I didn't hear any of it. Which sister do you mean?'

'Anne, the surgeon's sister.' Pons twisted his stool more securely beneath his plentiful weight. 'It doesn't appear to be a very pleasant family. I had better give you the background, so far as I have been able to piece it together.'

'Have you worked out some theory about the murder? Anything that would point to the murderer?'

'So far as I can see, there is only one person with us who has a serious motive for doing away with Cutter, but

I don't want to begin by telling you who that is. I want to
give you a picture of the family relations first.'

Dr Pons leaned back against the wall behind him,
settling himself as comfortably as possible. At Lord's
nod he continued, carefully lowering his voice. 'I haven't
enough details for much of a history, of course, but
plenty to show the general situation between all of them.
The two girls feel quite differently about the family problems; by talking with both of them and checking one
against the other I have managed to get some idea of
what has really happened, irrespective of their personal
opinions.

'Anne Cutter, I think, is the keystone piece in the
whole puzzle. The family seems always to have revolved
around her, around her doings and her problems, while
at the same time she appears to be the least positive
member of it. From everything I hear she has a weak,
vacillating personality; but the others have been concerned about her, have quarrelled and plotted about her
affairs for years, apparently, and, of course, that's not so
unnatural. The habit of yielding to advice and con-
forming to the opinions of others has a way of offering
unconscious invitation to more and more interference.
Just the same, I should like to meet her; there must be
something about her that is extraordinary. She is said to
have been a great beauty in her younger days and still to
be very handsome. That is probably the magnet.
Woman's beauty, whether she wishes it or not, is a
tremendously powerful force and the inevitable centre of
other powerful forces.'

'One of her daughters,' Lord interjected, 'is not
exactly homely.'

'I doubt, though, whether the mother is at all the same
type. The girl is actively inducive and captivating; she
has an active, vigorous emotional personality. Of course,
she has probably inherited her good looks from her
mother, but her emotional strength comes from some-

where else; her father, or perhaps her grandparents.
Anne Cutter, on the other hand, I should imagine to be a
more passive, clinging type. She would be the uncertain,
helpless beauty – not a very popular kind of woman
nowadays, but one whose appeal to stronger people than
herself can be almost irresistible if she possesses sufficient physical loveliness. Incidentally, all the rest of the
family *are* strong personalities, except possibly the
brother who is Secretary of State.'

The detective stroked his forehead gently, where the
pain of his injured head still lingered. 'They are not very
likely to work up the protective intensity of a lover about
her, however, are they?'

'Why not?' asked the psychologist. 'Of course they
are. That is just what they have been doing for years.'

'The daughters, too?'

'Certainly the daughters. The whole lot of them.
There is a drastic difference between the emotional
involvement of the two daughters, which we will come to
a little later; but you must try to get these conventional-
ised notions out of your head, Michael. The love
responses, normal or distorted, do not follow the patterns of any temporary convention, nor are they limited
or confined in their real operation by any particular kind
of social organisation. A monogamous system, for
instance, such as we live under, can only change their
form of expression, but neither their force nor their direction. It may, of course, distort them. But, despite a
puritanical assertion that only some vague thing called
mother love or maternal instinct can be recognised, there
are actually strong inter-family responses between all
the members. Many of them are veritable love
responses.'

'I take it you are referring to the underlying basis of
incest.'

Dr Pons shook his head, while a frown gathered on his
broad brow. 'Now Michael, listen to me. Let's not go off

on a long tangent about the misconceptions of psychoanalysis. That deals only with perversions; even its norms are perversions, and psychoanalytic theory itself is based upon a perverted outlook. What you are calling incest is not a love response at all, since its final aim is the self-gratification of the so-called lover; but there are love relations between parents and children, between brothers and sisters, and it's no good whatever giving them names like incest and homosexuality until they have actually become perverted in these ways. That doesn't happen nearly as often as a lot of psychoanalysts, on the lookout for new clients, would like everyone to believe.'

The good doctor sighed a somewhat exasperated sigh, and continued. 'In the present case I deduce that originally we have two brothers in love, as you would say, with their sister. I am not sure about one of the brothers, but certainly the other one, Amos, was in love with her. It was not an especially normal love, either. While I am confident that it never went to the extent of incest, his objective behaviour pattern for years has evidenced an obvious jealousy of her other lovers; fundamentally it was the appetitive response of a strong appetitive personality. It was the continued and more or less exclusive possession of his sister's affections that has been his goal over the years.'

'But see here,' Lord interrupted. 'Aren't you taking a good deal for granted? You can't possibly be acquainted with all these details if you have never known the family before.'

'Oh, come now.' The psychologist shifted his position, as he felt in his pockets for a smoke. 'Well, here's part of the history I've dug up. See what you make of it . . . The first affair I have heard of was a boy and girl romance out in Reno long ago. Some young man had paid Anne Cutter attentions since their childhood days; finally it came to be generally recognised that she was his "girl."

They went about together continually, were always asked to parties together. That seems to have been the extent of it and, as they were both still very young, there was probably no immediate question of marriage between them. Nevertheless, Amos Cutter's jealousy of the young man became more and more extreme, until at length it issued into a physical fight. He gave his sister's boy-friend a thrashing, during the course of which he inflicted serious injuries. The young man very nearly died, and the affair developed into a scandal of large proportions in the still small home town.

'Probably as a result of this scandal the Cutter family, who seem always to have been well-to-do, sent the two brothers and their sister upon the Grand Tour of Europe. They were gone about a year, I gather, and during this time another suitor became attached to Anne. Amos' new rival was a young medical student whom they met in Germany. This time the situation was even more romantic. Anne and the German youth fell in love at sight – apparently she has rather a preference for Germans. There is no doubt that it was a serious affair, for the young man gave up his studies at some German university and followed her back to America to complete his education here. His persistence was rewarded, too; on the day he received his medical degree they became formally engaged. I am more or less guessing as to what happened next, because you must remember that my informants are two girls who had not yet been born when these events took place – '

'Considering that, these seem to be very circumstantial accounts,' hazarded Lord.

'Not at all. I tell you Anne Cutter's affairs have been of much importance to the rest of the family. There is no doubt that both the young women with us are well informed about her erotic history and the part played in it by their uncle. In the case I am telling you about the engagement was subsequently broken off. Fonda claims

that she has it from James Cutter that Amos accomplished this by means of an underhanded man-
oeuvre that was either blackmail or something closely
resembling it. She asserts that the fiancé was too honour-
able to resist the plot, since some sort of reflection would
have been cast upon Anne. Isa does not agree with her;
she admits that Amos was responsible for the breaking of
the engagement, but says he brought it about simply by
persuading his sister that the German was the wrong
man for her to marry. I don't know the details, and it is
hard to say which version is correct. On one hand Anne
is undoubtedly prone to yield to strong and repeated
persuasion. On the other hand the next series of events
makes me suspect that there may easily have been some
dirty work involved in this one.

'The next suitor was successful where the others had
failed. He was a brilliant young lawyer named Hardin
Luke, and he married Anne Cutter while Amos was
abroad taking a post graduate degree in Vienna. He was
probably smart enough to realise that the time to marry
her was while her brother was away.'

The detective had looked up at his companion's mention of the new name. He said, 'Hardin Luke? That name
is familiar, somehow.'

Pons' smile was unpleasant. 'Yes; you will recognise it
better in a moment. Luke married Anne Cutter toward
the end of 1903. He took her on an extended wedding
trip, not returning until the early summer of 1904. They
settled in New York, where Amos Cutter was now prac-
tising his profession and already beginning to specialise
as a surgeon. Within four months of his return with his
new bride, Hardin Luke was dead . . . Do you recall
anything now?'

'I should say I do,' Lord answered slowly. 'I recall
plenty. The Luke case is still on our Unsolved file.'

'I happen to know about it, because I recently did a
syndicate article on suspicious deaths. I didn't know the

police were still working on it, however. After thirty years I must give you credit for a good deal of tenacity.'

'The coroner's verdict was an open one,' the detective reminded his friend. 'The jury could not agree, but voted by a majority of one against a finding of murder. The Police Commissioner, nevertheless, was entirely convinced that murder had been done, and when he quitted office he left with the Department a long memoir setting forth the evidence as he saw it, and recommending strongly that the case be kept open in the Detective Division in the hope that some day further light might be thrown on it. His reasoning was so convincing that to this day the Luke case is still a current one so far as the Department is concerned. Naturally I am familiar with it to an extent.'

'Then you will remember the main features. Hardin Luke was found in his own dining-room one morning, stabbed by a knife belonging to the dinner service. The incision was a peculiarly expert one for a layman to have made. It was shown that his wife had gone to bed early, that the servants had retired, that he might easily have admitted someone to the house who later had killed him. All this, however, was merely negative; it was not shown that anyone *had* been admitted, but the chief point which was held conclusive of suicide, in spite of all lack of motive, was the presence of Luke's own fingerprints on the knife and the absence of anyone else's. Fingerprints were a new fad at that time, and criminals were unacquainted with the necessity of leaving none behind. Just the same, it occurs to me now quite forcibly that novel police methods, such as fingerprinting, had been first of all developed and utilised in Vienna, from which city Amos Cutter had recently returned.'

'H'mm,' Lord considered. 'You are building up a certain poetic justice in his own stabbing.'

'Let me finish; I have one more affair to relate. Anne seems to have been greatly shocked by her husband's death. So much so that she virtually went into retirement for a number of years. Eventually, of course, she again began taking part in social life. She was still young; she was still very beautiful, and Amos' troubles began once more.

'On her reappearance she was at once surrounded by a number of eligibles, but none made much progress until her present husband, Mann, appeared. Evidently he was a dashing young man of means who was leading an adventurous, cosmopolitan life, accepted socially both in Europe and America as a man of position in his own country, Germany. Even then he was acknowledged to have had many affairs with women, some of them of his own station in life, but never yet had he been intrigued to the point of marriage. Here certainly was a romantic figure, and Anne undoubtedly found herself first flattered by his obvious attentions, and then, as she found them sincere, inevitably responding to them. There was a whirlwind courtship of a few weeks, followed by what Mann's acquaintances never expected would happen. Early one morning he and Anne were married at City Hall after an all-night ball at which he had told Amos Cutter to his face to go to hell. He swept her off her feet and won his cause by offering her what no other woman had ever been able to bring him to offer – marriage.

'For a time there was a definite estrangement between Anne and her brother. Mann, every bit as strong a personality as Amos, refused to allow the latter in the home which he bought in New York, and his influence over his wife was now stronger than her brother's. Mann, however, had not changed his nature, and his nature was to be attracted by attractive women.

'In this,' went on Dr Pons quite seriously, 'I am not disposed to blame him. Any man who does not respond to actively inducive women who captivate him is in one of several conditions: either he is already so strongly captivated by someone else as to have his responses fully taken up, which is so rare a permanent occurrence that it is almost unheard-of, or else he is physically weak or physically out of kilter, or else one part of him, under the external influence of an artificial and quite unnatural "moral code," is preventing his normal emotional responses. The final possibility is that he merely appears not to respond because he restrains his actual behaviour toward the woman who captivates him, for her own benefit in a society which is thoroughly perverted in respect of social recognition of the love responses, but in which society, nevertheless, it is necessary that the woman live.'

The psychologist paused and Lord looked over at him. Like most people, he had been paying an interested attention to the subject of love. He said, 'That's an unusual notion about restraint. I doubt if many women would appreciate it. It seems to me that any man strongly enough captivated, as you call it, soon becomes incapable of such restraint. The degree of his lack of control, in fact, is used roughly as a measure of his captivation.'

Pons shook his head, in the mournful manner of a professor sadly disappointed in the performance of one of his brighter pupils. 'Michael, Michael, will you never learn about these things? Of course women are miseducated to mistake possessiveness for love; sometimes they even welcome the perversion of jealousy. Nevertheless, they have strong emotions which frequently permit them to recognise a love response without understanding it. The greatest love response, *of course,* is that which is prepared and able to renounce self-gratification for the benefit of the person toward whom it is directed. That is, really, a final and objective test of love; fortunately it seldom becomes necessary. But a so-called love response, so feeble as to yield to the immediate desire for self-satisfaction, and the devil take the beloved, is not strong;

it is weak and it is the response of a weak, undeveloped personality.'

'Well, sorry I interrupted you. You were saying that a man who does not respond to captivation is either already captivated or physically on the rocks, or moralistic, or actually responding but not showing it, at any rate to the public.'

'Right. Of these conditions only the first and the last are normal, but Mann's responses are obviously much too quick and too general for him to be emotionally monogamous; and as to the last condition, it is plain that a carefree adventurer – they are not a very brilliant type – is unlikely to appreciate the necessity of restraint in a world which he has always treated successfully as his private oyster.

'His alternative is to be tastefully promiscuous, and I should consider that for such a person this was reasonably normal. He is not clever about it, however; he is too straightforward to take the trouble either to conceal or deny his indiscretions. From this it is again apparent that he may injure a woman with whom he has a real love relationship, not because there is anything wrong about his own emotional responses, but simply because he fails to take account of the social forces against her which he himself is quite strong enough to override. In other words, his lack is intelligence rather than emotion.

'It is plain that a man like that will stray, and he did soon begin to stray. Just the same, his is a type very attractive to almost all women; sometimes even its infidelities add to its charm. I think Anne has been in love with him ever since she met him; the birth of Fonda in 1910 shows that there could have been no serious quarrel at that time, despite the fact that Mann had again become notorious for his affairs with other women. Isa was born in 1912 – more evidence to the same effect.

'Then came the war, and he returned to Germany; he was wise enough to take his family with him. He served in the German Air Force, where he won all kinds of decorations and in general lived up to his reputation as a daredevil and hero. Afterwards he returned to New York and resumed his former life. But you will remember that for some time after the war there was a continued anti-German sentiment here, and no doubt Amos began taking advantage of that. Together with Mann's mode of life, which will never change until he wears out physically, and with his absences on hunting trips, which he now took up for the excitement he found lacking after his military experiences, some very good opportunities were offered to Amos for interference. He capitalised them shrewdly and well. Once he had his sister's ear again, quarrels were fomented leading to temporary estrangements, for the brother probably estimated quite correctly the effect of a wife's tearful reproaches upon a man of his brother-in-law's temperament. Several years ago he succeeded in bringing about a formal separation, and the divorce action has now been started.'

'You agree in laying this entirely at Amos Cutter's door?' Lord asked.

'Yes,' said Pons, 'I do. Both the young women agree about that, if about nothing else, and that brings us to them and their part in this last matter. Fonda first. You will agree that Fonda Mann is physically beautiful; she has also the emotional beauty of highly-developed feminine captivation which, like her father, she exercises with more force than discrimination. She is very much like her father, the adventurer, I think, but she is purely feminine, whereas he is purely masculine. Their understanding of each other's recklessness and their complimentary emotional sequences would both draw them together. Fonda is rather contemptuous of her mother, but she is definitely in love with her father. My God, no, Michael,' the doctor raised a protesting hand, 'I am not hinting that this is an abnormal relationship. I am asserting that they are emotionally in love with each other, and I mean by this that their mutual responses are more like what is called romance than like some pallid parental affection. I think there is very little that Fonda would not do for her romantic father; and she is quite reckless enough to do it.

'Isa is another story entirely. Again, if you can get it out of your head that I am referring to physical acts, Isa is emotionally an active homosexual. For us her personality is important, and her personality is a mannish one; emotionally, which is the main thing, she is more masculine than feminine. She is uninterested in men, and I doubt if she cares a snap of her fingers about her father; but her mother – ah, there is something different. I believe she is in love with her mother, with the same kind of jealous, protective "love" that Amos has always manifested. Anne's very uncertainty, her weakness, her female rather than feminine dependency, all of this would be an irresistible magnet to Isa, just as to a certain type of appetitive male. Accordingly, she is Amos' ally; she is all for the divorce, where Fonda is all against it, and she is plainly hostile to the absent husband.

'Well,' Pons stretched, got up, ground out a cigarette and sat down again, 'there is the Cutter-Mann set-up. With a situation like that, with a man like Amos Cutter pursuing his jealousies in the main successfully, there is nothing to be surprised at in what has happened. He has thwarted the strongest responses of human beings and his own appetitive behaviour has inevitably raised against him the appetitive hatreds of other men, with what most people would say was good reason. I have told you only the cases I know, but there are doubtless many other men who bear him something more than an ordinary grudge. I am not surprised that he should be found one day with his throat cut; certainly any one of the four men whose stories I have told had just the kind of motive that is to be looked for in a case of murder.'

Lord observed quizzically, 'What surprises me is that,

after your long recital and analysis of all these emotions, we are not a bit advanced. Of your four suspects, the first two are God knows where, the third is dead and the fourth is in Africa. You are not suggesting, are you, that either of the first two young men, harassed by Cutter so many years ago and long since without any connection with the family, probably with families of their own by now, are travelling on this 'plane with us?'

'How do I know?' asked Dr Pons.

'But it has been years – forty years or more. That is a longer time to hold even a very serious animosity than I can easily credit.'

'Rarely, very rarely, indeed,' the psychologist remarked, 'the love responses of a man toward a particular woman are really permanent. Then they continue over absences and over years of separation. Presumably they would continue to reinforce his hatred of the one who caused the separation.'

The detective sat thinking for a short period. Then, 'No. Aside from the rarity of such an occurrence, which you admit, there is more than that against it. Cutter was not killed in a large city where anyone could have access to him; he was killed in our baggage compartment on the Medicine Bow field. Someone in the 'plane killed him, but he himself had carefully observed everyone and had recognised no one of you. Had he seen one of his enemies, he would surely have told me of him. Therefore – '

'Of course they might have an altered appearance after forty years. They might even be disguised, and he hadn't seen either of the pilots we took on at Cheyenne. Yes, I know they have alibis . . . Well, to stop fooling about it, Michael, there is someone else right here who had the motive and who has the ability and who has a close and intimate connection with the family.'

'Do you mean Tinkham? You haven't mentioned him at all yet.'

'I don't mean Tinkham. It is agreed that he took no

part in the family affairs, was uninterested even in the daughters, is altogether wrapped up in medical research. Why look into the far distance and avoid what is straight before us?'

'And who,' Lord inquired, 'is straight before us?'

'Fonda.'

All along he had guessed at Pons' selection, but, put into words, it was still a shock. He said, 'Yes? Fonda is not a rejected suitor or an estranged husband.'

'She had the motive, and the motive in this case is too plain to overlook. Cutter's interference with his sister's love affairs is certainly what caused his death. Fonda was acting for one of Anne's lovers, for her father. She is in love with him, really in love with him, and wants his happiness, which she is convinced lies in a reconciliation with her mother. She would do anything for him; and she has all the recklessness necessary for her to have done this.' There was an inexorable reasoning in the answer, and the detective stared down the cabin to where the girl they were discussing slept quietly in one of the forward seats. Her hat and scarf had been removed and placed in the little hammock above the chair; the small curls of her blonde, bright hair reflected the dim light in a rumpled confusion.

'Has she an alibi, Michael?' Pons added after a moment.

Lord said miserably, 'No, she hasn't an alibi.'

'I know how you feel, Michael,' his friend told him. 'She is beautiful and she is captivating. All the same, you have your duty, and murder is murder. There was provocation – more than enough. But no matter how abnormal Amos Cutter's behaviour has been, murder is more abnormal still. Murder must be punished. You will have to pull yourself together and do a distasteful but a necessary thing.'

Lord still continued to stare down the cabin. He was casting about desperately in his mind for another, some different, lead. The slip he must have made. The weapon. With the suddenness of lightning an idea flashed into his mind. Before he had even considered it, he had gotten up, walked quitely along the aisle and returned with Fonda's scarf in his hand. Attached securely to the scarf was the large and gleaming clip, four and a half inches long when folded. He unfastened it with difficulty and opened its two leaves which, hinged at the centre, allowed it to clip two layers of material together. He raised it to the light and brought his eyes close to the shining metal.

Along the sharp edges of one of its pointed blades were unmistakable traces of dried blood; caught in the projection of a setting on the reverse side was a tiny, torn piece of flesh.

9500 FEET

Michael Lord sat alone on his camp stool in the rear of the cabin. He was bent forward with his head in both hands, and his head ached horribly. Pons had retired to his chair ahead, where he reclined stretched out at full length. Below, the Grand Island beacon welcomed them out of the night, was drawn under the 'plane and vanished. In the open skies they flitted through patches of moonlight, slipping into darker areas, where only the wing-tip aviation lights and the yellow bulb above the cabin made three small pin-points in a black void.

One of his hands still clutched the soft silk of Fonda's scarf; between this hand and the other he stared at the little section of carpet between his feet. He was vaguely aware that he felt wretched, sick and discouraged. She couldn't have done it. He couldn't imagine the slim daintiness of her hands digging that thing into a living throat. God, what a rat the man had been if Pons were

only partially right about his history! What if she had
done it? He deserved what was coming to him – plenty.

That wouldn't help her, though; it wouldn't help her a
bit. He had seen murder trials. He knew they weren't
pageants of dramatic interest, that they were sordid,
hateful crucifixions, justified only by the sordid, cruel
people who there were brought to book. Even if she were
acquitted, which would be likely enough, the experience
would either break or lastingly embitter her; and if he
expected a jury of other men to have the decency to bring
in acquittal, what about himself, cast for the first rôle in
the course of this torture?

'The hell with it,' muttered Michael Lord through a
dry mouth. He swayed with a sudden dizziness and
brought himself up sharply just as he felt the stool slipping from under him. Into his headache came the notion
of wiring in his resignation and getting out of here, getting the hell anywhere out of here. It jingled around in
his head for several moments, until he saw that that
wouldn't help Fonda, either. Someone else would come
out on the job, some hard-faced dick to haul her up
before a judge who, as Craven had put it, was paid every
thirty days to thunder orthodox stupidities.

He straightened himself and brought out a flask. He
took a stiff peg of brandy, then a small chaser of water
from the faucet beside him in the rear wall. There, that
was better. He must snap out of this. The girl was in a
jam and no fooling about it. All these theoretical motiva-
tions. The trouble was that they were so entirely reasonable. People would believe them; more than that, they
would probably be quite right in believing them. Pons
had been wrong before, all the same. Pons had been
wrong twice within Lord's experience. It was true he
hadn't been very much wrong, and this time he probably
wasn't wrong at all. Of the four without alibis, Fonda
had so much stronger motive than the others that no one
in his senses would look at them twice. Isa, no motive;

Tinkham, no motive; Craven, not even connected with any of them, except the distant father. Still, logic aside, Pons might be wrong. It occurred to Lord that that was just exactly what he had to prove.

Reasonable doubt.

And what about justice? What about the oath he had taken when receiving his commission? What about a crime that was no mere technical evasion of a technical law but a true crime against humanity and against all human beings? Fonda had probably committed this crime. Murder is murder, Pons had said. Clichés, platitudes. 'The hell with it,' Lord's mutter repeated. 'All right, I'm a damned cluck . . . It suits me.'

Now that he had cleared up his course, his thinking cleared up also. What was the case against Fonda? A simple one, and a nicely damning one, too. She had a strong and obvious motive for killing Cutter; she had the strength to have done what had been done; she had had the opportunity, for during the crucial period no one else had been found who had seen her; finally, the murder weapon was hers and had been found in her possession. That was the case. Part of that, at the very least, had got to be upset.

He began carefully going over so much of the crime as he actually knew. He had come out of the cabin and gone around the nose of the 'plane to the baggage compartment. It had taken him some time to open the door. Well, there was nothing there; that would have given her just about time to arrive when he had been hit. Agh, he didn't like the idea of Fonda hitting him from behind, although at the same time he realised, wonderingly, that if she had, that was all right, too. His surprise at this discovery delayed his thoughts for a full minute, while he remembered Fonda's ankles and her face and the lines of her trimly clothed figure and the changing expressions in her blue eyes.

All right, he had been hit from behind on the right side

of his head. There was something there. Now, what was it? The right side of his head, that reminded him of some obscure point, but the more he thought, the less it reminded him of anything. That she was strong enough to have hit him had been established, he went on. He had fallen in the snow, and the murderer had entered the compartment and slashed Cutter's throat. That, definitely, was incredible when she was put in the rôle. Yet she might have done it in the dark, he supposed, nerved to the act by her determination to help her father. 'I'll bet anything you like she would have been sick afterwards, though,' he murmured. There had been no sign of illness.

The right side of his head! Of course. He had it now. He saw a picture of Fonda catching the matches he had thrown across to her on the bed in the field keeper's little room.

'Why, Michael, what are you doing here?'

He looked up suddenly, to see the girl he was thinking about standing before him. Her eyes were sleepy and her coat a little wrinkled where she had been lying on it, but as he got to his feet he couldn't decide whether she looked more or less attractive in this condition. She looked damned attractive, he knew that. His desire to exonerate her received prompt reinforcement.

'Michael, please, won't you lie down? You look as pale as a ghost. I don't think you're well a bit. Come on, lie down for a little while, anyway.' She held out a hand to take one of his.

He leaned against the wall, pretending not to notice the hand. He asked, 'You didn't come back here for that, did you?'

Fonda said, 'No. I didn't imagine you weren't resting. I came for a drink of water. Whatever are you doing with my scarf, Michael?'

'I – Here is your clip.' He handed it to her, and she took it automatically. He watched her closely as he said,

'Do you see the blood along the edges? That is the weapon that hacked the life out of Amos Cutter's throat.'

The girl took a step backwards and involuntarily looked at the object in her hands. 'Oh!' She dropped the clip to the floor as if it burned her. 'I don't want it. I never want to see it again. It – it's just horrible!'

After a moment he asked, 'Well, what about it? It's your clip.'

Fonda looked at him with eyes that now were wide. 'You don't think I did it. I *didn't* do it! I don't know anything about it. Oh, I don't care about that hateful man, but . . . Michael, I don't *want* you to think I did it.'

'You had better be thinking about other people than me. The prosecutor, for instance.'

'Oh.'

'I'll do the best I can for you, Fonda.'

'What do you mean by that?' She looked at him with growing bewilderment.

'I'm trying to find everything I can to throw doubt on the case against you. It's strong, strong as hell.'

Fonda actually smiled; and strangely, under the circumstances, her smile seemed to hold a measure of contentment. 'You're a dear boy, Michael, but you're awfully silly. No one can prove I did something that I didn't do. Now, come, please lie down. You'll see how foolish all this is in the morning.'

He shook his head. 'You don't understand. You've never been in a jam like this before. It's a murder case; you just don't know . . . Tell me, how do you play tennis? With which hand?'

'I play left-handed,' was the surprised answer. 'Do you always change the subject as quickly as that?'

'Can you prove that you play left-handed?'

'Why – why, of course. Lots of people know that. I play in tournaments. I'm not a bad player; you won't mind playing with me, really, Michael. I have a good backhand, too.'

There was a short silence. Lord's face had fallen abruptly and its grimness, momentarily relieved, had returned. Ordinarily it could be shown that the blow from behind against the right side of his head had been delivered by a right-handed person. Why in God's name had she had to make that addition about her backhand? That tore it. Any prosecutor with high school wits could make hash out of Lord's attempted point. Lord said 'Hell' softly.

'Won't you please lie down now?'

'I can't. I've got to think.'

'About getting me out of a jam? But that's silly, I tell you.'

'It's not silly, I assure you.' He spoke with certainty. He gave an impotent shrug. 'I've got to get you out. I'll do it, too, somehow; but there's no time for sleep.'

Fonda recognised the signs of masculine decision. She said, 'You're a dear, obstinate boy. Can I sit up with you?'

'No.' His lips held the hint of a smile. 'I can think better, I'm quite sure, if you'll just go back again to your chair.'

'All right, I'll go back if . . . '

'If what?'

She looked at him for seconds that seemed like very long seconds indeed; and her blue eyes, even in the little light there was, were very blue.

'Michael . . . kiss me.'

9900 FEET

For minute after minute the detective sat on his stool, and during this time he thought only of Fonda's kiss. It is doubtful if he would have noticed an outbreak of fire. Bridger Butte slipped away beneath them and Salt Lake

City was only thirty minutes away.

Finally the glint of the clip on the floor caught his eye and brought him back to his problem. He reached forward and retrieved it, dropping it into his pocket. It was evidence. It crossed his mind with a sudden shock that he might have to do away with it – if the worst came to worst.

It hadn't come to that yet, thank God, that he, Captain Michael Lord, should become an accessory after the fact to the crime he had been assigned to prevent and to solve. Well, where was he? The four-point case; motive, ability, weapon, opportunity. Which of these points could he disprove? Could he disprove any of them? Or, if not, could he at least procure something to cast reasonable doubt upon some of them?

He turned his attention to the first point – motive. Very carefully he went over Pons' construction of the Cutter family inter-relations, Fonda's position in respect of the various members who made it up. Constantly he found it necessary to check his own prejudices, to view the situation as someone else who had never seen or heard of Fonda would view it. He came to the conclusion that it was tight and logic-proof. Whether or not she would ever have done it, the girl possessed a powerful and consistent motive for murdering her uncle.

While he was on the subject, had anyone else a reasonable motive? Isa, the ally of the murdered man, would seem to be excused, certainly. As for Tinkham, it was only too plain that his connection with the family as such was hardly more than that of an entire outsider. It was hard to believe that he could have been involved in the pros and cons of Anne's divorce action to the extent of contemplating a serious crime. What else, then? Was there any reasonable possibility of professional rivalry between him and his patron? Of course, there might be; but, again, scarcely to the extent of murder. The vivisection crusade had seemed to offer a much greater chance

of intense opposition between the two, but that was still a
wide guess, with all the probabilities favouring Cutter's
allegiance to the same cause that claimed his assistant.
Cutter, when he had been called away, had even then
been engaged in dissecting the brains of apes.

Was Craven a foreign spy, with a purchased motive in
the surgeon's death? Pretty wild stuff, that. He was, however, an admitted friend of Mann's, whom he felt the
brothers had treated badly. He went a good deal further
than that, too; he was prepared to condone openly Cutter's murder by Mann, for he had done so. That was
foolish, though; however entertaining as an abstract
argument, Lord could not take seriously the proposition
that Mann, from the continent of Africa, had committed
so long-distance a crime. The possibility, to put it
plainly, was that Craven had done it for him, but Craven
was no more than a chance acquaintance who, at most,
had developed a certain degree of friendship for Anne's
husband on a hunting trip. If such a motive could be
imputed to him, with how much more reason might it
apply to Fonda herself. He knew he was grasping at
straws. It was useless to waste time trying to break down
Fonda's motive; she had it and that was that.

She had the ability. Well, of course, everyone on the
'plane had the ability to hit an unsuspecting man from
behind on the head and to mangle the throat of an
unconscious person securely strapped down to a
stretcher. It wasn't much of a point, one way
or the other, and nothing could be done about it,
anyhow. There were plenty to witness that Fonda had
not been physically incapacitated at the time of the
crime.

Her possession of the actual weapon was much more
serious. She said she had left it in the cabin, and only
returned to recover it at a time when the murder had
already been accomplished, and for that statement there
existed no proof at all. Lord considered what the
prosecution would do with it. They would allege that

Fonda, after killing her uncle, had schemed to divert suspicion precisely by this dodge of coming back and pretending to find the weapon under her seat. She had, of course, brought it back with her in a pocket of her dress and herself placed it on the floor from which she claimed to have retrieved it, and they would make good use of the stewardess's evidence that she had gone through the cabin previously to Fonda's return and seen no sign of it. It was damning, this matter of the clip! It was direct evidence, and it was just the sort of bungling weapon that an inexperienced amateur, a young woman of breeding, for instance, without any experience of injuring people physically, would take. It was an extraordinarily poor tool for the purpose, and its very selection pointed to naïve inexperience – and thus to Fonda.

As he considered the various points about the weapon, Lord found his earlier incredulity as to Fonda's guilt vanishing. It became increasingly likely that all these indications could not be incorrect. Maybe she had done it. What did not vanish, however, was his determination somehow to save her from the consequences. All he had to do was to think for a moment about Fonda herself to have this determination strengthened to its original intensity.

Nevertheless he could see nothing to do either about motive or about the weapon. Opportunity was the single item that offered any possibility of attack. The point against her here was merely negative. No one knew for certain where she had been during the crucial period; there was no direct evidence against her. Here, if anywhere, something might be accomplished to raise a reasonable doubt; but in view of the other incriminating factors it would have to be something fairly drastic, something much more than mere negativity. He realised that the necessity for real accomplishment precluded too much finesse. In trying to extricate her, in investigating more closely her actual movements, he might only succeed in procuring the direct evidence that still was lacking. He would have to chance that, though; he would have to chance everything. Otherwise she was caught.

The criminal had come around the tail of the 'plane and returned that way, as shown by the trail in the snow. Could he show that Fonda had not made that journey? He did not see how. It struck him, now that he thought of it, that this was the only part of the criminal's movements which was definitely known. Maybe the point could be made to mean something, although it was not at present apparent how to do so.

The detective drew out his note-book and took from it the sheet headed 'Reported Movements,' which he had spent so much effort in constructing. He looked down Fonda's column in the chart with attentive care. She had gotten up from her chair at 8.32, and left the cabin at 8.33; and 8.33 was the beginning of the crucial period. From that time until seven minutes later, namely at 8.40, when she returned to the cabin, she was unaccounted for except by her own story. By that time the crucial period had ended, and it was this that caused her lack of alibi.

But the crucial period had ended at 8.37, according to Lord's calculations, and Fonda had not reached the cabin until 8.40. It should not have taken her three to four minutes to walk around the tail of the 'plane from the baggage compartment. And then he saw that this meant nothing, for she could easily have stopped for a minute or so at some point on her return journey to recover her composure after so violent an experience. In fact, one would expect her to have done so. There was nothing in her favour in the delay.

It occurred to him that he had better decide just what he was trying to do. Her movements, as they appeared upon the chart, constituted an alibi, of course, just as did everyone else's. Was it this alibi that he was trying to establish beyond doubt, or another? After a moment he saw that his best course was to work for the alibi she herself had asserted. Either it was true or it was a fabrication. If true, it would be easier to prove than any invented one; and even if false, it was still the best one to adopt, for it had then been devised by a person who was undoubtedly intelligent and who, moreover, could judge, from her knowledge of what had really occurred – a knowledge that he lacked – how best to make it appear plausible. Yes, it was the alibi as it appeared in Fonda's column on the chart that he must firmly establish in some fashion or other.

How far could he rely on the chart, now that he was trying to confirm it rather than break it down? He knew that in most cases only the sequence of events could really be relied upon. The scheduled minutes were mainly calculated and he had calculated them himself without confirmatory observations of clock or watch time. Better than anyone else he knew the amount of guesswork that had been part of the schedule. While they remained the most probable times at which the various movements had taken place, still some of those essential minutes in Fonda's column might be changed. He could change them arbitrarily, naturally, but could he change the essential ones in that way? The stewardess, for example, was fairly sure of Fonda's return at 8.40, so that could not be altered. Marjorie Gavin had also seen her leave the cabin, but here the time was more or less approximated. He saw that if Fonda's departure from the cabin could be put back far enough, until 8.36, for instance, she could be shown to have left too late to commit the crime. It would be no good to offer merely an unconfirmed estimate, however, for in her case there were already far too many other items against her. If it were to be alleged that she had not left till then, corroboration became essential.

Without hesitation Lord rose from his seat and approached the chair on which the stewardess reclined.

8600 FEET

Marjorie said, 'No, I can't be sure. I told you that. When you bring it down to this minute, and the next one, and the one after that, I just didn't take these times, and so I can't swear to them. I do know that everyone except Dr Pons did leave the cabin within a few minutes of the time we landed, and I know he left within ten minutes, but that is all I can say.'

'You are certain that everyone else had left at least some minutes before Pons went out? You are so certain that you will swear to it on the witness stand?'

Marjorie hesitated, and finally admitted, 'No-o. I am not as certain as all that. Some of them stood around in the rear space where we are now for some little time, and one of them may have stayed longer than the others. I can't testify that someone did not leave a little before Dr Pons, because I was in the forward part of the cabin then, and I wasn't watching. I can only swear that, when he went, everyone else had already gone.'

'Then Miss Fonda Mann, for example, might have remained and only gone out a minute before he did? Or perhaps even at the beginning of the same minute?'

'I suppose so, but I don't believe it. One of those girls did stay back here longer than the other, but the last I noticed either of them was considerably before the time you are speaking about.'

'Which one went out first, then? Please try to see if you can remember that.'

'I can't,' Marjorie pronounced, after some moments in which she frowned seriously over the question. 'I think it was the good-looking one that asked me the way to the house, but I am not even sure of that. I just haven't the slightest idea which one jumped out first. If anything, I should guess it was the one who had asked for directions, but I certainly wouldn't say so as a witness.'

'And whenever the first one did leave was a good while before Dr Pons got up?'

'Oh, yes. It was four or five minutes before, anyhow.'

Lord shrugged his disappointment, and passed on to another point. 'About that clip of Miss Mann's. You told me you had been through the cabin before she had returned and had not seen it. Now, how much importance should I put on that? After all, you weren't looking for it, but only straightening things up in the cabin. Very probably it would have escaped your attention under those conditions, don't you think so?'

'That's a funny thing,' she answered slowly. 'I have thought it over since I talked with you before. I saw where she picked it up, beside the seat behind her own, although I was then in the rear of the cabin, but I had looked under that seat myself only a few minutes earlier, and I am positive it was not there then.'

'How can you be so sure you had looked under that particular seat?'

'Because there was a book with a funny title, *Wild Talents*, lying there. I picked it up and put it back on the seat.'

'And when was it that this happened?'

'It was just after Dr Pons went down the aisle.'

'Then it was at 8.36, or 8.37, and you are entirely certain. You would be willing to swear to that, and to be cross-examined on it in court?'

'I would swear to it,' said the girl simply.

The detective said, 'All right, Marjorie. That's all, I guess.' He watched her go back to the rear chair on the port side, adjust it uprightly after a glance at her wristwatch, and sit down. She looked up and down the cabin at her temporary charges.

And a lot he had accomplished by that questioning, he reflected – nothing at all about Fonda's departure; he had merely succeeded in uncovering plain evidence that she had brought the weapon back into the cabin with her. About as damaging evidence as could well exist on that point. It was cold comfort to realise that at least he knew what he had to meet. It would probably still be best to work on the time of her leaving, he conjectured. Where could he find someone to corroborate the desired delay? Isa, possibly? The two girls, he recalled, had come together to the cabin's rear, at any rate.

He walked between the sleeping figures until he came to Isa's chair. He shook her gently by the shoulder, and she woke with a start, raising herself on one elbow to stare with half-opened eyes into the detective's face.

'Sorry to wake you up,' he apologised. 'But would you mind coming back here with me for a few minutes? It is really important, or I wouldn't have disturbed you.'

Shortly afterward Isa emerged from the lavatory, where she had splashed her face with cold water, and took the camp stool beside Lord. Now that she was here, he thought, he might as well confirm for himself some of that story of Pons about the family. So far, he only had Pons' word for most of it, although that was probably enough, worse luck.

He began without much hope. 'I shall have to ask you some rather personal questions about your family, Miss Mann. I hope you will not consider them impertinent. It is very necessary that I understand clearly everything in the situation as it bears upon Dr Cutter.'

'Go ahead,' Isa replied in her husky voice.

'About this divorce action of your mother's. I have been given to understand that it has caused some intense disagreement.'

'There is no disagreement among us, except on Fonda's part. She has always mooned about her father. Everyone else knows that Anne has no choice but to divorce him.'

'You don't feel that it could be patched up, that there

is any possibility of a reconciliation.'

'With that man?' Isa demanded. 'I should say not. He's nothing but a handsome flibberty-gibbet and not five cents' worth of brains in his head. With his absurd posturings and posings, he's like a male dress model, if there is such a thing.' Her lip curled contemptuously. 'A tin-pot hero, with his big-game hunting and swarms of silly, empty-headed women tagging around at his heels.'

Lord did not fail to note the intensity of her feelings, nor that Pons had not exaggerated the emotions engendered by the situation. He suggested, 'Your sister doesn't seem to have the same opinion.'

'Oh, Fonda. I like her, but she's a silly fool sometimes. She's crazy about men, makes eyes at every one of them she meets, and she has always been super-silly about *him*. I believe she'd marry him herself if he wasn't her father.'

Just in time and with some difficulty Lord restrained what seemed to him an appropriate comment and proceeded, 'But isn't it true, Miss Mann, that your uncle has made a practice of interfering in your mother's relations with other men for a long time? The present instance is not an isolated one by any means.'

She said, 'I don't call it interference at all. You would have to know Anne, to understand it. She is the sweetest woman in the world, but men have always taken advantage of her. They're forever chasing after her, some of them for her money, some of them for her body. She never sees through them, and they're such damn fools that they imagine no one else does, either. Somebody has to take care of Anne, or she would always be in some mess or other. She is too good-hearted to see what kind of animals men are, and she *is* easily flattered. I don't know what would have happened to her if Uncle Amos hadn't looked out for her all this time.'

'I see how you view it,' the detective confessed. 'But what about this attack upon him? None of the men he has been "protecting" your mother against are with us here.'

'Wotan Mann did it, as sure as shooting,' Isa asserted.
'I'm sure of it. It is just like his idea of melodramatic
revenge.'

'But he isn't here.'

'I don't care. He hired someone to come along and do
it. Oh, you'll find that out if you ever find anything out at
all about it. He has just about wits enough to go to Africa
and arrange for Amos' murder while he is away.'

'You are really serious about this? You accuse your
own father of this crime?'

'Certainly. He's nothing but a man – a little worse
than most of them, that's all. I tell you, Mr Lord, and I
assure you I am right, that he is at the bottom of this
business somewhere.'

'You would not think it possible that Tinkham had
anything to do with it, would you?'

'That laboratory worm! Grow up, Mr Detective, grow
up. This is Wotan's little trick of being he-man again. I
am only surprised he didn't do it himself with a flourish
of a duelling pistol. But I suppose even he knows there
are some laws left.'

'We'll let it pass for the moment,' said Lord. 'There is
something else I want to find out from you.' He waited,
and then went on, 'When we landed back there at
Medicine Bow field. You got up out of your seat a few
minutes after we landed and went to the rear of the
cabin. I think your sister got up at about the same time.
Is that right?'

'Yes, that *is* right. She came down the aisle right after
me.'

'But you didn't leave the 'plane together. What happened when you got back here?'

'Why, she said something to the stewardess, I think;
and I got a drink of water. I waited a minute and then
took some tablets in another glass of water to settle my
stomach.'

'And which of you left first? Did you go out on the field

before she did?'

'No, Fonda went out first. She hardly waited at all. The door was open and she jumped down right away before I had even finished my first drink of water.'

'You are positive she left first?'

'Absolutely.'

'That's all, Miss Mann,' said Lord dejectedly. 'Thank you. I will think over what you told me about your father.'

'You'd better.'

Isa walked back to her seat, where the stewardess followed her and rearranged the blanket after she had lain back on the chair again. Lord sat disconsolately alone. Pons had been utterly right about the Cutter situation, and Fonda had left the cabin early, in plenty of time for the crime. Here was another witness he had dug up against her.

He couldn't get anywhere with it. Slowly he spread out the chart once more and gazed at it, cudgelling his brains. Yes, she had left the cabin at 8.33 all right, if not sooner, and then it was borne in on him that he had been trying to do just what he had decided against; he had been endeavouring to change Fonda's alibi, to upset her own story as to when she had left the 'plane. Well, it hadn't worked, anyhow; willy-nilly, he would have to come back to his first idea of confirming her story.

He glanced across the parallel columns lining the page. Somewhere he must find someone who could be brought to admit he had seen her during the crucial period. Pons? No. Bellowes or Didenot? It didn't look likely, and then he saw something that almost made him jump out of his seat. By God, that was it! That was the one chance, not only of raising reasonable doubt, but of –

The cockpit door was quietly opened and Lovett's low voice called down the cabin. 'Margy, we're landing. Salt Lake City. See the belts are all right, will you?'

4250 FEET

Lord was down the aisle before the transport had come
to a full stop. He bent over Isa Mann, who was still
awake.

'Something I forgot to ask you. When you went from
the 'plane across the field to the house, did you walk right
across? I mean, did you stop at all or turn around or drop
anything?'

'No, I walked straight across.'

'You didn't at any time bend down to pick anything
up, for instance, from the ground? Please think carefully;
you must be absolutely sure.'

'Of course I'm sure,' said Isa. 'I walked right across
without any stops at all.'

Lord sighed excitedly and hurried back to the cabin
door without another word. Isa, screwing herself around
on her chair, watched him with surprise in her face as he
unlocked it and jumped to the ground. The senior pilot
was already coming back through the cabin.

The three walked toward the Amalgamated Air
Transport building, Lannings, Lord and Marjorie
Gavin. Behind them a field attendant stood guard before
the locked door of the cabin while mechanics swarmed
over the motors and wings, refuelling the 'plane,
checking the controls in the glare of the airport lights.
Lovett, too, had instructions to let no one leave the
cabin. The time was 3.33 a.m.

A police sergeant lounged in the entrance of the buildings, smoking a cigar whose aroma matched its frayed
and unhappy appearance. To him Lord gave a small
object wrapped in one of the sheets torn from his note-
book. 'You'll have to get someone up at the hospital, or
rout out one of your own men. It's important; I *must* have

a report within an hour or so at the most. Bring the report out here to Amalgamated, and they'll send it to me. Got it?'

The sergeant put the little package carefully in his pocket. 'Yes, sir. We'll get it for you.' He saluted and strode out to the police car waiting for him beside the main entrance.

'Now,' said Lord, 'I want to go to the Control Room.' Together with Lannings he mounted the stairs and came into the room at the top of the building where the night staff of dispatchers and weather men sat at their desks, the Teletype machines clicking busily away beside them.

While Lannings scanned the weather maps and looked over the latest reports from farther west, Lord addressed himself to the chief dispatcher. 'I want to get in touch with the field keeper at Medicine Bow,' he explained. 'I have a number of questions to ask him.'

'Telephone's best, then. I'll get him for you. Wait a minute.' The dispatcher reached over and took up one of the 'phones beside him on his desk. After a short interval he extended the instrument to Lord. 'Here he is. Sounds a little sleepy.'

'Ginty, this is Captain Lord speaking from Salt Lake City. On 90. You remember who I am?'

. . .

'Yes, Captain Lord, the detective.'

. . .

'You will remember, Ginty, that you went into your room with Lannings, the pilot, when he sent a message off for me on your Teletype. Do you remember that?'

. . .

'And while you were there you looked out the window and saw a woman on the field. Now, was that woman good-looking or homely, was she a blonde or a brunette?'

. . .

'Well, I didn't really expect you could tell, through the snow, but she was close enough to the house so that you could see her without any question?'

. . .

'Fine. Now tell me this: When you were watching her, was she walking toward the house or was she standing still? *Did you see her bend over toward the ground as if she had dropped something or as if she were picking anything up?*'

. . .

'Now listen here, Ginty, this is far more important then you think. You are certain she was bending over and searching for something on the ground. You will swear to that or make out an affidavit to that effect?'

. . .

'That's all, then, Ginty, and thank you plenty. That evidence is just what I was looking for.'

Lord got up from the desk, over the side of which he had thrown a leg while talking into the 'phone. His expression, intent and strained at first, had cleared as the conversation progressed. Now, as he handed the instrument back to the dispatcher, his face broke into an elated grin.

'And right there,' he told the room at large, 'is one of the best and tightest little alibis that was ever sworn to. No one will break that down. I'm telling you.' He lit a cigarette and walking across to Lannings, slapped him heartily on the back.

'Well, old boy, how does she look? Are we off to Reno?'

Part V – Explanation

High above the waters of the Great Salt Lake the transport swung through a sky that still was only partially clear. The highest ranges, the most difficult part of the ocean-to-ocean flight, had been passed, but other great mountains bulged from the desolate land ahead, Pilot Peak, Mount Lewis, Mount Moses, Battle Mountain and Sonoma Peak. Between them the line of airway beacons threaded a sparkling path for the 'plane. From Elko, half-way on the Reno hop, came reports of low temperatures and the likelihood of occasional squalls but the ceilings had been reported satisfactory, at least as far as their next stop.

Several of the passengers had wakened at Salt Lake City, but now, with the resumption of the flight, they had settled back in their reclining chairs and dim quiet once more pervaded the cabin. Of all of them only Dr Pons had elected not to return to slumber; his short nap had greatly refreshed him and he felt no desire for further sleep. At the rear of the darkened cabin he again sat next to the detective on one of the camp stools. The feeling of motionless isolation crept up once more as they conversed in low voices three thousand feet above the resting earth.

The psychologist had not failed to remark Lord's rejuvenated appearance when he had entered the cabin just before the take-off. The detective seemed almost jubilant and his air, as he had mounted the accommodation steps beside the 'plane, suggested jauntiness rather than fatigue. Nor had Pons long to wait to discover the cause of the transformation. No sooner had the transport settled into its steady flight after climbing away from the airport than Lord had confided his new finding.

Dr Pons was not immediately convinced. He said, 'That's all right, but any alibi at such a time and under the conditions that obtained must be largely guesswork. It's not as if it really could be accurately checked, and the other points are – '

'No, doctor, you are wrong. Fonda Mann simply cannot have committed the murder. Here, take a look at her schedule and let me show you how it *is* checked.' He spread out his chart and directed Pons' attention to the elements in question. 'She got up from her seat at 8.32 and left the cabin at 8.33. The – '

'And right there,' Pons interrupted, 'you're beginning to guess. You don't actually know that it was 8.33 when she left.'

'I don't know that it was exactly 8.33,' Lord admitted freely, 'but consider the position. If she left later than that, it is entirely in her favour, so the question really is, did she leave earlier? I submit that that is impossible. We know she didn't jump up the moment the 'plane stopped and as a matter of fact Isa, who didn't either, will testify that Fonda came down the aisle after her. Moreover, no less than five persons had left the cabin before she did, as the stewardess's evidence, along with their own, shows. These five were myself, the two pilots, Craven and Tinkham. None of us left together (except the pilots), and most of us were so far separated that we did not even see any of the others. Fonda was the sixth person to leave and it is obvious that 8.32 or 8.33 was the earliest time she could have done so.

'Now at 8.36 a woman approached the house and was seen by the field keeper through his office window. Originally I put this woman down as Isa, but I have telephoned the keeper from Salt Lake City and he positively identifies her as Fonda. Without going into it, I can tell you that Fonda's testimony, Isa's and the keeper's so match as to make this identification certain; also, it agrees with Fonda's own story. But if she left the 'plane

at 8.33 and was close to the house at 8.36 – and that
minute is definitely set by the Teletype machine – it is
certain that in those three or four minutes she could not
have been around to the port side of the 'plane, hit me
down and murdered Cutter. It is true the criminal didn't
need much time for the crime, but two minutes at least
must have been used up. That would give her only one
minute to reach the house, to say nothing of the trip
around the 'plane and back.

'As to her having done the crime *after* she approached
the house, that is out, too. I was hit at 8.34 at the latest,
and she was still near the house at 8.37, hunting for her
scarf in the snow. She says she then returned to the
'plane, and Marjorie Gavin confirms her return at 8.40,
which would be just about right . . . She's out, doctor;
she's out of this case for good.'

Pons took the chart and held it close to his face in the
meagre light. He grunted as he followed out the minutes
of Fonda's movements and checked them as the detective had done already. Finally he pronounced, 'Well –
ugh – if this really checks – Just the same, Michael, I'm
certain about the motive in this case. It is foolish to doubt
that Amos Cutter's jealousy is at the bottom of his death.
He's been asking for it for years. If you let Fonda Mann
out, where does that leave you?'

Lord's face sobered quickly. 'It leaves me with about
three hours in which to discover who killed Amos Cutter
and in which I must also find the proof,' he observed
quietly . . . 'and the only way to do it is to think. I
examined the compartment at Salt Lake City with a
floodlight. There is absolutely nothing in it to give any
clue to the murderer. I am still hoping for some information from New York, but it hadn't come in when we left
the airport. It may not come in until too late.'

'But nobody else had the motive,' Pons objected.
'Nobody, that is, who was with us, at that field. I've no
doubt that there were others besides Mann with a

motive, but certainly none of them had an opportunity. Mann is the only one directly connected with those on the 'plane, and the girl was his natural agent. Who else could be?'

'Some one could be, that's certain. Some one had this motive, if you're right about it. Well, let's see what we have. There are Isa, Craven and Tinkham. Did you know that Craven was a friend of Mann's and very sympathetic to his cause?'

'No,' the psychologist admitted, 'I didn't. Of course that might make a difference. Still, it's weak. I haven't often heard of friends volunteering to do a murder for each other. You'll have to keep sight of it, naturally, if that's the case, but I should call it an outside possibility just now.'

'He gave me a phoney theory of the crime. That Mann had killed his brother-in-law by "projection" from Africa.'

'Yes, I heard part of it; but that was before any real crime had been committed. At that point I think both of you were trying to kid each other. You were asking him to point to a criminal when there wasn't any and he thought it would be fun to give you an outlandish theory for your pains.'

'By golly, I wonder if he had guessed the truth. It's possible, you know, that he is the one who had an inkling Cutter wasn't dead then. That would be real indication, for whoever killed him must have reasoned that he still needed killing, and at the field he amended his "projection" theory so as to make it fit the real crime. He rather went out of his way to do it, as a matter of fact.'

'I still don't see how he could have guessed,' Pons replied. 'I didn't mean that he had, when I said he was fooling with you, but he's still sticking to that stuff of his, eh? That will make a hot defence in court, if it ever goes so far.'

'It holds me up,' Lord confessed. 'I know it's an

important point, the way the criminal found out about my fake attack on Cutter, but I'm positive I hadn't said a word to Craven that would put him on the track. I can't think of any other way he could have suspected, either . . . Well, what about Tinkham?'

'I can't see it,' Pons shook his head negatively. 'Both the girls say he had nothing to do with the family, Fonda said she didn't even think he had ever seen Anne. They're opposed on enough things; when they're in agreement, it's fairly certain they are right. At any rate, it's all there is to go on, so it will have to be accepted.'

'There's the chance of professional antagonism. In the research game.'

'A big surgeon and his disciple? I should doubt it, but, of course, I don't know. On the other hand such a motive is insignificant in comparison with this divorce thing. I've seen a good deal of professional rivalry and sometimes it gets pretty fiery, but, except in a most unusual case, the emotions springing from such a source will not be nearly as strong as the love and jealousy ones.'

'All right. The only other person without an alibi is Isa. It has to be one of those three. It's time I looked over Isa's movements again, at that. If she wasn't the woman seen by the keeper through the window, there is no check of any kind for her story.'

'But Isa,' Pons pointed out, 'was Cutter's chief confederate in the family.'

'How do you know she was?'

'Why, that's the whole set-up as I got it.'

'Sure; and you got it from Isa. So did I, to tell the truth. Now that I think of it, I didn't get any confirmation from Fonda on that, because I never asked her about it. In view of what you had told me, it seemed to be all fitting together properly; but Isa is no simpleton. What if she has been painting the picture for the very purpose of avoiding any possible suspicions?'

'You can find out any time you want by asking Fonda.

From my analysis of her, though, I think she *was* his ally.'

'Maybe so; but it's high time to see where the keeper's evidence puts her.' Lord bent over his paper again and for a little time there was silence as he followed his notations, not only up and down, but horizontally also, across the chart. When he finally looked up and hitched his chair over closer to the psychologist's, there was a new note of doubt in his voice.

'See here, doctor,' he sketched out with his pencil the points of his reasoning as he proceeded, 'this is beginning to look more than a little funny. That girl's story is pretty well shot to pieces by what has turned up; I expected it might need a bit of amendment, but there's nothing left of it now to be amended.'

'That's interesting, if you're right.' Pons bent down in turn and his eyes scanned the sheet on Lord's knee.

The detective went on, 'Just look what she told me. That she got up at 8.29 and was out on the field at 8.30 or 8.31, to start off with. Now that's simply impossible, because – '

Lord's voice ceased with the approach of the junior pilot. Lovett had quietly opened the cockpit door and was coming down the aisle toward them. As he drew nearer, it was to be seen that he brought a lengthy memorandum with him in his hand. He lost no time in addressing the detective.

'I want to get back to the cockpit,' he said rapidly. 'On a night hop both of us should be there all the time, but I thought I had better bring this back to you myself.'

'It's a pretty long stretch for you boys, isn't it?' Lord inquired. 'I thought you would probably leave us at the last stop.'

'We should have, ordinarily; but when we were forced down at Medicine Bow, they let the relief pilots go and, rather than wait for them, we are going through to Reno.'

'Well, let's see what you've got there. A message for

me, I take it?'

'You're right,' Lovett confided. 'It came into Salt Lake City from New York just after we had taken off. They sent it along over the air. The thing is, it's in code. I checked it back twice with the Control Room, but I thought I'd better let you see if it looks all right; it's just a mess to me.'

Lord ran his eye along the lines of jumbled letters and numerals on the paper the pilot handed him. The signature, although likewise in code, told him that Felix, Darrow's secretary, had sent it out; that young man, he thought, is up pretty late. He said, 'Well, I can't tell, of course, until I've decoded it. So far as I can see now, it's O.K.. If I get in a jam with it, I suppose we can check it back again with Salt Lake City?'

'Sure. Maybe we can get it out on the tape, if it's important enough. I'll get up forward, then. Let me know if you need anything else.' Lovett left them and the little cockpit door, with its momentary glimpse of the green-dotted instrument panel, closed after him a moment later.

Lord moved up to a rear seat where he turned on the individual reading light and bent to his task. The dim bulb above the lavatory door was not sufficient for his work of transcribing the coded message. Dr Pons got up and stretched, but apparently decided against returning to his own chair farther forward. He sat down again on his camp stool and presently, to the monotonous drone of the 'plane through the air, commenced to nod.

Gradually, under the detective's pencil, the words from New York were taking shape. Several times he hesitated, eventually transposing a letter here or there which almost surely had been changed from its proper place in transmission to the 'plane. At the end of fifteen minutes he had the message before him.

'Your advice Medicine Bow,' it read. 'Arrest criminal all costs. G-2 reports Craven British agent Near East during war. Believed resigned 1920. Vivisection: President A.M.S. alleges Cutter strong opponent vivisection extension; planned leading fight convention this year. Draft his address recently missing. Restrained by President from making accusation vivisectionists because scandal lack proof. Tinkham not suspected by Cutter although strong vivisectionist but without comparable influence. Checking further morning. Isa Mann injured girl quarrel Greenwich Village last year. No other items party.'

So. It was a long message and Lord found considerable food for thought in it. He remembered, especially, Tinkham's voice, strained with passion when he had spoken about the scientific value of the vivisection technique. The march of knowledge onward from Galileo. There had been a crusading fanaticism about that passage; he wished he could recall more of it. The Englishman's notion that priests and scientists were identical at heart had an obvious bearing. When one considered scholasticism and the heated controversies over abstract, purely theoretical matters; and the merging of the scholastic tradition into the violence of the Inquisition, again a violence over no more than intellectual acceptances; when one considered these things, it was plain enough that a mere difference of theory, let alone practice, was capable of arousing very destructive emotions. Those times were happily over for the Church, but that was only because the Church was now, all but a very few exceptions, like Bellowes, a broad-minded enfeeblement of religion hardly distinguishable from Ethical Culture. Science, however, was young and vigorous; science, now that it had no longer to fight religion directly, might well be taking over the intense kind of intellectual combats that the Church had abandoned. At all events there could be no doubt that this vivisection cause was just the sort of crusade that had always brought up furious passions, and men were certainly no better now than when they had tortured each other about the Virgin Birth. Whether they did it in the name of a religion of love or in that of scientific benefit to mankind, scarcely altered the question. In both these names they were prepared to kill their fellows.

It appeared that Tinkham might well have had a motive worthy of serious consideration.

Lord continued to think about the surgeon's assistant. There were a number of suspicious circumstances. Of course, he had had access to the weapon, but that was not a very telling point. Fonda could not remember when she had lost the clip, nor even where it might have dropped off. It could just as well have fallen near Isa or Craven and have been picked up by them as by Tinkham. The matter of Cutter's missing address was much more to the point. Whatever Cutter may have thought of it, Lord now had little doubt that his co-worker had stolen and either destroyed it or handed it over for study to the other camp. Perhaps he had concealed from the surgeon the full extent of his interest in vivisection; but with Lord, the bars had been inadvertently lowered and a fighting zeal had been behind them.

Still, theft was one thing and murder another. It was certainly easier to see the man as a thief than a killer. Would he advance from the one to the other, if circumstances necessitated? But this was entirely theoretical, such questions as these. What other points were actually against him? The alibi that he lacked, of course. That, however, might have a perfectly natural explanation, for Tinkham wasn't the only one whose time was unaccounted for on Medicine Bow field. All the unsupported stories, except one, were true.

That brought Lord back abruptly to Isa, and the very curious situation in which the field keeper's testimony had left her. He looked for his chart and didn't find it. Well, that was funny! Where could it have gone? He

looked under the seat, but it had not slipped out and
fallen there. Maybe Dr Pons had kept it when he, Lord,
had come to his present seat to decode his message. He
got up and prodded the doctor gently with a finger. Pons
woke up with a sudden start from his doze and said,
'Hah!' sharply.

'I think I left my time chart with you. Didn't I? I want
to finish looking into that business about Isa Mann that
we had begun when the pilot interrupted us.'

'Yes – ugh,' Pons reassured him. 'You left it with me
and I put it in my pocket when you took that seat. Didn't
want to disturb you; it's safe enough in my inside
pocket.' He rubbed his eyes sleepily and reached within
his coat.

'Now let's see where I was.' Lord drew his stool up
close to the other's, so that they could both follow his
reasoning on the paper. 'I had been over this once in my
own mind and it was a damaging situation. I have been
thinking of other things now; I'll have to try to recon-
struct it.

'The first thing is obvious enough. Isa said she left the
cabin at 8.30 and was on the field at 8.31 and that is
entirely out of the question. You see,' he indicated the
column next to Isa's, 'we have now established that
Fonda did not leave until 8.33 and, at the time she left,
Isa was still in the rear of the cabin taking some digestive
tablets or something of the kind. The stewardess is not
very clear about the detailed movements here, but she is
clear enough to confirm that; and both Fonda and Isa
confirm it, too . . . Any way you look at it, that's a queer
beginning.'

Pons said, 'What's so queer about it? Suppose she was
off a bit in the time she said she left. She was only guessing, in all probability.'

'It's not as if she were wrong by a minute or so; she's
four or five minutes, maybe more, out of the way. The
point is, she said she left as soon as the 'plane came

down, practically, and she did nothing of the sort. She
didn't leave until long after it came down, until seven of
us, at least, had preceded her. So we find out now. At the
time she gave me her evidence, it was impossible to check
it at all and she may have thought that in the confused
circumstances a false statement would be able to stand
by default.'

'Oh, come now,' the doctor protested. 'Even granting
all you say as to the actual facts, you are going out of your
way to put them in the worst possible light in your
deductions.'

'Let us put the worst face on it that we can, and see
where we come out.'

'Really, Michael, that's not the way you viewed the
case against Fonda, is it?'

'Fonda and Isa are two different people,' Lord assured
his friend, and Pons grinned openly, remarking as if to a
banal child, 'I'm sure that is true. So abrupt a change of
tactics, however, would lead me to think that they did
not even belong to the same species of animal, let alone
the same family of humans. Is it possible that this altera-
tion has more to do with you than with them, by any
chance?'

The detective could not prevent the slight flush that
spread over his face. He knew well enough that the
accusation was just and that he had had no thought or
purpose concerning Fonda Mann except to clear her,
honestly or dishonestly. But with her out of the way, his
accustomed part had returned; his only interest now was
to discover which of the three remaining suspects was
guilty and then to jail the guilty one. All this, of course,
he could not confide, even to Pons. He had to content
himself with the feeble retort that 'You yourself said they
were almost opposites.'

'It's a bad way to do,' Pons insisted. 'It's unscientific.
You ought to look at these people objectively; you ought
to be neither for them nor against them, until you get

some proof . . . You act as if you had something against
Isa. What is it?'

'What I have against her is just what we are going over
now. I am interested, so far, mainly in two things. First,
in what I suspect was the deliberate falsification of her
story right at the beginning, in view of how far wrong it
has turned out to be. It's not so much the few minutes,
even, as the fact that she must have meant to be misleading. And second, I am impressed with the notion
that, if one is setting out to be confusing about a train of
movements, the clever place to do it is at the commence-
ment of the train. If it begins wrongly and that much can
be put over, everything subsequent will be thrown out of
focus. We shall be looking for Isa, to put it explicitly, at
times and places where it will naturally be impossible to
find her . . . I think Isa is a clever person.'

Lord paused as an earlier thought recurred to him.
'We shall be expecting Isa to turn up where she wasn't,
and we may even mistake some one else for Isa at such a
point.'

'She couldn't have planned anything like that. She
couldn't have known where any one else *would* be.'

'Possibly she didn't plan it; maybe it was luck. All I'm
saying is that she put herself in a position where such
lucky breaks could easily occur; and I think she did that
on purpose. It's not foolish; after all, holding a lottery
ticket does at least expose one to luck. You'll see what I
mean in a minute.

'This brings us to Isa's trip to the house. She said she
didn't know the way and was confused by the snow; she
admitted that she might have taken a rather longer time
to get there than most of the others. Originally I gave her
four minutes for it, putting her arrival down at 8.34, and
then the keeper's evidence of a woman's approach at
8.36 made me change it to that. It was two minutes later,
but it seemed just possible when I was talking to her and
I was looking pretty desperately for some sort of check on

the stories at that time.'

'But that is six minutes,' Pons remarked slowly. 'Six minutes for an average walk of three minutes, even allowing for the snow-storm. I agree that that is stretching it a bit.'

'Well, of course the whole thing was wrong. It wasn't Isa that the keeper saw at all, but that's what I meant; that's how her mis-statement at the beginning made me jump to a false identification. I was expecting that Isa would show up at the house about the time that Ginty actually saw a woman through the window. For a while it led me so far astray that I not only put down her arrival for 8.36, but considered it as one of the few points on the whole chart that could be relied upon, since it was confirmed by independent testimony that could not be questioned. Naturally Isa wasn't anywhere near the house at that time, but I think she wanted me to believe she was.'

'Yes, I see your point now. You mean that by making you think that she had left the 'plane at a time other than she did, you would not only be looking for her at mistaken times and places, but that, in the haphazard state of affairs, she might easily be confused with her sister who might have been noticed at such places. Hm . . . well . . . it wasn't a very nice trick on the sister.'

'You're damn right it wasn't,' said Lord, and felt his animosity rising. 'This Isa isn't a very nice girl. Did you know she had a fight down in Greenwich Village last year and injured some other girl badly?'

'Rather along Amos' lines, eh? I'm not greatly surprised. No doubt they were both fighting over a third girl . . . But all this about the false times would have been fairly complicated to have figured out ahead of time.'

'Not when you're thinking of nothing else. Oh, lots of them are clever enough for that sort of thing, and it worked temporarily, at least. You see, as long as I thought I had Isa identified near the house at 8.36, that

let her out of any complicity in the crime, just as it let out
Fonda later, when I discovered it was she who had actually been seen there. 8.36 at the house means innocence
so far as concerns the crucial period at the 'plane.

'Incidentally we know now that Isa didn't reach the
house close to 8.36 from further evidence. She wasn't
there at 8.37 when the keeper returned to the front room
and when Bellowes entered. She wasn't there at 8.39
when Didenot arrived; and finally, you went in at 8.40
and she wasn't there then, either.'

'When did she arrive, anyhow? I wish I could
remember her there, but it's too bad; I just can't.'

'Yes, and I don't know either,' the detective added.
'She seems to have flitted about as if she didn't want to be
seen. There were eight people in that room, at least,
when she finally came in – three pilots, the keeper, yourself, Craven, Didenot and Bellowes. She must have
sneaked in like a ghost. Absent one minute, there the
next. It's a small point, perhaps, but her entrance must
have been unobtrusive, to say the least of it.'

'Did I tell you she wasn't in the room when I got there?
I certainly don't remember now whether she was or not.'
Dr Pons wrinkled his broad face in unsuccessful recollection, while Lord consulted his notes on the testimony
taken in Ginty's bedroom.

'No,' he said presently, 'you didn't. Nor did Bellowes,
as it turns out. Didenot is the source of the evidence. He
stated positively that when he entered the house at 8.39,
no one was there except the pilots, the keeper and Bellowes, but he was sure of it. I think that settles the point.'

'Maybe she was in one of the other rooms. That might
have been why no one noticed her come in the front door
later. If she came in through one of the other doors to the
main room, I mean.'

'If Isa was in any other than the main room of the
keeper's house, then she was hiding there,' the detective
surmised. 'What legitimate purpose could she have had

in wandering about his house? If that's the case, it's more suspicious than ever.'

Dr Pons asserted in a definite tone, 'We're just guessing, Michael. This sort of thing won't get you anywhere. It's no good your trying to imagine all kinds of incriminating items against Isa Mann. Even if you were guessing right by some remote chance, you would still have to prove it. What's the use?'

'You're right, doctor. All I know now is that she misled me badly about her movements, but I haven't the slightest idea what her movements really were. I shall simply have to try to find that out. She can't just have vanished, after all. Some one *must* have caught a glimpse of her somewhere, and that is what I shall have to uncover. I'll do it, if I have to wake up every one on the 'plane.' Lord rose from the camp stool, folded his notebook and put it into his pocket with an air of determination.

The psychologist got up too. He said, 'If you are going to interview them, you'll want this seat I'm using, I suppose. A nap for me in any case. Mind you, I don't believe you're on the right track with this case you are trying to build up against Isa, but you'll have to go further with it now, if only to satisfy yourself. Well, luck.'

Dr Pons lumbered forward cumbersomely on the none too firm footing of the narrow aisle, steadying himself tentatively against the chairs on which the passengers slept.

Michael Lord stood thinking. Where to begin? The whole series of the girl's actions on Medicine Bow field was blank, no indication even for a starting point. For no reason that notation he had about Tinkham's bag occurred to him, the man's statement about dropping it on the field as he came across. He had said it had come open and that he had picked it up and looked in it to see whether anything had fallen out.

It kept the detective motionless in thought at the rear

of the cabin for more than a minute.

For, you see, Tinkham could not have looked in his bag.

7900 FEET

Between the two lines of restless figures Lord made his way quietly to the cockpit door. It struck him that a transport 'plane at night, with the lights out and the stewardess dozing in a rear seat, might offer more opportunities for an attack by a criminal than would have appeared likely in view of the confined space and the proximity of the passengers to each other. The one who had planned Amos Cutter's murder would not have been hampered, in the ordinary course of events, by an unduly difficult setting for the crime. Previously he had supposed that the contemplated assault was to be made *in spite of* the air trip, that some urgent requirement of time might possibly lie beneath the fact that April 13th had been chosen as the day.

Now it seemed possible that the plan had been made to coincide with Cutter's flight by choice. The threatening note had specified noon, of course, instead of night; and at noon the conditions in the 'plane would much more closely resemble the publicity and difficulty one would expect to encounter in a transport cabin. It wouldn't do, though, to take everything about the note too seriously. The hour it named had always been viewed more dubiously by Lord; it was far too specific. More likely all around that it had merely been meant, with the harmless passing of time named, to lure the victim into a false feeling of security. The inclusion of the words 'Central Time,' was an added factor; it had seemed to indicate almost a straining for exactitude, a deliberate calling of attention to that very hour and thus to no other hour. The night would have been chosen for the actual attempt, without doubt; he was still surprised to see what a difference it made, now that he had noticed it. The forward part of the cabin was in nearly complete darkness.

The detective looked behind him, down the dim lines of chairs. He would wager that in the morning not one of the passengers – except possibly Pons, who might not have dozed off as yet – would be able to say he had passed up and down the aisle. He mounted the two small steps and put his hand on the knob of the cockpit door.

Both pilots looked around quickly and Lovett's hand slid toward his holster. Evidently the junior pilot was alert to further possibilities within the cabin. With his eyes accustomed to the dark, however, he recognised Lord immediately and asked, 'Message garbled?'

The detective shook his head. 'No. It came out very nicely, considering. We won't have to repeat it. I'm looking for another, though. Hasn't anything come in for me?'

'Not a thing,' Lannings assured him. 'I've just taken over the ship; I've been running the 'phones for the last trick. There hasn't been anything at all except the usual routine reports.'

Unconsciously they were speaking in low voices. From the cabin behind Lord's back, as he stood in the doorway, came a few slight sounds, as of some one moving about quietly, but the motors drowned it out effectually from all three pairs of ears in the cockpit.

'That's too bad. If it doesn't come in within the next hour, I wish you would call Salt Lake City and ask about it. It should come through the police department to the field. Can you do that?'

'Sure. Glad to. I don't think it will be delayed, though, once it gets to the field.'

The detective looked around the cockpit with interest. Most of it was lost in obscurity, for the lights on its rear wall were out. Directly in front, the instrument panel glowed with its indirect, green lighting illuminating the dials and pointers on its crowded surface. Behind its glass the little 'plane in the Sperry instrument hovered dimly above its artificial horizon, evidencing a slight climb. The pilots, he thought, must be so familiar with their levers and controls, that any other lighting was unnecessary.

Through the glassed sides nothing of the earth below was visible, not even a pinpoint winkled. From ahead a beacon flashed, and was extinguished. 'Nice and snug,' Lord commented. 'Am I mistaken or is it beginning to get a little grey outside?'

'Not yet. We're up pretty high, but it will be another hour before the false dawn.' Lovett reached into his pocket for the microphone. 'Will you excuse me; it's time for our twenty-minute report.'

'Go ahead, of course. You won't forget about my message, will you?' Lord's head and shoulders withdrew, and the small door closed.

As he turned about, he saw there had been a change in the cabin. Upon the camp stool he himself had occupied next to Pons at the rear end, Hugh L. Craven was sitting propped back against the wall. He was peacefully smoking his pipe.

8000 FEET

Lord looked at him doubtfully as he stepped down into the aisle.

Had Craven been prowling about the darkened cabin? And if so, what for? He was certain the Englishman had been lying back, to all intents asleep, when he had passed forward a little while before. So the man had certainly gotten up and passed along the aisle, in order to reach his

present position. Lord realised that his suspicions were
on the alert. Maybe the man's purpose had been no more
than his ostensible one of going back to enjoy a smoke.

'What woke you up?' he asked, approaching the
seated figure.

Craven looked up lazily. 'Nothing special, I imagine,'
he responded in a casual tone. 'I found myself awake and
thought I'd have a bit of a pipe before lying down again.
Didn't want to disturb the chaps next to me.'

'I see.'

'Aren't you going to get any sleep at all to-night?
Better have a spot of nap yourself, hadn't you, old chap?'

'Not to-night,' said the detective grimly. 'To-night
I'm working.'

'How's your head? Rather a bump you got.'

'It's O.K. now,' Lord lied. 'I wouldn't know it had
been scratched.'

A short silence. Then, 'You haven't solved the mys-
tery, what? No arrest?'

'H'm.' Well, he might as well make use of the fellow,
now that he was here. 'By the way, Craven, you can't
remember seeing Isa Mann anywhere, either in the
cabin or on the field, back at Medicine Bow, can you?
I'm especially anxious to establish just when she left the
cabin.'

'Afraid I can't help you with that. I got down just after
the pilots, y'know. I'm certain she must have been in the
cabin when I left, and I've no idea when she may have
decided to come out on the field . . . Of course I know
when she reached the little house, but I've told you that
already, I believe.'

'What's that? You know when she reached the house?
You haven't told *me* about it, that's sure.'

Craven blinked with apparent surprise. 'Oh, didn't I?
Well, you may be right, I had a notion I'd told you back
there when you were asking where I'd been myself. Why,
she came in the door just after me; no sooner had I closed

the door than she opened it.'

'So that was Isa,' said Lord, with satisfaction. 'I knew
some one had entered behind you, but I didn't know who
it was. That anchors down one end, anyhow. You and
Pons went into the room at 8.40 and, if she was right
behind you, that makes 8.40 for her also and puts the
question as to what she was doing all that time. She
didn't go out to investigate the combat 'plane, I'm positive.'

The playwright's attention was caught by the suspicion in Lord's tone. 'Are you really still tryin' to pick out
one of us for the dock?' he inquired curiously. 'You won't
be able to do, y'know . . . Your chap's in Africa, what?
Rather out of your jurisdiction for the moment.'

The detective in turn observed his companion with
curiosity, as he spoke. 'A joke's a joke. It gets silly after a
while. You don't seriously entertain those absurd
theories about "projection" and all the rest of that stuff,
of course.'

'My dear fellow,' Craven retorted easily, 'of course I
do, because, y'see, they're not theories, but merely
phenomena that occur and are reported circumstan-
tially. There is as much evidence for them as there is for a
goodish lot of so-called scientific "facts." More, for some
of them.'

'Pshaw.'

'Well, there you are; that's as intelligent an argument
as I've ever heard brought against them, and I'll wager
you would believe anything a "scientist" told you just
because he had letters after his name and was a sup-
porter of currently fashionable ideas . . . But I don't
want to shake your confidence. It's comfortable to stay
hypnotised.'

There ensued a short silence while Craven puffed contentedly on his pipe. Lord was trying to frame a question
that would not seem too leading and the task was proving difficult. It was to be an important question.

'That stuff – what do you call it, Fortean? – was all right as long as you thought Cutter had been killed by the bulb I gave him this morning, but it's washed up now.'

'I never did think you poisoned the man,' the other reminded him.

(There, that was the thing!)

'Why not? It happened right in front of your nose and every one else thought so.'

'But I told you why.' Craven, at ease, shrugged. 'Probably every one else did think so; this atmosphere of scientific credulity surrounding the educated ends up by making them credulous all along the line. But detectives don't poison the persons they are guarding. They don't do it even in stories; certainly they don't do it in actual circumstances. Wotan Mann wanted Cutter's death and Cutter died, in full view of all of us, without being attacked by any one present. The only man near him was, in fact, guarding him. Well?'

'Oh surely; but we have passed beyond that set-up. Cutter met his death in a quite different fashion. His throat was cut.'

'And again, curiously enough, in the absence of a weapon.'

'Not at all. I have the weapon in my pocket . . . No, I found it to-night, while you were asleep.'

'You found the knife?'

'Not a knife, Mr Craven,' said Lord softly, 'not a knife. It was Fonda Mann's scarf clip and I found it hanging on her scarf with Cutter's blood on it.'

The Englishman twisted his long body into a more upright position. He spoke sharply, 'It's ridiculous, and you call my ideas fantastic! No one could cut a man's throat with a scarf clip.'

'It could be done with this one, all right,' he was assured. 'The thing is more than four inches along one blade and the blades are spade-shaped. Also they are of some strong, rigid metal and the edges are as sharp as the point. Not as sharp as a knife, it's true, but plenty sharp enough to slash an unconscious man's throat.'

'Well,' Craven drew a long breath, 'if you think Fonda Mann went out and cut her uncle's throat with her scarf clip, you're batty. It's unpleasant work, slitting throats; they bleed like hell. A girl like Fonda Mann? By Jove, you might as well bring Wotan before a jury as bring her.'

'For once I agree with you.'

'Oh, I see. Fonda is not suspected.'

'As I have pointed out before, that leaves the rest of you. Especially the rest of you who have no alibis for the period in question. You can't strengthen your own, I suppose? You have had some more time for recollection now.'

'Can't do. I can't get very worried, either . . . There is one thing I forgot to tell you about my journey, though. I only remembered it after we had got back in the 'plane. When I was coming up to the house on the field, just before I met up with the Pons chap, I saw some one scrabblin' around in the snow about fifty yards back as if he'd lost something and was damn anxious to find it.'

'Who was that?'

'Don't know, I'm sure. I had only a glance through the snow and didn't think much about it. Just gave it to you now because you seem to be interested in anything you can find out about that field. I've something more amusin' than that for you, if you want it.'

'Yes?'

'Yes. Since I've been asleep, some one's hopped it with my gun.'

The detective's interest was evident in his voice. 'Suppose you tell me all about that right now.'

'There's not much to tell,' Craven responded. 'I had a gun, a little German thing with eight bullets in it. It was in my coat pocket when I lay back and went to sleep after we left the emergency field. When I woke up just now, it wasn't there. That's all.'

'It didn't merely drop out, I suppose?'

'It did not merely drop out. I looked about a bit with a flash.'

They sat for some moments pondering this situation. Lord said finally, 'I've been here all the time. Of course I got out at Salt Lake City, but a number of you were stirring about then, which would more or less count that time out . . . I have been working, of course, but most of the time Pons has been with me. Although he went to sleep back here once. I suppose it could have been done while I was working on that message. The only other time was when I was speaking with the pilots just now. Do you think you could have been awakened by the thief? Just now, I mean.'

'It's possible, I imagine. I don't recall anything of the kind, however. It seemed to me that I merely woke up, not that I was awakened by anything.'

'It's a foolish thing to have done,' Lord considered. 'Very foolish. The murder is finished, and no one can possibly get away from this cabin with your property. Do you want me to make a search for it now?'

'Wouldn't think of it, old chap. Wakin' everybody up; there's no such hurry as that. If it doesn't turn up by the time we reach Reno, that's soon enough for searching people. As you say, it can't get away.'

'Just the same, there's something very funny about this.' Lord fell silent, turning over several possibilities in his mind, until the other rather abruptly got to his feet.

Craven knocked the ashes from his pipe into a container. 'I'm turning in again for an hour or so,' he announced. 'Sorry you can't see the light about the main thing. Mann could easily have transported that clip to his enemy's throat and then have transported it back to a scarf when it had done its job of work. Trans-mediumisation can be about as "miraculous," when viewed by "scientists," as they want it.'

Lord's only answer to that was a grunt. Craven walked easily down the aisle and subsided skilfully into his reclining chair. The detective strained his eyes to see whether or not he pulled a blanket over him. He did not. As doubtfully as when he himself had come down the aisle to find the novelist at the rear of the cabin, Lord continued to stare at the reclining figure in the seat.

8100 FEET

Craven (Lord considered from the little camp stool that now was becoming definitely uncomfortable) was most assuredly a cool customer. Just a touch too cool for compatibility with complete innocence. His theories possessed a patness to any emerging factor in the situation, which suggested that they had been considered beforehand in anticipation of such eventualities.

And such theories! He didn't know which was more incredible, the theories themselves or Craven's calm assurance that he could get any one else to take them seriously. Was it possible that the playwright himself took them seriously? Hardly. As an intellectual pastime, yes. Undoubtedly he was intrigued by them; his intimate acquaintance with their details showed that he had spent some time, at least, over the bizarre notions of this fellow, Fort, but as a significant basis of explanation for real occurrences, for a murder that had been committed not ten feet from this very cabin – no, Craven struck him as far too well balanced for that. 'If he found himself in my place with a criminal to catch,' Lord muttered, 'I'll bet he wouldn't waste much time thinking about Africa.' Transmediumisation – the 'transportation' of the clip from a scarf in the cabin to Cutter's throat and back to the scarf again! My God!

Of course, Craven didn't know the circumstances of the clip's loss and subsequent discovery on the cabin floor. Or else he was pretending not to know. For he, as well as the other suspects, had had an equal opportunity to pick it up and plan its use . . . He hadn't inquired about the details of the clip, how Fonda had happened not to have it when it was being used, where Lord had found the scarf, or anything else; which in itself was surely peculiar under the circumstances. It rather looked as if Craven had not been anxious to discuss the matter of the clip. A few questions would have been more natural. No discussion, no possibility of slips, perhaps?

And yet when he was talking, he seemed so entirely convinced of his strange viewpoint that it was difficult to doubt his sincerity at such times. What if he did actually believe in 'projection' and the rest of it? Well, no use mulling that over again. It could have nothing really to do with the case; it was either an aberration or it was a clever smoke-screen. If the latter, it was suspicious. What else was suspicious, that was the point now.

The Englishman had been a British secret agent during the war, Felix wired. A spy, in short; and at the very beginning of the case there had been reason to think about spies. A British spy, naturally, was out of the question; Lord found it impossible to conceive of the British Foreign Office being involved in an attempt, even an indirect one, upon the life of the American Secretary of State. They had, in fact, far more reason to protect his life, for James Cutter was as notoriously pro-British as he was anti-French.

That, however, hardly altered matters. Craven had once been a British agent; why not now a French one? Or even an Oriental one? The detective had vague ideas that, once in that game, one's services were generally on the market for the highest bidder. The playwright had pooh-poohed spy rings in peace times, and, ordinarily, Lord would have felt inclined to agree with him; but if he were actually a spy himself, the pooh-poohing became a natural reaction to such suggestions. Another pat attitude.

A corroboratory remark edged its way into the detective's consciousness. Craven had spoken not only calmly but with familiarity concerning throat cutting. No doubt spies inevitably learned something of this art; or became casualties instead of spies. His unruffled treatment of the murder was certainly not entirely assumed. There was no doubt that he felt reasonably at home in an atmosphere of violence and sudden death. That much could be said anyhow, for it was established that Craven had lived among the vicissitudes of the Secret Service for some time at the least. The question was whether his real profession now was literary or semi-military.

And, in addition, he might have had another motive. Even if he were totally innocent of foreign employment, there remained his friendship with Wotan Mann; and it became increasingly plausible that a man who had certainly killed in the past, who had in fact been a legalised criminal during the war, would not hesitate to revive his abilities on behalf of a friend if the affair appeared safe. As he had probably accomplished far more difficult feats in the past, there was no reason why he should lack confidence here. Confidence was a quality possessed especially by deliberate murderers, by those, for example, who dispatched death threats in advance of their deeds. Whatever else might be said, it was growing clear that, of the three suspects left, Craven was by far the best equipped, both temperamentally and by experience, for the commission of the crime.

And he lacked an alibi as completely as either of the others, now that Isa's arrival at the house had become known. Or had it? Could Craven's evidence be trusted on this or any other point? After a little reflection Lord saw that, so far as concerned the case against the girl, it could be. If Craven were guilty, it could not be, but if Isa were the criminal, then it could be, for that meant the Englishman's innocence.

And Isa, now that he thought of it, had the temperament, if not the experience, of her fellow suspect. She was disagreeable, she was appetitive; more than that, she was plainly rude and quarrelsome. She went out of her way, when talking with people, to sneer at them and insult them. She did with men, at all events. Even if she had wanted to, she could not have concealed her violent antipathy to them from any one. Without exaggeration it could be said to go to the extent of hatred . . . That crude slashing of Cutter's neck had been an act of hatred rather than a job of workmanlike competence . . . The actual details of the murder fitted Isa better than they did Craven. From this angle.

Her motive? Lord was beginning to see the outlines of a possible motive for Isa. He would have to get more on that, though, before it shaped up into anything. Incidentally, he had better set about getting it. Time was slipping past. He looked at his watch – good heavens, yes! Too bad to wake them up. Nevertheless, there was no choice now; he would have to do it.

8000 FEET

Fonda moved restlessly as he touched her. She opened her eyes and said, 'Michael,' in a soft murmur. She smiled sleepily.

They whispered together for some minutes. At first there seemed reluctance as well as drowsiness in her manner, but then, more fully awake, she answered his questions with accurate detail. At their conclusion he patted her shoulder, avoided provocatively upraised lips (for which he was sorry an instant later), and stepped back to Dr Pons' chair.

The psychologist, snoring gently on his back, was more difficult to arouse; but he stumbled down the aisle after Lord, grunting and grumbling, once he was awake. 'Hell, Michael, is this a trip or a laboratory experiment of some kind?'

'Sorry, doctor, but time is drawing short.'

'It must be nearly morning.'

'It is. That's just the trouble, and I haven't got my three suspects sorted out yet at all.' The detective ran a hand over his injured head and paused, as Pons drew off no less than six cups of water from the wall fixture and gulped them down in rapid succession.

'There, that's better,' Pons announced, as he crumpled the cup and sat down, with a final grunt, on the little camp stool. 'Well now, what is the present emergency?'

'Isa Mann,' said Lord definitely. 'I'm going to go through with her case this time until it makes sense. Or until it doesn't. You know about her false story at the field and her misleading statements; we've been over that. By the way, I've found that she reached the house at 8.40; she was the one who came in just after you and Craven. That leaves her unaccounted for between 8.32 or 8.33 and 8.40. Those are eight very important minutes.'

'But why ask me?' Pons rolled a longing eye in the direction of his comfortable chair.

'Because you are supposed to be an expert on personalities. Has she the sort of personality to have done this murder and can she be said to have had a credible motive? Those are two questions that it is necessary I discuss with you now.'

'H'm,' said Pons, noncommittally. 'As to her personality, I haven't had time to study it properly. You must stop making me guess about people without adequate data. I've done that before, sometimes at your instigation, and the results were not promising . . . I'd hate to have some of my colleagues hear about that Summerladd fellow . . . Personality. Well, Michael, all I can say is this: aside from a small appetitive sub-type – the gunman, gangster type – murder is an extraordinary and unusual abnormality. You won't find many types of personality that will screw themselves up to the actual point. On the other hand all sorts of impulses or fundamental emotions can reach an intensity, under the apposite conditions, that will cause a person to perform actions that ordinarily would appear to be, and in fact would be, out of the question for that person. It becomes really a question of the degree of the motivation involved, and as to that you have to know, not guess, the actual circumstances as they bear upon a definite personality history . . . You know that it's my opinion that Isa didn't have any sufficient motive for this crime.'

'Sure. That's another reason I got you up. I know your opinion, but, meantime, I've dug up more information, and I have what looks to me like a reasonable motive for her to have done it. I want to build my story up and have you criticise it. You know more about motives than I do. If you can't knock down my hypothetical one, it ought to be a pretty good example.'

'I'm listening,' the psychologist informed him.

'First of all,' Lord began, 'I *do* think she's the sort of person who could easily be imagined taking part in violence. All the time I've seen her she has been rude and nasty; it's undoubtedly her general attitude.'

'Her emotions are directed homosexually,' Pons interrupted. 'She has always had to be on the defensive against conventions and conventional attitudes on the part of others, especially men, who scorn and abuse her. It is not surprising to me that she has developed the technique advised by the phrase that the best defence is attack.'

'I don't care how she developed it; there it is, and, of course, she goes far beyond mere rudeness, sometimes at all events. That fight she had down in Greenwich Village, when she laid out another girl, can't be her only experience of physical animosity. That is evidence, anyhow, that she is capable of becoming as violent as her manner indicates.'

'A rough and tumble fight is a far cry from a murder, and she had a reason for that, I've no doubt, a reason that appeared vital to her, no matter how it would have looked to you or to me. The point here is that she had no motive, that, if anything, she was in alliance with the murdered man.'

'Ah, now we come to it.' Lord offered a cigarette, lit one of his own. He drew several puffs, marshalling the details of the motivation he had in mind. He commenced his exposition slowly.

'You admit that Isa's emotions are homosexual. Yes, I know; I'm speaking about her *emotions*. The whole Cutter family seem to be excellently supplied with emotions and there is one of them who, if we are to judge by everything that has been said, is an emotional magnet if ever there was one. Anne. To put my notion in plain words, it is that Isa is as wildly in love with Anne as Amos was or as any of the others. That's plausible enough, isn't it?'

'It's practically certain, from what we know,' Dr Pons shrugged at the obvious, 'and for that reason she was allied with Amos in getting rid of outside rivalry. Probably had been for years, when the occasions arose.'

'But when the outside rivalry had been done away with, then what? Then she became, in turn, the rival of Amos; Amos, with the violently jealous disposition, with the desire and the brutal force to monopolise his sister completely. Within the family it's as plain as the nose on your face that the natural rivals for Anne's attention were Isa and Amos. Fonda certainly has an entirely different feeling about Anne and the Secretary, so far as appears, has been a more or less unwilling participant all along. Even if he once had any such desire, he has had to abandon it long ago for the duties of his political

career . . . No, there were two jealous and possessive
people in that family, the daughter and the brother. Isa
and Amos. The more I think of it, the more sure I am
that they have been at each other's throats – er – for
years. They simply must have each been scheming how
to shut the other out, how to get more of Anne for themselves.'

'Well,' Pons halted his reply and stopped to consider
the view expressed by his friend. 'Yes,' he said finally, 'so
far as the general situation goes, there is nothing much
wrong with your analysis. I can easily see both Isa and
Amos as jealously appetitive and so, if left with only the
family circle to contend with, I see them as naturally in
opposition to each other. Since they both wanted the
same thing and since the condition of having what they
wanted, was that they should have it *exclusively*. In
general, yes; but we're not confronted with a generality.
The occurrence you're interested in is specific, and the
specific case was that Isa and Amos were temporarily
allied in order to dispose of an outsider intruder . . .
Also, where is there any evidence that we are talking
more than unconfirmed theory? Have you asked Fonda
about this yet?'

'Just finished. She wasn't particularly anxious to discuss her sister, but I finally got something out of her. She
as good as admitted that the theory is correct. In general,
Isa and Amos have been jealous of each other ever since
Isa was old enough to understand that her uncle wished
to divert her mother's attention away from her and to
himself. In other words, from childhood on. Most of the
time they have been enemies and, I should judge, rather
underhand ones. Then, whenever an outsider
threatened to come into their warfare as a third candi-
date, they combined against him until he had been
pushed out – or otherwise gotten rid of. Fonda told me
this without too much lead on my part. She didn't especially want to tell me, either, and I'm sure we can take

that much of my theory as established.'

Pons said obstinately, 'All right. All right, take that much, but that doesn't give Isa motive. For at this point we find the alliance in full swing, even if temporarily so. Right now they are engaged, in fact, in getting rid of the most serious rival of all.'

'That's just what I doubt,' Lord responded slowly. 'You see, getting rid of some one can be accomplished long before the papers are signed. Wotan Mann has cleared out, gone to Africa. The divorce is in train and will go through almost automatically; so far as concerns their real problem – pushing out the husband – it is already accomplished. He is not contesting the divorce.'

'How do you know he isn't?'

'Fonda again. She would know, too.'

'Yes, she would know her father's plans, if any one did.'

'Well, she is certain. It's funny how all these men of Anne's, when it comes to a showdown, do what she says. One of them gave up his fiancée, and now Mann refuses to contest the divorce because, Fonda says, once he realised Anne had decided, he didn't want to put her to needless expense and difficulty.'

'They fall in love with her,' said the psychologist. 'Once in love with her, they will submit to her, against their own desires . . . They are really in love with her, of course, whereas neither Amos nor Isa, for that matter, love her at all. There is no love response where the gratification of the subject comes first.'

'Well, you see the bearing of all this. With Mann out of the way – and he is out of the way now to all intents and purposes – the truce is over and the Isa-Amos fight begins once more. They are actually on their way to see Anne, to renew their struggles with each other on the spot. Both of them have given it plenty of thought, you can be certain. I can well see now why Amos didn't want to bring his nieces out with him . . . It's another crisis, actually, in his long fight with Isa. It's a place where, if ever there was to be violence, it could be expected to happen.'

'Sometimes you are an apt pupil, Michael,' Pons had to admit.

'Then you agree with me that there was a logical motive for Isa to do away with her uncle? A motive that the prosecution could take into court without fear of being tripped up by your science?'

'There exists no such motive as that; nowadays you can hire an "expert" to testify to anything. Usually they're psychoanalysts . . . I will go so far as to say this,' added Dr Pons cautiously; 'the theoretical motivation you have been ascribing to Isa is perfectly sound psychologically. In theory, that is, but that's just it; it is entirely theorising, without a scrap of factual evidence to back it up.'

'Motives usually have to be theoretical, to begin with.'

'There is nothing else at all to connect her with the murder, is there? Her lack of an alibi, after all, is only a negative point. Have you gotten anywhere with the weapon angle?'

'There is nowhere to get,' Lord asserted ruefully. 'Fonda doesn't know when or where she dropped that clip. Certainly Isa could have picked it up, and so could Tinkham, and so could Craven. So that's that.'

'You haven't been able to get anything more on either of those fellows, eh?'

'You mean evidence connected with the murder? No, not a thing. Whatever I have gotten is no stronger than implication.'

'You had one more angle to work on, didn't you? That business about somebody realising Cutter was only unconscious, not dead. Nothing doing?'

'Hell, I can't get anywhere. Craven frankly admits he never believed that Cutter was killed by the bulb. A stupid man who was guilty would say the opposite, of

course – but would Craven? It seems to me he might say
just what he does say. It fits in with that junk about Cutter's having been killed from Africa, you see.'

'Still,' considered Pons, 'if he's the only one who had
any such idea – '

'Sure. *If* he's the only one. All I know is that he's the
only one who talks about it; but he talked about it to both
the others.'

'Really? Before the real murder? When did he do
that?'

'Oh, not directly. I've racked my brains to remember
this and I'm pretty nearly certain I'm right. Do you
recall when Craven first began giving me his notions
about the fake crime? You were sitting just across from
me, he was in the seat ahead of mine and I think Isa was
just in front of you. It was after Bellowes had finished
telling us about hell and damnation.'

'That's right,' Pons confirmed. 'I heard some of Craven's talk myself. I suppose Isa could also have overheard him if she had been listening. That's not to say she
took any more stock in him than I did, though . . . It lets
Tinkham out, anyhow; he wasn't there then.'

'No. But he was later. My conversation with Craven
was interrupted when we landed somewhere. When we
took off again, he went on with his stuff. Craven did, I
mean, and for that instalment, Tinkham was right opposite us. I definitely remember that I thought at the time
he was listening to us and pretending not to. He got up
after a few minutes and disappeared into the lavatory,
but I am almost positive that that was after Craven's
explicit assertion that I had not given Cutter a bulb that
would injure him . . . I'll admit I am not perfectly sure of
it. I've tried to remember the exact place when he left
until I can't recall anything definite now.'

'How did it seem when you first recollected the
conversation? First of all, when you considered it, did
you think Tinkham had been there or not?'

'First of all, I thought he had been there.'

'Then probably he was. When you get mixed up like that, the greatest probability is that your first recollection is the right one, and somehow I think that Craven's remark would suggest more to Tinkham than to the girl, if he did happen to overhear it. Yes, I'm sure it would. A research man's mind is far more accustomed to little hints denying the obvious, and a doctor could easily jump to the idea of a drug with similar effects. If he vivisects, he must know plenty about anaesthetics.'

'You're veering toward Tinkham?'

'Not really. No, I can't see his motive.'

'He had enough motive, maybe. There is a hot fight about extending vivisection to human subjects. Cutter was the leader of those who opposed it, and Tinkham, while not a leader, was strong as he could be on the other side. I don't mean simply an academic discussion; it was growing into a serious struggle. Papers had been stolen and so on.'

'Well – '

'I'll tell you, doctor; I have considered Tinkham seriously. Especially when I thought I had caught him out on part of his story. Just a little thing, but the kind that would show his evidence about his movements had been made up. Tinkham told me that coming across that field, after he had been back here for his bag, it came open and he dropped it. When he picked it up, he said he had looked inside to see if anything had fallen out. I had reason to think that he could not have done so . . . Yes, and now Craven tells me that at 8.40, just as he was about to enter the keeper's house, he caught a glimpse of some one reaching around in the snow as if searching for something. About fifty yards away. He doesn't know who it was, but I'm afraid it was Tinkham.'

'Why Tinkham?'

'Isa didn't drop anything and also she must have been closer to the house, for she came in right after you did. No one else told of dropping anything, except Fonda, and at 8.40 Fonda had reached the 'plane again. It must have been Tinkham and, as Craven didn't know of the other fellow's evidence, his testimony lets Tinkham out of a lie nicely. If he lied about his movements, he didn't lie about that detail. I'm quite sure he didn't know he was being observed. It's just the kind of little thing, too, that gives a colour of truth to his story.'

'Then you think now that Tinkham's testimony about his movements was correct? That gives him an alibi automatically.'

'No,' Lord observed, 'I'm not quite ready to leave him out as completely as that. Part of it is true, although it is not a very vital part, but the implication is in his favour. Craven is in the same boat. If he hadn't been over to the combat 'plane, at least he came to the house from a direction other than that of our 'plane. The fact is that Isa is the only one who told me what has been shown to have been false. The accounts of the others *may* be false; her account *is*.'

'Well,' Pons confessed, 'it's a tough one. It surely is. It's all so indefinite. Of course it may be this, it may be that, it may be lots of things. All theoretical. All of it, as you say, is a matter of implication, but some sort of real clue must have been left. I have never heard of a case when that didn't happen.'

'If it was left, I haven't found it. Yet.' Lord gave a discouraged shrug. 'Just for good measure, here's one more implication. The criminal sent Cutter a threatening letter. The criminal came aboard this 'plane, intending to murder him. The original plan for the murder could not be carried out because of the action I took and another plan had to be improvised on the spur of the moment. It is plain enough that the clip was an article provided by chance only, and used by some one who seized the opportunity it offered, but that doesn't alter the fact that the criminal, when he came aboard, must have provided himself with some weapon to accomplish what he had in mind.'

'Yes, that's all right. Well?'

'Well, the only person on the 'plane of whom I am certain that he started out with a weapon that can kill, is Craven, and I can't figure why he told me so. Was it chance? Or is he convinced that the plainer he makes himself, the less he can be seen?'

'Edgar Allan Poe's letter,' commented Dr Pons thoughtfully.

7300 FEET

It was light.

From the cockpit, Lovett, who was flying the transport now, watched the earth taking on outline and substance below him. They had passed over Elko eighteen minutes before and the Beowawe beacon beyond Emigrant Pass, which they were just entering, still flashed palely in the greyness ahead. A threatening morning, with dull, over-cast skies. Darker clouds to the south-west; there might be squalls or small hailstorms before they came down at Reno. Nothing serious, however, the weather reports assured them of that. Only a little more than an hour and a half now and he and Lannings could leave the cockpit and turn into billets for a well deserved rest. The thought gave him new energy for the last, short leg of the flight. Some one else would take the 'plane on from Reno. Well, let them, and happy landings at San Francisco.

The windows of the cabin were paling grey squares and the passengers were commencing to stir about. Marjorie Gavin had been second into the lavatory – Pons had been first – and she had emerged as neat and fresh as when she had crossed the field at Chicago the day before. Now she was adjusting Pons' chair for him while some one squeezed past her down the narrow aisle. The some one was Tinkham.

He came to the rear of the cabin and there he had to wait, for the Rev. Manly Bellowes was splashing his face with water at the little washstand beyond. 'Goodmorning, Captain,' said Tinkham. 'Have you made any progress with this outrage? You have been up all night, haven't you?'

The detective's face in the morning light was drawn with fatigue. 'Not much. Nothing definite enough to act upon.'

'What's the next step? We shall all have to stay in Reno, I suppose, until something is done?'

'You're staying there anyway, I thought,' said Lord.

'Yes. I meant the others.'

'I shall hold them all as long as I can.'

'It's damnable,' the surgeon's assistant asserted. 'A great man, a great scientist. Isn't there anything I can do to help find his murderer?'

'Not unless you want to confess.'

Tinkham gave a perceptible start. He said, 'Uh?'; then smiled wryly. 'You ask too much, Captain. No, I'm serious. It is unbelievable that Dr Cutter's assailant should escape his just deserts.'

'He won't,' Lord grated. 'I'll get him, but I haven't got him yet.'

When the other had left him, he sat thinking. Was it Tinkham? He could not forget that voice, strained with passion, cold with contempt, speaking of those who would obstruct scientific progress. Back at Newark Airport. Ages ago. The man had looked distinctly uncomfortable when requested to confess, but anyone else would probably have looked uncomfortable, too. He didn't appear to be a man of action, but these fellows, Lord knew, could act drastically on occasion; but would a surgeon – and undoubtedly Tinkham was a competent surgeon himself – have made those crude slashes in a

throat? Would he have selected such a bungling instrument as a scarf clip? Only if he were clever, very clever
indeed . . . And he had, it seemed, opened his bag.

'Mornin'. Craven's voice was cool and pleasant.
'Luck?'

'None that you could notice,' Lord admitted gloomily.

'Too bad; but you know, old chap, you're not looking
in the right direction at all . . . Any sign of it?'

The detective knew the other was referring to his
pistol. He shook his head in the negative.

'Well, there's a little time yet.' The novelist passed on.

Very collected, very calm, Lord noted. That business
of the gun, though, appeared sillier, the more one considered it. Had it been a real error, one of those inevitable
mistakes that ought to put him on the right track? Or was
there actually a criminal in the cabin who harboured
plans of further violence, who had seized another opportunity to provide himself – or herself – with still another
weapon? Why? The first murder was a success. There
could be only one reason for a second attack: if some one
knew who the murderer was, if some one else had to be
silenced. But no one knew. No one except Dr Pons had
even voiced suspicions. Perhaps, though, somebody held
a vital piece of evidence without knowing it and eventually Lord would dig that evidence out. If so, however, he
was still far away from it and both the time for silencing
such a hypothetical witness was becoming extremely
short and the conditions for doing so undetected were
now once more peculiarly difficult. The scheme hardly
seemed plausible.

On the other hand, suppose that Craven had originally intended to shoot Cutter during the night. The
gun, no doubt, had a silencer; and the shot itself, in the
noise of the droning motors, might well have been
unnoticed. Now he wanted to dispose of the gun; who
knew, there might be a search before the passengers were
permitted to land. It was not vitally important evidence,

even if found upon Craven, but how much better for him
either to tuck it away somewhere in the cabin or slip it
into some one else's coat or bag; and then to claim to
have been robbed. Suspicion would thus be divided, at
least, between himself and the alleged thief. Yes, that
was the calm and competent thing to have done, and
surely as plausible as the idea that some one had stolen it
too late to use it except in full view of them all.

And why had Craven volunteered all that additional
information during the night? Lord had received a dis-
tinct impression of stealth when he had turned around in
the cockpit doorway and discovered the novelist seated
at the cabin's rear. Had Craven right then been engaged
in planting the gun upon some one? He realised, however, that he was going out of his way to look for trouble
now. The man might well have been doing just what he
appeared to be doing; and the new evidence he offered
might also have been simply a matter of further recollection, subsequent to his first examination in Ginty's
room.

That evidence had definitely shown the extent of Isa's
unaccounted time, Lord remembered, veering again.
Assuredly she had sufficient motive. What a family! Pons
could say what he wanted – and almost surely the things
were altogether emotional – but just the same, to the
detective's mind, incest and homosexuality were not
pretty, any way you looked at it. Because he had built up
the theory of it himself, Isa's motivation suddenly
seemed very strong to him. What was murder to a person
as twisted as that?

And just then Isa came down the aisle. Lord looked at
her closely. He masked the distaste in his mind and
asked, 'Did you have a good sleep?'

She put her hand on the lavatory door before replying.
She turned and said, 'Thanks, I had a hell of a night.'

So there they were, all three, and mighty little to
choose between them.

7400 FEET

The passengers were upright in their seats now, the blankets folded and stowed away by the stewardess; all signs of the night had vanished. It was brighter outside, although still dull and cloudy. Mt Lewis and Mt Moses loomed to the south, their peaks jutting high above the 'plane, while Battle Mountain, north, was well below it. Only about an hour now to Reno, for some of them the end of their trip. An air of expectancy already hung about the travellers.

Michael Lord sat stupefied.

He had wondered, while the others were moving about and coming back to settle into their chairs, if he were really going to fail. The first big case he had flopped on. Of course he could hold them all for a little while at Reno, but there the difficulties would be enormously increased and gradually, on one pretext or another, they would disperse. The time to achieve a solution was here on the 'plane, in this cabin, while he had them all under his eye with no possibility of escape. He had no idea how to do it.

Fonda had come back and fussed over him. She had made him wash his face. She had said, 'Michael!' several times, had said 'poor boy' once. Fonda had been quite proprietary and he had been surprised to realise how much he had liked it. She had left him then, but the revival she had brought to his senses had lingered while he sat looking up the cabin at her hair under the little hat.

Then he had slumped again. It occurred to him that he had had no sleep for the last twenty-four hours and that the last time he had slept, it hadn't been for long. A lot of things had happened, among which he had taken a good knock on the head and fallen rather violently in love. It appeared a bad combination as a background for clear reasoning.

Marjorie had brought him a message from the cockpit and for a brief moment hope had flared up. Until he had read it. It was addressed to Cutter and said: 'Patient had excellent night. Recovery assured. MacKenzie.'

In angry despair he had crumpled the paper and flung it into the aisle. What did he care whether the other Cutter recovered or not? If it had to be one of them, he would much have preferred James dead and Amos alive. It was just the other way around.

Desperately he went back to the three possible criminals. It seemed to him that he had spent his whole life in going over their motives, their missing alibis, their evasions, their bluffings. His head ached, God how it ached!

And then he saw it. As clearly as if the printed name had been held before his eyes, he knew at once and finally who the murderer was. He sat stupefied.

It was so simple, all the time it had been so obviously simple! It was no theory that disclosed the criminal, no implication far-fetched or close. It was a staring fact; a fact so easily established and so readily appreciated that he could not now believe that any one could miss it, and he had missed it all along; he had thought of this fact and even discussed it with Pons. Pons had missed it, too.

'Well!' He drew a long breath and expelled it slowly. Then he got to work, going over the whole case with the criminal in mind, no longer a shadowy X but a definite name and a definite figure at which, every once in a while, he glanced to assure himself of its presence. He fitted things together; this element and that one fell into their orderly places. Only one detail remained unexplained and that one, he felt certain, would prove easy of ascertainment. He could practically prophesy it, as a matter of fact.

Finally, he brought out his note-book, unfolded the

chart over which he had pored so often. He scratched out the word 'Reported' in front of 'Movements' and substituted 'Actual'. He went over it carefully, confirming the alibis that were correct, two of them, and changing the false one to accord with the real movements of the criminal. They fitted again. Of course. They had to. Everything fitted.

Michael Lord got out of his seat and walked steadily up the cabin.

7600 FEET

As he reached the door to the cockpit and faced around, the 'plane bumped in a sudden gust.

He said, 'Ladies and gentlemen, this case is over.' His hand went into his pocket and when it came out it held an automatic.

He looked down the two lines of faces, turned toward him attentively. With his bald announcement all conversation had abruptly ceased. He noted the locations of the various passengers as he faced them: to his left, Fonda, Pons, Isa, Didenot; to his right, Tinkham in the forward seat, then Bellowes, Craven, an empty chair and the stewardess at the rear. Tinkham was getting up.

'Where are you going?' asked Lord. 'Don't you want to hear who killed Dr Cutter?'

'I most certainly do,' the surgeon's assistant assured him. 'I'll be right back, give you more room here, too. Hold it up just a minute, will you, please?'

Lord said, 'Sure.' But during the minute or so Tinkham was in the lavatory, he addressed the others. 'Practically all of you have been under suspicion,' he told them. 'Some more than others, of course, for some of you had alibis back there at Medicine Bow, when this murder took place. Dr Pons I have known personally for some years; he was never considered. And Bellowes and Didenot could clear each other. Miss Fonda Mann, it turned out, also had an alibi, although that was not evident at first. It would have been foolish to suspect the stewardess or the pilots. That left three of you, Miss Isa Mann, Dr Tinkham and Mr Craven. An explanation is due to all of you, particularly to those who have now been cleared; and I am sure you are all interested.'

In the pause, Craven's voice drawled, 'Quite.' Tinkham re-entered the cabin and took the last vacant chair on the left, across the aisle from Marjorie Gavin. It was doubtful if he had heard anything except the last sentence.

Isa said, 'Please,' in an unaccustomedly subdued tone. 'I want a glass of water. Can I get it?'

The detective nodded and she stepped back to the faucet in the rear. When she had finished she, too, remained in the after half of the cabin, taking the seat just ahead of the stewardess.

When she was in the chair, Lord went on. 'I am not going to take your time with a recital of the cases against the two innocent suspects. Theoretically they both had motive, opportunity and means. So did the guilty person, of course.

'I want to recall to you the circumstances of the crime. As soon as we had made our emergency landing, I left the cabin and went around to the baggage compartment on the other side of the 'plane to reassure myself about Dr Cutter. I had a little difficulty in getting the baggage door open and I had just done so when the criminal, coming around the rear end of the ship, struck me on the head from behind and knocked me out. It was not more than one or two minutes' work to enter the compartment and slash the unconscious man's throat. The criminal's steps were then retraced and eventually the field keeper's house was reached, where, in the confusion, every one finally made his or her way.

'The crime was committed with Miss Fonda Mann's scarf clip, a peculiar weapon but a more dangerous one than you would suppose unless you examined it. Unfortunately the choice of this instrument gave little indication as to who had used it, for Miss Mann had dropped her clip some time after we embarked on our present 'plane at Cheyenne and she didn't know either when or where it had been lost. Any one could have picked it up, even while we were getting into the 'plane, perhaps.

'There were other angles to the case, however, which at first sight appeared more promising. Dr Cutter had received a threat of death through the mail the day before we left New York; therefore it was plain that the criminal had planned the crime in advance and must have come aboard armed with some sort of weapon with which to accomplish the purpose. Had there been no solution during the flight, you would all have been searched when we landed, but, of course, the possession of a weapon with which the crime had *not* been committed, would be no more than an indication. It would be of no use as evidence. As a matter of fact, now that I know who the murderer is, I am almost certain I know the original means decided upon.

'This means could not be used, due to my plan of carrying Dr Cutter out to Reno unconscious and in a trance; and not in the cabin with the rest of us, furthermore, but in the baggage compartment to which, under ordinary conditions, no access of any kind is available to the passengers during a trip. I adopted this plan without Dr Cutter's knowledge for two reasons: first, because he was an obstinate man who could not be trusted to follow my instructions; and second, because of the safety of the situation. An unexpected snow-storm and the exhaustion of our escort flyer combined to make my precautions useless.'

The 'plane bumped again. The passengers were

becoming restless and, despite all they could do to conceal it, a little frightened. Bellowes raised a stentorian voice. 'Have done, my man,' he demanded. 'Who is this criminal who is sitting among us?'

'The murderer,' said Lord calmly, 'is Dr Tinkham.'

There was a surprised silence. Then, with one accord, most of the passengers turned to stare at their fellow traveller. Almost at the same moment Pons and Fonda both said, 'Are – are you sure?'

Tinkham sat apparently at ease and returned the looks focused upon him by the others. Lord knew now that he had been prepared for the accusation; was that why he had gotten as far away as possible?

The detective said, 'Hood Tinkham, I place you formally under arrest for the murder of Dr Amos Cutter. When we land, you will accompany me immediately to the police station at Reno, where you will be held for the time being, until arrangements can be made to return you to New York for trial. Any statement you may make now, may be used in the case against you.'

'You haven't got any case against me,' Tinkham answered coldly. 'I had no motive for such an act. Where is there any evidence against me, more than against any one else?'

Lord permitted himself a grim smile. 'The case against you is so complete that I will tell it to you . . . As to motive, you are prepared to go to any lengths in your fanatical support of the vivisection crusade. You stole Dr Cutter's address for the summer convention and when you found how hopeless his determined opposition made your cause, you decided to kill him. You then, with the confidence of many fanatics, sent him a note foretelling his death, which you knew would not deter him from his plans but, if anything, make him play into your hands.

'Your original idea was simple enough, when you found that both of you would fly to Reno. Under pretence of apprehension over his heart, you insisted upon bringing along a hypodermic with which you would have found some means of injecting into his blood a poison, not glonoin solute. Trusting in being the only physician present, you would have certified death from heart failure, due to altitude. You would probably have tried to poison him at the time mentioned in the death note; in fact I had some trouble in preventing your doing just that.

'I found a chance to open your bag and secure that hypodermic when you left the cabin for a few minutes. It is now being examined in Salt Lake City and I have no doubt of the eventual report. That is why I did not think you had dropped your bag on the field at Medicine Bow and then looked through it. You did, however, and so you have known for some time that the game was up. You had no opportunity to escape at Salt Lake City. Maybe you didn't realise that the tests were already being made or maybe you hoped that any report would be delayed until after we reached Reno. You would certainly have tried to disappear there.

'When your original plan for the murder fell through, you were constantly on the alert for another chance. You, who had planned to kill Dr Cutter just when he seemed to have died, must have found something very peculiar in the circumstances, and Craven confirmed your suspicions by insisting that I had not given him anything harmful, in a conversation which you overheard. From then on certainly you sought to carry out your first intention.

'When you found Miss Mann's clip and slipped it into your pocket, you were doubtless only playing a long chance, but your surgeon's eye saw its ability to cut and it had the double advantage of belonging to some one else and of being an unlikely weapon for a professional surgeon to use.

'The chance to use it came fortuitously and fairly soon

after you had procured it. We made an emergency landing under confusing conditions and you found it possible to get out of the cabin and follow me to Dr Cutter. Then you put me out and murdered him, but the mistake you made was so absurd that I cannot yet see how you came to do it. I suppose you wanted to implicate Miss Mann and get the full benefit of your weapon. Why didn't you throw it away in the snow? You brought it back to the cabin again; and that is conclusive proof that you committed the crime.

'The chart of our movements show this without any possibility of doubt. For at 8.34 the clip was in the baggage compartment being used against Dr Cutter and at 8.41 it was back in the cabin where Miss Mann found it. She was within sight of the keeper's house at the time of the crime so that she could not have had the clip in her possession to bring back with her, *and you were the only other person to enter the cabin between 8.34 and 8.41.* That convicts you, I think.'

Lord's voice ceased and in the silence Fonda asked, 'Can I see the chart, Michael?' He reached for it with his left hand and gave it to her, keeping a watch meantime on Tinkham at the cabin's rear.

The latter sneered openly. 'A very pretty case, no doubt. However, you've got the wrong man. I didn't kill him.'

The detective's answer was cut short by the opening of the door behind him. Lanning said, 'Oh, there you are. Here's your message from Salt Lake City finally.' Lord reached back again with his left hand, and felt a paper put into his palm. The paper said simply, 'Weak solution HCN. Lethal.' The case was complete.

His eyes were dropped for a moment while he read it, and in that moment Tinkham acted. He sprang out of his seat, jerked Marjorie Gavin from hers. In the space at the rear, from behind the stewardess's shielding body held before him, he raised Craven's gun and fired.

ACTUAL MOVEMENTS.

TELETYPE "PX" 90	TIME	LORD	FONDA	ISA	TINK-HAM	GAVIN	PILOTS	PONS	CRAVEN	BELL-OWES	DIDE-NOT	KEEPER
	8.28	seat	seat	seat	seat	seat	seats	seat	seat	seat	seat	house
	8.29	getting up	→	→	→	lights	Lovett in aisle	→	→	→	→	field
	8.30	out door	→	→	getting up	rear	out door	→	getting up	→	→	→
	8.31	nose	getting up ↕	getting up ↕	out door	→	carrying Philips	→	out door	getting up	→	house
	8.32	baggage door	out door	out door	tall	→	→	→	field	getting up	getting up	→
(Crucial period)	8.33	→	field	rear	tall	→	→	→	→	rear	getting up	→
	8.34	snow	→	→	baggage door	→	→	→	→	out door	rear	→
	8.35	→	→	→	baggage compartment	→	→	getting up	→	field	field	→
	8.36	→	approach □ house	out door	tall	→	house out door	out door	army plane	→	out door	□ window
Lord's Message	8.37	→	return	field	cabin ◇	◇ Tinkham	→	field	→	house	field	house
	8.38	→	→	→	bag etc., leave	→	→	→	field	→	→	→
	8.39	→	→	→	field	→	→	→	→	→	house	→
	8.40	→	cabin	house +	→	Fonda	→	house +	house +	→	→	→
	8.41	→	search	→	house	→	→	→	→	→	→	→
	8.42	→	find and leave	→	→	out door	→	→	→	→	→	→
	8.43	→	field	→	→	field	→	→	→	→	→	→
	8.44	→	→	→	→	→	→	→	→	→	→	→

In the instant before he was hit, the real explanation of
the theft of the preceding night flashed across Lord's
mind. Then he fell backwards.

The passengers sat aghast at the startling change of
affairs. Craven, who was nearest Tinkham, turned in his
chair, but it was only too plain that he could do nothing.
The shots were going into the cockpit now, through the
little window in the pilot's door, and suddenly the 'plane
began to sway; gradually at first, then with a dizzying
rapidity it went into a spin. No one could do anything
except hold on.

The motors were cut and the sighing rush of the wind
made an eerie prelude to the coming crash. At the foot of
the whirling cabin the cockpit door jerked open and
Lovett, clinging to one of its sides, raised his automatic,
just as both motors roared again, full open. The junior
pilot fired and missed, but the spin was lessening now,
they seemed to Craven's trained senses to be coming out
of it.

In the cockpit, Lannings had been staring ahead,
watching the earth come toward them. They were over
Carson Sink, a flat expanse of alkali desert, fifty miles
long. Foolishly he thought of Reno, only thirty minutes
away; they had nearly made it. Then he brought his
attention to the turning transport; he was not dizzy, he
recognised death grinning at him and his passengers, he
summoned all the skill of his long flying experience to
meet the sudden problem.

He waited as long as possible, but there was not much
time to wait. He knew what would happen when he
opened the motors, shut off temporarily to let him per-
ceive the action of the crippled 'plane. He thought, no
more time – he gave 'em both the gun simultaneously.

The ship jerked, shot downward with augmenting
speed. The earth rushed up at him. He didn't look at it
but the air speed indicator registered over 300 m.p.h.
when the spinning began to lessen. They were danger-

ously close and again he could wait no longer to straighten out, to try to straighten out.

He pulled back his stick, the ship responded; the snout, still circling slowly, moved over the ground below, gradually toward the horizon. He had it now, it touched horizon, he had it. A zoom would be hopelessly dangerous, but he must try it; he lifted the transport's head, cut the motors, the speed decreased rapidly. He levelled off and started a downward glide.

Lovett, equally undizzied, was waiting another chance at the doorway. Marjorie had slipped away from in front of Tinkham, who still could do no more than cling to the rear seat, but this time he didn't intend to miss. His gun came up, he steaded it and pulled the trigger. Tinkham staggered and fell to his knees, still clung to the back of the chair and was hidden from the rest of the cabin.

The glide was not working out. The port ailerons, uncontrollable, refused to function; the port wing slid off. Then a lucky gust saved them, boosting the wing, levelling off the ship for a few seconds. And they were nearly down; a hundred feet below them lay the safe earth. It was the last chance and Lannings took it. The nose dipped, he touched the motors. The 'plane jumped toward the ground. Watch it, wait till the last instant; the tail controls were still working. Now! Once more the ship responded, but slowly, a little too slowly. The nose lifted, not quite enough. They came down hard as the senior pilot at the last moment switched off the ignition. There was a splintering crash as the landing gear hit. One wheel broke, the starboard wheel. The 'plane tried a lop-sided bounce – thank God the angle had been enough for that. Ten or fifteen feet in the air it hopped, then pancaked down on the cushioning remains of its smashing landing gear. The nose dug into the dry dust of Carson Sink.

Lovett, eager to get back to the cabin's rear, loosed his

hold on the doorway too soon. The final crash found him unsupported. He was thrown backwards against the cockpit partition and his head whacked soundly against the metal. He slid quietly down on the cockpit steps.

And Tinkham was on his feet before any one else had recovered. His left arm hung limply but there was no unsteadiness in the hand that aimed the pistol down the aisle. 'Bellowes!' he barked sharply.

The minister instinctively looked back, but had no voice to answer.

'There's a key in Lord's vest pocket, Bellowes. Get it and throw it back here. No nonsense. I'll drill your belly full of lead in five seconds unless you get that key!'

Bellowes hesitated momentarily and the gun came up to cover him unerringly. He was paper-white as he bent shaking over the detective's unconscious form, and with trembling fingers found the cabin key. He was making a peculiar, whimpering noise – 'weh, wegh . . . weh.'

The key came back. 'His gun now. Right beside him. Pick it up by the muzzle.' But Bellowes, collapsed in his chair, was capable of nothing more.

'The hell with you,' snapped Tinkham. 'Stewardess! Walk down there and bring that gun back by the muzzle . . . If any one tries anything, I'll kill her first,' he warned. They knew a killer; no one interfered as the girl hesitantly went down the aisle. 'Do what he says,' Pons grunted painfully as she passed him. 'He's on top now, but we'll get him sooner or later.'

She came back. Tinkham dropped his empty gun and took Lord's full automatic from her hand, as she stared at him with trembling lips and hatred in her wet eyes. 'Open that door. Throw the key out. Get away from it.'

He stepped to the entrance, glanced down. With a final threatening look about the cabin, he jumped out. The door slammed shut.

As Tinkham jumped, three things happened. Lord groaned and stirred in Fonda's arms as she knelt beside him in the cramped aisle. An idling propeller swished outside and dust flew as the escort 'plane landed, rolling toward the grounded transport. And Lannings' face, lined with effort, appeared over Lovett's body in the doorway.

The detective was on his feet, staggering. 'Michael, you can't,' Fonda cried. 'He has your gun. He took the key. We're locked in.' That last act of Tinkham's appeared to her now as a godsend.

'Key,' Lord muttered, swaying around toward Lannings. 'Gun.'

Long ago, when the case first broke, he had told Darrow that the flyers could be relied upon in a pinch. He had been right. The pilot's key and gun were in his hand a second later and he started toward the door.

Lannings had slid back a glass panel in the cockpit. He was leaning out, waving frantically to the other 'plane, shouting, yelling. The army man was half out of his cockpit when, from the ground, Tinkham's gun spoke twice – crack – crack! Just behind the lieutenant's leg, two neat little holes drilled through the fuselage.

The army flyer thought quickly, too, and his first thought was that he was a mighty poor revolver shot. The motor buzzed, then spat staccato sounds. The 'plane jumped ahead.

Dust swirled about it as it shot a hundred yards forward. Then the nose tilted and it climbed almost vertically. One more shot Tinkham had at it as it passed him some thirty yards away, but no effect was apparent.

From the ground beside the cabin entrance Lord and Fonda watched what ensued. He was leaning heavily on her shoulder, he was faint from loss of blood. Tinkham was running across the sandy ground, away from the transport, and above him the little combat 'plane circled and seemed for a moment to pause.

Then it dived. It streaked down out of the sky and a burst of machine-gun fire came faintly to their ears.

Drup-drup-drup-drup-drup-drup. The dust kicked up behind the running figure; the loose ground made a perfect indication of the fire, more perfect than tracer bullets. Drup-drup-drup-drup-drup-drup! The spurts reached the man below, crumped him in an instant, clung about the splotch he made against the yellow earth. The 'plane skimmed on, rose, banked and came to a landing a few yards away from what had just been Tinkham.

The pilot, after a moment's survey, stood up in the cockpit. He raised one arm against the distant skyline. His thumb was pointing down.

'Oh,' sobbed Fonda. 'Oh, Michael, Michael! You won't have to do it. We're safe, we're all safe. Michael!'

Lord summoned a twisted grin. He hardly knew what he was saying. What he said was, 'Fonda, darling.'

Prologue

BOUDOIR

Fonda Mann slipped off the backless evening gown and walked across to her dressing-table. It was two o'clock on the morning of April twelfth. As she crossed the room, she wondered for the hundredth time why lingerie was always so much more intriguing than any gown, no matter how low or how fashionably the latter might be cut. Not, as a matter of fact, that there was much lingerie; once out of her dress, there remained only the silver-heeled mules, sheer, clocked French stockings, a very brief pair of panties and the new, tricky bra.

She regarded her face in the triple mirror without any pretence of denying its beauty. Thank God it was beautiful. Why did she always make it up at night before, instead of after, getting into her pyjamas? It was a queer habit, really. She supposed it came from the time when, as a young miss, she had first begun using nightly cosmetics and had hated those long, white nightdresses that Anne insisted on buying for her a half dozen at a time. If her father came in to kiss her good night, she wanted to be more fetchingly attired; and a young miss's lingerie, while nothing to write home about, was still a cut above a shroud.

She wished her father would come in now, although now, of course, he would knock discreetly on her door and wait to be admitted until she had thrown on one of her negligées. Which were not bad, either, and then he would kiss her hand instead of her cheek, and look as if he would so much rather have kissed her lips. Gallant restraint; always the right gesture, both entering and leaving. He was wonderful, that man, he really was; she was crazy about him.

But now he was way off in Africa with that silly Mitzi.

Not that Mitzi wasn't all right; and Wotan was probably all right, too, for the time being, but he wanted Anne, she knew he wanted Anne terribly. Anne was as beautiful as any of these others and, besides, he was in love with her. Further, Anne was in love with him and didn't really care, a bit more than did Fonda, about a few other women at a properly vague distance.

An ugly look came over her face and one manicured hand commenced to clench. 'Damn,' she muttered, 'people who get in the way of love, *smell*! I *know* it's fair to put them out of it.' What right, she continued, had that disagreeable old Amos to break up a real love affair, to make two sweet people miserable, just for his own damned selfish satisfaction. Fonda was glad she had sent him the anonymous note that afternoon; that would take him out to Reno, beyond any shadow of doubt, the obstinate old fool. And she was glad she had those two little, white tablets, so innocent-looking and actually so deadly.

The young chemist from whom she had cajoled them would never give her away, no matter what happened, but poison in the home was so – indicatory. Especially in a home like Amos'. A trip was better, and a hotel, say at Reno, with lots of other people about. Almost anybody could logically be suspected of killing such a man. He had plenty of enemies in Reno, and none of them would be caught because she would have done it.

But what if she were suspected? 'Oh, hell,' said Fonda with a reckless shrug, 'I won't be.' And if she were, if some policeman or detective found her out, if she were really cornered, why she'd marry the man. 'And that,' opined Fonda, as she undid the bra and let it fall, 'will settle *him*.'

HOTEL

He came out of the little shower bath, rubbed vigorously and pulled on a comfortable lounging robe. He lit a cigarette and crossed over to the table next to the window where breakfast had been laid by a waiter.

Why should a playwright rise early? No reason at all; nine o'clock was plenty early enough. It had been quite a show at the Lamb's Club the night before, and to-morrow he had to leave, to fly out to California for that confounded lecture tour. He regretted it now. One show playing on Broadway and another on the road some-where; what a fool he was to have told the bureau he would talk and talk and talk to more of those dull-faced club women. Still, this was no time to turn down an honest quid. Just a morning slump, doubtless; he knew very well that all club women were not dull-faced. Sometimes one met very charming ladies. He remem-bered, even in the suburbs –

New York was best, if one couldn't be in London. Well, he had to go, anyhow; no use grousing about it now. He finished his breakfast, got up, strolled about the room, pulling contentedly on a pipe. Flying out to-morrow. Suddenly the snatch of conversation he had had with that physician the evening before came back to him. Amos Cutter was flying out, too; they might find them-selves on the same 'plane.

The name had meant nothing to him at first. He had only remembered later that this must be the fellow who was the enemy of his friend, Mann. Yes, there couldn't be much doubt of it, a surgeon and with that name. And Mann had saved his life, not once but twice. 'I'll look out for that chap. Maybe I – '

Another thought flashed abruptly across his mind. He

stepped over to one of his bags, unlocked it and took out the curious little pistol he had picked up in Germany last year. It was small; the whole thing fitted into his own large hand as he stood weighing it with speculation in his eyes. It had a built-in silencer; also – and this was the significant point – it was demountable in such a fashion that none of its small parts, when disassembled, bore any likeness to a pistol. Even the tube broke open at one end. It had taken him half an hour under competent instruction to learn how to put it together. He had bought it as a curiosity and had never even taken the eight bullets from their carrying compartment in the grip. Of course, he only had the eight bullets. One would be enough.

The idea added to itself, grew automatically without special effort. On a 'plane. No need to make a fool of himself; he wouldn't do any public shooting, but he had flown enough to realise that opportunities might arise, were sure to arise, in fact, and to know, also, how to dispose of small objects in such a milieu. The pistol would never be assembled, or probably recognised, even if found. It was untraceable, too. Life was pretty much of a joke at best and he had never thought it worth the value solemn asses put on it. He had seen too much murder, not general slaughter but cold-blooded individual murder, during the war to be greatly concerned over that. Rather a temptation to do a real friend a turn.

It could never be proven that he had any connection with Cutter, for he hadn't. Never seen the man . . . A crime without a weapon. It reminded him of something. Yes, that was it; it reminded him of Charles Fort's stuff. Lots of cases in those books of the very thing. Entirely circumstantial accounts, as he recalled them.

'I think I'll take it with me,' he said; and locked the bag.

He walked over and bent down beneath the tablecloth by the window. From the shelf below he selected, after a moment, a book and sat down in one of the chairs, turning the pages attentively. Hugh L. Craven was familiarising himself with the accounts of uncanny deaths contained in *Wild Talents*.

Private Chamber

Fonda had gone to the hairdresser's and by ten o'clock the maid had finished her dusting in this section of the apartment. With an assured three hours of solitude Isa sat writing in her very personal diary under the date of 'April 12th.'

'I shall burn this page when I have finished' (she wrote) 'but most good minds think better on paper. I am getting very tired of Amos and his overbearing insolence. He is interfering more and more between Anne and me. He will be better out of the way. We are going by 'plane, to-morrow, and it would be best if he did not reach Reno at all. The divorce is practically settled; I can carry it through without him. James? He will do as well with MacKenzie as with Amos. Fonda is quite right about that. What difference does it make which clumsy male works over him? Either he will get well or he won't, that is the size of it. No, Amos had better not reach Reno. God, why does he come between dear, dearest Anne and me? Oh, I know why; he wants her to himself. Men are foul animals. I think Amos is the foulest I have ever seen. I would put out his light – like that! Of course I have supported him in the divorce; there's a point in my favour. No one would suspect me, anyhow. I should be the last suspected, but how to do it? We are going by air. Well Lowenstein, that Belgian, fell out of a 'plane. They said he couldn't, and they made tests, but the fact remains he did. Some fool men made the "tests," probably. They *are* such fools, proving that what is so, can't

be so. I don't believe I need worry being caught out by
that sort of dunce. Could I get him to open a door and
give him a shove? I have never been in a 'plane, but I
suppose it's a possibility. No one could prove he hadn't
slipped himself. Then there must be airports where you
get out and walk around to change 'planes. Probably
there will be a good many people about but that won't
hurt anything. It might be better. There will be a chance.
If I watch carefully, I shall find it. God knows, all women
are cleverer than men, and certainly I am; and every
time I think of Anne, I will be strengthened. Yes, I have
decided now. I shall watch for my chance, and I shall get
it, somehow . . . '

LABORATORY

Dr Gesell entered the new quarters of the College of
Physicians and Surgeons, far uptown, and passed the
entrance desk with its little calendar proclaiming 'April
12th.' He nodded to the girl who sat behind it in her
white nurse's uniform.

The elevators. 'Fifth floor, blease.' A white corridor.
An archway – 'Physiological Pathology and Chemis-
try'.

His little laboratory was small, but it was bright and
beautifully equipped. A range of shelves bearing bottles
of chemicals, liquid and solid, retorts, pipettes, the most
newly developed microscope; even a spectroscope,
rather cumbersome, at the end near the corner. Below, a
copper basin set in a broader, zinc-covered shelf, waist
high; hot and cold water, two gas outlets to one of which
was attached a Bunsen burner, several electric outlets.
Various instruments were stacked neatly against the
wall at the back. An electric stopwatch, in its metalled
motor case, was attached by a slender cord to one of the

outlets. At the end of the shelving a window looked down on the broad thoroughfare beneath.

Dr Gesell beamed his approval of this orderly room.

He hung his overcoat on a hook and followed that by his bowler hat. Stripping off the coat of his suit and donning a laboratory apron, he got to work without delay. 'This bulb; only one inch for diameter.' He pressed a bell and pouring three powdered chemicals into a retort, set it above the Bunsen burner.

There came a knock at the door. 'Come,' said Dr Gesell without turning around. 'Three glass bulbs, blease, one inch diameter. Number two glass.' He plugged in a small electric clock and set it going as the bottom of the retort began to glow with heat. Another retort went over an electric grill.

As he worked, he muttered to himself . . . 'What for obbortunity. This *Gott* must give . . . Once I have let it slip; not now . . . *Ach*, Anne, for this I subbose I have lived . . . Anne . . . What was that boy who love you, that Franz? Hardtly could I remember him now; how he thought, what he do, how he suffer. *Nein*, he is not I; that boy is deadt, many years now is he deadt. Quite another is it what now make a bulb for Amos Cutter . . . Come in, blease.'

The door opened. *'Bitte.* Thank you, blease.' He laid the bulbs carefully beside the retorts. He crossed the room and locked the door to the corridor.

'When that Franz die, what is left give himself to Science. Science, I subbose, is my mistress; but she is a coldt bedfellow, too.' Dr Gesell took up two pipettes; carefully he annealed to their ends two one-way, glass valves, as carefully manipulated two of the bulbs, annealing the valve to these. He bent over the retorts, sniffed gently, turned down the gas beneath the first one after a brief glance at the electric clock . . . 'Something there is much wrong with this Science; power she give but not knowledge. A mistress what is coldt and also deceive you, what good is that mistress? . . . *Nein,* I leave her now; that Franz is deadt, but now I do somethings for that Franz what so many year is deadt . . . What is it to me, to cut them ub or not to cut them ub? It is nothing. Brobably it will now be cut them ub.'

With precise fingers he inserted a pipette into the first retort. He sucked in and a bluish vapour filled half the first bulb. The second retort yielded a yellow gas, but when they blended in the bulb, it became quickly clear and transparent. The pipette was broken off skilfully at the valve, the valve annealed.

'This young man what come for a bulb to put Amos Cutter into a trance, *Gott* has sent him . . . Or berhaps it was Eros; vengeance also belong to Eros, berhaps . . . What could put him into such a trance? He is a foolish young man . . . From this trance Amos Cutter will come out – never!'

Unlock the door, ring the bell. He walked to the window and stood gazing downward; a police car was drawing up to the curb. Dr Gesell started nervously. Then recovered himself. 'But this can with me nothings have to do.' He walked back across the room.

Two little boxes, cotton wadding, the bulbs on the wadding. More wadding, then the boxes were covered and neatly tied. One into Dr Gesell's pocket. For the other, 'You will sendt this, blease, at once to Cabtain Michael Lordt, by the Bolice Headtquarters, Center Street. Here is the address written. This goes, blease, at once.'

APARTMENT

11.15 p.m. on April 13th. Dr Gesell paced the floor of his sitting-room, to which a tiny hallway made a preface from the second floor landing. The apartment was

untidy and unkempt, in complete contrast to his spick
and span laboratory.

He paced the floor nervously, his small legs carrying
him now to the window overlooking the street, now
around the table in the middle of the room. 'What, then,
could it be? One telegram have I this noon to Chicago
sent; already before noon the bulb was to be given . . .
Why do I wait? Have I not decided? Never alive will I be
taken; only then Anne's name into everything must
come.'

He placed the little box from his pocket on the table;
cut the string, took off the cover. On its bed of cotton the
second bulb reposed comfortably. Dr Gesell looked at it,
then resumed his pacing.

Out the window a patrolman was making his way
down the street, flashing his light into the darkened area-
ways as he passed along. Gesell drew back, trembling, as
the patrolman passed the house. He muttered, 'Everything I have decided alreadty. If to the telegrams there
no answer is, then must the crime be discovered.
Without reply alreadty have I telegraphed Chicago;
berhaps for some reason only after Chicago is the bulb
given, but at six-thirty I telegraphed Cheyenne and still
no answer do I get.' He pulled out a large, gold watch
with a hand that shook. '*Halb zwölf.* No reason could
there be but it is found out. Berhaps even that young
man he see at once that Cutter is deadt. Or some one tell
him there is no such trance . . . He telegraph the bolice,
perhaps, instead of me . . . I am lucky not yet they have
come.'

Up the front steps ran a telegraph boy, in his hand a
yellow envelope addressed to Dr Gesell; in the envelope
Lord's telegram from Medicine Bow through Cheyenne
– 'All O.K. according to plan.' As the boy approached
the front door, a fellow lodger of Gesell's came out. The
boy went in, after inquiring from the lodger the number
of the chemist's apartment. He mounted to the second

floor and rang the bell.

Gesell stiffened sharply; with difficulty he walked back to the table and stood leaning against it heavily with both arms. 'It is the bolice. Never will I alive be taken. Courage, Franz, this is for Anne. Courage.' Outside the door the telegraph boy was writing on a blank form from his pad; 'An effort was made at 11.35 p.m. to deliver – ' He finished writing, waited a moment for any sounds from within. Then he gave the bell a long, insistent peal.

Dr Gesell bent over his handkerchief. 'Good-bye, Anne. Fare you well, *liebe* Anne.' He broke the bulb.

There was only a slight thud as his body struck the floor.

The telegraph boy, tired of waiting, slipped the printed form under the door sill and departed, whistling through his teeth.

The Clue Finder

Do not peruse until after you finish the story.*

*Isn't there enough cheating in the world without this
    sort of thing?

As is his custom
the author seeks permission to impose upon
the reader's patience by hinting that the
arch-criminal hereinbefore has been suggested by sundry indications:

As to the murderer's anxieties:

	PAGE	LINE
He seeks information	97	11*ff.*
He seeks it again	121	36
His information is delayed	122	13
But finally given	140	9
And is never corrected	143	29

As to the time of the victim's death:

	PAGE	LINE
Another suffers ill effects at the same time	80	17
And asserts their origin	88	29*ff.*
Still another is puzzled	103	30
Stating his reasons	104	3
One admits the truth	123	27
But qualifies it considerably	124	10
And refers to the essential time	160	19
To which he sticks	233	16

A CATALOG OF SELECTED
DOVER BOOKS
IN ALL FIELDS OF INTEREST

A CATALOG OF SELECTED DOVER
BOOKS IN ALL FIELDS OF INTEREST

100 BEST-LOVED POEMS, Edited by Philip Smith. "The Passionate Shepherd to His Love," "Shall I compare thee to a summer's day?" "Death, be not proud," "The Raven," "The Road Not Taken," plus works by Blake, Wordsworth, Byron, Shelley, Keats, many others. 96pp. 5³⁄₁₆ x 8¼.   0-486-28553-7

100 SMALL HOUSES OF THE THIRTIES, Brown-Blodgett Company. Exterior photographs and floor plans for 100 charming structures. Illustrations of models accompanied by descriptions of interiors, color schemes, closet space, and other amenities. 200 illustrations. 112pp. 8⅜ x 11.   0-486-44131-8

1000 TURN-OF-THE-CENTURY HOUSES: With Illustrations and Floor Plans, Herbert C. Chivers. Reproduced from a rare edition, this showcase of homes ranges from cottages and bungalows to sprawling mansions. Each house is meticulously illustrated and accompanied by complete floor plans. 256pp. 9⅜ x 12¼.
0-486-45596-3

101 GREAT AMERICAN POEMS, Edited by The American Poetry & Literacy Project. Rich treasury of verse from the 19th and 20th centuries includes works by Edgar Allan Poe, Robert Frost, Walt Whitman, Langston Hughes, Emily Dickinson, T. S. Eliot, other notables. 96pp. 5³⁄₁₆ x 8¼.   0-486-40158-8

101 GREAT SAMURAI PRINTS, Utagawa Kuniyoshi. Kuniyoshi was a master of the warrior woodblock print — and these 18th-century illustrations represent the pinnacle of his craft. Full-color portraits of renowned Japanese samurais pulse with movement, passion, and remarkably fine detail. 112pp. 8⅜ x 11.   0-486-46523-3

ABC OF BALLET, Janet Grosser. Clearly worded, abundantly illustrated little guide defines basic ballet-related terms: arabesque, battement, pas de chat, relevé, sissonne, many others. Pronunciation guide included. Excellent primer. 48pp. 4³⁄₁₆ x 5¾.
0-486-40871-X

ACCESSORIES OF DRESS: An Illustrated Encyclopedia, Katherine Lester and Bess Viola Oerke. Illustrations of hats, veils, wigs, cravats, shawls, shoes, gloves, and other accessories enhance an engaging commentary that reveals the humor and charm of the many-sided story of accessorized apparel. 644 figures and 59 plates. 608pp. 6⅛ x 9¼.
0-486-43378-1

ADVENTURES OF HUCKLEBERRY FINN, Mark Twain. Join Huck and Jim as their boyhood adventures along the Mississippi River lead them into a world of excitement, danger, and self-discovery. Humorous narrative, lyrical descriptions of the Mississippi valley, and memorable characters. 224pp. 5³⁄₁₆ x 8¼.   0-486-28061-6

ALICE STARMORE'S BOOK OF FAIR ISLE KNITTING, Alice Starmore. A noted designer from the region of Scotland's Fair Isle explores the history and techniques of this distinctive, stranded-color knitting style and provides copious illustrated instructions for 14 original knitwear designs. 208pp. 8⅜ x 10⅞.   0-486-47218-3

ALICE'S ADVENTURES IN WONDERLAND, Lewis Carroll. Beloved classic about a little girl lost in a topsy-turvy land and her encounters with the White Rabbit, March Hare, Mad Hatter, Cheshire Cat, and other delightfully improbable characters. 42 illustrations by Sir John Tenniel. 96pp. 5³⁄₁₆ x 8¼. 0-486-27543-4

AMERICA'S LIGHTHOUSES: An Illustrated History, Francis Ross Holland. Profusely illustrated fact-filled survey of American lighthouses since 1716. Over 200 stations — East, Gulf, and West coasts, Great Lakes, Hawaii, Alaska, Puerto Rico, the Virgin Islands, and the Mississippi and St. Lawrence Rivers. 240pp. 8 x 10¾. 0-486-25576-X

AN ENCYCLOPEDIA OF THE VIOLIN, Alberto Bachmann. Translated by Frederick H. Martens. Introduction by Eugene Ysaye. First published in 1925, this renowned reference remains unsurpassed as a source of essential information, from construction and evolution to repertoire and technique. Includes a glossary and 73 illustrations. 496pp. 6½ x 9¼. 0-486-46618-3

ANIMALS: 1,419 Copyright-Free Illustrations of Mammals, Birds, Fish, Insects, etc., Selected by Jim Harter. Selected for its visual impact and ease of use, this outstanding collection of wood engravings presents over 1,000 species of animals in extremely lifelike poses. Includes mammals, birds, reptiles, amphibians, fish, insects, and other invertebrates. 284pp. 9 x 12. 0-486-23766-4

THE ANNALS, Tacitus. Translated by Alfred John Church and William Jackson Brodribb. This vital chronicle of Imperial Rome, written by the era's great historian, spans A.D. 14-68 and paints incisive psychological portraits of major figures, from Tiberius to Nero. 416pp. 5³⁄₁₆ x 8¼. 0-486-45236-0

ANTIGONE, Sophocles. Filled with passionate speeches and sensitive probing of moral and philosophical issues, this powerful and often-performed Greek drama reveals the grim fate that befalls the children of Oedipus. Footnotes. 64pp. 5³⁄₁₆ x 8 ¼. 0-486-27804-2

ART DECO DECORATIVE PATTERNS IN FULL COLOR, Christian Stoll. Reprinted from a rare 1910 portfolio, 160 sensuous and exotic images depict a breathtaking array of florals, geometrics, and abstracts — all elegant in their stark simplicity. 64pp. 8⅜ x 11. 0-486-44862-2

THE ARTHUR RACKHAM TREASURY: 86 Full-Color Illustrations, Arthur Rackham. Selected and Edited by Jeff A. Menges. A stunning treasury of 86 full-page plates span the famed English artist's career, from *Rip Van Winkle* (1905) to masterworks such as *Undine, A Midsummer Night's Dream,* and *Wind in the Willows* (1939). 96pp. 8⅜ x 11. 0-486-44685-9

THE AUTHENTIC GILBERT & SULLIVAN SONGBOOK, W. S. Gilbert and A. S. Sullivan. The most comprehensive collection available, this songbook includes selections from every one of Gilbert and Sullivan's light operas. Ninety-two numbers are presented uncut and unedited, and in their original keys. 410pp. 9 x 12. 0-486-23482-7

THE AWAKENING, Kate Chopin. First published in 1899, this controversial novel of a New Orleans wife's search for love outside a stifling marriage shocked readers. Today, it remains a first-rate narrative with superb characterization. New introductory Note. 128pp. 5³⁄₁₆ x 8¼. 0-486-27786-0

BASIC DRAWING, Louis Priscilla. Beginning with perspective, this commonsense manual progresses to the figure in movement, light and shade, anatomy, drapery, composition, trees and landscape, and outdoor sketching. Black-and-white illustrations throughout. 128pp. 8⅜ x 11. 0-486-45815-6

THE BATTLES THAT CHANGED HISTORY, Fletcher Pratt. Historian profiles 16 crucial conflicts, ancient to modern, that changed the course of Western civilization. Gripping accounts of battles led by Alexander the Great, Joan of Arc, Ulysses S. Grant, other commanders. 27 maps. 352pp. 5⅜ x 8½.　　　　0-486-41129-X

BEETHOVEN'S LETTERS, Ludwig van Beethoven. Edited by Dr. A. C. Kalischer. Features 457 letters to fellow musicians, friends, greats, patrons, and literary men. Reveals musical thoughts, quirks of personality, insights, and daily events. Includes 15 plates. 410pp. 5⅜ x 8½.　　　　0-486-22769-3

BERNICE BOBS HER HAIR AND OTHER STORIES, F. Scott Fitzgerald. This brilliant anthology includes 6 of Fitzgerald's most popular stories: "The Diamond as Big as the Ritz," the title tale, "The Offshore Pirate," "The Ice Palace," "The Jelly Bean," and "May Day." 176pp. 5⅜ x 8½.　　　　0-486-47049-0

BESLER'S BOOK OF FLOWERS AND PLANTS: 73 Full-Color Plates from Hortus Eystettensis, 1613, Basilius Besler. Here is a selection of magnificent plates from the *Hortus Eystettensis,* which vividly illustrated and identified the plants, flowers, and trees that thrived in the legendary German garden at Eichstätt. 80pp. 8⅜ x 11.
0-486-46005-3

THE BOOK OF KELLS, Edited by Blanche Cirker. Painstakingly reproduced from a rare facsimile edition, this volume contains full-page decorations, portraits, illustrations, plus a sampling of textual leaves with exquisite calligraphy and ornamentation. 32 full-color illustrations. 32pp. 9⅜ x 12¼.　　　　0-486-24345-1

THE BOOK OF THE CROSSBOW: With an Additional Section on Catapults and Other Siege Engines, Ralph Payne-Gallwey. Fascinating study traces history and use of crossbow as military and sporting weapon, from Middle Ages to modern times. Also covers related weapons: balistas, catapults, Turkish bows, more. Over 240 illustrations. 400pp. 7¼ x 10⅛.　　　　0-486-28720-3

THE BUNGALOW BOOK: Floor Plans and Photos of 112 Houses, 1910, Henry L. Wilson. Here are 112 of the most popular and economic blueprints of the early 20th century — plus an illustration or photograph of each completed house. A wonderful time capsule that still offers a wealth of valuable insights. 160pp. 8⅜ x 11.
0-486-45104-6

THE CALL OF THE WILD, Jack London. A classic novel of adventure, drawn from London's own experiences as a Klondike adventurer, relating the story of a heroic dog caught in the brutal life of the Alaska Gold Rush. Note. 64pp. 5³⁄₁₆ x 8¼.
0-486-26472-6

CANDIDE, Voltaire. Edited by Francois-Marie Arouet. One of the world's great satires since its first publication in 1759. Witty, caustic skewering of romance, science, philosophy, religion, government — nearly all human ideals and institutions. 112pp. 5³⁄₁₆ x 8¼.　　　　0-486-26689-3

CELEBRATED IN THEIR TIME: Photographic Portraits from the George Grantham Bain Collection, Edited by Amy Pastan. With an Introduction by Michael Carlebach. Remarkable portrait gallery features 112 rare images of Albert Einstein, Charlie Chaplin, the Wright Brothers, Henry Ford, and other luminaries from the worlds of politics, art, entertainment, and industry. 128pp. 8⅜ x 11.　　　　0-486-46754-6

CHARIOTS FOR APOLLO: The NASA History of Manned Lunar Spacecraft to 1969, Courtney G. Brooks, James M. Grimwood, and Loyd S. Swenson, Jr. This illustrated history by a trio of experts is the definitive reference on the Apollo spacecraft and lunar modules. It traces the vehicles' design, development, and operation in space. More than 100 photographs and illustrations. 576pp. 6¾ x 9¼. 0-486-46756-2

A CHRISTMAS CAROL, Charles Dickens. This engrossing tale relates Ebenezer Scrooge's ghostly journeys through Christmases past, present, and future and his ultimate transformation from a harsh and grasping old miser to a charitable and compassionate human being. 80pp. 5³⁄₁₆ x 8¼. 0-486-26865-9

COMMON SENSE, Thomas Paine. First published in January of 1776, this highly influential landmark document clearly and persuasively argued for American separation from Great Britain and paved the way for the Declaration of Independence. 64pp. 5³⁄₁₆ x 8¼. 0-486-29602-4

THE COMPLETE SHORT STORIES OF OSCAR WILDE, Oscar Wilde. Complete texts of "The Happy Prince and Other Tales," "A House of Pomegranates," "Lord Arthur Savile's Crime and Other Stories," "Poems in Prose," and "The Portrait of Mr. W. H." 208pp. 5³⁄₁₆ x 8¼. 0-486-45216-6

COMPLETE SONNETS, William Shakespeare. Over 150 exquisite poems deal with love, friendship, the tyranny of time, beauty's evanescence, death, and other themes in language of remarkable power, precision, and beauty. Glossary of archaic terms. 80pp. 5³⁄₁₆ x 8¼. 0-486-26686-9

THE COUNT OF MONTE CRISTO: Abridged Edition, Alexandre Dumas. Falsely accused of treason, Edmond Dantès is imprisoned in the bleak Chateau d'If. After a hair-raising escape, he launches an elaborate plot to extract a bitter revenge against those who betrayed him. 448pp. 5³⁄₁₆ x 8¼. 0-486-45643-9

CRAFTSMAN BUNGALOWS: Designs from the Pacific Northwest, Yoho & Merritt. This reprint of a rare catalog, showcasing the charming simplicity and cozy style of Craftsman bungalows, is filled with photos of completed homes, plus floor plans and estimated costs. An indispensable resource for architects, historians, and illustrators. 112pp. 10 x 7. 0-486-46875-5

CRAFTSMAN BUNGALOWS: 59 Homes from "The Craftsman," Edited by Gustav Stickley. Best and most attractive designs from Arts and Crafts Movement publication — 1903–1916 — includes sketches, photographs of homes, floor plans, descriptive text. 128pp. 8¼ x 11. 0-486-25829-7

CRIME AND PUNISHMENT, Fyodor Dostoyevsky. Translated by Constance Garnett. Supreme masterpiece tells the story of Raskolnikov, a student tormented by his own thoughts after he murders an old woman. Overwhelmed by guilt and terror, he confesses and goes to prison. 480pp. 5³⁄₁₆ x 8¼. 0-486-41587-2

THE DECLARATION OF INDEPENDENCE AND OTHER GREAT DOCUMENTS OF AMERICAN HISTORY: 1775-1865, Edited by John Grafton. Thirteen compelling and influential documents: Henry's "Give Me Liberty or Give Me Death," Declaration of Independence, The Constitution, Washington's First Inaugural Address, The Monroe Doctrine, The Emancipation Proclamation, Gettysburg Address, more. 64pp. 5³⁄₁₆ x 8¼. 0-486-41124-9

THE DESERT AND THE SOWN: Travels in Palestine and Syria, Gertrude Bell. "The female Lawrence of Arabia," Gertrude Bell wrote captivating, perceptive accounts of her travels in the Middle East. This intriguing narrative, accompanied by 160 photos, traces her 1905 sojourn in Lebanon, Syria, and Palestine. 368pp. 5⅜ x 8¼. 0-486-46876-3

A DOLL'S HOUSE, Henrik Ibsen. Ibsen's best-known play displays his genius for realistic prose drama. An expression of women's rights, the play climaxes when the central character, Nora, rejects a smothering marriage and life in "a doll's house." 80pp. 5³⁄₁₆ x 8¼. 0-486-27062-9

DOOMED SHIPS: Great Ocean Liner Disasters, William H. Miller, Jr. Nearly 200 photographs, many from private collections, highlight tales of some of the vessels whose pleasure cruises ended in catastrophe: the *Morro Castle, Normandie, Andrea Doria, Europa,* and many others. 128pp. 8⅜ x 11¼. 0-486-45366-9

THE DORÉ BIBLE ILLUSTRATIONS, Gustave Doré. Detailed plates from the Bible: the Creation scenes, Adam and Eve, horrifying visions of the Flood, the battle sequences with their monumental crowds, depictions of the life of Jesus, 241 plates in all. 241pp. 9 x 12. 0-486-23004-X

DRAWING DRAPERY FROM HEAD TO TOE, Cliff Young. Expert guidance on how to draw shirts, pants, skirts, gloves, hats, and coats on the human figure, including folds in relation to the body, pull and crush, action folds, creases, more. Over 200 drawings. 48pp. 8¼ x 11. 0-486-45591-2

DUBLINERS, James Joyce. A fine and accessible introduction to the work of one of the 20th century's most influential writers, this collection features 15 tales, including a masterpiece of the short-story genre, "The Dead." 160pp. 5³⁄₁₆ x 8¼. 0-486-26870-5

EASY-TO-MAKE POP-UPS, Joan Irvine. Illustrated by Barbara Reid. Dozens of wonderful ideas for three-dimensional paper fun — from holiday greeting cards with moving parts to a pop-up menagerie. Easy-to-follow, illustrated instructions for more than 30 projects. 299 black-and-white illustrations. 96pp. 8⅜ x 11. 0-486-44622-0

EASY-TO-MAKE STORYBOOK DOLLS: A "Novel" Approach to Cloth Dollmaking, Sherralyn St. Clair. Favorite fictional characters come alive in this unique beginner's dollmaking guide. Includes patterns for Pollyanna, Dorothy from *The Wonderful Wizard of Oz,* Mary of *The Secret Garden,* plus easy-to-follow instructions, 263 black-and-white illustrations, and an 8-page color insert. 112pp. 8¼ x 11. 0-486-47360-0

EINSTEIN'S ESSAYS IN SCIENCE, Albert Einstein. Speeches and essays in accessible, everyday language profile influential physicists such as Niels Bohr and Isaac Newton. They also explore areas of physics to which the author made major contributions. 128pp. 5 x 8. 0-486-47011-3

EL DORADO: Further Adventures of the Scarlet Pimpernel, Baroness Orczy. A popular sequel to *The Scarlet Pimpernel,* this suspenseful story recounts the Pimpernel's attempts to rescue the Dauphin from imprisonment during the French Revolution. An irresistible blend of intrigue, period detail, and vibrant characterizations. 352pp. 5³⁄₁₆ x 8¼. 0-486-44026-5

ELEGANT SMALL HOMES OF THE TWENTIES: 99 Designs from a Competition, Chicago Tribune. Nearly 100 designs for five- and six-room houses feature New England and Southern colonials, Normandy cottages, stately Italianate dwellings, and other fascinating snapshots of American domestic architecture of the 1920s. 112pp. 9 x 12. 0-486-46910-7

THE ELEMENTS OF STYLE: The Original Edition, William Strunk, Jr. This is the book that generations of writers have relied upon for timeless advice on grammar, diction, syntax, and other essentials. In concise terms, it identifies the principal requirements of proper style and common errors. 64pp. 5⅜ x 8½. 0-486-44798-7

THE ELUSIVE PIMPERNEL, Baroness Orczy. Robespierre's revolutionaries find their wicked schemes thwarted by the heroic Pimpernel — Sir Percival Blakeney. In this thrilling sequel, Chauvelin devises a plot to eliminate the Pimpernel and his wife. 272pp. 5³⁄₁₆ x 8¼. 0-486-45464-9

AN ENCYCLOPEDIA OF BATTLES: Accounts of Over 1,560 Battles from 1479 B.C. to the Present, David Eggenberger. Essential details of every major battle in recorded history from the first battle of Megiddo in 1479 B.C. to Grenada in 1984. List of battle maps. 99 illustrations. 544pp. 6½ x 9¼. 0-486-24913-1

ENCYCLOPEDIA OF EMBROIDERY STITCHES, INCLUDING CREWEL, Marion Nichols. Precise explanations and instructions, clearly illustrated, on how to work chain, back, cross, knotted, woven stitches, and many more — 178 in all, including Cable Outline, Whipped Satin, and Eyelet Buttonhole. Over 1400 illustrations. 219pp. 8⅜ x 11¼. 0-486-22929-7

ENTER JEEVES: 15 Early Stories, P. G. Wodehouse. Splendid collection contains first 8 stories featuring Bertie Wooster, the deliciously dim aristocrat and Jeeves, his brainy, imperturbable manservant. Also, the complete Reggie Pepper (Bertie's prototype) series. 288pp. 5⅜ x 8½. 0-486-29717-9

ERIC SLOANE'S AMERICA: Paintings in Oil, Michael Wigley. With a Foreword by Mimi Sloane. Eric Sloane's evocative oils of America's landscape and material culture shimmer with immense historical and nostalgic appeal. This original hardcover collection gathers nearly a hundred of his finest paintings, with subjects ranging from New England to the American Southwest. 128pp. 10⅝ x 9. 0-486-46525-X

ETHAN FROME, Edith Wharton. Classic story of wasted lives, set against a bleak New England background. Superbly delineated characters in a hauntingly grim tale of thwarted love. Considered by many to be Wharton's masterpiece. 96pp. 5³⁄₁₆ x 8 ¼. 0-486-26690-7

THE EVERLASTING MAN, G. K. Chesterton. Chesterton's view of Christianity — as a blend of philosophy and mythology, satisfying intellect and spirit — applies to his brilliant book, which appeals to readers' heads as well as their hearts. 288pp. 5⅜ x 8½. 0-486-46036-3

THE FIELD AND FOREST HANDY BOOK, Daniel Beard. Written by a co-founder of the Boy Scouts, this appealing guide offers illustrated instructions for building kites, birdhouses, boats, igloos, and other fun projects, plus numerous helpful tips for campers. 448pp. 5³⁄₁₆ x 8¼. 0-486-46191-2

FINDING YOUR WAY WITHOUT MAP OR COMPASS, Harold Gatty. Useful, instructive manual shows would-be explorers, hikers, bikers, scouts, sailors, and survivalists how to find their way outdoors by observing animals, weather patterns, shifting sands, and other elements of nature. 288pp. 5⅜ x 8½. 0-486-40613-X

FIRST FRENCH READER: A Beginner's Dual-Language Book, Edited and Translated by Stanley Appelbaum. This anthology introduces 50 legendary writers — Voltaire, Balzac, Baudelaire, Proust, more — through passages from *The Red and the Black, Les Misérables, Madame Bovary,* and other classics. Original French text plus English translation on facing pages. 240pp. 5⅜ x 8½. 0-486-46178-5

FIRST GERMAN READER: A Beginner's Dual-Language Book, Edited by Harry Steinhauer. Specially chosen for their power to evoke German life and culture, these short, simple readings include poems, stories, essays, and anecdotes by Goethe, Hesse, Heine, Schiller, and others. 224pp. 5⅜ x 8½. 0-486-46179-3

FIRST SPANISH READER: A Beginner's Dual-Language Book, Angel Flores. Delightful stories, other material based on works of Don Juan Manuel, Luis Taboada, Ricardo Palma, other noted writers. Complete faithful English translations on facing pages. Exercises. 176pp. 5⅜ x 8½. 0-486-25810-6

Browse over 9,000 books at www.doverpublications.com

FIVE ACRES AND INDEPENDENCE, Maurice G. Kains. Great back-to-the-land classic explains basics of self-sufficient farming. The one book to get. 95 illustrations. 397pp. 5⅜ x 8½. 0-486-20974-1

FLAGG'S SMALL HOUSES: Their Economic Design and Construction, 1922, Ernest Flagg. Although most famous for his skyscrapers, Flagg was also a proponent of the well-designed single-family dwelling. His classic treatise features innovations that save space, materials, and cost. 526 illustrations. 160pp. 9⅜ x 12¼. 0-486-45197-6

FLATLAND: A Romance of Many Dimensions, Edwin A. Abbott. Classic of science (and mathematical) fiction — charmingly illustrated by the author — describes the adventures of A. Square, a resident of Flatland, in Spaceland (three dimensions), Lineland (one dimension), and Pointland (no dimensions). 96pp. 5³⁄₁₆ x 8¼. 0-486-27263-X

FRANKENSTEIN, Mary Shelley. The story of Victor Frankenstein's monstrous creation and the havoc it caused has enthralled generations of readers and inspired countless writers of horror and suspense. With the author's own 1831 introduction. 176pp. 5³⁄₁₆ x 8¼. 0-486-28211-2

THE GARGOYLE BOOK: 572 Examples from Gothic Architecture, Lester Burbank Bridaham. Dispelling the conventional wisdom that French Gothic architectural flourishes were born of despair or gloom, Bridaham reveals the whimsical nature of these creations and the ingenious artisans who made them. 572 illustrations. 224pp. 8⅜ x 11. 0-486-44754-5

THE GIFT OF THE MAGI AND OTHER SHORT STORIES, O. Henry. Sixteen captivating stories by one of America's most popular storytellers. Included are such classics as "The Gift of the Magi," "The Last Leaf," and "The Ransom of Red Chief." Publisher's Note. 96pp. 5³⁄₁₆ x 8¼. 0-486-27061-0

THE GOETHE TREASURY: Selected Prose and Poetry, Johann Wolfgang von Goethe. Edited, Selected, and with an Introduction by Thomas Mann. In addition to his lyric poetry, Goethe wrote travel sketches, autobiographical studies, essays, letters, and proverbs in rhyme and prose. This collection presents outstanding examples from each genre. 368pp. 5⅜ x 8½. 0-486-44780-4

GREAT EXPECTATIONS, Charles Dickens. Orphaned Pip is apprenticed to the dirty work of the forge but dreams of becoming a gentleman — and one day finds himself in possession of "great expectations." Dickens' finest novel. 400pp. 5³⁄₁₆ x 8¼. 0-486-41586-4

GREAT WRITERS ON THE ART OF FICTION: From Mark Twain to Joyce Carol Oates, Edited by James Daley. An indispensable source of advice and inspiration, this anthology features essays by Henry James, Kate Chopin, Willa Cather, Sinclair Lewis, Jack London, Raymond Chandler, Raymond Carver, Eudora Welty, and Kurt Vonnegut, Jr. 192pp. 5⅜ x 8½. 0-486-45128-3

HAMLET, William Shakespeare. The quintessential Shakespearean tragedy, whose highly charged confrontations and anguished soliloquies probe depths of human feeling rarely sounded in any art. Reprinted from an authoritative British edition complete with illuminating footnotes. 128pp. 5³⁄₁₆ x 8¼. 0-486-27278-8

THE HAUNTED HOUSE, Charles Dickens. A Yuletide gathering in an eerie country retreat provides the backdrop for Dickens and his friends — including Elizabeth Gaskell and Wilkie Collins — who take turns spinning supernatural yarns. 144pp. 5⅜ x 8½. 0-486-46309-5

Browse over 9,000 books at www.doverpublications.com